Randolph's Challenge

– Book One –

The Pendulum Swings

by Chris Warren

Strategic Book Publishing
New York, NewYork

Strategic Book Publishing
An imprint of AEG Publishing Group
845 Third Avenue, 6th Floor - 6016
New York, NY 10022
www.StrategicBookPublishing.com

ISBN: 978-1-60693-827-0
SKU: 1-60693-827-4

Printed in the United States of America

Book Design: Rolando F. Santos

Contents

Acknowledgements

TO ALL those who have taught me about the tapestry of life but particularly to my many friends and colleagues who value the art of clever, beautiful, and meaningful writing. My first tutor in the process of putting words together in a creative way, Susan Knight, must take a substantial slice of the responsibility, and then, my family in the form of my wife, Hester, and my sons, Jay and Damian, who have provided continued encouragement. I must mention the founder members of Eblana-Writers Group especially, again my wife, Hester, my very good friends Mary Honan, Fiona Price, and Caroline Brady, all of whom have given endless support in my literary endeavours. Then there are those outside that immediate writing circle who have, nevertheless, provided me with guidance, given me feedback, and listened with tolerance to endless drivel in my efforts to bring together words into a coherent and readable format. Of those, Tony and Penny Reid stand out among the crowd, if for no other reason than that they have that unusual blend of wisdom and literary madness essential to a budding writer. Thank you all.

Chris Warren
Dublin, Ireland 2008

To Hester

My loving and tolerant wife, best friend, and playmate.
*This is for you, **to** say thank you.*

The Prologue

THE PENDULUM of fate swings slowly through time. Goodness on the one hand, periods of darkness and hatred on the other. But the evolution of humankind throughout the galaxy has provided destiny with imbalance in the forces controlling darkness and light. And so it had been for many millennia; the pendulum hung suspended on the side of good; for it must be said that humankind grew out of goodness and positive thought and was not created to maintain the dark force.

Thrung was not amused by this predominance of goodness. Thrung was an amorphous mass with a predisposition, in the perception of humankind, to selfish badness. Thrung's formless, shapeless, unstructured self lived by sucking energy from other life-forms—that's what made him (and we shall called it "him" for the sake of ease of reference in this text) grow and gain strength within the confines of his vile and unpleasant world. In the earlier years, many of those he influenced never aspired to more than petty crime, thievery, and mild villainy but, over time, greater works of skulduggery were becoming known. His power to attract those with natural strength was becoming a matter of concern to some who, although unaware of the source of this evil, were conscious of a growing movement directed against the forces of noble morality.

ô⊷ô

"Farewell my friends," King Petre of the house of Dondrenton in the Kingdom of Alusia addressed the closing ceremony of the Council of Kings of the Western Realm. "Farewell King Jute of Rú, goodbye my friend Karm of Obor, and you my colleague, Huthê of Lanah, and to all other noble monarchs gathered here today. My blessing goes with you all and with my son, Atha, who will be your host for future gatherings. I ask that you honor him with the same friendship and support you have all shown me these past years. My time for this world is now but short and you will not see me again. But weep not for me, my friends. I have lived a long and worthy life and my illness has been bearable. Galdore, my advisor and counsellor, will remain in office and as mentor to Atha. His wisdom will continue to protect and guide you in our quest for good."

King Petre was weak and staggered a little. Atha and Galdore stepped forward to support him, but he waved them away, determined to close this, his last Council, in a demonstration of strength, for that was his way and the way of his forebears.

"My last words to you are in the form of counsel and my last request is for you to heed it well."

The Kings turned their gaze to one another briefly, and looks of puzzlement and query were exchanged.

"We have touched on the matter briefly here during this our last council together. But I close now with dire warning of a rising threat to peace in our lands. Forces of darkness are stirring, and I feel a growing menace in our midst. I fear that even those who would once have sought to use their powers only for good may be enticed to subscribe to evil ways. We must seek a champion, one who can be trusted to counter the forces of evil. We must protect our realm. This I know."

King Petre sank slowly to his seat as a great weariness engulfed him, but he had spoken his warning and those who heard his words would not treat them lightly.

ନ୍ଧ

And so it was that later that year, Good King Petre passed peacefully to the Great Halls of the Everafter, leaving behind him a brave and worthy but youthful successor. As predicted, Galdore maintained a watchful presence over the affairs of state and, indeed, over the young king himself. There were many experienced and trusted supporters in the Council of Knights and in the more mysterious and magical overseers of Alusian providence, the Council of Worth, over which Galdore also presided as lord high wizard. It seemed for some years that King Petre's words of warning had been issued in error, or at least prematurely, and that the powers of darkness had not manifested themselves as he had been inclined to believe. Alusia and King Atha's subjects continued to thrive and prosper, and thoughts of evil and doom-laden prophecies faded into the background. It seemed that harmony and peace in the land were destined to remain forever.

Map of the Kingdom of Alusia

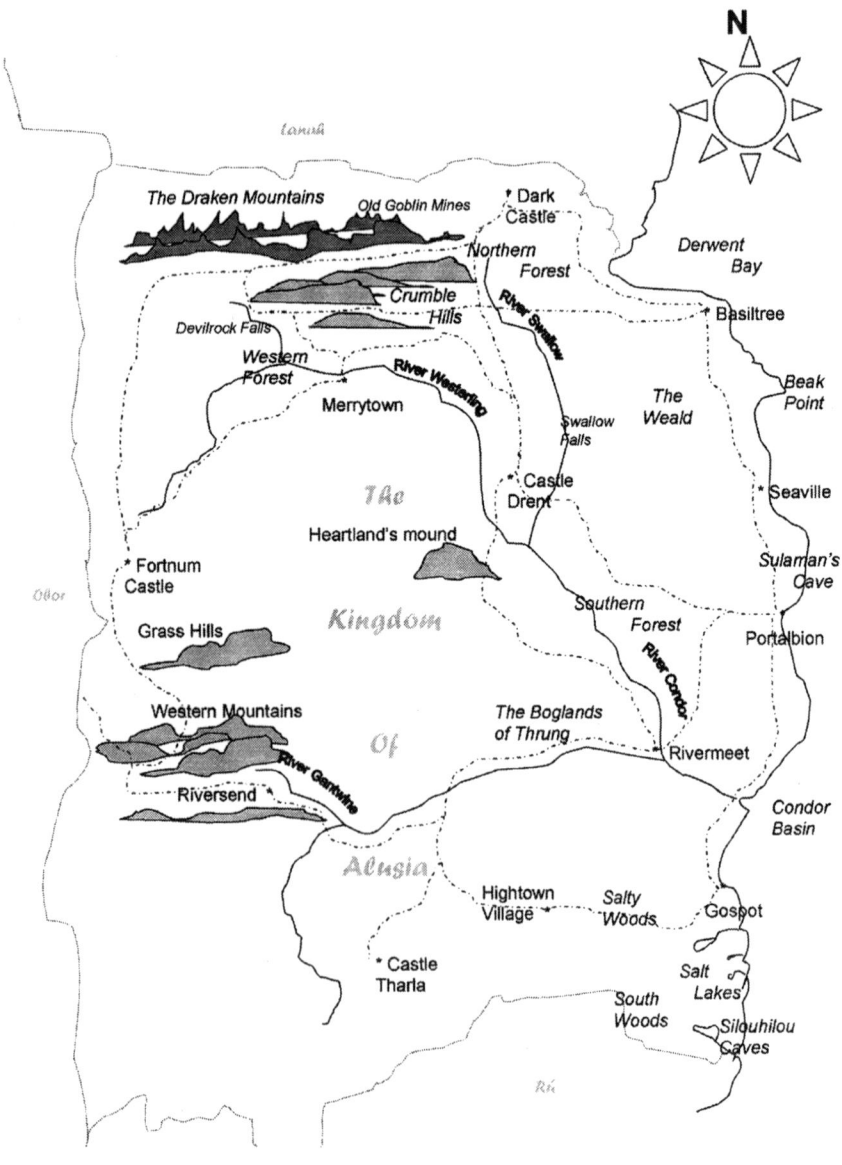

Alusia Today

THE KINGDOM of Alusia is a green and fertile place. There has been no poverty since many years past, and all the citizens of the land enjoy a tranquil life, but they are not idle folk by any stretch of the imagination. That everyone makes a useful contribution, according to their ability and particular skill, is seen as the backbone of their happy existence. Nobody expects reward other than fair return for a fair day's work. This applies whether a traveling entertainer, a village smithy, a local grocer or, indeed, a king. King Atha, of the Royal House of Dondrenton is loved by his people and good to those who respect the ways of peaceful existence. However, he is a formidable opponent of those who represent warlike ideals or decline to live in harmony with his subjects. Notwithstanding his peaceful and generous ways, Atha is known for his intolerance of things that conflict with his desires. His petulance is, to an extent, a product of his relative youth; for although he is a full grown man, he is yet early in the years of his reign. His advisor and mentor, the Wizard Galdore, is therefore an important member of the court and regarded by all, including the king, as a source of wisdom in the affairs of state. Castle Drent is a place of joy where all travellers are welcomed with friendship and camaraderie. Alusia is a land of fun, laughter, opportunity, and freedom—in the most part—for goodly as Alusian folk are, there are forces of evil present in their land. Malevolence, as it does in all places, waits only for a chance to overthrow and dominate goodwill.

Chapter One

Lucky Breaks

The Crumble Hills and
Northern Forest of Alusia

THE HAZY purple mountains behind him were beautiful in the evening calm. Graceforth's mail tunic weighed heavily on his shoulders. The jewel-studded handle of the broadsword, strapped to his saddle, glinted in the setting sun, shooting red and gold rays to the south, as if guiding him forward. But Castle Drent and the Council of Knights were still two days' ride at a moderate pace; he had many miles yet to face. Not tonight though; he had journeyed this way from Dark Castle many times before and was familiar with the safe caves that lay no more than a few furlongs on along the valley track. As he tensed his leg muscles for gentle encouragement to the horse's flanks, he detected movement on the way ahead and paused, reining the stallion to a standstill rather than urging him forward. Squinting into the gloaming, darkened by the canopy of the forest edge, Graceforth saw a flaxen-haired maiden who, by her demeanor and dress, he judged to be of uncommonly high breeding and rank. As she hurried toward him, limping a little, Graceforth perceived she was a comely wench. The maiden called.

1

"Good Sir Knight, save me from my peril and I will be forever in your debt."

Her soft, sensuous voice captivated Graceforth and even before she reached him, he felt drawn to her.

Aye, Graceforth thought, *having this lass forever in one's debt could be substantial comfort to a tired and weary soul—particularly if that tired and weary soul's personal mark be Sir Lionel Graceforth of Dondrenton.*

"Pray, tell me fair maiden, what is your plight? What ails thee, for I see naught but the glow of the setting sun and peace and tranquility in yonder hillside, rivaled only by your own perfect beauty."

"My plight is behind me my liege, in more sense than one, for I have been abused by a serpent, mistaken in its belief that I showed aggression, when in truth I merely wished to share the fallen tree on which it rested. Had I known of its presence in a hollow in the log, I would have selected an alternate resting place, but it lay hidden."

"My poor child, where exactly did he strike?"

The maiden turned slowly, indicating with a gesture the area around her left buttock.

"And," she confessed, "I caught sight of the beast, recognizing it as one venomous viper. The poison must be removed from my body without delay if I am to survive this encounter. Already I feel the creeping effects of the bane."

Graceforth burbled. He was a man of the world, much experienced in matters of the backwoods and knowledgeable in administering assistance to those afflicted with a venomous bite. He knew what had to be done and beautiful as the maiden was, his mouth went dry at the prospect. Being also well acquainted with affairs of etiquette, he was somewhat at a loss as to how to approach this particular situation. However, that must be put aside. He was a knight of the realm, sworn to defend the king and his subjects, avowed to uphold law and order, defender of the faith, and protector of maidens in distress. But, he would require this maiden's full cooperation in throwing her dignity to the four winds if he was to save her from her present peril. The application of the herbal poultice would be an insignificant issue in comparison to the extraction of the poison.

ॐॐ

High on Crumble Hill, perched on a ridge overlooking the valley, sat Randolph. He sang softly to himself as he brushed away the golden curls that hung loosely around his handsome face. He crooned gently to the hills and valley and to the setting sun in all its glory—with a "fah la la and a hey nonnie no."

As Randolph's brown eyes gazed idly down into the valley, he espied a good knight mounted on horseback, sporting the crest of the house of Dondrenton on his shield, symbol of his lordship King Atha. He appeared to be in earnest conversation with a fair young maiden whose manner indicated some measure of concern and urgency. As he watched, he observed the knight dismount and drop to his knees as if in prayer. He also saw, to his astonishment and amusement, the fair young wench lift her skirt, exposing for all to see that part of her womanhood that he guessed had been the subject of the negotiation he had just witnessed.

"Fah la la and a hey nonnie no isn't in it," whispered Randolph to himself. "Here is the making of a fine tale for the telling on my first visit to Castle Drent, and no mistake."

Randolph rolled into a more comfortable observing position in the soft turf, balanced himself precariously on the edge of the ridge, rested chin on cupped hands, and eagerly awaited developments.

ॐॐ

Lifting her skirts coyly, the maiden proffered her posterior to the gallant knight who, although having fought many a foe and been honored in numerous encounters with enemies of good King Atha, had never been subjected to an experience of such proportions, for attractive as she was, she displayed a substantial area of posterior flesh. What, he wondered, would be more likely to draw ridicule from his peers than the sight of him kneeling in the dusty road, lips pursed, addressing the exposed rump of a buxom, if comely, wench. His only consolation was the thought that nobody was there to observe his antics. Had he known then what he came to know some time later, he might have welcomed the keen interest of a minstrel perched on a ridge on the hillside. As his mouth came in contact with the wound and he sucked,

Graceforth was overcome with dizziness. He felt a powerful force pulling him in toward the maiden. It was as if he were defenseless against her charm, enveloped by her voluptuous form. He tugged his lips from the embrace, for he knew that the toxin must be ejected; to swallow the venom would be only to translate the maiden's plight into his own sorrow. But no sooner had he rid himself of the contents of his mouth than he felt his face involuntarily wrenched once more and buried deep in the generous proportions of the maiden's abundant buttocks. Once more he sucked, once more he tore away to spit, but again he was directed by an irresistible attraction to clamp his lips back in this now overly demanding and unorthodox embrace. It was as if some spell had been cast, demanding he become one with the maiden in this unseemly fashion; as if the very sands of time ran through the narrow link made between lips and derriere. The knight felt his strength being sapped; he was powerless to oppose the contact. His head swam and all about him dissolved into a mist. He was unaware of anything bar the unexplained, vital obsession to maintain this physical bond. He was oblivious to the commotion behind him, as a minstrel, with tears of laughter streaming down his cheeks and shaking uncontrollably, overbalanced from a ridge high on the hill above him and, complete with traveller's pack and instruments, came tumbling down the grassy slope. Neither Randolph, because of his preoccupation with not being bounced and slithered to death, nor the knight, due to his close attachment by the lips to the now offending hide, saw the comely maiden transform into a wizened, wart-encrusted crone. Randolph, as a consequence of his preoccupation with self-preservation, was also not aware of the hag dragging the semi-conscious, stupefied, and still firmly attached knight off the track, into the woods, and away. Randolph rolled to a stop, he judged in his disoriented state, just a few feet from the couple. However, on jumping up from his prone position, dusting himself down, and gently investigating his bruises, found himself and the stallion the only occupants of the otherwise lonely track.

"Ah," Randolph muttered to the stallion. "At last, Sir Knight has discovered which side is up and has taken the wench into the woods for a bit of eventide rumpey pumpey."

4

The stallion tossed his mane as if in disgust at the proceedings, turned toward the grassy verge, and commenced a noisy meal. Randolph slung his pack on his shoulder, recovered his lute and silver piccolo from the ditch nearby, bid the stallion adieu, turned on his heel, and went on his merry way into the sunset, whistling and already composing a ditty, with a "fah la la and a hey nonnie no."

Sir Lionel Graceforth was no more getting rumpey pumpey than he was flying in the air.

ॐॐ

"Where is Graceforth?" stormed the king. "The Knights' Council starts tomorrow."

"Word of his whereabouts has not been received, my lord."

"Then send in a minstrel. Let me at least be entertained if my cousin cannot find his way home, and even Galdore's sorcery cannot detect his location."

"Sire, there is a new man in court. I have heard tell he is worthy of a hearing."

"Then let him sing for his supper," Atha said. "Send him to me, and get Galdore to join us with some of his more colorful magic."

Randolph hurried to the hall where the king sat impatiently, his fingers drumming the arm of the throne on which he fidgeted.

"I am told you sing a good song with some flair and style," Atha said. "What is your name, minstrel?"

"Randolph Kettle, Sire."

"Then Randolph Kettle, sing me a ditty; I grow weary of the sameness of this place. Ah, Galdore, there you are. Come, join us. Listen to a song, then after, enthral us with some fiery spectacle."

Randolph sang for the king and the old man with flowing gray beard and sparkling eyes.

> *"How to handle a woman?*
> *There's a way . . ."*

Atha looked bored and irritated.

"No, no, no!" he shouted. "Every minstrel that passes this way sings me that song. By now, I know how to handle every blessed woman in the whole kingdom. Have you no new songs? Something different, maybe even something about how not to handle a woman."

"I have one such song in the stage of preparation, Sire, but in truth it may not be to your majesty's taste and, as yet, has no ending."

"Sing it to me anyway," commanded the king. "I will be the judge of whether or not it pleases me."

Randolph started his new song, telling the tale of the knight he had seen some few days earlier. He kept a watchful eye on the king to judge, as best he might, whether it pleased or offended. He planned to stop singing at any point and plead unfinished verses if the king looked dissatisfied.

> *"As I was walking out one day*
> *Among the hills so green, oh,*
> *I looked down on the valley track*
> *Where, proud Sir Knight did go.*
> *With a fah la la and a fah la la la la*
> *With a fah la-la ha and a hey-ey nonnie no."*

Randolph looked up, the king smiled and nodded for him to continue.

> *"Toward him ran a fair young maid;*
> *She would not let him pa-ass.*
> *She spoke with him in an earnest way,*
> *Then proffered him her arse.*
> *With a fah la la and a fah la la la la,*
> *With a fah la-la ha and a hey-ey nonnie no."*

The king chuckled at the bawdiness of the ditty, and his drumming fingers took up the tempo of the song. Galdore's face grew troubled, as if some concern played suddenly on his mind, but Randolph was focused on the king's mood and decided it was safe enough to continue.

"Then good Sir Knight descended from his horse.
On such luck he had not counted.
For all the world, I swore that he
Would swiftly be re-mounted.
With a fah la la and a fah la la la la,
With a fah la-la ha and a hey-ey nonnie no.

But he dropped down in an attitude of prayer
While the maiden was untucking.
But then he did just pucker up his lips
And her rump he started sucking.
With a fah la la and a fah la la la la,
With a fah la-la ha and a hey-ey nonnie no.

A more distasteful foreplay could not be,
And he soon discovered that.
For he pulled his lips away to the side
And very firmly spat.
With a fah la la and a fah la la la la,
With a fah la-la ha and a hey-ey nonnie no."

Atha was delighted with the entertainment. Tapping the rhythm with his foot, he turned to Galdore, whose look of grave anxiety displeased him.

"Galdore, where is your sense of fun? Does the minstrel not amuse your ear? Have those dusty books and that celibate living finally turned you into an old man?"

"Sire, 'tis not the quality of the minstrel's song, nor his skill at delivery that troubles me, but the tale itself that brings on a foreboding," Galdore replied. "Let us listen a while longer and then I will quiz the minstrel. I have a sense that the tale is not such a jest as it might first appear."

"Well good Sir Knight still didn't get it right
And looked a trifle grumpy.
The diff'rence it seemed, he did not know
Twixt rump and rumpey pumpey.
With a fah la la and a fah la la la la,
With a fah la-la ha and a hey-ey nonnie no.

> *At last, the knight he seemed to get the gist*
> *Of the maiden's prime desire.*
> *After two more sucks, each followed by a spit*
> *To the woods he did retire.*
> *With a fah la la and a fah la la la la,*
> *With a fah la-la ha and a hey-ey nonnie no."*

A page entered the hall and hurried to the king's side. "Grave tidings my liege. Sir Graceforth's mount has crossed the drawbridge alone. It is tethered in the courtyard below."

The king went quickly to the window to confirm that the riderless horse was indeed that of his cousin, Sir Lionel Graceforth. Galdore followed and, not to be left out, the minstrel also peered down from the window.

"But that is the stallion I saw not three days ago," the minstrel said. "That is the mount of the knight in my merry tale."

"Now less merry because of the truth in it," Galdore cried. "Come minstrel, tell me all that you observed; we may yet be in time to save Sir Lionel."

As Randolph related the happenings of three days earlier, the wizard's expression grew darker and more worried.

"Did you actually see them go into the woods?" Galdore queried.

"No indeed, sir, they must have gone while I was engaged in my unexpected acrobatics."

"Then you did not witness any transformation of the maiden?"

"No sir, I did not."

Galdore turned to Atha. "Nevertheless, we have no time to lose," he said. "Sire, I cannot be certain, but I believe Sir Lionel has been captured by the black witch, Griselda. She was banished to the forests of the north many years ago by the Lord High Wizard Sulaman. Rumour has been rife these past months that she has broken free of the magic bonds placed on her. Although not yet fully restored to her awesome power, it would seem she is preying on unsuspecting travellers, appearing in the form of a fair maiden and enticing them by various ruses into capture, where she is extracting their vital life force to restore her evil energy. The serpent bite is one such fabrication used by her, seducing victims to engage in intimate body contact, a circumstance, in her now reduced capacity, necessary for her to bring them under her spell."

"We ride north immediately," cried the king. "Saddle horses, call together an escort of ten of the bravest knights, and prepare a mount for the minstrel. He rides with us; his knowledge of what took place may be invaluable in saving Graceforth, and he may yet find an ending for his song."

Randolph's protestation that he was a minstrel and not a witch stalker or knight rescuer, was lost in the hubbub as he was ushered away to be kitted out with armour and weaponry.

శ్రీ

The woods were dark and cheerless and now, disengaged from the witch's rump, Graceforth slowly regained his senses to find his hands and feet bound. He lay in an uncomfortable, crumpled heap at the foot of a large oak. Sensing rather than seeing a movement to his left, he turned his head to find the ugliest old hag he had ever encountered. She squatted beside a bubbling cauldron, the contents of which Graceforth dared not imagine, but from which exuded a smell so loathsome it made him retch. The witch cackled and chanted in a rasping voice as she tended the stinking brew.

> *"Stir the pot and make it fine,*
> *Five days to be ready, then we dine.*
> *Suck the life from those we caught,*
> *Pint by pint, and quart by quart.*
> *Build our power and make it grow,*
> *Make it strong, then we can go*
> *And seek revenge; revenge is sweet.*
> *Reclaim position, our rightful seat,*
> *From where we'll rule, from where we'll strike,*
> *Enslaving all, make evil like*
> *The world has never seen before.*
> *We'll make it ours, lay down new lore.*
> *Black wisdom is what will be seen,*
> *And o'er the world we'll reign, as queen."*

As consciousness continued to drift back, Graceforth began to take in more of his surroundings. The witch's lair, hidden deep in the forest, was a foul and filthy place. Rotting vegetation, slime, and gruesome remains of previous victims lay all around. The air hung thick and still with the stench of death, and no sunlight penetrated this evil place. The hideout was bathed in a pale green glow that emanated from a large crystal globe suspended in mid air in the center of the lair, flanked by two black candles mounted on tall gold candlesticks. He watched as the crone shuffled to the globe and passed her hands over it in a gesture as if massaging some force that lurked within. He lay still, not wishing to attract the hag's attention, assessing what chance of escape, if any, he might have. The glow from the globe intensified and the witch peered into it as if seeing pictures and scenes from another place.

"Galdore, I sense your attention, but don't believe you can stop me now," she croaked. "My powers are soon to be regained; my strength returns. I am nearly ready to dominate the world and crush you in the process. I will rule; I will rule."

Graceforth listened to this ranting and knew that escape was imperative.

Not only is my own life threatened, but Galdore must be warned of the plans of this evil witch, he thought to himself.

ॐ

Randolph was of two minds about his membership in the Graceforth rescue party. On one hand, he was flattered and honored to be included in such an adventure. He was excited, as would be any young man, at the prospect of basking in the glory of a noble deed of rescue. On the other hand, he was apprehensive, perhaps terrified, at the thought of going into battle against a powerful and, what was that word Galdore used? —*awesome* black witch. He considered the jewels and dragons of the situation and finally decided that, on balance, he was a "reluctant participant in this venture," as he said to Sir Nigel, the master of arms, when he collected his weaponry and armour from the stores.

"Well my friend, if the king says you're going, then going you are," Sir Nigel declared. "But my advice would be to have a chat with Galdore before setting off. He'll complain and moan at being interrupted, he always does. But he's all skin and no scales when he's got to know you, and he'll give you some tips about what to do and when to do it. I'll be one of the party as well, so stick by me and I'll do my best to keep you out of trouble."

"Thanks Sir Nigel, " Randolph said as he left the store, laden with what felt like more than his own body weight in kit.

ॐॐ

Galdore was busying in his study, when there was a tapping on his door.

"Who is it, I'm busy," he shouted, but of course, he already knew who it was. He wouldn't have been much of a wizard if he didn't.

"It's me, Randolph. Can I talk to you before we go, sir?"

Galdore opened the door, displaying an irritated manner. "Can't it wait?" he said, huffing and puffing. "There's important things to do before we go, mustn't forget to bring all the bits and pieces we might need to defeat Griselda's wicked magic. We don't know what she might have up her sleeve—a sly old bat that one."

"Well I was hoping that before we went I might . . ." Randolph's words trailed off as he looked past Galdore into the wizard's study and saw the most amazing collection of books, glass tubes and phials, engraved wooden and ivory boxes, pearl-studded canes, embossed cards, pictures and charts, and all kinds of paraphernalia that one would expect of a wizard's room, but the like of which Randolph had never seen before.

"Don't just stand there blathering and gawping man, come in; you can help me pack."

Randolph entered as instructed. He stood, gaping at the strange room. Coloured jars with contrasting labels festooned the main workbench behind mixing bowls, dishes, cups, and glass beakers, some of which bubbled and churned liquids, enjoying their own private, self-contained storms. Clumps of dried and drying herbs of every type imaginable hung from bars suspended on chains from the high, beamed ceiling; boxes marked with mysterious hieroglyphics and symbols were neatly shelved in pigeonholes that stretched from the floor up to a level twice Randolph's height. And candles; everywhere there were candles,

11

white, green, red, blue, and two that each contained all the colors of the rainbow mixed in streaks and swirls that sent Randolph's head spinning just to look at them. These two multicolored candles stood on gold candlesticks about four feet tall, each side of a shimmering crystal orb that hung suspended in mid air. Beyond the orb, on the far side of the chamber, directly opposite the door, was an enormous fireplace in which burned a bonfire of logs under a soot-blackened cauldron. A huge oak beam formed the mantle across the hearth area, which contained alcoves on either side with small seats built into the stonework. The floor of the room was of polished slate, looking as if it should be cold as gray ice, but from which Randolph felt a warm, welcoming glow. Bright sunlight streamed in through the windows from the early autumn day outside, playing catch with the dancing shadows created by the blazing fire. Furnishings in the room were sparse, but the dark, carved desk and the few chairs dotted around were of impressive quality and style. Against the far wall stood a tall wooden cabinet. It had a round dish positioned at the front, on which were painted numerals and pictures. Two pointed arms pivoted on a spindle sticking out in the middle of the dish. Suddenly, it started to whir and clank, and then it emitted a loud chime as if a gong had been struck somewhere in its depths. Randolph leaped several inches into the air, startled.

"Mechanical time measuring device," Galdore said. "Built it myself. Only one other exists, but I gave that to a friend."

Randolph went over to one of the bubbling glass urns.

"Love potion," Galdore explained.

Randolph investigated a second steaming jar.

"Wealth spell," Galdore offered.

A third pot brought the description, "Sleeping draught."

Randolph crossed to the bubbling cauldron and sniffed at it.

"Rabbit stew," Galdore said, smiling at the curiosity.

By the door stood a large wooden chest, the hinged lid folded back. Randolph peered into it. The inside seemed about ten times the volume that should have fitted into the outside dimensions.

"Just a little trick I learned for packing lots of things into a small space," boasted Galdore, amused by the look of bewilderment that had replaced Randolph's previously smiling countenance. "Now come along; we don't have much time and there's still a lot to do. You collect that pile of blue boxes over by the hearth and load them into the chest. I'll check that we've got all the spell and charm ingredients."

"Mind yourself, Dragon." Galdore addressed a jet-black cat that was showing more than a passing interest in the packing. "Don't get in the way while we pack."

The animal obediently moved off and took up a supervising position, perched high on a pile of books on the desk.

Soon they were finished, and Galdore carefully lifted the glass orb and the rainbow-colored candles, placing them last in the chest before he closed and bolted the lid. Randolph hadn't even started to ask Galdore all the questions he had prepared in his mind, but it didn't seem to matter anymore. He felt that he had been promoted to wizard's helper, and that gave him a feeling of ownership in the quest. He had somehow been whisked from *reluctant participant* to *you're not going without me*. Galdore chuckled quietly to himself. A wizard's job wasn't always thunder and lightning spells.

"Come, then," Galdore said. "Just time for a quick bowl of that stew and then to the horses."

Wiping his mouth on a multicolored handkerchief, Galdore eventually announced that it was time to depart. "And bring the chest," he instructed.

"But I can't carry that," Randolph complained. "It'll be too heavy for even three men to lift."

"Nonsense," Galdore said. "Pick it up, man."

Randolph, if only to prove his point, went over to the chest. It was as light as a feather and seemed to float on the air, as a cork would bob on water. Randolph had only to push it along. Dragon sat, as if driving a carriage, on top of the floating chest.

When they got to the courtyard, the knights were already mounted, and Randolph thought, an impressively fearsome band they looked. It gave him some comfort to be traveling with such protectors. Randolph was helped onto his horse by the stable lads, who also took the chest full of magical supplies and, under Galdore's strict supervision, strapped it to the back of one of the pack animals. Galdore mounted his horse, a magnificent white stallion that bore no saddle or reins.

"Doesn't need them," Sir Nigel explained to Randolph. "The animal understands every word he says to it."

Atha came out of the castle and his horse, a sleek black mare, was brought forward. Leaping athletically into the saddle, the king cried, "Forward men, to the rescue of our brother knight and the destruction of Griselda."

He raised a chainmailed fist above his head, signaling for the castle gates to be opened and the rescue party to ride forward. Evening was approaching as they departed the castle, and they rode hard through the night northward, the king setting a fast pace at the head of the party and Galdore bringing up the rear. Randolph was put in charge of the pack-horse carrying Galdore's strongbox and placed toward the middle of the party riding with Sir Nigel. It seemed that Galdore had unofficially appointed Randolph as his helper, a fact that made him feel important, but also a little anxious about whether he would be equal to the task. In the early morning light, the group rested on the bank of a river where the horses were watered and grazed. Galdore called Randolph and bid him walk with him to the water's edge some short distance from where the main party sat eating their breakfast rations.

"By my calculations, we are about five hours' ride at a fast pace from the point where Sir Lionel was kidnapped. We have made good time, which is well, for Griselda grows more powerful by the day; I can feel her strength tugging at the fabric of the world. It will not be long before she equals me, and I will be unable to deal with her alone. As it is I will need all my reserves to counter her evil force, and I will need you to assist me."

"Mmm… me?" Randolph stammered. "I know nothing of wizardry and magic. What can I do?"

"You will know at the time," was all that Galdore would say. "Trust in yourself and the magic of your music. You will know at the time. You are destined to be the One."

"What one?" Randolph asked.

But Galdore was already striding off toward the others.

Randolph looked down at Dragon, who gazed unblinkingly back. If cats can smile, Dragon smiled. It didn't make Randolph feel any easier.

෨෦ඏ

Graceforth became aware that he was not the only uncomfortable-looking bundle trussed up and stacked around the base of the large oak tree. As the green light from the globe intensified, he could see others lying close by, all bound and gagged in similar fashion to himself; all with staring, terrified eyes; all awaiting their fate as Griselda's fodder. Graceforth noted that the style of dress of his fellow prisoners indicated they were common folk, merchants and journeymen, unlikely to have any training in dealing with capture, kidnap, and escape. His fate, and theirs, rested on his leadership. If escape was to be achieved, it would be down to him. The witch finished viewing the scene she had called up in the globe, and as the light faded again, she came to where her prisoners lay. She poked one or two with a bony finger and squeezed their flesh with grotesque, horny hands.

"Only a few more days my lovelies," she cackled. "Only a few more days."

The witch screeched with laughter and returned to her cauldron of stinking brew, which she stirred vigorously, releasing a foul stench that enveloped the whole lair, bringing bile, once again, to Graceforth's throat.

At least, he thought, *I have a while to think. I will be missed at court; they will come seeking me, and even witches must sleep. I will await my chance and prepare for rescue.*

He rolled sideways to ease the developing stiffness in his immobilized limbs, the unauthorized movement drawing a string of abuse from the witch's mouth, the like of which he wouldn't even have heard in the back room of the Castle Inn on a knights' night out. However, in rolling, he encountered a sharp fragment of bone, probably from a previous victim, but which would serve as a blade to sever his bonds. He lay still, covering the bone, lest the witch or her black raven, perched close by, should discover his lucky find.

෨෦ඏ

"My bum's sore," Randolph announced to the world. He was not used to riding so hard or so long, but they must be close now.

"Yes," he called back to where Galdore still protected the rear of the group. "I recognize the valley and the hillside where I tumbled. We are close to the spot where Sir Graceforth must have entered the forest."

Galdore urged his horse forward to the front of the party and spoke with Atha.

"We camp here," Atha called to the men. "Rest now, for it is tonight that we attempt rescue of Graceforth. Galdore has preparations to make. Give him whatever assistance he requires."

Galdore's wooden chest was unstrapped from the pack horse and taken to his marquee, which was being erected close by. In Atha's tent, plans were being made for the assault on the witch's lair from sketches and diagrams Galdore had provided. The strategy was for the group to move, with maximum stealth, as close as was possible to the witch's lair without detection. At that point, Galdore would launch an attack of magic on the witch and while distracted by this, the knights would storm the lair in search of Sir Lionel Graceforth. On establishing that he was still alive and securing his release, attention would be switched to the destruction of the witch. Galdore's counsel was that her death could be ensured only by boiling her alive in her own cauldron. He also told how both her crystal orb and her familiar, the black raven, must be destroyed to guarantee that she would never be able to resurrect. Randolph wandered aimlessly around the camp, helping here and there with tent erection and then went to the kitchen area, where cooks were organizing a meal for the whole party. Most rested in preparation for the attack, but Randolph wasn't tired: He drifted toward Galdore's tent, curious to know what the wizard was doing and hoping to get another look at some of the treasures they had packed in the chest. He was still several yards from the wizard's marquee when a voice in his head said,

"Stop lurking about outside and come in here, will you, I need some help."

Delighted to have something positive to do, he went into the marquee and stopped in his tracks, staring dumbfounded at the construction he saw before him.

"Close your mouth, will you," Galdore said. "Every time you come into my rooms, you stand around gaping. Haven't you ever seen a spell generator before?"

Randolph admitted that he hadn't as he gazed, still open mouthed, at the contraption. It was about the size and shape of a large barrel. On the front, connected to a pipe that went in through a hole in the casing, was a trumpet type of arrangement, and mounted on top was a large swiveling mirror. On the opposite side from the trumpet were what looked like levers and handles, each located under a magic symbol, but the most startling thing about it was the color. It was fluorescent pink.

"Why is it pink?" Randolph asked.

"All my machines are pink," Galdore said, as if this answered the question. "This is the machine that you will operate while I use the magic orb to drain Griselda's power. We need to distract her while I twin with her orb and set up a force field and an earth connection that will give a reverse loop, directing her evil power back on herself. It'll take her a while to make compensating adjustments to break through the force field, and while she does that she will be powerless—you see?"

Randolph nodded, but Galdore could tell from his expression that he didn't see at all. "It'll all become clear at the time," he offered in comfort at Randolph's obvious unease.

But Randolph was not comforted in the least. He had a feeling that while he was doing the distracting with the spell-making machine, he was going to be in direct line of fire; he was going to be the target for Griselda's wrathful response. He didn't like that one bit and said so to Galdore.

"Don't be such a milksop," Galdore said. "What do you think the mirror is for?"

Randolph didn't have a clue what the mirror was for, a fact that Galdore quickly interpreted from Randolph's shaking knees and whiter-than-normal complexion.

"You use the mirror to reflect back the bolts of enchanted lightning that Griselda will hurl at you. Look, I'll demonstrate." And without warning, Galdore directed a stream of colored flashes from the index finger of his right hand at the mirror on top of the spell generator. They bounced from the mirror's surface and shot off at an angle, narrowly missing the cat, which scampered from the tent with a howl of surprise.

"See? As long as you stay behind the mirror, you can't be harmed."

"You better tell that to the cat," Randolph mumbled.

"Well you'll have to do it," Galdore said. "There's no-one else, unless you'd like to swap places with one of the knights and rush the lair while Griselda's distracted."

Randolph opted for working the spell generator. He'd come this far, and Galdore obviously wasn't going to take no for an answer.

"All right," Randolph said reluctantly. "Show me how to work it then."

ठ∘ऽ

Dragon, having recovered from the near miss, was off on an errand. Wizard's familiars, as well as being friends and companions to their masters, were also unseen eyes and ears. They often collected information, passed messages, and observed situations that required stealth. As Dragon approached the witch's lair, she felt apprehensive. She sensed the presence, not only of Griselda, but also of the black raven, guarding the area. This must have been the same bird that Dragon had noticed earlier, when they arrived at the campsite. It had circled several times high above them, screeching, then flown swiftly off in the direction of the deep forest. The witch would know of their close proximity. Dragon knew she would have to proceed with extra caution. Moving slowly and carefully through the undergrowth, the cat picked her way to within a few feet of the lair. Peering into the pale green gloom, she could see the witch stooping over the steaming cauldron. The huge black raven, perched on a branch, seemed to be sleeping; well, one eye looked closed, which Dragon knew was about as close to sleeping as ravens came. Any sudden movement and it would be instantly awake, beady eyes alert, pointed beak ready to stab and thrust at any foe, clawed feet ready to tear and rip at the flesh of intruders — and it was far too big for Dragon to overpower. Past the witch, on the far side of the clearing, stood a large oak at the foot of which Dragon could just make out what looked like bundles of old rags, but then she saw one of them move and realized they were people, lying bound and tethered, but they were definitely human forms. It was only a few minutes later that Graceforth felt the silken rub of soft fur on the back of his hand. He opened his eyes to meet the gaze of the cat.

"Dragon," he whispered, immediately recognizing Galdore's familiar.

As soon as she knew her presence had been acknowledged, the cat was gone, leaving Graceforth for an instant wondering whether he had been dreaming. But he knew in his heart that it was real, and he knew Dragon couldn't risk lingering any longer than necessary. But he also knew that if Dragon was there, Galdore and probably Atha and his brother knights were not far behind. Rescue was imminent, probably only hours away. He must start preparations to distract the witch and that evil-looking bird. He must give Galdore the best chance to get close and attack the old hag before she realized what was happening. Of course, he did not know of the raven's flight; he did not know that the witch was already aware of the exact size of the rescue party and of the precise location of their camp; he did not know that she was already making preparations for their reception.

Galdore sat, in what appeared to Randolph to be deep conversation with a cat. Two days ago, he would have classified the behavior as, at least, eccentric, probably bordering on insanity; now he accepted it as relatively normal. He mused on whether this might mean that he, himself, was becoming mad. Before he had time to draw a conclusion from his reflections, Galdore called him over.

"Randolph. Run to Atha and inform him. Good news. Sir Lionel is alive. Off you go quickly. Tell him to prepare the group to leave in an hour. Tell him the witch's lair is several miles from here, deep in the forest. Quickly Randolph; we have no time to waste. Tell him and then come back here as fast as you can; we have our own final preparations to make."

Randolph did as the wizard bid and was soon back, feeling both excited and afraid—this wasn't what minstrels were built for, but it was an adventure worthy of great song and story. This was the stuff of legends, and he was in it. For a minute, he was flying with the birds in a blue sky, flitting between white clouds, swooping down to the green treetops below, floating on air, and all the while singing of the legend of Randolph the Great, Randolph the Explorer, Randolph the Adventurer, Witch Killer, and

Rescuer (not rescuer of maidens in distress, although he would do that too, but of knights in distress). And below him thronged the crowds, waving, cheering masses, applauding his deeds of daring, honoring his prowess, glorifying him and his feats of incredible heroism.

"So what do you think?" Galdore's voice cut sharply across this personal journey of fantasy. "Can you do it?"

"''Course I can."

Randolph, still in part responding from his flight of fancy, winced at his own agreement to something unheard.

"But just go through it again to make sure I understood it properly," he added quickly, hoping to discover what he had just contracted to.

"All right," Galdore said, looking a bit puzzled. "But I don't see the difficulty in making two cups of chamomile infusion to warm us before we leave."

Randolph heaved a relieved sigh and went off to the camp kitchen to make the brew.

In the kitchen area, Randolph encountered Sir Nigel.

"Randolph, or should I say Apprentice Wizard Randolph? For that is the reputation you have quickly gained amongst our number. And yet I remember your words of not two days past—reluctant participant in this venture—you had us all fooled, I'll confess. And there was I, offering to protect you, when all the time it was you coming along to help protect the king, me, and all my brother knights."

Sir Nigel threw back his head and roared with good-natured laughter, slapped Randolph on the back with a heavy swipe that sent him spinning across the kitchen, and disappeared off to his tent chuckling,

"Reluctant participant," Randolph heard him chortle. "That's a good one, ha."

Randolph stretched and waggled his shoulders to make sure they still worked. He made two mugs of steaming chamomile infusion in a thoughtful mood and carried them carefully back to Galdore's marquee. He was fascinated by all the wizard's paraphernalia and very taken with his way and his manner, but Apprentice Wizard Randolph was sure he was not.

Anyway, he thought, *I could only be such a thing by the agreement of Galdore, and he'd never consider a minstrel as a suitable candidate for a prestigious role like that—would he?*

Back in the tent, he handed Galdore one of the mugs.

"Hhmmm," Galdore said. "That smells like a good brew. You're quite a natural when it comes to herbal infusions. Hhmmm." He eyed Randolph in a thoughtful and penetrating way. "Anyway, get that down you; we must leave in a few minutes."

Randolph's mind quickly reverted to a position of reluctant participant as they moved the spell generator, plus a box of additional things that Galdore had carefully packed, to join the party assembled outside Atha's tent.

"Good," Atha said. "Here are the wizards; now we can get started."

Off they went. A somber bunch, for they knew the seriousness of their mission and the difficulty of their task. Dragon led the way, followed closely by Galdore and Randolph with the spell generator, which floated in much the same way as the chest had done when they moved it from Galdore's study. It seemed like weeks, if not months had passed, rather than just two days since he sang for the king and since Sir Lionel's riderless horse had arrived back at court. On through the woods they tramped for more than an hour. Suddenly, Dragon stopped and sat down on the forest track. Galdore picked up the cat and appeared to be listening to something, but Randolph, close as he was to the two of them, heard nothing at all. It was dark now, and the deep forest removed any chance of light from the moon, even though it shone brightly on the canopy above. Their only light was a faint red glow, risked from Galdore's wand, but even this would soon need to be extinguished for fear the witch might, too soon, detect their approach. Closer they crept, nearer and nearer, until they could smell the foul stench of the lair. Galdore, still at the head of the group, held up his hand to signal a halt and then waved them to keep down low lest their heads should be seen above the bushes and prove to be targets for lightning bolts thrown by Griselda. They gathered around Galdore in a small clearing just yards from the boundary of the lair, shielded from the witch's view by the dense undergrowth and shrubs that protected the boundary of the hideaway.

"Now," Galdore whispered to Atha. "Let's go through the plan one final time."

"Yes," Atha said. "The plans are laid well. When you have done whatever magic is to cause the distraction of the witch, give the word. We will rush the lair, release Graceforth, grab the witch, and throw her into the cauldron. Our archers will shoot down the raven and throw that into the pot on top of the witch. Lastly, as we get Graceforth and any other captives away to safety, you will dismantle her orb, throw that into the cauldron, under which Randolph will have stoked the fire and have a real blaze going."

"Good," Galdore said. "Any questions from anybody? Randolph, I'll give you your final instructions in just a minute, as soon as the men are spread out."

"That's fine," Atha said. "Take up your positions."

The knights crept quietly away from the clearing, each moving to his allotted place, surrounding the lair on all sides. Galdore turned to Randolph.

"Right, now you go to the spell generator, take off the cover, and start it up. Remember all that I showed you back at the camp. Generate the spells one at a time and hurl them into the lair. If you can actually hit Griselda, even better. Don't forget, stay behind the mirror so that she can't strike you down, and turn it to reflect her lightning bolts back into her camp. Then, as soon as the knights attack, you rush into the lair behind them and start stoking the fire under the cauldron. We need a terrific blaze going to get the pot as hot as possible and to give us light to work by. Any questions?"

Randolph had nothing to ask, other than how to stop his knees quaking, but he felt this wasn't the time or place to pose this particular question to Galdore. He shook his head to indicate no questions and turned to take up his position behind the machine.

"Oh," Galdore said, reaching into the box of tricks he had brought and producing Randolph's lute. "You best take this and keep it with you; you never know. We can't be too careful."

Randolph opened his mouth to ask for what earthly reason he might need his lute, but thought better of it, took the instrument from Galdore, slung it on his back, and went over to the spell generator. He crouched behind the machine and gently pushed it forward until he was within ten feet of the lair boundary. There he stopped, turned the mirror toward the witch, whom he could see in the dim light, crouched over the cauldron, and watched for Galdore's signal, a brilliant blue flash that was to indicate the start of the attack.

బు⊸ఫ

Graceforth had managed to use the piece of sharp bone to free his hands and was now wriggling slowly, so as not to attract the attention of the hag, into a position where he might sever the bonds restraining his legs. His plan was to free himself and his fellow captives but not to attempt escape until Galdore arrived. He had just freed his legs when he heard a gentle purr. Dragon was back.

"Galdore must be here," Graceforth mouthed the words. He could have sworn the cat nodded affirmation.

Suddenly, there was a blinding blue flash followed by explosions all around the lair as Randolph activated the spells. The witch jumped from her position tending the bubbling cauldron and in one bound reached the green glowing orb. Her hands moved like lightning across its surface and she chanted words that Graceforth had never heard before.

"Misadola alfecto gradium," she cried, raising her bony, wrinkled, claw-like hands to the unseen sky. "Incresendo maximosa alforscum me paro."

An aura of incandescent yellow light grew to surround the witch. Her hands clasped and kneaded it into a ball of luminescence and she turned, throwing it with a mighty force into the forest in the direction of Randolph and the spell generator. The lightning bolt, for that was what it was, passed by Randolph and the machine, shot about one hundred yards into the forest, executed a neat 'U' turn and hovered, poised to strike from the rear. As it gathered speed, aimed directly at the machine, Randolph's only thought was, *Turn the mirror, turn the mirror.* He shouted to himself and launched himself forward to swivel the post on which the glass was mounted, but he slipped on the damp mossy soil, fell against the machine, and knocked the mirror to the ground. The lightning bolt was almost on him, he grabbed his lute from his back and using it like a bat, as the yellow ball of brilliance

23

came past him, hit it straight back into the witch's lair. He sank to his knees proclaiming, "Saints be praised—the power of music."

Griselda, knowing from the raven's reports about the spell generator and, from this, guessing most of Galdore's plan of attack, was convinced that her reverse-thrust heat-seeking lightning force bolt, which she had developed specially for this sort of attack, would destroy the machine. Having launched the bolt, she had therefore turned immediately back to access her orb before Galdore had a chance to link into it and earth out her power, which she realized correctly, would be his next move. She didn't see the yellow ball streaking from Randolph's splintered lute; she didn't know what it was that burst on the tree trunk just inches from the back of her head, stunning her senseless; she didn't see Graceforth lead the charge of the prisoners, pinning her face down in the mud; and she didn't hear Galdore's command to the knights to attack the lair; and she never knew it was Randolph who stoked the fire up to the blaze that boiled her away to oblivion.

❧

Back at court, Randolph was the hero of the day. Galdore was impressed that he hadn't even been needed to drain the witch's power; Atha and the knights were delighted that there had been nothing left for them to do but pick up the unconscious old hag and dump her in the cauldron. The archers laughingly complained that Randolph had forgotten to take over their jobs as well and they had still been required to shoot the raven down. Galdore had taught Randolph some party tricks to perform at the banquet table and every available young lady in court was jostling to get closer to him. Sir Lionel had given the hero's welcome speech and showered thanks on all his friends and colleagues who had participated in his rescue, but he had reserved special thanks for Randolph.

"How much we are all indebted to our new resident apprentice wizard for the bravery he has shown and the skill demonstrated in slaying the wicked witch," he said.

Randolph suddenly felt sad and, when Sir Lionel had finished his speech, went over to a window in an alcove at the back of the hall were Dragon sat on the windowsill in the evening sun.

He looked out over the forest and the hills beyond. He felt the still warm rays of the setting sun as they played on his face; calling him.

"I'm not sure I can be these things," Randolph said to Dragon. "Not sure I want to be these things. I'm not really an apprentice wizard or a hero. I'm just an ordinary minstrel who happened to get a lucky shot at a passing ball of fire and destroyed his lute in the process. None of Sir Lionel's rescue or the death of the witch was because of anything I did. I just happened to be in the right place at the right time and got a lucky break."

Dragon looked up at the minstrel. He could have sworn she smiled at him again. The cat jumped down from the sill and went to the door. She looked back as if to indicate to Randolph that she wanted him to follow. He took a last look at the party, which was still in full swing, and slipped quietly through the door behind Dragon. Only an old wizard with a long gray beard and sparkling eyes saw him leave. The minstrel followed the cat back to the room he had been allocated. On the bed lay his old clothes where he had left them when he donned his new finery for the banquet, but beside them lay a new lute, of the finest and most delicate rosewood imaginable. It was inlaid with mother of pearl design, and in the center around the hole into the sound chamber were engraved the same magic symbols that Galdore had shown him on the spell machine.

"Thank you Galdore." Randolph addressed the absent wizard. "Now I can finish that song. Oh, and thank you for not making it pink."

ॐ∘৯

When Galdore entered the room, all that remained were the fine clothes, neatly folded and laid on the bed with a note that said, "Thanks." Gone were the minstrel clothes, gone was the lute, gone was the minstrel. Galdore crossed to the window, where Dragon sat, and gazed onto the hillside beyond the castle wall. He could just make out a solitary figure climbing the steep track leading to the pass and on toward the southern forest and the sea. As he watched, the figure stopped and turned, looking back at the castle, and for a while seemed to hesitate, almost as

25

if he might turn back. But he didn't, and Galdore was pleased at his bravery.

"Too soon," he said to Dragon. "He has much world to investigate before he returns here. But one day, one day Castle Drent will see him again my friend, and then he might be ready. In the meantime, we can but guide and support him in his quest. Come, the party awaits."

Chapter Two
Adventure by the Sea

Portalbion Harbour

IN THE dusk, the pine-scented air smelled sweet as Randolph climbed the steep track. He stopped and looked back toward the castle where, just an hour earlier, he had been honored by knights, applauded by the king, and treated to a new lute by a wizard of great standing. He pulled the instrument round from where it hung on his back and looked at it. He raised his eyes to the castle again. The lighted windows showed warmth and shelter. Friendship and maybe even romance were contained within those walls. So why was he leaving?

"Am I mad," he said to himself. "There lies comfort, convenience, and a promise of success. Should I return? I could slip back to the party; no one would even know I'd been gone—except maybe Galdore."

The minstrel took a step back down the track, then stopped again and turned, looked on up the hill away from the castle. An owl hooted somewhere in the forest.

"But, there lies my path," Randolph said.

27

He cleared the top of the hill twenty minutes later and before starting his descent into the next valley, threw one last glance back to the castle.

"I can go on," he said to himself. "Because now I have a home. I have a place where I can always return and be welcomed."

And with that thought and a "fah la la and a hey nonnie no," he strode on, down the far side of the hill, on toward the southern forest and the long walk to the sea beyond. "Ah, the sea," he crooned to himself.

> *"Take me back to the sandy shore,*
> *Where love's lost shadow evermore*
> *Will haunt the cliffs*
> *And roll with the mist,*
> *Where I was treated to youth's first kiss.*
>
> *There let me tarry, there let me stay.*
> *There let me find again love's sweet way.*
> *In the coves and the dunes,*
> *Oh hear my plea;*
> *Show me the way, the way back to the sea.*
>
> *In the valleys and hills and rolling plains,*
> *I can walk, and sing, through the sun and the rains.*
> *But nearer to thee, oh my love,*
> *Let me be*
> *Where my soul can look out, look out over the sea."*

Sadness engulfed Randolph as he sang, for although few had ever known it from his lips, as well as holding fond memories of childhood sweethearts, the sea had also taken his beloved twin sister from him. He and Lydie were both six years old when she left him. He still returned time and time again in the vain hope that, one day the sea nymphs might return Lydie to him.

How much further to the coast? he wondered, wiping his eyes dry. "I seem to have been traveling forever through this forest."

It was two days later he heard the screech of a gull and knew that this part of his journey was nearing an end. An hour later, he was standing on the quay of a small harbour town.

"Randolph?" a voice behind him queried, and he turned to face Nicholas Freedom, his boyhood friend from many years past in Gospot.

"Nick, what on earth are you doing here?"

"I might ask the same question of you, Randolph Kettle. I live here, but you don't. What brings you to Portalbion?"

"I just followed the road to the sea and this is where it brought me," Randolph said. "Portalbion, is that what it's called?"

"Certainly is," Nick confirmed. "And you have the honor of addressing Nicholas Freedom, purveyor of fine wines and beers, and the best food and most comfortable beds in the town—one of which I hope you will occupy tonight."

"I can't afford to . . ."

But Nick stopped him in mid-sentence.

"As my guest. In recognition of past service as good friend and colleague. Come on Randy, you don't think I'm going to charge you for food and a bed do you? Has it been so long that you've forgotten our friendship?"

Randolph looked embarrassed at the reminder of how long he had not been in contact with his old friend, not since they had spent a few days together five years ago on one of Randolph's infrequent visits back to Gospot.

"And, if it wasn't for you, I wouldn't be here now," Nick said.

"No," Randolph replied. "And if it wasn't for me, Lydie might still be here too."

"Look Randy." Nick was earnest all of a sudden. "You can't go on forever blaming yourself for that. There was nothing you could have done to stop that boat being washed out to sea; the current was too strong. If you'd gone in after it, there's no doubt you would have been drowned and so would I, because you wouldn't have been there on the rocks to haul me out. I still don't know where you found the strength to lift me."

"It wasn't anything, really," he said. "Just a lucky break. I was in the right place at the right time."

"Lucky break or not, you saved my life and there's no denying that. Come on, come and meet the Black Swan. We've some catching up to do over a pint or two of good ale. And then, if you insist on paying for my hospitality, you can entertain the customers this evening."

Randolph felt easier accepting food and lodgings with this arrangement.

"That's fine, then." He smiled at Nick. "Don't just stand there, show me the way."

The Black Swan was set about half a mile from the harbour, to the north side of the town square and up the hill on the road leading out to Sulaman's Cave. It took Randolph and Nicholas only ten minutes to reach the tavern. As they entered through the front porch, the bell in the old mechanical timepiece in the entrance rang five times. Randolph stopped and examined it.

"Bet you've never seen one of those before," Nick ventured.

Randolph didn't have time to comment before Nick went on. "I'll show you where your room is. You can wash the journey's dust from your feet. I'll get the bar open and the kitchen warmed up for our man, Fat Ham. He has a reputation for producing the finest plate of food in town. When you're ready, come on down and we'll have an ale together before we eat. I'll stick up a notice saying, 'Entertainment tonight at half past eight.' Is that all right for you?"

"That's perfect," Randolph said. "I'll sing a few songs, tell a tale, do a few tricks that an old friend taught me, then a few more songs that folk can sing along to."

"Sounds ideal," Nick said. "Come on, I'll show you your room."

Up the old carved wooden stairway they went, into a long corridor that ran the whole width of the tavern, off which there were eight doors, each leading, Nick told Randolph, into bedrooms. They went to the last door, which Nick opened into a well-appointed, homely room.

"Best room in the house," he announced. He continued, jokingly, "So, you better do a good performance later. See you downstairs in a while. Anything you need, just let me know."

Randolph looked around the neat room. The whitewash providing the main decor contrasted with the old oaken beams that adorned the ceiling and divided each wall into framed panels. In the biggest of those hung a tapestry. Randolph was fascinated by the picture and studied it in detail.

"The weaver," he murmured to himself, "Must have hung suspended in the air out over the sea to get that view of the cave entrance. I wonder who stitched it. I wonder if it's a real cave somewhere or the product of somebody's imagination."

He sat on the wide double-sized bed and gazed at the embroidered wall hanging. He felt drawn to the cave. It seemed familiar, and although he knew he'd never been there, he felt it was a real place and that somehow it was calling him. Unseen hands lifted him, beckoned him, calling. There was someone calling with a silent voice, as if to say, "Here must you linger, here must you tarry a while."

In his mind's eye, he floated down to the little cove, where the waves lapped the stony beach, tossing and rolling the smaller pebbles in and out of the ocean. He glided across the shore right up to the mouth of the cave and hovered there, listening. Rising above the sound of the bubbling waves on the beach, he heard a soft, crooning voice drifting from the darkness before him. The melodic, hypnotic voice gathered pace and rhythm as he listened.

> *"In all the world,*
> *In time and space,*
> *In here and now and eternity.*
> *Give all thyself,*
> *Give mind and form,*
> *Give thought and strength and understand.*
> *Take all of life*
> *Take heart and soul*
> *Take time and care, and know thy way."*

A tap on the door startled Randolph back into conscious awareness. "Who is it?" he called, but he already knew it was Nick. He sensed his presence. "Hang on, I'll let you in."

"Thought I better come up and get you," Nick said as he entered the room. "You've been so long I wondered if you'd dropped off to sleep. Look, you haven't even unpacked; what have you been up to? Are you still the same old daydreamer you used to be?"

"What's the time then?" Randolph asked.

"Nearly seven," Nick replied and, as if to add confirmation, the mechanical timepiece in the entrance porch chimed laboriously. "If we want to get a couple of ales and some food inside us before you start your act, we need to get our toes tapping."

A little later, after a quick wash, Randolph sat opposite Nick at the window table in a front alcove of the tavern. Fat Ham had lived up to his name as well as his reputation of encouraging the same amount of flesh as he personally enjoyed to grow on all Nick's customers. He thumped heaped dishes in front of Randolph and called for a jug of ale to be brought. The ham he served was as tasty a lump of meat as Randolph had enjoyed for many a moon. He examined the contents of his platter with enthusiasm. His journey from Castle Drent had left him weary with hunger, and the plump, fried mushrooms and thick wedges of potato complemented the griddle-cooked meat perfectly. The delicious fare was balanced flawlessly by the jug of foaming ale that arrived to form the centerpiece for their table. Relaxing into his meal and between mouthfuls, Randolph broached the subject of the embroidered drape with Nick.

"Who did that interesting tapestry hanging in my room?" he asked.

"Which one is that?" Nick quizzed.

"It's a cave set on a beach," Randolph reminded Nick.

"Oh that one," Nick said. "Yes, lovely piece of work. Done by a local woman. She's a bit strange, but her stuff is well liked by people around here. Some folk say she has magical powers—that she weaves charms and spells into her pictures but, of course, that's a load of tosh. She's just a very good artist. Actually, she owns the mechanical timepiece in the entrance porch. She told me it was a gift from a friend and, as it was too big to fit in her cottage, she asked me if I'd keep it here for her."

Randolph was glad he'd said nothing about the timepiece earlier. He didn't now either. He just smiled at Nick's dismissal of any possibility of the existence of things magical. He had always held that view. His pragmatic approach to life had been the root of many deep discussions between them in their younger years.

"Maybe you'll understand when you grow up," Randolph joked. "I don't know how you can just dismiss the magic of life, it's all around you; you don't even need to seek it out. It will come to you if you let it."

"Nuts," Nick retorted. "You get what you earn in this life. Nothing more, nothing less."

Randolph was not of a mind to repeat the same debate they had had many times before, not tonight anyway. He was due to do his turn shortly and, as well as finding out a bit more about the tapestry, he wanted to quiz Nick about a few of the characters that were drifting into the tavern and would soon be part of his audience. For the moment, he stayed with the subject of the tapestry.

"What's her name?" he asked, steering the conversation away from the magic of life topic. "The weaver?"

"Oh, Martha," Nick answered. "She lives in a cottage just up the road from here, out toward Sulaman's Cave."

"Is that the cave in the tapestry then?" Randolph asked.

"Certainly is," Nick replied. "Supposed to be haunted. The local folk won't go near it and anyway, it's virtually inaccessible on foot; the only way to get to it is by boat. People who have been close say they hear voices coming from the cave, but it's obviously just the sound of the sea moaning deep down in the rock crevices at the back of the cave. Voices, my bottom," he scoffed, stuffing another mouthful of meat into his face.

Randolph smiled again and made a mental note to visit both Martha and the cave before he left the area. They continued chatting and eating and after a while, the timepiece coughed a single chime, the signal for half past the hour. Without further ado, Randolph took up his lute from behind him and launched into his first song; a raucous ditty that he often used in these barroom settings to get the attention and participation of the audience. He had written it so that the words could easily be adapted to take on the location in which he was singing and details of some of the local personalities. While they were eating, Nick had already divulged a few names of his regulars, some of the reputations they had, and pointed them out to Randolph as they had arrived in the bar.

> *"I only go to the good places*
> *Where posh folk spend their dough,*
> *Where they talk of matters of import,*
> *Chatting politely with those they know.*
> *And now I've come to Portalbion*
> *And looked for where to go,*
> *But there ain't no 'igh-class places,*
> *So the Black Swan had to do."*

Hoots, jeers, and shouts of "We've been found out" and "Who told on us?" indicated to Randolph that his audience were with him already.

> *"And so I have to sit here,*
> *Among thorns, I am a rose.*
> *I have to sit and watch, while*
> *Joe there picks his nose."*

As fortune would have it, Joe's habit of picking his nose when he thought others weren't watching was in full swing and, to the absolute delight of the crowd, he was caught in the act.

> *"And as I suffer silently,*
> *Pretending I'm not here,*
> *I look away for an instant*
> *And Gilbert drinks my beer."*

Again Randolph got a lucky break and Gilbert, Nick's potman, was discovered carrying out his usual practice of "accidentally" drinking somebody else's beer. Various projectiles, including half-eaten potatoes, chicken bones, and apple cores were directed toward Gilbert who, laughing and bowing to the audience in an exaggerated way, proceeded to defend himself, responding in kind with anything that came to hand. Randolph quickly started another verse in order to regain some measure of control.

> *"I came down here, but I didn't know*
> *I'd have to play this part,*
> *I didn't know I'd have to sit*
> *And hear Jemerma fart."*

34

The room disintegrated into howls of laughter. Jemerma, a greasy-haired woman with a black toothy grin, ruddy complexion, and larger-than-average nose, leapt to her feet, climbed, with the help of several cavorting customers up onto one of the long trestle tables, lifted her skirt to knee level and, accompanied by a little jig, let rip a thunderclap of a fart. The volume of her trumpeting was matched only by the jubilant applause and cheering of the crowd. Randolph continued.

> *"Now Nicholas is our jolly host*
> *For whom there is no hope.*
> *But all the ladies like him,*
> *'cause he always has a grope."*

At this point, some half a dozen or so young wenches descended on Nick and carried him, helpless with laughter, out from the bar into the street, returning with his breeches as a trophy, which they waved high in the air. The de-bagged Nick was seen darting back in through the front porch and up the stairway, only to return when he had regained his composure and donned a pair of deep red velvet knickerbockers to protect his modesty. However, he then began a rather seductive slow walk down the center of the barroom, hands on swinging hips, displaying his scarlet pantaloons, stopping only as the troupe of young wenches threatened a repeat attack. By this time, Randolph, having abandoned the idea of trying to tell a tale to such a boisterous bunch, was proudly displaying some of the colorful and explosive fireworks that Galdore had shown him how to make. He shot streams of florescent sparks in all directions, making the audience duck and dive for cover as they whooped with joy at the spectacle.

"Forsooth," Gilbert cried. He was in the process of collecting empty pots from the long communal tables when a bolt of blue and orange lightning made him dive for cover behind Jemerma's billowing skirts.

"Wouldn't get behind there," Joe yelled. "You'll be off work for a week if she drops one on you."

Gilbert emerged with a soot-covered face where the magical blast had dusted him.

35

"Too late," Nick screeched. "She got him. Is there an apothecary in the house?"

Laughter scented the air, and frivolity caressed the assembled friends. The party spirit continued into the small hours with songs, dancing, jokes, and more magic, all led by Randolph who was in good form and full of more ale than he had consumed for many an evening. It was three in the morning, endorsed by the rusty whirring and cranky whining that proceeded the three clanking chimes of the mechanical timepiece, when Randolph, having bid a snoring Nick "Goobdite, sheep tiiii (hic)ght" in the corner of the barroom and, moving carefully on all fours, negotiated the carved staircase and the endless corridor to his room.

"Musht remember to gotothecaveinthemorning," Randolph informed the large wooden knob on top of the bedpost before collapsing in a heap on the soft, fleece-filled mattress and down pillow.

√●√

Randolph woke with a jump, as if he had fallen to the bed from the ceiling. His head felt like he had swapped it for somebody else's—someone who had had far too much to drink recently. It was still dark but a bright moon kissed the earth with her gentle light, painting the sill outside Randolph's window with silver. He peered through bleary eyes and was sure he saw a black cat glide silently from the ledge. As he drifted back into slumber, his mind wandered to the tapestry cave, then out from the neat room in the Black Swan, following the cat, and away into the moonlit night. The dream cat led him to Sulaman's Cave. He listened to the sound of waves gently lapping the shoreline, the sea breeze rustling the grasses and heather that clung in desperate clumps to the rock face around the cave mouth, the low moaning echo of the hollowness of the cave itself, and there, there rising above all those sounds, he found the melodic chanting of that voice again.

Oh, such sweet harmonies you sing. Why do you call me? What do you want of me? Who are you? Randolph thought.

"Why, Randolph, do you not know your own song when you hear it? Are you deaf to your own calling?"

"In all the world,
In time and space,
In here and now and eternity.

Give all thyself,
Give mind and form,
Give thought and strength and understand.

Take all of life,
Take heart and soul,
Take time and care and know thy way."

Randolph looked down to where the dreamed cat sat at his feet. He met her eyes, and he could have sworn she smiled.

෨෬

It was well past midday when Randolph eventually joined the daylight from a fitful and restless sleep. He recalled the last few words of what the voice had said. "Know thy way."

He had traveled many times to the cave that night in his dreams, answering many calls, worried, floated, dived, flopped, been absorbed and regurgitated by the deep darkness of the black hollow; he awoke exhausted, but knew he had to go there in his waking hours. Whatever was meant by, *know thy way*, he was sure it included going to the cave. A rather pale-looking Nick was already at the table, staring blankly at a piece of bread and a glass of water when Randolph shuffled gingerly into the barroom.

"Bin like 'at for hours," Ham said, gesturing with his head in Nick's direction. "Think he be tryin' to remember 'oo he is. You want some breakfast . . . or would't be lunch? A nice bowl o' oats with honey? That'll sort out both of 'ee."

Randolph nodded agreement, as his mouth didn't seem to work, and he went over to where Nick sat. Nick left his trance-like state and even raised a feeble smile as Randolph joined him at the table. After a while, Randolph attempted speech.

"Good evening," he ventured.

"Question, statement, or greeting?" Nick groaned.

"Dunno," Randolph said.

Further need to convert thought into coherent speech was eliminated by the reappearance of Fat Ham behind a large

37

wooden tray, on which perched two steaming bowls of oats and two large mugs. Words remained unexchanged for the next fifteen minutes as they consumed the life-giving gruel and mugs of brew. With something solid in his belly to soak up the remaining alcohol, Randolph felt a little revived.

"Think I'll wander up the track a way and get some fresh air," Randolph said to Nick. "Coming?"

"Nope. Can't anyway," Nick said. "I've got to give Ham and Gilbert a hand to clear this lot up." He gestured around the bar. "Ready for opening in a couple of hours. Look, before you go off. I meant to say yesterday and then never got round to it. You will stay on for a few days, won't you?"

"If that's all right," Randolph said. "There's one or two things I'd like to do around here. But I'll only take up your room if I can do something in return. As payment."

"I think you've done quite enough already," Nick said, nursing his aching head. "I haven't had a bender like that for years, in fact, not since . . ." He paused to think. "Not since the last time I saw you in Gospot. You're a danger to mankind, Randolph Kettle. Now clear off, I've got work to do."

They laughed, then wished they hadn't, as their heads complained bitterly.

"See you in a few hours," Randolph said as he left the room. "We'll just have some gentle ballads tonight then."

"Don't worry if you don't get back in time," Nick said. "We can do it tomorrow evening. Bye."

It was nearly half past two, according to the mechanical timepiece, as Randolph crossed the tavern porch and walked out into brilliant sunshine. He felt the warmth embrace his still less-than-well head and he smelled the fragrance of the earth as he trudged up the track, leaving the Black Swan and the town behind him. The track was wide enough to allow two carts to pass easily. It was bordered by high hedgerow, through gaps in which Randolph could see neatly ploughed fields. The track meandered uphill toward a white cottage, clearly visible at the crest about a mile away.

I'll aim for there, Randolph thought as he looked up the hill toward the cottage. *I bet that's where Martha lives.*

He pictured she would be quite old, homely in appearance, maybe a little plump with ruddy complexion. In fact, a good solid, wise country woman who would know about nature. Also, being a friend of Galdore, which Randolph had assumed was the case because of the mechanical timepiece connection, he had automatically endowed her with the same sort of busy, preoccupied, scatterbrained but slightly dominating characteristics that he displayed. He envisaged her in her workroom where she created her tapestries, it being on the same lines as Galdore's study, full of intrigue and fascinating bits and pieces. Her style of dress would be of garments with lots of pockets containing bobbins of different colored threads, packs of needles, scissors, squares of material. In fact, he had an image in his mind of her being made out of patchwork. It took Randolph nearly an hour to trudge to the cottage. The hill was steeper, the track was windier, the sun was hotter, and he was groggier than he had expected. At last he got there, puffing in spite of the many stops he had had on the way; although the climb had served to clear his head a little and he felt somewhat better than when he had left the tavern.

"How fresh autumn air, sunshine, and the smell of the bare earth revives the soul," a voice said.

Randolph turned to see a woman leaning on the low gate to the garden of the cottage. Randolph studied her without speaking. She was certainly not a patchwork woman; maybe this wasn't Martha's cottage after all. Randolph's mouth dropped open as he observed a beautiful, feminine form of, he judged, about ten years more than his own age. Her long raven hair, framing her high cheekbones and perfect facial features, Oriental almond eyes, and full red lips, accompanied by her silken-soft musical voice were only the top piece. As his eyes drifted lower, he absorbed bare brown shoulders, firm rounded breasts only partially covered by a low-cut, ruched, snow-white linen bodice that hugged her shapely contours and followed them into one of the slimmest waists that Randolph had ever seen.

"I'm Martha," she said. "You must be Randolph. Yes, you must be Randolph; Galdore said you would stand around with your mouth open."

He shut it quickly and swallowed hard, suddenly conscious of his red and sweating face, puffing lungs, and general morning-after-the-night-before appearance.

"Come on inside," Martha invited. "You look like you need to sit down for a while, and I've got something here I want to show you."

Martha took Randolph by the hand and led him into the cottage. Her touch was gentle and soft. Randolph felt coarse, ugly, and awkward in her presence. Once inside the cottage, she turned to him. Brushing his tangled golden curls away from his face with her fingers, she said,

"Now let me look at you properly. Hhmm, I can see what Galdore meant by promising eyes. They have the look of wisdom. Maybe you are the One."

"What one?" Randolph asked.

But Martha didn't reply; she led him into a back room of the cottage where a long pine table and four chairs filled the center of the room. The far wall hosted a fire and griddle on which perched an array of cooking pots and kettles. One of these contained boiling water that Martha ladled into two mugs, adding a yellow powder to each. A smell of dandelion and burdock reached Randolph, but it was tinged with another fragrance that was strange to his senses. As if reading his mind, Martha said, "Saxifrage. It's a herb I often use to soothe the fever, but it also works well to reduce the after-effects of a good night at the Black Swan." Her smile revealed pearl-white teeth that served only to increase Randolph's magnetic attraction to the alluring beauty of this woman.

Martha carried the steaming mugs to the table and sat close beside Randolph. The nearness of her warm body and her sweet breath excited him, and he felt the redness of his cheeks from his uphill climb extend to his neck, jaw, and ears. She touched his arm and he felt a stirring desire for her, deep within his loins, more powerful an urge than he had ever experienced before.

"No, your thoughts are transparent to me," she said. "Your eyes may have the look of wisdom but, remember, they are also windows to your soul. Guard your feelings. Exposure of your innermost desires may not serve you well."

Randolph felt uncomfortable. He didn't want to be transparent. He closed his eyes in an attempt to elude Martha's probing vision.

"It's not for me you feel such deep yearning," she said, "But for all that I represent. Fulfillment of your passion can only be achieved through a joining of your soul with all that is life and eternity."

Randolph wasn't sure. At this moment, he was more of a mind to favor a steamy session of passionate love making with Martha than a profound and intense affair with life and eternity.

And she's the one who started it, Randolph thought to himself. *She came and sat close to me and got me all horny. She can't possibly think she can just pour cold water on my ferret with some hogwash about finding my destiny.*

Eyes still closed, he visualized a scene where he floated off with Martha to a place of infinite peace and beauty. He now playing hard to get, and she, unbridled and begging in her rapacious desire to possess him. There were woods. There was warm summer sun. Birds sang and muted music played. A carpet of bluebells sprang up before his eyes and he lay Martha gently on it, caressing her expectant body. Teasing her just a little, he touched and stroked the curves of her form, almost reaching the most sensitive parts of her body and then, then at just the last moment, sending his dancing fingers off on some other sensuous exploration of her person. She moaned with pleasure, her lips inviting him to kiss her tenderly. As she moved, turning her head slowly from side to side, the taut white bodice revealed the erect nipples of her firm breasts. She pleaded for him; she begged for him to enter her.

"More dandelion tea? And maybe a piece of sweetcake before we go."

It was the right voice, but the wrong words. Desperately clinging to his vision, Randolph turned to touch Martha. She got up from the table, unaware of Randolph's extended arm but then, sensing his movement, she turned and came back toward him, thrusting another mug of hot brew into his clasping hand. Randolph landed with a bump.

"We shouldn't be leaving it too long before we go," Martha said. "Not if we want to get down to the cave and back before dark. I can show you the maps tomorrow. Come on finish your tea up."

"Maps?" Randolph asked. "What maps? Are we going to the cave? What, now?"

"You haven't been listening to a word I said, have you? It must have been a really good party last night. No matter, I'll show you the map tomorrow when you bring your brain up with you."

Sulaman's Cave was only half an hour on along the track, but as they went downhill, Randolph kept thinking that the way back was all uphill again. He had really had enough of hills today, and he thought that he had promised Nick he would sing some ballads this evening. But being beside the beautiful Martha was, in Randolph's mind, time well spent and his other thoughts drifted into oblivion. He would climb hills for her all day and any day; he was besotted, but Martha didn't seem to care about his rampant desire. The only hint she had given that she viewed him as anything more than a boy was her comment about his deep yearning and that it wasn't for her, but Randolph thought different. Martha began to sing. Her sweet, honeydew voice embraced the notes of the ballad, a haunting lullaby that encircled and caressed the breeze. As they made their way toward the little pebble beached cove and Sulaman's Cave, Randolph noticed the wind strengthening; it swooped and tumbled in time with Martha's song. Randolph suddenly realized that Martha commanded the wind, it was she that enticed it forth, encouraging it from zephyr to youthful whistling breeze, then tempting it on to mature wind. From wind, she lured it into blustery currents that tugged at Randolph's hair and clothes, as if to strip him bare. By the time they reached the cliff edge, they had to lean into the gale to make any forward step, and still Martha sang.

"How are we going to get down the cliff?" he yelled over the raging torrent of air.

But no sooner had the words left his lips than Martha took his hand and they flew. The wind lifted them, supporting them with graceful eddies, whisking them upward. High above the ground they rose, like birds they played on the melody of the swirling waves of air. They danced with clouds, waltzed with gulls who viewed them with quizzical looks, and frolicked with floating leaves and jetsam of the air. They flew so high that Randolph had trouble locating the tiny cove way below them in the wild array of coastal curves, but then Martha lowered the tone of her crooning and they started to descend, until Randolph could pick out the pebbly beach and the black blob in the cliff face that was the cave mouth.

"You do it," Martha said all of a sudden, and she stopped her song.

They started to fall faster, to plummet toward the ground.

"Go on," she urged, laughing. "Go on, sing, you have a voice to charm and command the wind."

"What shall I sing?" Randolph screeched as they fell faster and faster and the ground rushed up to meet them.

"Anything that you think the wind will listen to," Martha replied.

Randolph sang the only song that came to his head that was anything to do with the wind; one of the first ballads he ever composed; a rhythmic, lilting, tuneful piece that told of his love of natural things.

> *"The breeze and I were lovers once.*
> *The wind and I, we kissed.*
> *But I grew old and the wind stayed young;*
> *My love I sorely missed."*

As he sang, Martha joined in harmony.

> *"The trees and I we were as one;*
> *The woods became my friend.*
> *I yearned to stay forever young,*
> *Our friendship not to end."*

How she knew the words Randolph didn't understand. Their descent slowed and then Martha fell silent again, leaving only Randolph's voice for the ears of the wind; but it was content and accepted the magic of his words.

"Come stay with me, come be my love,
Whispered Nature to my ears.
Our love will be forever true,
However long the years."

They drifted gently earthward and set down on the pebble beach a few paces from the cave mouth. Randolph looked down to check that his feet really were in contact with the ground. His mouth still moved as if in song, but no sound came forth from his lips. His arms flapped a little as if providing a back-up, in case he needed a boost in flight.

"The wind likes you," Martha declared. "A good song for wind wooing; where did you learn it?"

"I wrote it," Randolph said, regaining the power of speech for an instant, then suddenly realizing that he should be terrified after what just happened, and then realizing he *was* terrified. "Bbbbbb . . . bbb . . . bb . . . but . . . wwww . . . wwweee . . . ffffffffffffffflew," he stammered.

Martha gave him an "I'm impressed" and "Well aren't we the clever one then" look and turned to the cave entrance. "Just remember, that the song you used is now your windsong," she said. "Each time you sing it, the wind will gather force and lift you into the air. The louder you sing, the higher you will go, and the softer you croon the lower will you be flown."

"Hhhhowww . . . ddoo . . . I . . . ch . . . choose a dddd . . . direction," Randolph burbled, his knees still shaking.

"Oh, just think where you want to go and it will happen," Martha said, as if it were a stupid question. "Now come along, stop flapping your arms like a chicken. It's getting late and we don't want to keep him waiting, do we?"

"Who?" Randolph said.

"Galdore, of course. You weren't listening at all up at the cottage were you? He'll be here any minute, and he gets very testy if people are late."

Inside the cave was chill in comparison to the warmth of the air in the evening sun outside. As they went further, the light faded until total darkness surrounded them. They stopped, Martha holding Randolph's arm.

"Listen," she whispered, and Randolph again smelled her sweet breath as she brought her face close to his ear. A shiver went down his body and goose bumps raised on his neck as he fought the urge to turn and kiss her.

Randolph was saved from further sensual torment as a pale blue haze appeared from further inside the cave. It slowly grew in intensity and then Randolph saw a black shadow dart from behind a rock, and he felt the soft nuzzle of a cat's head around his legs. He looked down at Dragon, who smiled her cat smile at him.

"Randolph," Galdore's voice boomed in the echoing confines of the cave. "Randolph, how good to see you."

He came striding up to Randolph and embraced him heartily in a gesture of true friendship.

"Thought you could sneak off without saying goodbye, did you? Never mind, I made your apologies to everybody. Said you'd been called away urgently on a matter of great importance. Which, of course, is true. Well the important part is true, and it becomes more urgent by the day." He chuckled, and Randolph felt a warmth toward this wise old man.

"How did you get here?" Randolph asked Galdore.

"How do wizards get anywhere?" Galdore responded, as if the answer was obvious.

"We flew," Randolph boasted. "We flew from the cliff top right up into the clouds and then down again and landed on the beach. Martha showed me how."

No sooner had he said it than he felt silly. He felt as if he was a little child, telling his father what he had learned at school today. He blushed at his own naivety in the presence of these two great and wise people, and he was glad of the dimness of the cave to hide his embarrassment. Dragon nuzzled his leg as if to say, "It's all right."

Randolph bent to stroke her, pleased to have a diversion while he composed himself. As he straightened again, Galdore met his eyes with a serious expression.

"Randolph, the time has come for me to divulge the purpose of your journey here. I had hoped we could avoid this, but the path you chose was the one that was right for you, and that must be. An easier way would have been for you to remain with me at Castle Drent and, for a while, I thought that possible, but the easier way was not your chosen way. If you truly are the One, then your chosen path, although not always the easiest, will be the right one."

"There you go again," Randolph said, "Telling me I'm the One. Martha said it as well. What is the One and why do you think I'm it? I'm only a poor minstrel; I'm only Randolph Kettle. I might have slain a witch, I might have rescued a knight, saved a friend's life, learned how to fly . . .," he paused, realizing what he had just catalogued. "Fine, so I might have had a few lucky breaks, but I'm Randolph the minstrel. How can I be anything special?"

Galdore looked at Martha, Martha looked at Dragon, Dragon looked at Randolph, and smiled. Randolph became aware that he had already answered his own question.

"And so you see why you might be the One?" Dragon said. "You are special, Randolph. You may be Alusia's champion."

"She spoke," Randolph said to Galdore. "Dragon spoke to me."

"And you can add that to your list of special things as well," Galdore replied. "Randolph, like it or not, you are special. We don't yet know if you are the savior, and that is something we will not fully discover tonight. We don't even know if the savior has yet been chosen, but tonight we will know if you have the potential to be the One, if you have what it will take to become the One destined to save Alusia from the rising forces of evil."

"But defeating Griselda was a good start," Dragon said.

"We cannot guarantee you success," Martha said. "But Galdore and I, the other members of the Council of Worth, and Sulaman will watch over you as best we can and lend what support and help possible. However, the overthrow of the rising evil will ultimately be the responsibility of the One."

"The urgency is now growing," Galdore told Randolph. "With the destruction of Griselda, the evil forces have been warned. We must ensure Alusia does not fall and leave Rú, Obor, and Lanah exposed to the threat of darkness. We are certain that the forces, which have come out of the Boglands of Thrung, will not be content with a prize of Alusia alone, but will strive toward domination of the whole of the Western Realm."

Randolph stood, gaping again. He didn't want to be the One. He hadn't asked to be involved. He had a million questions fighting in his head, each wanting to be asked first.

"Close your mouth before Galdore sees," Dragon advised quietly.

"Council of Worth? Rising Evil? Boglands of Thrung? Western Realm? And anyway, who is Sulaman? Why has he got a cave and where does that fit in? Why are we here?" all tumbled out of Randolph's mouth. "Saints alive," he said. "Tell me I'm dreaming. Let me wake up asleep in the woods."

"You can't wake up asleep," Galdore said. "Now stop talking drivel man and pull yourself together. There's work to be done before this night is older. All your questions will be answered in good time."

Randolph raised his eyes to the domed roof of the cave chamber and sighed. He really didn't want to be the One. He just wanted to be Randolph the minstrel and to excite people with his music, intrigue them with his tales, make them happy with his jokes and jesting. But he knew that could not be so. He knew that however he had got himself into this confounded messy business, it was no use resisting Galdore. He would just have to go along with it for the moment and hope he turned out not to be the One.

"That's it!" he muttered to himself. "I'll act a bit stupid and fail whatever test they've got in store for me. I'll prove that I'm not the One."

"Oh no you don't," Dragon said. "You can't fool Sulaman by pretending to be simple. And anyway, you enjoyed the flying, didn't you? Don't you want to be able to do it always?"

"I'm going off cats," Randolph said.

Dragon just smiled.

"All right," Randolph said as he turned to Galdore. "What's next? I'm obviously not going to wake up in the woods."

"Let's start by answering a few of your questions." Galdore's tone shifted from that of master to friend. "Sulaman was lord high wizard of Alusia. His transcension to etherical status . . ."

"Whoa, whoa, whoa," Randolph interrupted. "If you're going to explain things, you'll need to do it in my language. Transcension to etherical status?"

47

"Sorry," Galdore said. "When he passed on to a higher plane." He looked at Randolph to gauge understanding.

"That'll do for the moment," Randolph said, mentally converting the phrase to, *when he died.*

"He needed to maintain some sort of contact with the council," Galdore continued.

Randolph revised his translation back to *passed on to a higher plane.*

"He also needed a way of talking to other people and having others talk to him. He uses the cave here as a sort of communication channel. It's a link, a vortex, a whirlpool, to the higher world where he now exists—you understand?"

"Oh," Randolph said, not understanding at all.

"It is Sulaman who has the wisdom and ancient knowledge to select the one most likely to succeed. The one in whom the future of good in the Western Realm will be vested. The one who, by natural affinity with all that is truth and light, will have the chance of overpowering the natural force of evil—you see?"

Randolph was beginning to see. He was becoming aware that all this was somehow a sort of compliment to his way, to his understanding of rightness and truth.

"But why can't you or Martha, or some of the other council members you mentioned be the One? They must be better qualified than me, surely. And they would all be much more experienced at giving evil a good flogging. Wouldn't they?"

"You're right in what you say," Martha agreed. "But that is the very reason we of the council cannot bear the burden of the One. Purity of heart and innocence in knowledge of mystical ways are essential to the struggle between good and evil. We council members know too much to be trusted to natural response when faced with the force of darkness. You still have the virtue of clear vision, untainted by past gained insight."

"Thanks a lot," Randolph said, feeling as if he had just been branded as an infantile dimwiddy.

"Don't take offense," Dragon counseled. "What Martha tells you is a great compliment and you should be proud of your adept ability and your fitness for consideration as the One."

"Look," Randolph said. "I mean, it's a great honor and all that, but I still don't see how I can even be considered as a possible one. I'm a humble peasant, born in Riversend, raised by my Aunt in Gospot, and then given to a life of wandering as a minstrel. Admittedly, a good one, but at the end of the day, merely a minstrel."

"The day is not yet ended," Galdore replied. "It may be that come nightfall you will be proved right, and maybe no. Sulaman will decide. Come now, he awaits us."

Deeper into the cave they went, Galdore leading the way, his glowing wand held high to give them light. They passed from the cathedral-like cavern where they had met into a narrow tunnel, well hidden behind boulders and rocky outcrops. The tunnel wound its way into the hillside, up a gentle incline to another chamber, smaller than the first great cavern but still of a scale to accommodate a small army. As they entered, Galdore's wand grew brighter, revealing sparkling and glinting crystal surfaces on the walls and ceiling of the grotto. Galdore signaled them to stop and he raised outstretched arms toward the center of the high ceiling.

"Sulaman," Galdore's voice chanted, echoing around the chamber and rumbling into the distant crevices and cracks. "Revealatum benefactrus annointement. Join us. Give your pronouncement on this mortal. Gaze into his soul and determine his prowess. Determine for us his fitness to take on the challenge. Advise us of his strength to bear the responsibility of the One. If he is to carry the lamp bringing light to places of darkness, then give him your blessing."

"What's all that about carrying lamps and going into dark places," Randolph whispered to Martha. "Nobody said anything about carrying lamps and dark places until now. I don't like dark places. I'm only in here because you brought me."

"Ssshhhh," Martha said.

A soft orange glow lit the cavern, gaining in brilliance until the full splendor of the crystal formations glittered like diamond stars in a sea of foaming silver and gold strands. Galdore fell silent, his deep ruby-colored tones replaced by the pure sound of tumbling streams of water as they cascaded through the cave. And then emerged a vision of white light that slowly took form and substance until, there before them, stood a tall white-haired figure, robed in rich silken fabric of shimmering radiance. In his right hand, he held a staff of yew and from his waist hung a golden-handled sword.

"Galdore, my friend," the vision said. "Let him come forward that you judge worthy of the challenge of the One."

Martha gave Randolph a gentle push from behind.

"Go on," she said. "Go forward and let Sulaman see you."

Randolph was frightened, but he stepped forward cautiously.

"Come closer," Sulaman said. "Let me look into your eyes, young man."

Randolph glanced back over his shoulder, seeking confirmation from Martha that it was safe to go closer. She nodded and gently waved him on. He was struck again by her beauty and took confidence from her smile. Turning back toward Sulaman he stepped boldly forward, stuck out his hand in greeting and said, "Good evening, sir. I'm Randolph Kettle. I assume I have the honor of addressing Mr. Sulaman. Nice cave you've got here."

Galdore raised his eyes skyward in disbelief, Martha giggled, Dragon's tail bushed in fear. Sulaman looked at Randolph. His face broke into a smile, then a grin, and finally into a hearty gale of laughter that billowed and bounced around the walls, bringing showers of crystal stardust floating down through the still air.

"Come sit by me, Randolph Kettle," Sulaman invited. "We have much to discuss."

He waved his staff. A stone table and benches to seat all four of them materialized, grown from the rock floor on which they stood. Once seated, Sulaman regarded Randolph more closely, looking deep into his eyes.

"It seems they think you may have the potential to take on this awesome task. They think you may be the One."

"I keep telling them that I'm only a simple minstrel," Randolph said. "But they won't take no for an answer, and so here we are. I'm afraid we've wasted your time and brought you all this way, from wherever, just to meet a simple minstrel."

"Your guise may be that of a minstrel, Randolph, but simple you are not. You have the eyes of wisdom and the heart of a lion. And what is more, Galdore tells me you're prone to getting lucky breaks."

"Would that were true," Randolph sighed. "I don't think Lydie would agree."

"Ah," Sulaman said. "Yes, your sister, Lydie. She too may suffer at the hand of darkness if the evil is not thwarted."

"But Lydie is dead," Randolph said. "She was swept out to sea and drowned because I didn't get a lucky break. That's why I can't be the One. If I was, then I am sure Lydie would be with us today. I let her down. I didn't have the power or the strength to save her. How can it be then that I might save Alusia?"

"Lydie was swept out to sea," Sulaman confirmed. "But her life-force is still present within the Western Realm. She did not perish as you believe. Although her whereabouts are beyond the reach and range of my power to determine, I do know that she is entwined with your destiny in some mysterious and yet-to-be-discovered manner. I do believe, Randolph, that you have the power to become the One and in accepting the challenge, you may once again be united with Lydie. I can promise nothing as nothing is certain and the path of destiny is not yet firmly laid."

Randolph could not believe his ears. To know that Lydie, maybe, was alive somewhere and there was a chance he might, one day, see her again gave him great strength. But then suddenly he was overcome with weariness and knew that the time to say goodbye to Sulaman's Cave and, indeed, Portalbion was approaching. Slowly he felt himself drifting; his eyelids became heavy, so heavy that their closing was the only option. Voices melted together, awareness dulled as the sound of rapidly cascading water once again echoed around the cavern, and Randolph slept.

He awoke refreshed. The morning sun streamed through the window and nine chimes alerted Randolph to where he was and when it was. But his head had a problem—how had he got there?

"I remember . . .," he said slowly to himself. "I remember going to the cave with Martha, and flying, and being in the cave. I remember meeting Galdore and Dragon and Sulaman. We talked. We talked about Lydie. We talked about me being the One. I remember feeling very, very weary and then, and then . . ."

But no further memory could be coaxed from his brain.

"Must have all been a dream. Thank the saints for that.".

"You were good," a voice said.

Randolph leapt several inches off the bed, startled by the unexpected voice in his ear. When he landed, he turned to find Martha beside him.

"Saints alive," Randolph said. "You scared the doo-doo out of me. How? . . . there . . . get . . . yoodledid? I mean, how did you thereget?"

"I think you mean, 'How did I get here?'"

"Yes," Randolph said.

"I flew," Martha said. "How did you get here?"

"I don't know," Randolph confessed. "Do you?"

Martha laughed, a sweet musical laugh that lit up her face.

"I brought you home after you went to sleep on us. It was late, you were exhausted, out cold, sleepwalking. Nick was busy in the bar, so he said it was fine for me to bring you up to your room and put you to bed. I was tired too and couldn't face the walk up to the cottage."

"Couldn't you fly on the wind?" Randolph quizzed.

"Too many people around. Can't be seen flying. So I popped in here beside you. You looked so peaceful."

"Did we? . . . Did we? . . . Did we? . . . Did we?

"Do it?" Martha helped out.

"Yes. Did we do it?"

"You weren't capable of saying it, let alone doing it."

"What did you mean 'I was good' then?" he asked.

"In the cave, with Sulaman; he was really taken with you. Very impressed and quite confident that you have the power to become the One."

"So we didn't do it then?" Randolph said sadly.

"No," Martha replied. "We didn't."

ॐॐ

The smile on Randolph's face stretched from ear to ear as he bounced lightly down the old wooden staircase. Martha had slipped nimbly from the window of his room, down the vine that decorated the side wall of the Black Swan and, fleet footed, skipped away up the lane, turning only to wave quickly before she was gone from sight behind the tall hedgerow.

"Oh, good morning to you," Nick said as Randolph came into the bar. "If it isn't old sleepy head himself. I had to get Martha to put you to bed last night. You were dead to the world. But you look pretty pleased with yourself this morning—happy dreams were they?"

"Something like that," Randolph replied. "Is Ham around anywhere? I'm starving hungry."

"In the kitchen. Go on through, he'll get you something. Then maybe you'd give me a hand. I need to get the barroom here organized for tonight. When I told the customers that you were singing again they were thrilled; we're expecting quite a crowd. But don't panic, I've told them it's not party night again—this is more of a quiet concert for folk who appreciate good music. You can do good music?" Nick joked.

Randolph grinned, picked up a half-eaten bread roll that was lurking on the bar, and aimed it at Nick's head. The rest of the day was spent cleaning, polishing, changing barrels, setting out chairs and tables, and generally preparing for the evening. Ham was preparing special dishes of nuts and fruit, baking bread of various sorts and, in the yard, where he kept disappearing, Randolph discovered two spit-roasting wild boar. Every now and again, Ham would have to attend them to turn the carcasses and to dowse them with ale.

"Brings ou' flav'r," he had informed Randolph.

But every time he dowsed the boar, he took a swig and by late afternoon the ale had brought out Ham's flavour as well. Randolph found him snoring loudly in a corner of the yard and had to shake him several times and wash him down with cold water before he could get any sense from him at all. The evening came and went all too quickly, and as the time arrived for Randolph to close his show, he felt overcome with a sadness. Tomorrow he must leave and he liked these people, he liked the Black Swan, he liked being in Nick's company, and above all he liked being near Martha. He would see her tomorrow before going on his way and he sang to her in her absence.

> *"When we're walking and we're talking*
> *And I'm listening to your voice,*
> *Then beside you is the place I want to be.*

When we're touching and we're kissing
When we're in each others arms,
Then your eyes are the only thing I see.

So love, love me true,
I do so love you.
Your eyes are the only thing I see.
So love, love me true,
I do so love you.
Your eyes are the only thing I see.

When you put your arms around me,
Then I know that love has found me,
And your eyes tell me all I want to hear.

And when I'm alone, or without you,
Then it's cold in that dark place,
But still your eyes are the only eyes for me.

So love, love me true,
I do so love you.
Your eyes are the only thing I see.
So love, love me true,
I do so love you.
Your eyes are the only thing I see."

The applause was deafening, and Randolph was tempted to close the evening there and then on that high note. But no, he couldn't finish without singing the song. The first song he had ever written. The words of which told more of his destiny than he realized even now.

"I'm the storyteller; I come from here and there.
I say, I'll give you rhyme and rhythm, then go, I know not
        where
Oh yes, I'm full of tales and legends of far off times and
        lands.
You know, I talk of things like dragons and spells and
        magic plans.

I bring you golden stories and songs of silvery seas.
I'll tell you things of faeries and tricks of birds and bees.
I'll show you how to spin a web and sail up to the moon,
And tell you why the leaves turn brown and how birds
sing in tune.

You'll wonder at my fancies, you'll marvel at my deeds,
You'll laugh at jokes not funny, you'll satisfy my needs.
If I should be so lucky, my music and my voice
Will rivet you with fantasies—but you ain't got no choice,
because . . .

I'm the storyteller; I come from here and there.
I say, I'll give you rhyme and rhythm, then go, I know not
where.
Oh yes, I'm full of tales and legends of far off times and
lands.
You know, I talk of things like dragons and spells and
magic plans.

Oh yes, I am the storyteller; I come from here and there.
I say, I'll give you rhyme and rhythm, then go, I know not
where.
Oh yes, I'm full of tales and legends of far off times and
lands.
You know, I talk of things like dragons and spells and magic
plans."

Bowing, and amidst much cheering and chanting for more, Randolph left the bar and made his way up to his room. He could hear the happy voices of the people in the bar below, which served only to heighten the feeling of loneliness and responsibility that now weighed heavy on his shoulders. There was a tap on the door.

"Come in Nick," Randolph called.

"Fabulous, brilliant, wonderful," Nick gushed his thanks to Randolph, clasping him firmly by the hand. "They think you are just the greatest and all want to know when the next show will be."

"Not for a while," Randolph said. "Tomorrow, early, I must be gone."

"But why?" Nick was startled by the sudden announcement. "There's no need to go, you can stay as long as you like. Stay forever."

"In other circumstances I wouldn't hesitate. This could easily become a place for me to live and be happy, but . . ."

"Oh, I know, the call of the open road," Nick said.

"It's more than just that, Nick. It's what it is calling that makes it impossible for me to stay. I can't explain, but I can promise I will come back if at all possible."

"What do you mean, if at all possible? You sound like you're going into battle to fight the powers of darkness," Nick joked.

Randolph just smiled a weak smile. There was nothing he could say, certainly nothing Nick would understand. All their boyhood exploits, all their companionship, all the friendship Randolph felt for Nick flooded his mind, and he wished there was some way he could explain. Nick didn't understand; his refusal to believe in anything that he couldn't see and feel meant that he couldn't even start to understand. There was no way Randolph could tell him the truth of what was happening.

"Whatever may happen, wherever my path may lead, I will remember these days here at the Black Swan, and I will return just as soon as I can," Randolph said.

Chapter Three
The Chronicles of Sharn

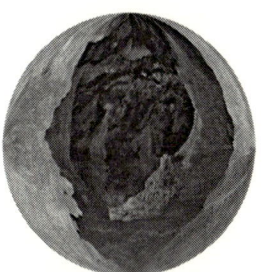

Inside the Caverns of Doom

"C'MON YOU lazy good for nothings," boomed the gang master.

His snaking whip cracked and a red welt opened up on the back of the nearest slave.

"C'mon," he repeated. "Faster."

The work gang pushed the heavy trolley along the track rails. It was laden with booty that had been brought down the main shaft leading from the boglands of the overworld. Not much had changed since the days of Sharn.

"Don't none of you get no fancy ideas 'bout gettin' outta here. There's not bin an escape for an 'undred years, and there ain't gonna be one now. Move, you dogs, faster."

The gang master wasn't quite accurate in his 'undred years' estimate. In fact, it was only fifty years previous that the unfortunate Sharn had been spirited away from his happy existence as a journeyman in Alusia.

"You're not 'ere to 'ave fun," the gang master shrieked. "You're 'ere to work."

Again the whip cracked and the gang of miserable, dirt-encrusted workers picked up their pace a fraction in a futile attempt to avoid further beatings. The Caverns of Doom were places of toil and sweat. Captives laboured under the command of Thrung's cronies. Those who had been lured or stumbled into his clutches existed in torment as they were forced to work in the construction and maintenance of palaces and halls for the pleasure of Thrung and his cohorts; to toil in the building and deployment of his machines and weapons of destruction; to fight in his battle against what he called *the soft*.

"Out of the way," bellowed the gang master as they turned a corner of the tunnel to encounter another group digging and chipping away at the tunnel wall. "Out of the way," he yelled, scattering them with his whip.

They dripped blood, toiled unceasingly, died, and were discarded as empty, useless shells to be replaced by others drawn from the pool of humankind to do Thrung's bidding.

Much deeper in the labyrinth of tunnels and caverns of the halls of doom, Thrung festered in his vault. He slumbered and dreamed of times past and yet more powerful times to come. In his dream he stood high on a dais, the masses of his unwilling population gathered cringing below him. In a booming voice, he commanded them to know his power.

"Hidden deep in the mists of time," he roared, "Beyond the dawn of creation, beyond the evolution of humankind, beyond the emergence of the power of good, lies my inheritance."

He watched as the dreamed masses groveled at his feet and clawed each other in their attempts to fight for space and air.

"Know that my heritage is vested in the power of evil, in the fires of time before existence, in the distrust of all that has now matured into the soft underbelly of existence, into humankind."

He spat the last word with a vengeance and venom that echoed around the great hall where he delivered his address to these inadequate beings.

"My legacy of dominance through darkness was sanctioned in the very creation of the universe, fired by the forces of eternity, as the particles of matter combined to form all that was to be. I am invincible."

Thousands of millennia had passed in the evolution of humankind but, for Thrung, this represented no more than a short slumber. As humankind thrived in the overworld, Thrung grew more restless in his slumbers. For him, his sensing of the rise of goodness was like the beginnings now of some bad dream, replacing his vision of supremacy, tugging at his mind, calling him from his sleep to a watchful awakening. In the beginning, he believed the emergence of humankind had been but a blister on his domination of all things. His power was not diminished, merely resting.

"Take heed, Thrung," a voice in the dreamed masses below him shouted. "Goodness is about you. The soft hardens. The witches and goblins of the material world, your enlisted representatives and collectors of energy, are persecuted and hounded by those who understand only righteousness. The lore of selfish independence has been pushed aside and is at risk of being forgotten."

Thrung was aware of a growing need to reestablish his presence. Deep within the Caverns of Doom, he stirred. His awakening heralded the need for humankind and faerykind alike to beware. While he had slept, his needs had been few and the mysterious, occasional disappearance of folk from their normal daily lives had gone virtually unnoticed. His needs had been met by his followers in the overworld preying on those choosing an itinerant life, their passing being attributed to their travel away to far and distant lands or, at times, to accident and misfortune. In his awakening state, his demands would grow. His unsatisfied need for labouring masses would escalate in proportion to his wakefulness, and he would want more; only a few at first, but his hunger would increase. In his dream, he answered the voices of defiance.

"Total domination of humankind is to be the way," he cried. "For they, with their lust for love and procreation, will provide an inexhaustible supply of labour to build and develop my realm. And, if they fail to keep pace with my hunger for fresh hands, there are others; faeries, gnomes, elves. They are all potential sources of energy to satisfy my demands."

❧❦

Few in the overworld knew of Thrung's existence or of the underworld realm that he commanded. Most had not even an inkling of the reality of evil, seeing it more as a manufactured tale of humankind invention used mainly as a deterrent for naughty children. None subscribed more so to this misguided belief than the gentle folk of Alusia. Was it then by coincidence or design that Thrung's principal doorway to the overworld was situated in the kingdom of Alusia? Was it also by coincidence that the few who knew of the Chronicles of Sharn were also inhabitants of Alusia? The Council of Worth, formed initially under the Lord High Wizard Sulaman and now, since his passing, working under the guidance of the Wizard Galdore, were those people. A gifted and magical group who, in tune with nature, posed the only threat to Thrung; the only group with the knowledge and ability to mount a resistance to his campaign against Alusia, the Western Realm and, ultimately, all races inhabiting the overworlds.

Extracts from The Chronicles of Sharn

Let it be known that I, Sharn of the kingdom of Alusia, in the Western Realm, be of sane mind and disposition. Though broken and crushed in spirit and abused to an extent where even the scribing of this parchment brings agony to my body, I must record my experience in the hope that knowledge of what is intended will reach those in my world who can prevent its occurrence. Let the Mystics be praised who make this so.

While I still have some small strength, I will take what time I can to prepare this text in the hope that an opportunity may arise for me to smuggle it from this forsaken place into my own world.

My account begins in the years of the rule of good King Petre; in the time shortly after the passing of the Lord High Wizard Sulaman and the appointment to the service of the court of the young Wizard Galdore. My happy existence and my life as a journeyman brought me to many places and frequently to Castle Drent. There as everywhere, I was treated always with friendliness and welcome and hospitality fit for a prince. I was just a journeyman, given to travel and wandering; to carrying of information and, occasionally, goods and wares between the towns and villages of our humble province.

It was by misfortune that on one such journey through the Weald that I encountered the black witch Gremolda, sister to the legendary Griselda who had been banished to the north by the lord high wizard prior to his passing. She had been sentenced to live in shackled isolation, her power to act as consort to wicked forces destroyed.

Gremolda tricked me by a cunning ruse to drink from a magic cup, rendering me helpless and unable to resist transport to the underworld realm of what I now know to be Thrung's kingdom of blackness.

In truth, I reveal now the horror and the terror that lurks below our world and promises to rise and overthrow it.

I awoke from the stupor induced in me by Gremolda's potion to find that all about me was rich with a shining blackness of high walls. Steamy heat encased me, making breathing a painful and arduous task. As I lay there, an orange glow of fire made from hot coals and other matter filled the cavern. The stench of burning flesh reached my nostrils, and I turned to witness a horned creature tossing broken bodies into a pit of molten lava.

As I was dragged roughly past this gory spectacle by a troll of huge proportion, it assured me this would also be my fate if I was not to do its bidding, and that when I was spent and no longer able to work this would, in any case, be my destiny. I resolved at that point that I would do my utmost to escape and to bring warning, of the existence of this terrible place to those in power in Alusia. Little did I realize just how terrible and dangerous was the story I was to discover.

My allocated work was with a group of other unfortunates assigned to the cutting and lashing of wooden struts to build platforms and decks that supported stairways to the surface.

Here the text becomes damaged and difficult to read due to water spillage on several pages. The few decipherable words and sentences suggest Sharn witnessed the building and construction of terrible machines and equipment designed to convert the natural resources of the overworld to energy and power to feed the underworld kingdom. There also seem to be reports of unimaginable creatures charged with duties of extracting maximum labour from the work gangs, ensuring minimum sustenance and rest was provided, sufficient only to prolong their agony. They administered regular beatings and batterings to ensure the continued diligence of their charges to the tasks in hand. The text goes on.

> *I was, for some time in my misery, also forced to work on the cleaning and restoration of a great underground cavern or hall in which creatures who appeared to be in league with a master they called Thrung were plotting and scheming in the formulation of plans ready for his imminent awakening from his slumber. It seemed that his aim would likely be to vent a wrath most terrible on the goodness of the overworld, bringing to account the soft and making all that was worthy a target for his venomous passion of domination.*
>
> *I was later moved to toil again on the higher platforms close to the surface, where fuel and provender stolen from above was brought below to satisfy the needs of the creatures of Thrung's domain.*
>
> *It was at this time, with what little strength remained in my beaten and exhausted body, that the opportunity to gain my freedom presented itself. The changing of the watch on working gangs was often a confused and argumentative affair, with vile gang masters claiming their own selfish demands of when and where they would conduct their duties. But this was the nature of the society in which they lived; others' needs or wishes did not feature in their repertoire. It was one such exchange that diverted the guards' attention and gave me the opportunity to drag myself over the top of the platform, where I hid in a crevice in the shaft wall.*

Again, damage to the parchment makes several pages un-readable, but then it goes on.

> *Emerging into the light at the top of the main shaft, after what seemed like an eternity in hiding, I found myself stranded in some quagmire. I was surrounded by black muddied, stinking waters in which grew naught but stubby outcrops of reed and marsh grasses. The mist swirled and danced about me and as it parted, I saw a narrow track, raised a few inches above the surface of the bog, winding away into the marshland. Following the track, I dragged myself away from that dreadful place to where I now lie. I am weak, scarcely able to scrawl these last few words. I do not know how far I may be from human company.*

May it be that this parchment is found. May it be that my warning reaches those who will heed it and have some knowledge of the precautions that must be taken to protect the future of humankind.

Little did he know, and little good it may have done him if he had, but the parchment was discovered only half a mile from the Bogland Road. Of Sharn there was no sign. The peasant who discovered the parchment could neither read nor write. However, in his belief that parchments meant official business, he duly delivered his find to the aging mayor of Rivermeet who, by a lucky break was, prior to his retirement from office, that very day entertaining the Wizard Galdore to a visit to the town. The mayor, in his enthusiastic attempt to avoid any additional administrative hassle that might delay his retirement, passed the scroll to Galdore, unread. It was not until some months later that Galdore first opened and read the parchment, initially dismissing the writings as some fantasy scribblings of an overactive mind. However, later, he realized that it was consistent with other strange, seemingly unrelated happenings, and he brought it to the attention of the Council of Worth. And so matters remained, until more frequent and regular changes in the balance of harmony in Alusia triggered Galdore and the council into action.

Chapter Four
The Road to Who Knows Where

The Road to Rivermeet

"I DON'T pretend to understand why it is you must go," Nick said as he shook Randolph's hand. "Just know that you are always welcome here. Go well my friend."

"Thank you," Randolph said. "Nobody could wish for a better companion."

As he walked slowly up the hill toward Martha's cottage with his pack, lute, and piccolo slung on his back, Randolph played over in his head all the events of the last few days. In some ways, he found it difficult to believe all that had happened to him. Maybe Galdore was right, maybe he was special in some way; but how could it be that he, Randolph Kettle, was destined to be some sort of champion for good in the Western Realm? How could he, Randolph Kettle, be the savior of souls from the powers of evil and darkness? But fate seemed to have taken a hand in marking him out for special treatment; and then there was Lydie. Could Lydie be alive? Could it be that Sulaman was right and they might find each other? Confusion sat heavily on his mind as he reached the little white cottage at the top of the hill. He knocked on the front door, but there was no answer. He knocked again and when there was still no response, he went through the pretty garden, around the side of the cottage, to the back door. It stood ajar and a note was pinned on the frame. As he read the script penned neatly on the parchment, he could hear Martha's voice in his head.

"Randolph," it said. "I had to leave before you got here. I had the most urgent call to meet with the other members of the Council of Worth. Sulaman sent you the things on the kitchen table—they weren't appropriate to bring down to the Black Swan. Also, take the map that I've left for you; it will be useful. Please feed the cat and shut the back door when you leave. I'll see you soon. Love, Martha."

Randolph turned over the parchment, and on the back was a further note.

"Galdore suggests you head for the Boglands of Thrung."

Inside the cottage, Randolph went to the table to find the parchment map rolled into a leather pouch, a yew staff, and the gold-handled sword and jeweled belt he had seen strapped to Sulaman's waist in the cave. He drew the sword from the scabbard and admired the sheen of the blade. He had never owned anything so precious or handsome in his whole life. He strapped it on and admired his reflection in the long glass hanging in Martha's kitchen. He picked up the note and read it again.

"Boglands of Thrung?" he said to himself. "Why would I want to go there? There's nothing but bog—that's why they call it bogland. I've heard that people have gone there and never been seen again."

He got out the map from the leather pouch, unrolled it on the table, and located the Boglands of Thrung.

I'll need to go down to Rivermeet to cross the Condor, he thought. *And I've never been there before. So, all right Galdore, we'll go to Rivermeet first and see what transpires.*

Folding away the map again and sliding the pouch onto the belt alongside his sword, Randolph picked up the stout yew staff, pointed it forward, and announced to the world, "Off we go, then."

He couldn't believe his ears when a voice came from the staff.

"You'll have to be more precise than that young fellow," it said. "How do ye think I can be properly doin' my job if you don't be tellin' me where we're headed? Off we go to where? And what's more, would you mind not holdin' me so tightly or at that precarious angle, or in that particularly sensitive place. It fair makes me head spin."

Randolph dropped the staff in surprise.

"Ouch!" it cried as it clattered on the stone floor. "Now listen here laddie, there's one or two things we need to be gettin' straight before we leave this cottage. I'll be askin' you to pick me up and put me carefully back on the table, then sit yourself down and we'll have a wee chat afore we 'off we go then' anywhere. Enthusiasm is a fine enough thing to be havin', but it has to be handled; can't just let it run riot. See what I mean, laddie?"

Randolph was a bit taken aback; he'd never encountered a speaking stick before, particularly one that had such a prominent will. He didn't really know what to say. So he said nothing. He picked up the staff and placed it carefully on the table before seating himself.

"Better," said the staff. "Now, laddie . . ."

Randolph was treated to a lengthy and tortuous soliloquy that amounted, in his mind, to an unnecessarily complicated and over-comprehensive guide on how to use a stick. He was tempted to leave it behind but, at the last moment, thought better of it, picked it up, and told it to be quiet and not speak again until it was spoken to. It appeared to take offense and went into a sulk, which suited Randolph fine. Having closed the cottage door firmly behind him, Randolph started up the track he and Martha had walked two evenings previous toward Sulaman's Cave. At the crossing of the paths, however, he turned southwestward toward the town of Rivermeet and the two- or three-day journey he was facing to the joining of the Rivers Condor and Gantwine. What lay ahead he did not know, but he was on the open road, which, as Nick had rightly suggested last night, was one of his favorite places. The clouds had gathered, blocking out the sun, but that met with Randolph's approval. For traveling any distance in a day, he preferred not to have the sun beating the track in front of him. In fact, he sometimes enjoyed a little light rain to water down the dust of the path and to freshen the air. That was good, because that was what he got. Twig, for that was what Randolph had dubbed the yew staff, was less impressed.

"Shelter, laddie," said the staff, unprepared to suppress its loquaciousness any longer. "That's what we need now laddie, shelter. You'll catch yer death of chill awalking 'roond in this dampness."

Randolph ignored it for a while as it prattled on about the wet and the wind, until he was sorely tempted to throw it in the ditch. But, then it fell silent for a while, and he did appreciate the support of a stout staff in walking. So, he spared it the indignity of being cast aside and, after all, it wasn't just an ordinary stick, it was a wizard's staff, and that isn't something you discard lightly, even if it is an irritating growth.

"Look Twig," he said. "If we're going to journey together, I'd like to get a few things sorted out."

"Aye, laddie," the staff said. "No point in sweeping your dead leaves under the moss, or we'll all end up barking up the wrong tree, and we've both got our job to do."

The staff chuckled at its own humour and Randolph felt a little less animosity toward it.

"The fact is," Randolph said, "That I often like to enjoy the peace and quiet of the countryside. I like to walk in silence, listening to the birdsong, feasting my eyes on the greens, browns, yellows, reds, and purples of the forests and the hillside. I like to tarry a while beside babbling brooks and watch the wind as it plays chasing games with the leaves. To be absorbed by all the natural forces of the land and to feel as one with the earth, that's why I've chosen to be who I am. I pass through places, touch others lives, make them laugh, enjoy their company, sing with them, bring them music . . ."

"Hold on a minute, laddie," Twig interrupted. "I thought you were about to chastise me for too much verbiage? And there y'go yourself. I think we may find that any disharmony between us is built out of similarity, not difference. For I too enjoy much that you have mentioned. But I do have to say I don't like the wet ground and the puddles. Water gets up under my bark and chaffs something dreadful."

They laughed together and Randolph realized he had been too harsh in judgement of Twig.

"Tell you what," he said. "If I carry you on my shoulder when it rains, will you support me when it's dry?"

"Done," Twig said. "And if I promise not to talk too much when you're enjoying the peace and tranquility of the countryside, will you listen when I've got something important to say?"

"It's a deal," Randolph said. "Twig, do you know any songs?"

Twig huffed and puffed a bit and then started in a slow tuneless, rasping voice.

> *"Honk the horn, blow the flute, and ring-a-ding the bell.*
> *Bang the drum, and make it heard right over hill and dell.*
> *Pots and pans, and lids and cans, and tins and all will do,*
> *'Cause music is a part of us, so play the kettle too.*
>
> *Honk, honk, honk, toot, toot, toot, ring-a-ding a ling,*
> *Rat-a-tat-tat, well fancy that, howl like dog and meow like*
> *   a cat.*
>
> *Honk the horn, blow the flute, and ring-a-ding the bell.*
> *Bang the drum, and make it heard right over hill and dell.*
> *Pots and pans, and lids and cans, and tins and all will do,*
> *'Cause music is a part of us, so play the kettle too."*

"Did you know my name is Randolph Kettle?" Randolph said. He had never seen a stick blush before. "But it's a good song, Twig." Randolph added quickly, "With your permission I'll use it next time I do a turn. Go through it again, will you, so that I can learn it properly."

And off they went, singing together, down the wide open track.

ॐॐ

"Whaja fink Spike?" said the ugly goblin-like creature that slobbered and drooled over a plate of sloppy food at a corner table in the dark and dingy barroom of the Traveller's Rest.

"Dunno Toady," Spike replied. "Dunno if it's wuuurf it? If we go nickin' and the marshal's around, and we get caught, we'll be for the gobbin' 'igh jump."

"We can find a wooser; there are lots travel this road and there's plenty in tonight, just look around yer. And anysaway, I've swiped the keys to a couple of the rooms near ours, so's they can't lock their doors tonight. C'mon, not lost yer balls 'ave yer?"

Toady delivered the word *balls* with a heavy emphasis on the *b*, accompanied by a liberal spraying of saliva and the cabbage that happened to occupy his mouth at the time.

"'Course I ain't," Spike retorted, the *c* of *course* refunding the investment of cabbage threefold.

"Stop gobbin' on me," Toady instructed.

"You gobbin' started it." Spike spat back with a heartfelt belch that vibrated around the whole room.

"Oi," yelled the brawny barman. "You in the corner! Watch your manners, you filthy pig! There's others in here trying to en-joy their food. Do that again and I'll clatter yer head for you."

Spike contorted his face into an even uglier grimace than his usual expression and turned into the dark corner away from the barman, pretending not to hear him.

"Bar steward," he mumbled under his breath. "Gobbin' bar steward."

It was at this point that Randolph chose to enter the Trav-eller's Rest. Having instructed Twig to remain silent while they were in the company of others, he had received a mild rebuke, in the form, "I won't tell you how to do your job, laddie, if you don't tell me how to do mine."

Randolph pushed open the heavy wooden door of the inn and entered the barroom.

The thickness of the air made Randolph cough, which in turn made every eye in the place turn toward him. Some were clear and bright, others were shifty and deceitful. Some invited you to come closer, some invited you to keep your distance. A few remained withdrawn under hooded cloaks that spelled out a stranger's desire to remain unknown, unobserved, and anony-mous.

"Fancy a good time, duckie?" came a voice directed at Ran-dolph from somewhere in the dimness of the smoky barroom.

The barman shot a sharp look in the direction of the voice.

"Keep yer negotiations privater and quieter," he said. "I've told you before. You'll get me closed down if the marshals think I'm running a whorehouse here."

"Go on," Twig whispered. "Don't just stand there with your mouth open. Ask him."

"Don't you start," Randolph said.

"Start what?" Twig whispered again.

"Oh, never mind," Randolph said, his attention swinging to the barman. "Got any rooms you might be willing to let out for the price of an evening's entertainment?"

"Entertainment?" the barman sniffed. "What sort of entertainment? You a fancy dancer or sumfin'?"

He laughed a choking sort of laugh at his own humour and was joined by hissed sniggers from several of the very shady looking characters lined up on high stools at the bar. Randolph looked at them. He had a sudden image of wooden ducks and pigs lined up on a stall at the village fete where you throw wet rags at them and get a worthless prize if you knock down at least three. He smiled at the idea.

"Look," the barman addressed the shady characters at the bar. "He's smiling; he likes my little joke. That makes 'im a good sort." He turned his attention to Randolph. "Sorry," he said, "Can't let rooms out 'cept for 'ard cash. And any decent entertainment be wasted on this lot anyway. You'd be pushin' water uphill wiv a broom."

Randolph turned to leave.

"Tell you what." He called Randolph back. "If you're of a mind to do a few kitchen chores, I'll give you some grub and let you sleep in the hayloft in the barn. Best I can do. I know what it's like to be down on yer luck."

Randolph smiled again. The evening was chill and the wind and rain would have made a night in the forest unpleasant. He tossed up in his mind whether it would be more unpleasant than a night at this place and a couple of hours in a greasy kitchen. He came down in favor of the warmth.

"Done," he said to the barman. "Have you got somewhere I can leave my pack and my lute?"

"Best keep it in the kitchen wiv you; keep an eye on it, otherwise it'll grow legs and walk, if yer know what I mean," said the barman, making eye movements and head gestures toward the two goblin-like forms squatting at the corner table.

He repeated the coughing sort of laugh, which developed into a full fledged choke. His face took on a purple hue, his eyes bulged, and he had to be tended by a couple of the shifty-looking characters with a thump on the back and a glass of water.

"Don't be alarmed," one of them said to Randolph. "'Appens all the time when 'is in one of 'is joking moods. You can see why we don't need no entertainment when we've got 'im 'ere."

Randolph thought that having 'im 'ere was a very good reason why they might enjoy some decent entertainment, but he felt that discretion and the possibility of a flattened nose were two very good reasons for keeping the thought to himself. He followed the direction of the waggling, pointing finger of the barman, who was not yet sufficiently recovered to speak, and found the kitchen. Randolph, taking the barman's advice, stowed his belongings on the top shelf of the larder in the far corner.

"Now, you can look after my things and guard them from any prying eyes and sticky fingers, particularly those ugly looking goblins in the corner of the bar," he said to Twig. "I didn't like the look of them at all."

The kitchen sink was full of dirty platters and dishes, and Randolph spent two hours scouring and cleaning them, along with a varied selection of pots and pans that contained the remains of that evening's cooking. He also scrubbed and polished all the table tops and even the greasy walls.

"Well," he said, partly to himself and partly to Twig, "By the look of it, it wasn't so much cooking as a way of making the food not raw. Say Twig, I bet you're glad you don't have to eat people food." Randolph stopped and thought for a moment. "Hey, what do you do instead of eating; you must need something to keep you alive." He stopped and thought again, his brow taking on the look of a freshly ploughed field. "You are alive? Aren't you?"

"Weeeeell," Twig said, winding up for a soliloquy on the relative and comparative elements of various perceptions of what constituted being alive, being dead, and the magical state of a wizard's staff, which was neither of these things, but which Twig called *aloof*. But he never got to deliver it, because just at that moment the barman came into the kitchen and he had to be quiet

"Tweeeee," the barman let go a long flat, between-the-teeth whistle. "Never seen the kitchen looking like a kitchen before; and hey, the walls are yellow. I always thought they wuz brown. Tell yer what lad, I'm not supposed to, but we got a room free and there won't be nobody else by ternight. I can't putyer out in the barn after yer dun all this. But only for ternight, mindyer. By the way, me name's Rumble, or that's what they call me hereabouts."

"Hi," Randolph said, trying not to wince at the bear-like grip of Rumble's hand, as he introduced himself.

"Eeeeeee," Rumble said, "That's a fancy name, owjacumbythat?"

Randolph told Rumble just enough about his travels as a minstrel to satisfy his curiosity and to convert his belief from that of him being some sort of nomadic reprobate to one of a traveling entertainer.

"So," Randolph said, "Seems like a bit of a . . ." He paused, searching for a phrase that wouldn't offend "Lively . . . place you run here," was the best he could come up with.

"Lively? I'd just call it rough, but didn't used to be," Rumble said, almost sounding wistful. "Most of the crowd that come here are good'uns, but seems t'me we get more and more roughnecks and villains by the month. Decent folk have taken to bein' very guarded. Take that lot sitting up at the bar; they's good lads all right, but t'take a look at 'em ya'd think 'em a mite shifty; but they ain't; just wary, just watchin' out for 'emselves."

"Yes," Randolph confessed, "I thought they looked like shady characters all right."

"Well they ain't. Them's me mates," Rumble declared. "Now take them two sittin' in the corner. Wouldn't trust 'em further'n I could chuck 'em. That's the sort we're gettin' more and more of. But waddayado?"

"Waddayamean, waddayado?" Randolph said, unable to resist mimicking the barman's speech.

"Well, I mean, ya godda take what ya can get. If they pays up front, then they can 'ave a room. But I tell ya Randolph, lad, I'd keep me door locked tonight—ifiwereyou."

"Thanks for the advice," Randolph said.

"Now, have a rummage in the larder and 'elp yourself to some grub, the barman said. "I'm just goin' to clear up a bit in the bar. Ya room's top o' the stairs, second door on left. Seeyain-amornin'."

"Night," Randolph said. "Seeyainamornin'."

"Saints," Randolph said to himself. "Wouldn't want his job. Not ferallthetreesintheforest."

Chuckling to himself, he found some cheese and bread in the larder and satisfied his hunger. When he had eaten his fill, he collected his belongings, woke up Twig (who seemed to have dropped of to sleep or whatever equates with sleep for wizard's staffs), and climbed the stairs. Passing the first door, he heard two voices coming from the room.

"Whaja mean, gobbin' scared? I ain't gobbin' scared, just gobbin' careful," one said.

"I fink y'er getting' a gobbin' streak o' yeller down yer gob-bin' back," the other shouted.

"Sounds like a couple of charmers," Twig said, making a mental note that he needed to be particularly watchful tonight.

Randolph went on past the door quickly. He could still hear Rumble crashing about in the bar below. It sounded more like he was breaking up the place rather than tidying it. Following Rumble's directions, he found a small and basic, but clean, room. By the time he had studied his map for a while, washed himself in the bowl on the washstand in the corner, stretched, and yawned a bit, all had gone quiet downstairs and the raised voices from the next room had been replaced by silence. Randolph lay doz-ing on the welcoming bed. Suddenly he thought about Rumble's warning.

"Must lock the door," he muttered in a sleepy voice.

But, when he shuffled to the door, there didn't seem to be any key.

"Oh," he said. "Still, I guess it'll be all right," and he shuf-fled back to bed, asleep before his head touched the pillow.

Outside, the rain clouds had mostly flown and left a clear sepia and silver moonlit landscape. Small nocturnal animals scurried hither and thither, rusting in the undergrowth. An owl hooted somewhere in the distance, calling to his friends with in-formation on good places to hunt. The wind tugged at the trees, encouraging them to shed more of their browning leafy mantle, and Randolph snored. In the corridor outside his room, the floorboards of the old inn creaked and groaned, singing a comforting lullaby of low growls and echoes that parodied the snorts and murmurs of the forest creatures as they went about their nightly business. But they also masked the creeping footsteps that moved slowly and stealthily down the moonlit passageway.

"Stop making such a gobbin' noise," hissed a sneering voice. "You'll wake the whole gobbin' place."

There was the sound of a slap and a stifled grunt as goblin hand made contact with goblin head.

"I'll smack yer gobbin' face for yer if yer do that again," the voice sizzled with anger, like wet bacon thrown into pan of hot oil.

"Ssssssh, gobbin' sssssssh, will yer."

The latch to Randolph's room lifted quietly enough, but the creaking door complained bitterly as it responded to the pressure of the goblin's push.

"Sssssssh, I said Sssssssh, didn' I?"

"You gobbin' do it then."

Randolph stirred and turned over. The goblins froze like stone statues caught in a flash of moonlight. Randolph snorted, but his breathing soon returned to a regular rhythm as he drifted back into deep, dreamless sleep, unaware of the intrusion. Twig, standing in the corner of the room, woke to instant vigilance but remained silent. From his position behind the door, he couldn't see what was happening, but he sensed the presence of the wickedness. The goblins continued their slithering, creeping entry, passing through the partly open door, past Randolph, who now slept soundly again with his head buried in the soft pillow, and over to the far corner of the room where his pack, instruments, sword, and cloak lay in a pile. As the goblins extended their clawing hands toward the booty, Twig pushed away from the wall, falling forward against the door and pushing it closed. He continued his descent, landing on the bed and waking Randolph into instant confusion. In one deft movement, he leapt from his prone sleeping position to an upright stance, his back to the door, blocking the exit for the startled goblins.

Unfortunately, Randolph was as startled as the goblins. His apparent readiness for action was just that; apparent. He didn't actually have a clue what was going on, his mind was only half awake, and his body was still three quarters asleep. But, of course, the goblins didn't know that and thought they were being challenged. Well, corner a goblin and you better be able to defend yourself. Spike moved in a flash. Fast as a rat up a drainpipe, he darted to one side to get out of the direct line of Randolph's vision. Toady, moving with the speed of a scuttling cockroach, jumped to the opposite side.

"Quick," Twig said. "Pick me up and I'll do the rest."

Randolph, luckily, had enough of his wits about him to do as Twig bid. He grasped the staff tightly and shook his head roughly to wake himself up.

"Ouch," Twig complained. "I said pick me up, not grind me to sawdust."

"Sorry," Randolph said, loosening his grip a little.

Twig acted fast. He twirled in Randolph's hands so fast that all Spike and Toady saw was a blur of movement. The thick end of the staff caught Spike a hard blow under the chin, knocking him backward in a heap into the corner by the washstand, which collapsed under his weight, emptying the contents of the water jug neatly into his lap. Instantaneously, Toady, in true goblin disloyalty to his friend, tried to make a break for the door while attention was directed to his flattened colleague. But Twig was too quick for him. A fast return to the horizontal position and a sweeping movement to the left connected with the back of Toady's skull, sending him crashing, face first, into the stout doorframe. Randolph turned to see what had happened to Toady, and Twig completed an acrobatic back flip over Randolph's head, landing a crunching thump straight onto the top of Spike's head. Spike's knees buckled and he sank to the floor, completely disoriented. Meanwhile, Toady had recovered enough consciousness to stagger to his feet, only to be laid out flat again by the heavy door as Rumble charged into the room to find out what the commotion was all about.

"What's goin' on 'ere?" Rumble shouted.

But he could see immediately that Randolph had been defending himself and his property against the two thieving goblins. Twig relaxed to being just an ordinary staff in Randolph's hands.

"I was goin' to say doyaneedny 'elp," Rumble said. "But it looks like ya've seen these two beggars orf good and proper. More to you than meets the eye, squire, eh?"

He picked up the two goblins, one in each hand, crashed their skulls together, explained to Randolph that this represented a gesture of goodwill in as much as he didn't mash them both to a pulp, carried them over to the large window, through which the serene moon still shed its silvery light, and tossed them out. There was a delayed thud as they hit the ground about twelve feet below and then a further short delay followed by a scrabbling noise and pounding footsteps disappearing into the distance.

The last noise they heard was a far-off rasping voice. "I gobbin' told yer, I gobbin' told yer."

"Don't 'spect we'll see them again," Rumble said. "You're pretty handy with that staff. Two of 'em, and you must've been taken by surprise. Come on, I think we can treat ourselves to a couple glasses of brandy. Wajasaytathat?"

Randolph said, "Yesplease," without any intent to mimic.

Breakfast the next morning was a fairly late affair, mostly due to the empty brandy bottle that still stood on the corner of the bar. By the time Randolph did appear, Rumble was telling the story of the night's events to the reformed line of wooden ducks and pigs perched at the counter. Except the two goblins had grown to a half-dozen, Randolph had fought like a tiger, there had been blood everywhere, Rumble had arrived in the nick of time to save the day, and the one bottle of celebratory brandy had expanded to two. Randolph accepted the admiring glances graciously as he tucked into the eggs and toasted bread that Rumble had prepared specially for "our champion of good."

"Just a lucky break," Randolph explained to the assembled company.

Saying his goodbyes and accepting the open invitation to come and stay any time he was passing, Randolph made his way out of the dingy barroom of the Traveller's Rest and sucked in several lungfulls of the fresh air offered by the watercolor October afternoon.

He said to Twig, "Well, you turned out to be more of a log than a stick, didn't you? Where did you learn to do all that fighting stuff?"

"All part of the basic training," Twig said. "Being a wizard's staff isn't easy you know; there's all sorts we have to learn."

"Hmmmm, well thanks," Randolph said. "And to think, I nearly left you behind! Right. Onward. Rivermeet, here we come."

As he went on his way along the road from the Traveller's Rest, Randolph passed the occasional cottage or farm. It seemed that news traveled fast in the province, for the beating of the goblins and Randolph's part in chasing them from the neighbourhood was the story of the year. Folk came up to him, inquiring if he was Randolph. The same Randolph who had lodged at the Traveller's Rest last evening? The same Randolph who had rid them of the curse of the thieving goblins? They thanked him, showered him with praise, and offered him many invitations to refreshment and accommodation for the night. As he walked, he was suddenly transported in his thoughts to knight in shining armour astride a white charger. He carried a shield bearing the emblem of the House of Kettle and the bright blade of his gold-handled sword was stained with the black blood of goblins. Dragons fled as he approached, children clamoured to touch him. They gathered to hear of his tales of brave encounters with the forces of darkness, where he thrashed all that was evil and threatening to the good folk of Alusia. Parents accompanied their children, pretending just to be there as caring guardians of their offspring, but in truth, also desperate to be close to the protector, Champion of Alusia, Lord of the Western Realm, Randolph the Great.

"You Randolph?" inquired a voice.

Returning to earth from his flight of fancy, Randolph turned to see an old man leaning on the gate of his garden, in which was set a small thatched cottage. The garden was bulging with autumn vegetables and fruits, ripe for gathering and winter storage.

"I said, you Randolph?" the voice asked again.

"Yes," he replied, crossing over the track to come closer to the old man.

Two piercing blue eyes shone out from underneath haystack eyebrows. The brown weather-beaten face housed a smiling mouth, a mountain of a nose and ears that could easily have doubled as wings in the case of emergency. The whole visage, in spite of the mismatch of the component parts, suggested a welcoming and gentle nature and was topped by a furrowed brow with ridges in which, Randolph thought, an entire season's potatoes could be planted. The whiff of strong fragrant baccyweed hung in the air, rising from a smoldering clay pipe clenched between the old man's teeth.

"Well done, lad." The old man offered his congratulations. "Sounds like you gave them Gobos a rollicking good hiding, and well rid. They bin hanging 'round here for several months now, a nicking and a thievin'. Well done lad, but I'm a'feared they won't be the last or the worst of what's to come. Mark my words, old King Petre, bless his soul, he knowed what was a brewing, and no mistake."

Randolph was intrigued by the old man and stopped to exchange a few words with him.

"Thanks," he said. "Thanks for your kind words, but it was nothing really. Just a lucky break, being in the right place at the right time, and having my trusty staff to hand."

He gave Twig a gentle squeeze by way of including him in the conversation. The old man eyed Twig and then his gaze drifted to the gold handle of Randolph's sword, which protruded from under his cloak and onto the lute slung on Randolph's back. He studied the lute, seeming to read the magical symbols that decorated its face.

"You're a strange one and no mistake," he said. "If I didn't know better, I'd say you was a minstrel and entertainer by trade, and yet you carry things." He nodded toward Randolph's staff, sword and lute, "Things that many folk wouldn't know the origin of. I think you best come inside for a while and join me in a fresh brew."

Randolph was ready for a rest. It was late afternoon and while he hadn't made much progress on his journey to Rivermeet today, the events of the previous night had left him weary and of little mind to cover a great distance. He gladly followed the old man into the small whitewashed cottage and accepted the invitation to sit at the pine table that filled most of the kitchen cum living room.

"Bottle," the old man said. "Me name's Bottle, Walter Bottle. Attendant to the late King Petre for many's a year."

Randolph smiled at the vision that sprang into his head. Walter as a bottle, with jug ear handles and a nose spout. He didn't think it appropriate to say his name was Kettle, so he just left it at Randolph for the moment.

"Bin a few changes 'round here the past few years," the old man continued. He busied himself at the fire, boiling water and removing fresh-baked bread from the small oven. Randolph's nose raised and his head tilted back a little as he caught the smell of the bread, which overpowered the fragrance of the baccyweed that pervaded the cottage. He felt the saliva flow around his tongue as he imagined biting on the crusty outer shell of the wedge of loaf that he hoped the old man was about to offer and the soft, warm, butter-soaked bread melting in his mouth.

"Changes?" Randolph asked. "What sort of changes?"

"The folk around these parts; well I mean, used to be that you knew everyone and everyone knew you. And not only that, there was never any business going on that folk weren't aware of. You know what I mean?"

He looked at Randolph to check that he did know what he meant and, apparently satisfied that the essence of his words had been grasped, he went on to explain further.

"Folk are getting wary these days. Too many strangers around. Too much going on that is kept secret. Too much being hidden and too many whisperins behind folks' backs. Suspicious, that's what folk have become, suspicious. And I know things, y'know. I know things that haven't even crossed other folks' minds. If you know what I mean."

Once again, he looked toward Randolph to check that his meaning had been grasped, but this time he didn't seem so satisfied. "You understand?" he asked.

"I think so," Randolph said, drawing out each word slowly and stretching it to its fullest extent.

In truth, his attention was more drawn to the loaf of bread that had just sent another waft of fresh-baked smell in his direction, and he had only half listened to the last bit. He retraced in his head the words that he had heard, back to where his attention had wandered to the bread.

"Wary," Randolph said. "What do you mean, wary?"

Luckily, before he answered, the old man filled two drinking horns with brew from the kettle, hacked two slices off the loaf, allowing small clouds of steam to puff from the bread, and pushed a share, and one of the horns, in Randolph's direction. With a mouthful of hot buttered bread and his hands clasped around the warm drinking horn, Randolph was, once again, able to give his full attention to the old man's words.

"By wary, I mean they don't trust each other like they used to. There's been too much cheating and lies told of late. I tell you, there's some darkness at work here. Some force encouragin' folk away from the old ways, away from good and toward doin' each other down. I heard King Petre tell of his fears of all this shenanigans and monkeyshines the year that he passed on, and now it's all beginnin' to happen, just like he said. If you know what I mean."

Of course, Randolph did know exactly what he meant, but he wasn't prepared to divulge his understanding until he had quizzed Walter further.

"So," Randolph said, "where do you think all this strange behavior is coming from then? Why do you think all this is happening?"

"Thrung," Walter said. "That's what's at the bottom of all this. Thrung."

At the mention of Thrung, Randolph's attention became very drawn to everything Walter had to say. He was conscious that maybe this old man had important information that would be of value to him in his journey to the boglands, if that was where he had to go, and it seemed to be more of a probability as he followed his destined path.

"I worked this out from things I heard around the court," Walter said. "Things I overheard from conversations between the Wizard Galdore and King Petre. Things said at the Council of Knights and other bits and pieces reported by journeymen and travellers who passed through Castle Drent. I probably gathered more snippets from more sources than any other person, and when I put it all together, the answer was Thrung."

"Why are you telling me all this?" Randolph asked. "Why do you think I would want or need to know?"

Walter's eyes narrowed a bit and a knowing smile consumed his face, stretching the skin so that his ears waggled and his nose seemed to stand to attention. "There's not much escapes the notice of Walter Bottle," the old man said. "There's not just fluid in here, y'know," he said, pointing to his head.

Randolph couldn't help himself and a chuckle escaped his lips, generated once again by the picture of Walter as a bottle full of some innocuous fluid, his ears as jug handles that tipped the vessel to pour from the spout of a nose.

Walter interpreted the chuckle as a knowing noise of confirmation from Randolph and he drew closer, dropping his voice to a whisper. "I'll tell you, I know a wizard's staff when I see one, and that lute and sword you carry; they ain't no or'nary minstrel's gear," he confided.

Walter's nose wagged and his ears flapped in excited gyrations as his head nodded self-agreement with his observations. Randolph was convinced that while Walter had lots of bits of information about matters relevant to the rise of the forces of darkness and the quest to find and destroy the source of the evil, he didn't really understand what was going on or have a complete picture of the state of things now, or to come. However, it would be foolish not to gather some of his knowledge; it could fill in some gaps and provide answers to some of the many questions that still filled Randolph's mind.

"So what do you know about this Thrung?" Randolph said.

Randolph's suspicions were confirmed as Walter prattled on for some time, saying everything and nothing. It was obvious after a while that Thrung was just a name he had heard. He didn't even seem to know of the boglands. Evening was drawing on and Randolph made some moves to take his leave. Walter however, insisted that he stay the night.

"Can't be sleeping rough in this chill," Walter said, "And there's a good five hours on foot to Rivermeet from here."

Randolph found Walter to be a congenial enough character and while he obviously wasn't going to answer many questions for him, that was no reason not to accept his kind invitation. In fact, an evening in Walter's company might be fun, and he did make exceedingly good bread. They sat that evening around the roaring log fire in the cottage, swapping tales of exploits and supping horns of delicious ale that Walter boasted he brewed from a recipe handed down for generations through his family. They talked long into the night. Randolph sang Walter some of his songs and Walter promised in return to teach Randolph a special wizard's song he had overheard once when Galdore had held a magician's convention at the court in Castle Drent.

"It's actually a spell-song for making you invisible," he said in a low whisper. "I know it works, 'cause I've used it once or twice, but it gives me a terrible 'ead for days after, so I don't use it regular. If you know what I mean."

"Now come to me you mists of time.
Now come and listen to my rhyme.
I command that all 'round me
A cloak is made that folk can't see.

Make it tough and make it strong;
Make it wide and make it long.
It needs to hide me from the world;
Around me gather, around me fold.

Cover me, shield my form from view.
Cover me, secret and invisible to
All the eyes that look my way.
I go unseen by night and day.

And now I command the powers on high
To work this spell, so that I
Will take your charm, will take it fast,
Three days the magic spell will last."

Walter said the words carefully, explaining to Randolph that they didn't work without the tune and so he was being careful to present them completely tunelessly to avoid disappearing. He also explained that in the last line, you changed the words to however many days, hours, or minutes you wanted to stay invisible.

"Now, I'll hum the tune to you and you can put the two together if you want to use the spell-song," he said. "But be warned, it's not to be used too frequently. If you overdo it, I heard tell, you could disappear and never be seen again, and anyway it gives a shocking head for three days after you reappear. I'd only use it very rarely and in extreme emergencies if I was you."

Walter hummed the tune to Randolph and made him repeat it several times until he was satisfied that he'd got it right. Randolph smiled inwardly. He didn't think for one moment the spell-song would actually work, but he didn't want to offend Walter. He was a decent man, one of the traditional old folk, kind and generous to a fault. This was the sort of person that made Alusia a good country. Randolph was moved to see Walter as one of the people he would be protecting by following his path to make some contribution to defeating the forces of darkness. But he was still convinced that he couldn't be the main counter-player in this scenario of potential doom; he still didn't believe he could possibly be the One.

∾•∿

The next morning, Randolph was up early. Walter made him a fine breakfast of fresh eggs and ham and packed up some bread and cheese for him to take for his lunch. He waved from the gate of the little thatched cottage after extracting a promise from Randolph that he would call and see him next time he came past that way.

"Bye," Randolph called over his shoulder. "Thanks for everything."

The journey to Rivermeet was uneventful, even a bit boring by Twig's reckoning, but that may have been to do with the fact that Randolph was in thinking mood for most of the way and Twig had to keep his promise to be silent—that wasn't something that came naturally to him. After nearly four hours of walking and a short stop to do justice to the bread and cheese, Randolph reached the wooden bridge that crossed the Condor. It was about a mile upstream from where the Gantwine joined and spanned the ten yards between forest-clad banks resting on four wooden pillars set into the riverbed. The structure needed to be sturdy because it bore considerable traffic in the form of horses, carts, and those on foot journeying to and from the town of Rivermeet to the coastal towns and villages in eastern Alusia. Randolph's thoughtful mood had been mostly to do with all that he had been told by Galdore, Martha, Sulaman, Rumble, and even Walter. More important was the fact that he had witnessed the first few indications of a rise of dark forces in the activities of Griselda, and now the goblins, and also, Rumble's information that more and more undesirable characters were passing this way. All this had made a deep impression on him.

"It's all beginning to fit together and make some sense," Randolph said.

"You talking to me?" asked Twig. "Am I allowed to speak now?"

Randolph laughed. "Poor Twig, had to be quiet for a while did we? About to burst are we?"

Twig harrumphed in pretence of sulkiness, but he couldn't keep it up and dissolved into a fit of chuckling that started Randolph laughing as well. They made their merry way over the bridge together. Halfway across, Randolph stopped and looked over the parapet down into the swirling river below. One minute the water gurgled and spun, cascading down over rocks and stones in a beautiful rainbow-tinted torrent. The next, it glided serenely in deep pools, majestic in its gentle twirling and mysterious depths. Then off again it dashed, tumbling again over rocky rapids.

"It's strange, that the soft water of the river can be so many different things," Randolph said to Twig. "That it has the power to carve away a whole deep valley; that it can travel so far from the mountains to the sea without rest and still arrive fresh and excited. That it can be either friend or foe depending on the respect that you grant it."

Suddenly, in his mind, Randolph was the river. He felt strong and knew how it was that he had the power to grind away the mountain and transform it into a deep valley. He understood how he had the energy to move over long meandering paths without tiring. He was aware that the route he picked as he traveled on was either to give him a rough and bumpy journey or might allow him to linger in those calmer, more peaceful pools. Two men came to his bank, one carried a gold-handled sword, the other a leather pouch. Randolph watched as the one washed his sword in the clear waters, while the other filled his leather like a bottle and drank deep of the cool clear water. He understood that, as a river, even though he had the enormous power to move mountains, part of him could be easily captured by something as small and insignificant as a leather pouch. Even though he had the strength to travel tirelessly, he could be made to undertake menial cleaning tasks as would a servant perform for his master. He continued to watch the men on his bank as first one and then the other took up their pouch and sword as if to leave but that, stumbling on the stony ground where he, the river, had thrown up a small pebble beach, dropped their possessions, which were grabbed and whisked away by his current. He watched over time as the leather pouch became sodden and sank and was tumbled and tugged, on and out to sea, where it was lost forever. He watched as the blade of the sword rusted away to dust, leaving only the gold handle, which lay covered by his silt at the bottom of his deepest pool, neither glittering or glinting and hidden from view for eternity. For the first time, Randolph understood how he could be the One, how he could have the power. He looked at himself and at the river, and he learned.

"Hello," a voice in his ear said. "I thought I might find you around about here."

Randolph stopped being a river and returned to being a Randolph, to find Martha standing beside him. She turned, gave him a hug and a welcome kiss on the cheek.

"Martha," squeaked Randolph's voice as it gave away his excitement at seeing her and then overcorrected to a deep drone. "What are you doing here?" He finally regained his normal pitch, and said, "Although don't misunderstand, I couldn't have wished for a better surprise."

"What's the matter with your voice?" Martha asked. "It's all up and down."

"Nothing," Randolph said, realizing that even though he may have river-power, he could still be caught unaware; he still needed to learn how to ride it. "I was just looking at the river and having a think."

"Did you come to any conclusion?" Martha asked.

"I think I might have done," Randolph said.

Martha didn't probe his thoughts any further. She linked her arm into Randolph's and they continued on over the bridge.

"I've come down here to meet the others," she told Randolph. "They're all looking forward to talking to you."

"Others?" Randolph asked. "What others?"

"The other Council of Worth members," Martha said. "They'll all be at Rivermeet tonight to see you before you go of to the boglands tomorrow morning."

"Am I going off to the boglands tomorrow?" Randolph asked, genuinely surprised.

He had planned on staying in Rivermeet for several days before even thinking about what to do next.

"Yes," was the simple and unambiguous reply.

Randolph didn't argue. He was happy just to be with Martha again. Delighted to be touching her, feeling the warmth of her body against his side. Excited that he might get even one evening in her company. At Rivermeet, Martha led Randolph through the entrance gates, nodding to the two sentries who guarded the doorway. Once inside the walled enclosure of the town, they passed through narrow cobbled streets, flanked by wooden-beamed houses, some with thatched roofs, some with slates or tiles, but all perfectly and neatly kept, brightly painted and cared for. The colorful shops, inns and taverns, markets and town squares, and the general hive of excited chatter that came from all around made Randolph wonder why he had never really heard anything of Rivermeet before. It seemed a friendly, enthusiastic place, a typically Randolph sort of environment.

"Why does it have such a hefty wall around the town with only one entrance?" Randolph asked Martha.

"It didn't always have," she said. "Not so long ago it used to be a very open place. People would come and go freely and often. But when the troubles started, the townsfolk took swift control and now, without being known or being able to prove you have honest business or contacts in the town, you're not likely to get inside the gates."

"Troubles?" Randolph queried. "Would I be right if I said Thrung?"

"You would," Martha confirmed. "But I wouldn't say it too loud; not out here in the open streets anyway. Wait until we get to the Leaping Horse and meet the others, then we'll explain everything to you."

The Leaping Horse proved to be a small tavern located, as far as Randolph could judge, somewhere around the center of the town. It occupied a corner where narrow lanes made it an island of welcome among many tall houses. The bottle-glass-paned bow-fronted windows, the low door with a step down into the entrance, and the beamed interior gave a warm, homely feel, enhanced by the roaring log fire that blazed in the wide hearth. Seated on stools, gathered around a low oak table containing six jugs of foaming ale sat Galdore and three other men whom Randolph had never seen before. Martha led Randolph over to the table where Galdore greeted him warmly.

"Let me introduce you all to Randolph Kettle," Galdore addressed the three men, speaking in low tones. "This is the man who slays witches, rescues knights, and whom Sulaman has proclaimed as a contender, but more of that when we have a less public setting."

Galdore's eyes shone out from under bushy gray brows, probing the room to check the other occupants. He seemed satisfied that none were giving undue attention to the small gathering around the fire, and he continued with his introductions.

"Randolph, I want you to meet Grafdun, baron of Dark Castle." Galdore gestured toward a stocky, black-haired man of swarthy complexion. His brown eyes, unshaven chin, scarred face, and black leather tunic gave him a menacing appearance. But then he smiled and his face lit up a cheeky, boisterous character hiding within that initially sullen countenance. He was roughly handsome and, Randolph thought, was probably blessed with a natural ability to ride, use a sword and bow, and command an army of men with ease. He looked in all respects a fine but tough leader. He stuck out his hand to Randolph.

"Good to meet you friend. We've come to expect powerful things from you."

"And this is Brock." Galdore indicated the next table occupant. "He's the wise one amongst us. He keeps notes about everything."

"If Galdore calls you wise, you must indeed sit on the throne of knowledge," Randolph replied.

Brock drew out a small parchment pad and wrote on it.

"Oh, and a diplomat as well," Grafdun laughed.

"Thank you for your kind words," Brock said. "But true wisdom is not the domain of any one of us, it is a combination of all our strength, in harmony. Galdore flatters me only to divert attention from his own greatness."

Randolph could see why Brock had acquired that name. His trimmed black beard and hair were patched and streaked with gray, giving him a very badger-like appearance. He turned to the last of the three awaiting Galdore's introduction.

"And this, Randolph, this is Prince Moraden of the Faery Realm. He will be your guide tomorrow on your journey into the boglands," Galdore said.

Randolph studied the athletic framed, blond-haired man who, it appeared, was to be his companion for the next few days. He judged the prince to be about his own age and noted the clear, cool blue eyes and fine features of his handsome face.

"Greetings," Randolph said.

Prince Moraden nodded acknowledgement to Randolph, but he seemed more serious and less easygoing than the other two. Randolph assumed that it was because he was being sent out to face Thrung's bogland home tomorrow. He looked like Randolph felt. However, as they talked generally of this and that for a while, Moraden seemed to relax a little and even became quite chatty. He and the other two members of the council used the opportunity to ask Randolph about his feelings and his ways. Randolph judged that Moraden would be a valuable and erudite companion to guide him on this next stage of his quest. Galdore related the concern of the council members about increasing frequency and scope of evil doings and skulduggery.

"As individual incidents," he said, "they each amount to no real matter of worry. However, taken in total, we fear that the escalation of the frequency of these acts of wrongdoing and the increasing levels of violence and aggression used in their perpetration point only to an imminent major attack."

Particularly Galdore recounted an event that happened only a week ago, the like of which had never been known before in Alusia—an open attack on Rivermeet by a band of brigands, who had marched up from somewhere in the boglands.

"If the town had not been protected by its strong outer wall and heavy gates, there is a chance we would not be sitting here now having this discussion," Martha explained to Randolph. "The need to act is becoming more urgent by the day. Thrung's strength grows and his circle of darkness tightens its grip on our land. We must oppose his plan now and defeat his intent before he grows too powerful and we fall to his wicked way."

Galdore looked about the barroom of the Leaping Horse. He had said more than he intended in this place. People had now filled most of the other tables, chatting in small groups, and one or two lone individuals sat sipping their ale thoughtfully, studying fellow drinkers or staring idly into space, lost in their own thoughts. Galdore glanced at Grafdun, Brock, and Moraden in turn and each nodded, acknowledging his unspoken question.

"I think we are all agreed that Randolph is to proceed as our chosen envoy."

There were repeated nods and affirmative grunts from all present. Brock scribbled some more notes on his parchment.

"Then," Galdore said, "the time has come for us to retire to more private quarters and share knowledge that may ease his difficult path tomorrow."

"Hang on a minute," Randolph said. "Don't I get a vote in the 'chosen envoy' election?"

"If you like," Galdore replied. "But we know you will accept, and anyway, the vote would still be five to one, even if you declined. Motion carried."

Randolph sighed. He knew that Galdore was right. He knew his destiny was to accept this mission, and he hoped that his destiny was to carry it out successfully, but he still felt mostly minstrel and not very much chosen envoy.

"I'll see if Mrs. Weatherspoon has the room prepared for us," Galdore said as he crossed to the bar.

"Come on Randolph, chin up, and best foot forward," Martha said. "We all have confidence in you. We would have liked to give you longer, but as you heard, we dare not delay. Think back to the river, trust in your inner strength."

Upstairs in the cosy parlour the group, seated on comfortable cushioned chairs and couches, related their experiences to date, told of their observations of rising black forces and dark ways, and confirmed their belief that action could not be delayed. Galdore told of the contents of the Chronicles of Sharn, how they gave information that greatly disturbed the council, but also that it had taken many years to determine the best manner in which the powerful Thrung might be defeated. He explained that seeking the One had been their ultimate conclusion and how their plan was now coming to fruition with the discovery of Randolph. The more Randolph heard, the more he wished he had never left Gospot in his youth, but the more he looked at Martha, the more determined he became to prove his worth. Like Martha had suggested, he thought back to the river and took strength from the knowledge that he could command his own power. Within the frame that destiny had set for him, he could pick his own way, choose his own path, create his own lucky breaks.

"And now, I think the time has arrived for us to have supper and retire to our rooms," Galdore announced. "Moraden and Randolph have an early start tomorrow and some distance to journey."

With those words, and as if she had been waiting for some secret signal, the door opened and Mrs. Weatherspoon entered with a heavily laden tray of pies, fruit, cakes, and other good things to eat and drink. The company took their fill and one by one bid goodnight until only Randolph and Martha were left. Randolph had many things to say to Martha of a more personal nature than those discussed that evening. He also felt a growing desire to hold her to him and to find himself once again awakening to the sweet sound of her musical tones beside him on the pillow. She started to sing softly, and Randolph lay back in the comfortable chair and let the sound of her voice wrap him in ecstasy. He was very tired after the busy day and sleep soon overcame his conscious thought. He dreamed of flying with Martha, of being carried on the wind, of touching and holding her. He awoke the next morning to find himself in a strange bed in a strange room. Memory flooded back and he turned, expecting to see Martha's face next to him, but she was not there, only a hollow in the pillow remained where at some time in the night a head had lain. Randolph sniffed the pillow and caught the sweet scent of Martha's hair. He dressed quickly and hurried down the stairs to find his five companions already seated around the breakfast table. Conversation centered on how Moraden and Randolph should approach and enter the Boglands of Thrung without being detected. Randolph bid good morning to each in turn with a special tone reserved for Martha's greeting, and settled down to a fine platter full of fruit, nuts, breads, and toasted biscuits. There was apple juice and milk to quench the thirst of the night and Mrs. Weatherspoon had made a special fruit preserve, which Randolph discovered was famous in Rivermeet and all the surrounding area for its quality.

"When are we leaving?" Randolph inquired of Moraden.

"I think we need to be out of Rivermeet and on the Bogland Road within the hour," Moraden said. "Then, the plan is we should move onto the side tracks to get into the main areas of the bog to try and discover the location of the source of the dark forces. The tracks are dangerous and none who venture there are likely to be seen again, well not of humankind. The faery folk have, until recently, used some of the inner tracks, although even they have avoided the center of the bog for many a long year."

"What do you mean, exactly, by until recently?" Randolph asked.

"Until about six moons ago," Moraden replied. "Since that time Thrung's workings have grown to such proportion that even we dare not venture on more than the outermost tracks."

"And we're aiming for?" Randolph's question was sort of rhetorical, because he knew before Moraden answered what the response would be.

"The center," Moraden calmly announced. "It will be essential that we travel light, so I've arranged with Grafdun that he will take your pack and instruments on his way back northward and leave them at Heartland's Mound. We will return there after our foray. Come now, we must make ready and be on our merry way."

"Merry?" Randolph mumbled to himself. "If this is merry, I'd sure not want to go on one of the less joyful outings."

"We'll time our approach so that we get toward the center of the bogland as darkness falls. That way, we'll be less likely to be detected."

Randolph thought the combination of Thrung, bogland, forces of evil, and dangerous tracks hardly needed to be embroidered further by nightfall, but he kept the thought to himself. Within the half hour, they finished their breakfast and Randolph had prepared himself to leave, strapping on his sword, fastening his cloak, and taking Twig in his hand. All his other possessions he packed up and handed over to Grafdun. The party said their various goodbyes to each other.

"Did we . . .?" Randolph had whispered to Martha as she embraced him warmly.

"No," she said before he had even finished the question. "No, you went to sleep and I had to put you to bed again. You slept like a baby."

Damn, Randolph thought.

৵৵

"Can you hear that?" Moraden whispered.

Randolph strained to pick out any other sound over and above the bubbling and gurgling of the bogland and the croaking and spluttering of the various loathsome, slimy animal inhabitants of the wetlands. His hearing was, of course, no match for faery ears, but he though he could just detect a slow drumming sound, a thump, thump, thump, like the regular fall of an axe biting into the trunk of a hefty oak. He nodded affirmation to Moraden.

"What is it?" he whispered.

Moraden shrugged, his face showing that he didn't know.

Randolph followed Moraden onto a narrow track, along which they meandered for some time. It became so narrow that they had to walk one behind the other, Moraden leading the way. The ground on either side became wetter, giving off more pungent and dank odours the deeper they progressed into the bogland. Soon their pathway disappeared into a haze of swirling mist that disoriented Randolph. Moraden held up his hand to signal a halt and with his other hand placed a finger to his lips. The thump, thump, thumping sound was now distinct to Randolph.

"Now that we've come this close, you must lead from here. You're the One. You must choose our path. If I influence the purity of your decisions, it may jeopardize our chances. I'll follow and do whatever you say."

"The faery prince is either very trusting in the force of good, misinformed about the power of innocence, or stark raving mad," Randolph muttered to Twig. He took up the lead position and felt his way forward along the pathway through the misty swirls. "I

93

don't know why he wants me to lead; he seemed to know where he was going all right."

Darkness started to fall and the swamp phantoms glowed away in the distance to the right and left of them, but at least they gave Randolph some point of reference on which to focus, and the sense of disorientation left him as the night took hold of the swamp. The sky had clouded over and no stars or moonlight were available to guide them. In fact, Randolph couldn't see his hand in front of his face, even though he knew it was nearly touching the end of his nose. Then all of a sudden he could see it, well a faint outline of it, silhouetted against a background of glowing orange fire away in the distance. He turned to look for Moraden and saw him some little way behind down the pathway. His form appeared and disappeared like some ghostly apparition in that faint orange glow, as the mists folded around him and then unfurled, only to return in seconds, unsatisfied, and seeking more play with him. Moraden saw Randolph turn but waved him on, indicating that he was not to be consulted or involved in any decisions about what to do.

"What do you think Twig? Should we go on?"

"I'm not here to make decisions," was Twig's firm reply. "I'm the stick, you're the One."

"What should I do?" Randolph said to himself in desperation. "Why won't anybody help me?"

He sat down on the track to gather his wits and to think. Should he go on? Should he go back?

"Twig!" he yelled, "Moraden! Something's got me. Help!"

Suddenly the decision became the furthest thing from his mind as the muddy waters beside him churned and the tentacle that had emerged and grabbed him grew tighter around his leg, pulling sharply. He was dragged toward the muddy waters, the creature's intent too obvious for words. However, Randolph found words.

"Get it off me!" he yelled.

Moraden sprang forward but slipped, stunning himself as he fell. Twig planted himself firmly into the soil of the pathway as if he had formed roots.

"Grab me, quick!" Twig shouted.

Randolph lunged sideways with his left arm as he slithered through the mud, dragged slowly but surely by the tentacle attached to who knows what vile swamp creature. Twig's footing held good, although Randolph's strong grip made him wince a little.

Twig dug deeper into the ground as Randolph grasped him. The swamp creature pulled with a mighty strength and Randolph thought he would be wrenched in two. He dare not release his hold on Twig, that would bring only one result, and he was not about to end his days as swamp creature fodder. Something hard jabbed Randolph's side as he clung on for his life.

"My sword," he called. He reached across his taut body with his right hand. "Twig, if I can get my sword . . ."

Randolph worked his fingers slowly between his own side and the ground, stretching his hand to clasp the sword handle. Drawing the weapon carefully, so as not to slice himself with the razor-sharp blade, he slashed at the tentacle wrapped around his leg. Green fluid oozed slowly from the wound, congealing almost immediately on contact with the air.

"Got it," he gasped to Twig.

But the creature continued its slow pull, and the tentacle clasped tighter around Randolph's leg.

"Again," Twig cried. "Hit it again; I can't hold on much longer."

Randolph gashed the tentacle again with a mighty swipe of the sword, coming close to lacerating his own leg. Still the creature clung to its prey.

"You'll have to cut it right off." Twig's voice now reflected the strain of clinging to the less-than-firm soil of the pathway.

With a last desperate swipe, Randolph cut the tentacle from whatever foul creature lurked below the black surface of the quagmire. There was a sucking noise as the stirring water lapsed into stillness, and the severed tentacle cavorted and squirmed independently on the track beside them, thrashing the ground until it jerked itself back into the steaming mud of the bog. Moraden struggled to his feet, shaking his head.

"What?" he called to Randolph. "What's the matter? What's got you? Ouch, my head?"

"It's all right now." Randolph panted. "It's all right now. Thanks Twig, Thanks my friend."

Randolph checked Moraden's head. He couldn't see any damage, but Moraden insisted he could feel a lump coming up where he banged it.

"Mmmh," Randolph grunted. "So, even faeries can get bumps. We'll watch that and see if they get bruises too."

He looked at Moraden and grinned.

"Are you able to go on?" he asked.

Moraden nodded.

"Lucky break you had your sword with you."

"That was no lucky break," Randolph replied.

Strangely, Randolph's bravery at defending himself left him proud and determined; he swiveled on his heel to face the distant glow and, with sword clasped in a firm grip, he moved stealthily forward, crouching low to take advantage of the cover of the swirling mist. He was no longer afraid. They soon reached the shaft head and slipped silent and unseen over the rim and down into the Cavern of Doom. Moraden took the lead without thinking as they descended through levels of platforms and down ladders into the dark depths. Randolph was happy to see that Moraden seemed none the worse for his fall and was more than content to follow, confident that his colleague's superior senses would be their best guide. Eventually they reached solid ground below and, in the dim orange light of the cavern tunnels, started their reconnoiter to gather what information they could concerning Thrung's plans.

Chapter Five
Inside Heartland's Mound

River Westerling with
Heartland's Mound in
background

FAERY QUEEN Charmila was holding forth on one of her favorite topics. "Well," she said, "I've nothing against humankind. In fact, some of them are quite nice really. You take that Galdore for instance. Intelligent, charming, wise, quite handsome, well, in a humankind sort of way."

"Hrmmmph," King Brodika said. He was not really listening, as he often didn't when his wife was spouting forth.

"You listening, dear?" Charmila, without waiting for an answer, went on. "Most of the Council of Worth members are nice people, although that Baron Grafdun, I'm not so sure about him; looks like he needs a good bath sometimes."

But Brodika still wasn't listening. "My feet hurt," he said as he gave his main attention to working on a puzzle game he had just invented involving clues and lots of words that criss-crossed on a page when you entered the right answers. "I'm not as young as I used to be, and that walk around the forest this morning made my feet hurt."

"I wonder how Moraden got on with that Randolph fellow they're all talking about," Charmila said. "They're supposed to be coming back here and we don't know anything about him. I mean, is it acceptable to just let him in to wander about? Aren't we dropping our standards just a bit too far? Where will it end? Why don't we just throw open the gates and invite the whole of humankind to enter, regardless?"

Brodika turned his attention from his link-word puzzle for a minute. "Look my dearest," he said. "There's no point in getting a hornet in your hair about it. Apparently, this Randolph fellow is something a bit special and, anyway, he's a student of Galdore, we're not exactly running an open day. But, if you insist, we can get him to take the test; I suppose that's only right; all the Council of Worth members had to go through it before they were allowed freedom of the realm."

"I'm glad you agree dear," Charmila said. "I'll get it organized then."

ॐ॰ॐ

Randolph didn't understand why their presence had gone undetected and unchallenged but, having emerged unscathed from their brief exploration of the Cavern of Doom and armed with the information they had gathered, Randolph and Moraden made their way toward Heartland's Mound on a bright, late October morning.

"So," Randolph said, "tell me something about faeryland."

"Well first basic rule, don't, whatever you do, call it faeryland," Moraden said. "My parents will go hoop de hoop if they hear you say that. It's the Faery Realm, or just the Realm."

This was a very different Randolph from the young lad who had stood gaping in awe at Galdore's magical study only a matter of two moons ago. He was now a young man with a confidence and a self-awareness that he was, indeed, someone a little special. But he was still occasionally prone to opening his mouth before engaging his brain.

"Don't really see the difference," he blurted.

"Well," Moraden said, ignoring Randolph's comment. "What do you need to know? First thing, I guess, is that my mother will insist you take the futtratfagh before you can wander about the Realm unescorted."

He pronounced the word *foot-rat-far*. Randolph assumed this was a faery language word, but he had not a clue what it meant.

"Until a few weeks ago, I knew nothing about faeries, other than what all humans know through legend and story," Randolph said.

"Well if you're coming to visit, there are some basic things that you'll need to learn," Moraden said. "So, listen carefully to what I tell you."

Randolph was astonished to learn from Moraden that there was a whole parallel world where faeries existed and lived life in a way not unlike that of humans. He was even more intrigued that he was to be allowed to meet faery folk and see a world that only a handful of humans had seen since what Moraden called "the split." Until he had met Moraden, Randolph had thought of faeries as spirit beings flitting, flirting, and flying in the woods and forests among the bracken and the bushes, hiding from people and pursuing mischievous and cheeky pastimes for their own recreation. They were mythical beings of fable and children's stories—they were not real people.

"Will I be able to learn some of the faery tongue?" he asked Moraden.

"I imagine we can teach you something of our language," Moraden said. "But fear not, the language of humankind is spoken freely by all of my people. Our roots are from common stock."

"What does . . . footrotfart . . . mean then," Randolph pronounced the word slowly. "That's not anything like any human word I know."

Moraden laughed.

"Futtratfagh. F.F.T.R.T.F.H. It stands for 'fitness for the realm test for humans.'"

"What?" Randolph said.

"Fitness for the realm test for humans," Moraden repeated. "It's just to ensure that only those humankind folk with the faery blood are given admission to our realm without the memory wipe when they leave to return to their world."

"But I don't have faery blood," Randolph said.

"You can't tell that until you've taken the test," Moraden said. "Galdore seems to think you probably have. Certainly if you are the One, then you will have inherited the blood from your forebears, who may have carried it for many generations, hundreds of years, without conscious knowledge."

"Wow," Randolph said. "Me a faery?"

"No," Moraden said, smiling. "I didn't say you might be a faery. I just said you might carry some faery blood in your veins, the same as other humankind mystics or wizards. The same as black witches and those goblins that still inhabit your world carry troll blood, or your humankind kings and queens are endowed with traces of elven blood."

"Oh," Randolph said.

"You see, there are many worlds that exist in time and space, in parallel with each other, some of which we are aware and, I assume, others of which we are not."

"I see," Randolph said, not really seeing at all.

"Some," Moraden went on, "are more hidden than others. Take Thrung's underworld as an example. We can't walk through that unnoticed or without seeing it. There's a direct physical connection to the world of humankind. It's actually still part of the same world, just hidden down under the ground in a labyrinth of caverns. It's only in the more advanced splits that the physical link becomes less strong. There are some that have drifted further apart and now have only a tenuous link, a void between them that can only be crossed by those with the necessary sensitivity or power."

"Oh," Randolph said again. "So faeryland . . . I mean the Faery Realm . . . is one of those that have drifted further away?"

"Yes," Moraden said. "We need to go through a special gateway, an opening that only half exists."

"Oh," Randolph said. He didn't really see how they could go through something that only half existed. It would be like having the top half of your jug filled with ale and a big gap of nothingness holding it up. He was saved from further speculation and confusion as they made the crest of a low hill and in the chill of that October evening saw Heartland's Mound ahead in the distance.

"Come on," Moraden said. "Not far now. If we hurry a little, we should be in time for supper."

They marched on down the open track in silence, Moraden absorbed in his own thoughts and Randolph transformed, in his head, into a faery. But not a faery like Moraden. Nothing so ordinary. Randolph imagined he flew on gossamer wings, dressed in dazzling, shining white. He carried a silver wand on the end of which sat a sparkling star, and in his leather pouch he had stardust that he spread by the handful on passing strangers, turning them from sour-faced miseries into beaming examples of gentlefolk. He flew past Walter Bottle's cottage and saw Walter standing at the gate of his neat garden. Offering him the granting of a wish, he watched as Walter thought long and hard while he, Randolph the faery, sat in Walter's kitchen eating wedges of fresh bread, dripping with melted butter. Randolph tried to guess what Walter's wish would be. Would he banish the goblins from the land, bring peace to the world, prosperity forever to the kingdom of Alusia? But no. "Think I'll be 'avin' smaller ears and a pert li'l nose, If you know what I mean," Walter decided.

Randolph chuckled a faery chuckle and granted his wish as he flew off on further errands of magical generosity. He looked back, but Walter had turned away toward his cottage door, so Randolph didn't see him with his new look, but that pleased him; Walter wouldn't be Walter without those ears and that nose. He was given to thinking, as he flew spreading stardust across the land, protecting the crops from failure, curing ignorance and disease throughout the kingdom, that banishing evil and darkness from every corner of the kingdom was a good thing for Randolph, chief faery, to do. He thought that Chief Faery of all Health and Wealth was a great thing to be. He thought that having such power was the key to domination of good over evil. He was so proud of himself that he used his newfound power to reward himself. He granted himself the skill to make bread as good as Walter's. However, even in his fantasy, selfish use of his power was not acceptable. He tumbled, head over heels, from the sky where his mind had flown, landing with a hard bump on the earth below.

"Randolph, you all right?"

Moraden's voice snapped Randolph back to reality, to find that fantasy and the real world had collided in a most unpleasant way. He lay face down in a cowpat, his forehead bumped on the ground, scattering surprised flies and dung beetles in all directions.

"Must've tripped," Randolph said.

"You might have picked a less messy place to fall," Moraden said. "Here, let's take a look at that head. Mmmh. So, even One's can get bumps. We'll watch that and see if they get bruises too. Mine's gone already."

He was right, when Randolph looked, there was not a sign of any bump or bruise on Moraden's head. It was if he had never even banged it. Randolph smelled nasty, in fact he stank, and the bump on his head hurt. He spent the next mile trying to wipe the cow dung from his shirt and breeches but succeeded only in spreading it further and wider around his whole person as he trudged the rest of the way to the foot of Heartland's Mound. Moraden drew a kerchief from his pocket.

"Thanks," Randolph said reaching for the kerchief, "Mine's completely useless now."

Moraden snatched the cloth away from Randolph's grasp.

"I'm afraid I'll have to blindfold you Randolph. It's the rules. Until you've passed the test. Then you'll be given the knowledge to find and open the gate to the Realm."

Once securely blindfolded, Moraden uttered some strange words and led Randolph forward. He felt rather than heard a sort of crackling in the air. His skin tingled, raising goose bumps down the back of his arms, and the hair on his neck stood up. Suddenly the chill autumn evening air gave way to a waft of warm breeze and the scent of spring flowers and apple blossom.

"Hello Mother, Father." Randolph heard Moraden's voice greeting his parents. "Thanks for coming over to meet me. I suppose they told you we were coming through the gateway."

"Welcome home, son."

Faery Queen Charmila, Randolph assumed.

"Good to see you, boy."

Faery King Brodika, Randolph guessed.

Randolph heard the smacking of a mother's kiss on the cheek of a son.

"So son, how did it go?" the queen said. "Did you meet this Randolph fellow and when is he arriving? And what's this, this … person you've brought with you now? Who's he?"

Randolph stood, still blindfolded. He could sense the disapproving look of Queen Charmila. He could feel distaste in the air.

"Oh," Moraden said as he removed the blindfold from Randolph's eyes, the bright evening sun making Randolph squint. "Let me introduce you. This is Randolph."

There was a long silence.

"But he's covered in cow's poo," Charmila said, "And he's got a funny bumpy shaped head. And has he got something wrong with his eyes? Why is he squinting at me in that fashion? What's that nasty rag he's clutching and why are all those flies buzzing round him?"

"Nice to meet you lad," said the king, ignoring the stench that shared Randolph's space and shaking him warmly by the hand. "Come on we'll get you cleaned up and get some food inside your belly. I'll bet you're starving hungry after your long trek. Then we can all get properly introduced."

Randolph and Moraden followed the king and queen, Charmila holding Brodika by the arm as if she was steering him through a heavy sea.

"He's not at all what I expected," Randolph overheard her loud whisper to Brodika. "I mean, shouldn't he at least be a prince: He looks like a common humankind minstrel or something."

"Now, now dear," Brodika counseled. "Let's not be hasty, we know nothing about the lad yet. Let's wait and see. I sense there's something a tad different about him, an air, and something about those eyes."

"Cow's poo and a squint, dear," the queen said. "Cow's poo and a squint. Still the test will sort it out. I don't see there's any way he can pass that."

She raised her chin into the air, adopted what Brodika called her regal gait and, releasing his arm, flowed on down the pathway toward the castle like a ship in full sail, leaving Brodika to steer his own course home.

"Come on," Moraden said. "Let's go and find you some hot water before you attract every fly in the Realm."

Moraden scooped up his father and the three of them made their way to the castle gates.

❧

Randolph relaxed into the deep tub of steaming water. He rubbed himself with the sweet-smelling salts and the sponge that had been delivered with the water. He felt clean for the first time in many weeks.

"How you doing, Twig?" he asked the staff, standing sentry duty by the door. "We've not had much time to chat since we left the boglands. How do you think we fared down in the Caverns of Doom?"

"It's not up to me to say really," Twig said humbly. "It's up to the council to decide what needs to happen when you report at tomorrow's meeting."

"Yes I know it is," Randolph agreed. "But I value your opinion; I'd just like to know what you think."

"I'll tell you one thing," Twig said. "I don't go a whole hog on Queen Charmila's attitude. I'd say a trip to the boglands or a night in Rumble's tavern would do her no harm at all."

"Oh come on Twig, she's all right. After all, she's a queen and look what was presented to her as the One. A scruffy, very smelly youth who had recently been dragged through the muddy bog, descended into the smoky Caverns of Doom, rolled in cow's poo, sporting a lump on his head the size of an egg, and squinting at her like a one-eyed parrot. I can't imagine I presented an image in which she could have much confidence."

Randolph surprised himself at his defense of Charmila. Certainly, he agreed with Twig that she might have given him the benefit of the doubt, at least until they had a chance to have a proper introduction, but his experience as a traveling entertainer had brought him into contact with many different people. Randolph had learned from an early age not to judge everybody by his own standards or expect them to behave in the same way he would.

"She'll come round," Randolph said. "She just needs a bit of time to get to know me. I just need an opportunity to prove my worth to her."

"What, you mean a lucky break?" Twig said.

"If you like," Randolph smiled.

He was beginning to see that lucky breaks were things he could have some influence on, not just random occurrences. There was a rap on the door and a voice called, "Master Randolph, supper is about to be served in the dining hall. Will you be coming down?"

"You bet I will," Randolph called back. "I could eat a horse."

"I believe it's only wild boar tonight," came the humourless reply.

"That'll do," Randolph replied.

He dried and dressed quickly in the ruffed white cotton shirt, very elegant faery-green silk tunic, and stylish brown knee-length breeches and stockings that had been laid out for him on the four-poster bed. Black polished hide shoes with a silver buckle completed the outfit. His now clean and untangled golden curls framed his suntanned face. He looked every part the handsome prince that Charmila had been expecting.

"Well Twig," he said. He flaunted himself in front of the stick, "What do you think? How do I look?"

"You're a queen seducer, Randolph Kettle," Twig laughed. "Go get her, laddie."

Randolph entered the dining area to find that he was not the last to arrive. The queen was conspicuous by her absence. However, gathered in the anteroom sipping from delicate glasses were King Brodika, Moraden, and a pretty young woman with bright features and smiling eyes who Moraden introduced to Randolph as his sister, Reeka.

"Charmed," Randolph said, as he took the proffered hand and gently touched his lips to the back of the princess' fingers.

She looked into Randolph's handsome sun-bronzed face and smiled a smile so sweet as to melt the heart of even the most unromantic man. Randolph, of course, not being by any stretch of the imagination unromantic, was smitten by her gentleness and beauty as she was by his handsomeness and strong athletic body.

But, she is a mere child in comparison to my beloved Martha. Oh how I wish Martha was here, Randolph thought to himself.

As if reading his mind, Moraden announced, "Randolph. The plan is that we will dine tonight, just the five of us, to give Mother and Father the chance to get to know you a bit. Then tomorrow you will need to take the Futtratfagh in the morning. The other council members are arriving about midday for a meeting in the afternoon. Then, after you have given them a report of our brief journey into the Caverns of Doom, we must decide what steps to take."

Queen Charmila swept into the room. "Are we all here?" she asked in a loud voice. "Where's that Randolph fellow; I guessed he'd be late."

She looked at Randolph standing proud and erect beside Reeka. Her expression changed to one of graciousness and charm, and she smiled. In fact, her whole face lit up and she did justice to the defense that Randolph had made in her favor earlier when he was talking with Twig.

"And who is this delightful young man?" she asked of Reeka. "A new admirer, Reeka? You haven't mentioned any new admirers recently."

"This is Randolph, Mama," Reeka replied. "I thought you'd met him earlier."

"Mmmmh," said the queen eyeing Randolph up and down. "Well, you do scrub up a treat, don't you Randolph; maybe I misjudged. Anyway, come now, let's sit down to eat, shall we."

Randolph bowed just slightly and, smiling, held out his arm in a gesture of escort to the queen. She looked at him, raised her eyebrows, placed her hand on his arm, and allowed herself to be escorted into the dining hall. Randolph seated the queen, ensuring her comfort and then as he turned to take his own place, heard her say to Brodika in a loud whisper, "You could be right dear; there is something about the eyes."

The meal was delicious and passed all too quickly for Randolph, who was reveling in the comfort and elegance of the surroundings. He felt quite at home and by the third glass of wine, had decided that maybe, after all, he did have quite a lot of faery blood in his veins. And if he didn't have, then he wanted some.

"Come on Randolph," Moraden said. "I'm told you have a voice to charm the birds from the trees. Won't you sing for us?"

"I would," Randolph replied. "But I haven't caught up with my lute yet; Grafdun was supposed to drop it off here with my pack and stuff."

Without delay, Randolph's lute was located and brought to him. He picked a song that he felt would be to the queen's taste; one that he had written using his previous idea of faeries, but luckily, it fitted the occasion.

"A special song for a special occasion, with my thanks for making me so welcome."

"See, Brodika," said the queen, so as not to be seen to be totally wrong. "See," she said in a loud whisper, "I said he was a minstrel."

Randolph just smiled and sang.

> *"If all the world were made of Stardust,*
> *If all was gold beneath my hand,*
> *If the sun was a shining jewel above me,*
> *Then I surely would be in faery land."*

Moraden winced a little at the faery land phrase and caught Randolph's eye as he did so. But when they both glanced at his mother, she seemed entranced.

> *"I'd travel to go to many places,*
> *O'er land, over sea I'd even fly,*
> *But the place I always will return to*
> *Is a place to which I have a tie.*
>
> *It's a realm where there is only beauty,*
> *A place in which my dreams come true.*
> *A world I'll always call foreverland,*
> *In sunshine with sky that's always blue.*
>
> *For when my mortal life is ended,*
> *When they say it's time to choose my way,*
> *It's to the place wherein I came and met you,*
> *It's to the Realm I want to go, I'll say."*

Randolph remembered, just in time, to switch faeryland to the Realm in the last line. He finished the song and looked up to meet the loving gaze of Reeka. She was, like her mother, enraptured by Randolph's voice, captivated by his soft tones and flowing notes. For her the song was personally written and personally sung. She had found her ideal in Randolph.

ॐॐ

Randolph slept soundly that night. The wine, the good food, the freshness of the warm air, the comfort of the huge bed, all combined to make the night seem to last but a few brief moments. However, he awoke refreshed, ready to take on the challenge of discovery, ready to determine if he had the knowledge and skill to be awarded the freedom of the Realm, as one of the few humans to be given the freedom to come and go at his pleasure.

"No doubt about it," Charmila announced at the breakfast table. "You can tell a mile off, the man's got faery heritage oozing from his pores."

Needless to say, Randolph had done a good job of converting the queen to his support. In fact, he had almost done too good a job and she was suggesting to Brodika that the test might not really need to be applied too harshly. Reeka spent the whole of breakfast gazing toward Randolph in that sort of moony worship of which only young people are capable. In the end, it made him uncomfortable, and he started to excuse himself to make preparations for the test.

"Preparations?" Brodika asked. "How can you make preparations? You don't know what you've got to do yet."

Randolph sat down again, but the disturbance had served its purpose to break Reeka from the spell of enchantment. She finished her toasted bread and honey with eyes cast down, aware that she might have been staring a bit.

Brodika wiped the last crumbs from his lips with a silk napkin. "Now Randolph, are you ready for the futtratfagh?"

"As ready as I'll ever be without knowing what I've got to do," he replied.

"All in good time," Brodika said. "First we must ask you to take the oath. Come with us to the Hall of Heritage."

Randolph followed the small party to a grand hall where the ceiling and walls bore the crests and emblems of every ancient faery family name. As they entered this amazing room, Randolph found himself standing beside Reeka.

108

"I hope so much that you pass the futtratfagh," she whispered to him. "That would entitle you to have your name painted here up among those others carrying faery blood."

"Now," Charmila said, as she seated herself on the throne in the center of the hall. "Come on over here and kneel before me on your right knee."

Randolph did as he was bid. The floor was hard and cold, and he hoped the oath ceremony wouldn't take too long. Reeka was looking at him in that moony sort of way again and Brodika was fiddling with a piece of parchment and a quill pen.

"Stop messing with that puzzle thing for a moment, will you dear, and pay attention," Charmila said. "Get the ceremonial long sword and take your place behind Randolph. Reeka and Moraden, stand one each side of Randolph."

They moved to their allotted places, Reeka standing closer than necessary so her leg pressed lightly against Randolph's shoulder.

"Randolph," the queen said. "Place your right hand over your heart and repeat after me."

A soft, melodic choir of voices filled the hall, chanting harmonies the like of which Randolph had never heard. They were almost discordant in their match but then came together in the most wonderful way, like the wind sighing in the trees as they mixed and mingled with the sound of waves tumbling on the sands and the flutter of autumn leaves drifting gently from the forest canopy. From where the voices came Randolph could not see, but they were as beautiful and pure as he had ever heard. He felt the blade of the long sword rest on his right shoulder from behind and, moving his eyes sideways, he could just see the tip glinting below his ear. The queen spoke the oath, stopping after every line to allow Randolph to repeat the words.

> *"By all the souls that ever lived*
> *In this realm and all others,*
> *I swear the test of time and space*
> *I will honor and complete with grace.*
> *I swear that by my heart and soul,*
> *The blood of my elders will be shown,*
> *And should it be that faery blood*

Flows in my veins and it proves good,
Then let all here confirm my bond.
To the Realm, I swear my allegiance now
Until the sands of time run dry,
Until my faery soul might die."

The choir voices faded and Randolph felt uplifted. He felt certain now that faery blood coursed in his veins. He knew that whatever test the faery realm might set for him, he was ready. He knew that he was one of the chosen few who by heritage enjoyed the right to walk free in both the land of his humankind forbears and in that of his distant and ancient faery ancestors. Brodika raised the sword from Randolph's shoulder and Moraden and Reeka bent forward, each placing a kiss on Randolph's cheek. He noticed that Reeka's lips came closer to his mouth than they might have needed and that they lingered a little longer than those on the other cheek.

"Your task," Brodika's voice took on a deeper tone and a note of greater authority than Randolph had noticed previously, "Is to locate the gems of Ornica, to access, undetected, the chamber in which they are housed, to select that which most attracts you and, bearing that stone, return here to this hall within the hour. It is from the completion of this task and from the choice of jewel that your heritage will be determined. But know this Randolph. Know that your detection by those who guard the chamber, or selection of a gem that has no root in the Realm will banish you forever from this kingdom."

Randolph stood, a little bemused, and looked first at Brodika, then at the queen.

"Go on then," Charmila said, making shooing motions with her hands. "Don't stand around with your mouth open. Get on with it. Your time starts from when you reach your room."

Randolph hurried off. He didn't have a clue where to start looking for the chamber.

"If I'm going to crack this one," he said to himself as he followed the corridors back to his room, "I'm going to need a really lucky break." But then a thought occurred to him. "Or maybe I don't. Maybe this is my way out of this whole situation. If I fail then I can't be the One. If I don't pass the test, I'll go back to being just Randolph the minstrel, wandering the highways and byways of Alusia. This is my way out."

All the old doubts that still lurked in the depths of his mind surfaced again to tussle with the newfound confidence of recent days. Did he really want to follow this dangerous and risky path? Was he not still just Randolph the minstrel? In a few days, he could be back at the Black Swan with Nick; it would be like he'd never left. He stopped outside his room, his hand on the latch. He knew that from the moment he entered, he had just one hour to await judgment. In one hour, he could be free. All he had to do was sit in his room for sixty minutes and this whole thing would be over.

কৈ

Back in the Hall of Heritage Charmila, Brodika, Moraden, and Reeka waited. The queen paced the room, reviewing the various heraldic symbols and shields that adorned the walls; Moraden sat quietly, reviewing his own thoughts about who knows what; Reeka fiddled with her hair as she dreamed of a night of pleasure in Randolph's bed; Brodika had extracted his parchment and quill and continued work on his link-word puzzle.

"There's no word from the corridor outside his room yet and it's been half an hour since he should have started," Charmila announced to the room. "If he doesn't come out soon there's no way he will achieve it."

Moraden grunted, Reeka looked very sad, and Brodika remained apparently totally absorbed by his puzzle. After three quarters of the allotted time, they still sat with no word of Randolph having left his room.

"Well that looks like that then," Charmila said. "Shame really, I'd quite taken to Randolph, and I think you had as well my dear, hadn't you?" She smiled at Reeka, a knowing sort of smile that only ever passes between mother and daughter when matters of potential suitors are being considered.

"We had better prepare the memory wiper so that he can be sent back clean."

"Hold on a moment," Brodika said. "Time's not up yet."

111

"You're right, Father," Moraden said, "But so is Mother. How can he possibly do it now with only a few minutes left if he hasn't even left his room yet?"

It was Brodika's turn to grunt, and he did.

"Stop making a noise like a pig, dear, and put that silly puzzle away. You need to get ready to pass judgment. He'll be here any minute," instructed the queen.

No sooner had she spoken than the heavy door to the hall swung open and Randolph entered. He walked slowly toward the center of the room where Brodika was now seated on the throne.

"Well," said Queen Charmila, "We are sorry . . ."

"Wait," Brodika said, cutting across his wife's interruption of the judgment ceremony. "Wait. Randolph must be allowed to speak before judgment is passed. You know that."

Charmila retired into silence. She quite enjoyed it when Brodika was so dominant with her. "But he doesn't do it often enough these days," she sighed to herself.

"Now Randolph, what have you got to say for yourself?" Brodika asked.

Randolph was silent for a while, gathering his thoughts before he spoke. He wasn't sure whether he had done the right thing or not. He had found it very difficult to make a decision. What choice to make? There were so many different options. But now he fumbled in the pocket of his breeches and held aloft a glowing deep red ruby.

"This is my choice," he said. "I do hope it's the right one."

"How?" said the queen.

"What?" Moraden said.

"Wheeeee!" said Reeka.

"Blurble!" said the king.

"Is there a problem?" Randolph said.

"Problem? Problem? No, of course not," Brodika blustered.

"I knew he'd achieve it," cried Charmila, clapping her hands with glee. "Didn't I say so? Didn't I tell you? That young man's got faery blood all right. I said that; didn't I say that?"

Randolph stood motionless, holding the ruby up high. Queen Charmila came over and embraced him warmly. "Welcome Randolph, welcome to the Faery Realm."

Reeka followed her mother's example, crossing to Randolph and, putting her arms around him, embraced him. Although, unlike her mother's welcoming gesture he felt the full form of her body against his as she pressed her hips almost imperceptibly toward him in a gesture that spoke private volumes but went publicly unnoticed. Her kiss of congratulation she planted full on his mouth, and he felt her tongue wipe quickly across his lips.

"Welcome," was the simple greeting, but Randolph recognized, in its tone, the unspoken words.

Once again, Randolph wished Martha was there so he might openly demonstrate his affection for her in the presence of Reeka and dissuade her from her loosely veiled demonstrations of passionate longing, before her parents became aware and the situation got complicated. He also felt that a direct rejection of the princess' affection might cause offense and undo all the effort he had put into building his relationship with the king and, particularly, Queen Charmila. Randolph was also concerned that such a rejection might impact on the friendship he had developed with Moraden and ultimately on the much-needed support from the Council of Worth members.

It's a tricky situation, one that would be better avoided than dealt with head on, he thought to himself. Of course, he was highly attracted to Reeka; she was exceptionally beautiful and very sexy. In different circumstances, he wouldn't hesitate to respond positively to her display of affection.

"However, Randolph," his head said to him, "This is neither the time nor the place. And anyway, your heart belongs to Martha, even if it might also be prudent to contain that at a relatively private level for the moment."

"So how did you do it? Tell us how you did it?" Charmila's excited squawk was quite un-regal in its enthusiasm.

Randolph smiled to himself. He suddenly had a vision of the queen jumping up and down, clapping her hands excitedly, like a young girl with a new toy at the festive season party.

"Charmila," the king scolded. "Stop that at once. You know we have no right to ask such a question of one who has successfully completed the futtratfagh."

In Randolph's mind's eye, the queen deflated from her state of puffed-up delight and resumed her royal demeanor.

"And a ruby," Moraden whistled a low, hollow note through his teeth. "The choice of a ruby signifies the highest affinity with faery heritage. None of the others of the council chose a ruby."

"This choice," added the now normal-sized Charmila, "Indicates that your kinship lies in the ancient faery line of the clan of Cyeattle; one of the oldest and most respected houses. Henceforth, within the Realm, you will be known as Randolph of Cyeattle."

"Come, kneel before me," Brodika said. Once again, he took up the long sword and, resting it this time from the front, first on Randolph's right and then his left shoulder, pronounced, "By the power invested in me, as king of the Faery Realm, I hereby proclaim, as witnessed by those here present, and on behalf of all citizens of this land, that Randolph of Cyeattle, although of humankind birth, be entitled to freedom in this land as brother, friend, and defender of the Realm."

"Thank you," was all Randolph could think of to respond.

"Well done, Randolph," said the queen. "I said all along you had faery blood; didn't I say it, didn't I?" Charmila looked around the room for affirmation.

"Yes Mama." Reeka came to her mother's rescue with a smile. "Right again, as usual."

The queen beamed in self-approval. "Tonight we banquet, with Randolph of Cyeattle as guest of honor. Come along Reeka, there are many preparations to make."

Charmila and Reeka went off; Reeka throwing a public smile and a private look of longing over her shoulder toward Randolph as they left the hall.

Brodika had already got out his parchment and quill and was absorbed in construction of his puzzle. Moraden looked to where Randolph stood, as if rooted to the spot, still clutching the gemstone.

"What do I do with the ruby?" he asked.

"That's yours to keep now," Moraden replied. "But I don't suggest you carry it around with you. Now that you've been confirmed as a Defender of the Realm, you will have a permanent room allocated to you in the castle and that is where you should keep it."

King Brodika suddenly became animated, as if stuck by a sharp point.

"Ahha!" he cried. "Got it at last. That finishes the puzzle and now I can intrigue and amaze Galdore with it when he arrives. I bet he won't be able to solve it. I think a small wager would be in order. But don't let on to your mother." Brodika winked at Moraden. "You know she doesn't approve of my small wagers."

Brodika lowered and furrowed his brow as he directed his words to Moraden, who just chuckled. "Would I give you away Father? Would I tell on you?"

"Only if it suited your own ends," Brodika laughed. "Now come along, time runs short. Take Randolph and show him where his new room is and arrange for all his belongings to be transferred from the guest room. Oh, and take him down to the tailor so that he can have his wardrobe prepared. We can't have him going about with only one set of garments."

Moraden and Randolph went off, leaving the king to return to the final details of tidying up his puzzle before challenging Galdore with it. At the west wing of the castle, Moraden led Randolph into an elegant entrance hallway on the ground floor. Up a grand carved stone stairway they went, into a long corridor that ran the whole width of the castle, off which there were eighty doors, each leading, Moraden told Randolph, into private rooms. They went to the last door, which Moraden opened into a well-appointed, homely feeling room.

"This is the main room to your suite," Moraden said. "That door goes into your bed chamber and that other one into your dressing room, where you will also find the bathing tub and washroom. It looks like they've already brought your luggage over from the other room."

"Wow," Randolph said. "This is really mine? A proper place for only me? To keep as my own?"

"Yes," Moraden said. "All the council members have the same. Their rooms are all along this corridor. So are mine and Reeka's, and my parents have a huge suite up the other end."

"So how will I find the others?" Randolph asked. "How will I know who belongs in which room?"

"Oh, we have a strange and mystical system for that." Moraden lowered his voice to a whisper and looked around as if to make sure they were not being overheard. "We put their names on the doors," he said, busting into laughter and jumping out of reach of Randolph's attempt to grab him.

Randolph picked up the nearest thing, which happened to be a large apple from a brimming fruit bowl, and aimed it at Moraden's head. Moraden ducked neatly and the apple flew past him and straight out of the window.

"Missed," Moraden taunted. "You'll have to be a better shot than that if you're going to get Thrung. But seriously, your immediate neighbours are Martha next door, then Grafdun, although he hardly ever uses it. Reeka's rooms are opposite your door. I'm about halfway down, and Galdore and Brock have suites up the other end near my parents."

"Right," Randolph said, making an excited mental note that lucky breaks were still holding up for him and Martha's room was just next door. "I expect I'll get to know who's where quite quickly."

Moraden plonked himself down into a huge chair that stood by the window. "Now, I know we're not supposed to ask, but how did you do it? As far as we could tell, you never even left your room."

"The ruby?" Randolph asked. He had almost forgotten about his test already. He chose not to tell Moraden of his indecision about doing the futtratfagh at all. That would remain a secret between him and Twig, who had listened with horror to Randolph's suggestion that he might fail the test intentionally. However, it took only seconds for Twig to convert Randolph's thinking. He merely pointed out this would involve losing Martha and the ability to fly; never again visiting the Faery Realm; possibly forfeiting his friendship with Galdore and Moraden; returning to an existence where the domination of evil over good would be his likely destiny and, above all else, having to give up his trusty staff. Randolph also chose not to mention to Moraden the fact that Twig, having been crafted in the Faery Realm, knew something of the gems of Ornica and was able to tell him they could be detected from on high by the brilliant glow they radiated, making the chamber where they were housed like a beacon.

"That was easy," Randolph said. "I once met a man who told me how to make myself invisible."

"What?" exploded Moraden in amazement. "You can be invisible?"

"Yes," Randolph confirmed. "I'm not supposed to use it very often and I'm waiting for the terrible head that he told me I'd get sometime afterward. In fact, I'd never used it before and I didn't really think it would work. But it does."

"But that doesn't explain how you located the chamber and the gems," Moraden said. "It only explains how you got past the guards without being detected."

"Oh," Randolph said. "I spotted it from up in the sky; the whole chamber glows like a beacon."

"How did you get up high enough to spot it?" Moraden asked.

"I flew," Randolph said in a matter-of-fact voice.

"Flew? What do mean you flew? Humankind can't fly."

"Well, not so much flew as rode the wind," Randolph confessed.

"I begin to see why Galdore suggested you might be the One," Moraden said. "I begin to understand." He lapsed into silent private thought for a moment.

"But all that aside," he said after a while, "Why the ruby? What made you pick the one gem that would link you to the most important faery bloodline?"

"Oh, I don't know," Randolph said with a shrug, "I suppose red's my favorite color."

A while later they went to the tailor and then on to the Great Hall, where they were to meet the other council members. As they approached the hall, Randolph turned to Moraden. "I just thought," he said, "Would you keep the way I did the test to yourself? I think it best that everyone doesn't know."

"That's fine by me," Moraden said, "My lips are sealed."

Inside the hall, they met the others, who had all arrived together. Galdore sported an unsightly bump on his forehead.

"What have you done to your head?" Randolph asked. "Did you fall or something?"

"Or something," Galdore growled, scowling at the world.

"He's not in good humour," Martha giggled.

"It's not funny," Galdore grumped. "It hurts."

"Don't be such a baby," Martha said. "It was only an apple; anyone would think Heartland's Mound fell on your head the way you're going on."

Martha turned to greet Randolph. "Some lunatic threw an apple out of a top floor window just as we were arriving and hit him on the head, but he'll be fine; it's more his pride than anything else that's been wounded. See, even wizards get bumps; we'll watch it to see if they bruise as well."

Galdore harrumphed. Randolph and Moraden said nothing, but both had to turn their faces away and hide laughter with synchronized coughs.

"Hello," Randolph said, turning back to Martha. He crossed to her and hugged her as greetings were exchanged between council members.

Soon they were seated around the table and Galdore spoke in serious tone.

"Randolph, I understand from King Brodika that things have gone well for you here. On behalf of the council, I congratulate you on your investiture as Defender of the Realm and hereby formally appoint you as honorary member of the Council of Worth. I declare the council in session."

Randolph and Moraden were both asked to recount their journey through the boglands and then to tell of what they had discovered of the intentions of Thrung. Randolph explained to the council how he had nearly been dragged into the swamp and how Moraden had slipped and fallen in his attempt to save him. He told how he had to use his sword to cut his way free from the tentacled creature. He went on to recount how they had descended into the Caverns of Doom, down many ladders and through numerous levels.

"Steam rose from the shaft," he told them. "So, it was impossible to see down more than a few feet, even thought there was a bright orange glow of fire somewhere deep down in the cavern."

"How did you find your way down?" Brock asked, preparing to note down the response.

"There was a sort of a platform construction just over the rim of the shaft," Randolph explained. "From that, steps led down to a series of lower platforms and eventually down to the cavern floor. Moraden picked a way down for us, I just followed."

"And you and Moraden went down by yourselves," Grafdun said. "That was an act of bravery; well done, you are truly worthy of praise."

"But we didn't get much further," Randolph continued. "As we descended, the sense of fear built to one of pure terror. Our minds became enveloped with an urge to run, not to any real purpose or in any particular direction, but just to run, to dash in blind panic."

"How did you overcome the feeling?" Martha asked.

"Moraden taught me some faery noise to focus my mind; to block out the fear," Randolph said.

"The Sun Chant," Moraden added.

"Yes," Randolph explained. "It's a sort of single note that you keep repeating over and over in your head to keep your mind focused."

"Yes, yes," Galdore said. "We know of that. Go on; tell us more of what you learned."

"Well, there isn't a lot more to tell, because I judged it too dangerous to go too far into the cavern without being more in number and without any link to the surface. If we had been detected and captured, we would have had no way of getting any information out to you."

"Wise decision," Grafdun said. "Knowing your limitations is as important as knowing your strength in any campaign."

"But you were able to suppress the feeling of panic with the Sun Chant?" Martha asked.

"Yes," Randolph said. "That worked very well. Moraden is well practiced at it."

"Did you get any more details of Thrung's intent?" Brock asked.

"We did," Randolph replied. "We got a lucky break. Just by chance, as we hid in a small hollow off the main tunnel, two of what I assume were Thrung's chief advisors came along the passage. They were discussing Thrung's plans and had come to inspect the work being done at the bottom of the shaft."

"These advisors, what did they look like?" Galdore asked.

"They looked of human form," Randolph said. "They looked identical, as if they were twins. They had wicked eyes and hooked, beaky noses. Their dress was of flowing black robes and their speech; a tongue unfamiliar to me, and Moraden said he couldn't understand it either. However, Twig had some scant knowledge of the language they used and was able to translate some of their words for me."

"Twig?" chorused the council members.

"Who the blazes is Twig?" Grafdun said.

"Oh, that's what I call my staff," Randolph said. "The one sent to me by Sulaman."

"Ah," Galdore said. "All wizards' staffs are trained in many tongues. Did he mention which language these advisors used?"

"He called it Anciental and said it was one of the trolltalk tongues. They spoke of plans to overthrow the kingdom of Alusia, to enslave the citizens and to drain them of their life essence to feed the growing energy demands of Thrung and his forces. It seems that enslaving humans for use as labour is a mere drop in the ocean of Thrung's evil intent; his main purpose is to command their life-force. His aim, starting with Alusia, is to overpower all humans and any other realms, including the Faery Realm, to consume the power of good and convert it to his dark purpose."

"This is grave news indeed," Galdore said. "It would appear that Thrung plots total domination of all things living in the overworlds. Our responsibility is clear. Thrung must be eliminated, and it must be before his power grows too terrible to resist."

"Battle plans will need be drawn," Grafdun said.

"But first the use of stealth to determine more detail of his intent," Brock offered.

"And we need to understand more of what drives his evil motive," Martha added.

"We should not act too quickly," Moraden said. "We should not rush into any course of action."

"All your words are wise," Galdore said. "But first, as Moraden counsels, it is important that we think. Let us adjourn for today and dwell on the matter. Tomorrow we will reconvene and decide on the first steps to be taken. Randolph, you have done well. It would appear you may indeed have the power to become the One, but it is early in the year of our battle and much water has yet to pass under the bridge of time. We have a duty to maintain and pursue all things good in our struggle against the dark forces. So, tonight we make merry and banquet in honor of Randolph of Cyeattle."

So saying, Galdore closed the council from session.

かくゝ

After the banquet, Randolph was tired. Much had transpired in the last days and he needed to gather his thoughts and come to terms with his own conscience in various matters. Until just a few moons previous, he had been a happy-go-lucky minstrel, following a path that led him from where he had been to where he decided to go. He had laughed, lived, and loved life, pleasing others with his songs and stories. In the space of a few short weeks, he had become embroiled in a tale more fantastic than any story he might have invented or any song he might have composed. He had found love for one who had shown him how to ride with the breeze; he had discovered his faery heritage and been pursued by a beautiful faery princess; he had gone from having no dwelling to at least three places to call home; and, above all, he had taken on a responsibility where, if matters did not favor him he could lose everything, including his own life, in battle against a force of darkness so great that it might dominate all living things. He needed some time to himself, and as soon as he felt it was appropriate to leave the festivities, he retired to his room, inventing an aching head as an excuse for his early parting.

"Goodnight," Moraden said. "Sleep well, and breakfast will be on the terrace in the morning, I'll introduce you to some proper Faery Realm food instead of all this humankind fare we've had since you arrived. It's different but I think you'll like it."

Randolph kissed Martha goodnight. Reeka kissed Randolph goodnight, and bidding the others a good rest of the evening, he took his leave of the party. Twig was understanding of his need for thoughtful solitude and was happy to rest that night in the dressing room of Randolph's quarters.

"You don't need to be watched over in this place," Twig had said. "There could be no safer haven, even in these troubled times. Goodnight."

"Goodnight my friend," Randolph said as he closed the door and made his way to his own bed chamber. "Thanks for all your help," he called through the closed door.

"No bother, laddie," came the reply. "No bother."

Randolph lay on the bed and dozed. The multitude of thoughts in his mind tumbled and jostled with each other for attention. He heard distant voices passing down the corridor outside. Called *goodnights* and wishes of *happy dreams* floated in abundance as the others made their way to their rooms. Peace descended on the castle, and night graced the world with her presence in the Realm. Randolph took off his clothes, slipped between the fresh bed linens, and slept, but for how long he did not know. He snapped to wakefulness at the click of the latch on his chamber door. He lay still, watching through half closed eyes, as a figure slid silently into the room and stood silhouetted against the tall arched window. The flimsy night garment was transparent in the moonlight and her nakedness under it was revealed by the luminescence streaming in behind her. The figure moved toward Randolph and slipped into the bed beside him. Randolph's heart beat faster at the thought of the warm body, and he visualized the contours making up the picture that had just emblazoned itself on his mind. He could hear and feel the throb of the blood coursing through his body as her hand drifted across the space between them and touched his naked flesh.

"Randolph." Reeka's soft voice matched the beauty of her form and set his pulse racing even faster. "Randolph."

She slid closer to him and he felt the smoothness of her skin. His hand, almost involuntarily, reached to her body and caressed the curve of her hip, sliding up under her nightdress and resting on her firm breast.

"We shouldn't do this," he whispered, in the full knowledge that shouldn't and won't were not interchangeable in the phrase.

"No," she replied. "But nobody will know; it can be our secret."

They both froze to statues as a gentle tapping on the door of the bed chamber echoed like a drumbeat in the stillness of the night and Martha's voice half called, half whispered. "Randolph, are you awake? I came to see if you are all right."

Randolph didn't think his heart could go any faster, but it did.

"Quick," he whispered to Reeka, "Under the bed."

In an instant, she was gone.

He lay still and quiet in the comfortless hope that pretending to be asleep might dissuade Martha from entering. It didn't.

The latch lifted and the door creaked lightly as Martha pushed it open. He continued his pretence of sleep, peeking through half closed eyes. She slid silently through the doorway and stood silhouetted against the bright moonlit window of his room. The flimsy night garment she wore was transparent in the moonlight and her nakedness under it was revealed by the luminescence from the window.

I don't believe this is happening. Please let me be dreaming, Randolph thought.

But he wasn't and to prove it, Martha moved toward the bed and slipped in beside him. Randolph's heart beat still faster at the thought of her warm body and he visualized the contours making up the picture that had just emblazoned itself on his mind. The blood now pumped through his body with the power of a waterfall as Martha's hand drifted across the space between them and touched his flesh.

"Randolph," Martha's soft voice whispered in his ear, "Randolph."

Randolph was conscious of Reeka under the bed. He didn't know what to do. He desperately wanted Martha, but the trauma of the last few minutes meant the ardor had left his body and he was neither capable of demonstrating, nor prepared to parade, his passion in the presence of an audience, even a hidden one.

"Mmmmmm," he groaned, feigning waking noises. "Oh my head, Oh my painful head," he faked. "Walter said this would happen. He said this was the price of using the invisibility spell."

He suddenly realized this was his way out of the difficult situation.

"And I feel sick. Oh Martha, help me to the washroom."

Leaning heavily on Martha's shoulder Randolph staggered from the bed chamber through the main room of his suite and into the washroom. Martha filled the bowl with clean cold water and Randolph made great play of splashing his face while he listened for the click of the latch indicating Reeka's escape. When he was satisfied she had gone, he asked Martha to help him back to bed. She tucked him in tightly, as a mother would swaddle a baby, kissed him lightly on the forehead and was gone, leaving him, once again, hot and carnal and quite sleepless for the rest of the long night, but any miraculous recovery would have looked suspicious. By the morning, he really did have a full-blown headache.

છ્જ

Randolph was first down to the terrace where he remembered Moraden had said they would be breakfasting on faery fare. The phrase amused him.

"Faery fare, faery fare, faery fare," he repeated to himself as he sat keeping lonely vigil over many bowls of strange-looking foodstuffs and victuals on the laden table.

The terrace looked out over the castle grounds and gardens. Immediately below, down a few steps, was the vegetable garden where Randolph could see Stumple the gardener lovingly tending his flock of cabbages. Randolph inspected the contents of the bowls on the table and sampled one or two pieces of what tasted like a fruit but was blue in color. He picked at another substance that looked like pieces of sausage but tasted sweet and sticky. There was another bowl on a separate table just next to where he sat.

"They certainly don't go short of food. They can't even get it all on the one table. I wonder how they all stay so slim and lithe," he mused to himself.

He inspected the bowl on the separate table. It contained soft, squeegee lozenge shaped pieces of what appeared to be meat of some description. Randolph popped one in his mouth. It was tasty but rather chewy and he found the best way to eat them was like he had been shown with oysters, just to nip them with his teeth to get the flavour and then to swallow them whole; he finished off most of the bowl full. There was still no sign of Moraden.

"Must have had a late night. Maybe he went on somewhere after the banquet," Randolph said to nobody in particular.

Stumple came up the steps with a trug of vegetables on his way to the kitchen. He was mumbling to himself, discussing, solo, some important topic concerning the growing of legumes. He spotted Randolph and stopped by the table.

"Mornin' to thee, Master Randolph. Lovely morning. Best part of the day. Bright and early and up with the lark, sleep is for time when all is dark. That's what I says Master Randolph. That's Stumple's little rhyme for mornin' time. Ha! There I go; there's another little bit of poetry for you. Still can't stop chatting all day, must get these veggies down to the kitchen or the cook'll be crowin'. And must find that bowl of slugs that I picked off the cabbages earlier. Put it down somewhere and can't find it now. They'll all 'ave escaped again afore long. Ah! there it is."

Stumple bent to the low table beside where Randolph sat and picked up the bowl containing the few remaining back lozenge shaped things.

"Well wouldn't you know it and there you go, if I didn't waste me time. The little beggars have nearly all climbed out and got away again," and off he went clutching his trug and the bowl containing the few remaining slugs.

Randolph only just made it to his washroom before emptying the contents of his stomach into his bedpan.

"That disappearing really doesn't agree with you, does it?" Twig said from the corner of the washroom. "Wouldn't do that too often if I was you," he advised.

"Won't," agreed Randolph as he heaved again, leaving Twig to believe what he believed and Moraden to breakfast without his company.

ॐ∙ॐ

At the council meeting later that afternoon, a rather white-faced Randolph sat and listened to the general opinion that he should make ready to continue his quest immediately.

"I think that we must mobilize a carefully selected band of fighters and strike directly at Thrung in his vault in the Caverns of Doom," Galdore proclaimed. "Randolph, you will lead the force with your purity of decision and I will, by my powers, construct such spells as may be necessary to defeat Thrung's evil magic when we reach his chamber. By my estimation we have no more than one moon cycle, two at the most, before we might see his armies emerging from the caverns in a first attack on Alusia."

125

Nods of agreement came from all council members. Brock noted down some words on his parchment and Randolph found himself joining in confirmation of approval of the plan.

"Grafdun, your battle skills, and Moraden, your swiftness of foot, will be necessary in the cavern. Martha and Brock, your task will be to maintain a bridgehead at the shaft entrance and command the force that will slay any escaping foe. The battle will surely be bloody. Our hope can only be that it is a swift and final affair."

Once again, nods around the table affirmed agreement to the allocated responsibilities.

"And now, we must away," Galdore said. "Randolph, you must go with Moraden once again to reconnoiter the Caverns of Doom and further discover what you might of Thrung's plans. Through your stealth and guile, you must discover the route through to Thrung's vault. Martha and Brock, your journey is to Castle Drent to advise the king of the matters that have been decided and, with him, select the force that will be located at the shaft entrance to defend Alusia from Thrung's fleeing armies. None must be spared. Grafdun, you and I will journey to Dark Castle, where we will select and train an elite force of your men to enter Thrung's domain and protect us in our passage through the caverns to an attack on his vault."

And so saying, Galdore closed the session of the Council of Worth, bidding each fortune in their respective tasks. "Go well my friends," he said. "For it is in our hands that the destiny of human and faerykind alike may lie."

ॐ

It was in the late afternoon of that day, after all farewells and some sadness at partings, that Moraden and Randolph set off for the gateway through which they had entered the Realm only two days previous. The others were to make preparations for departure the following morning. Grafdun and Martha went off to their rooms, Galdore disappeared to see Brodika, and Brock went off by himself to stretch his legs and take the evening air.

"I'll show you how to locate and open the gateway once we're on the other side, before we leave the Mound," Moraden said. "Then you will be able to come and go as you please."

126

Chapter Six
The Three Castles

King Brodika and Queen
Charmila's Castle

"THE MOUND isn't only the gateway to the Faery Realm," Moraden explained. "It serves as a link to two other worlds that, since the split between humankind and faerykind, have gone on to separate themselves from the Realm."

Randolph, having visited the Realm, didn't find this at all strange. If he had had the conversation even a few weeks previously he wouldn't have believed a word. But now, if a pig flew past, he would probably only bother to remark on it if the pig was green with purple spots.

"Which worlds are those?" he asked Moraden in a very matter-of-fact tone.

"One is the gnome world or, as they call it, Gnoma, and the other is the Elven Kingdom. Gnomes and elves are both originally from faery heritage and we still have much in common with them, but each race has evolved along different paths and has now been independent for many hundreds of millennia."

"Will we go to either the gnome or elven worlds?" Randolph asked.

"No," Moraden said. "We don't have much contact now, and we don't have the right to just wander into each others worlds. I did get invited to the Elven Kingdom once many years ago when Mother and Father were on a rare state visit, but I've never been to Gnoma, I've even heard say that the gateway to Gnoma isn't working properly anymore."

They emerged from Heartland's Mound into the chill autumn air of Alusia and Randolph turned just in time to see the rock face shimmer as if it were a pool into which a pebble had been tossed. The ripples slowly subsided, and the rock reformed into a solid wall of granite. The weather was looking unpleasant and Randolph wished he had been able to stay in the warm springtime of the Realm for a few more days. Thunder rumbled in the distance, and mountainous black clouds fought with each other for position in the threatening sky.

"So, how do I get through the gateway when I want to come into the Realm?" Randolph asked.

"There are three things to remember," Moraden said. "The first is position, the second is the right frame of mind, and the third is the password spell. Let's start with the right position."

Randolph learned how to read the rock face in such a way that enabled him to stand on exactly the right spot to access the gateway. Moraden went on to teach him how to use the same Sun chant that had helped them when they were in the Caverns of Doom, to focus his mind and project the energy in a way that was necessary to make the transition from solid rock to open gateway.

"It's all to do with mental power and focus," Moraden explained.

After several attempts, Randolph got the balance right and was able, just through concentration, to make the granite shimmer and ripple.

"Good," Moraden said. "Now for the final part, which will allow you to pass through the gateway leaving Alusia and appearing in the Realm."

"How do I know I won't end up in the Gnoma or the Elven Kingdom by mistake?" Randolph asked.

"Can't happen," Moraden reassured him. "The password spell is the part that opens up the right pathway. The Elven and

128

Gnome password spells are completely different and only known, like ours, to those who have right of passage to those places."

Randolph listened carefully and learned the password spell off by heart. Moraden made him croon it several times before he was satisfied that he had the right inflection and emphasis in the right places.

"There you are," he said. "You wanted to learn some faery language."

Randolph tried it one more time.

"Deranum Diramult Deridium
Corfarus am slyden throom slipenum
En realmardi tu grample y droverpool
Crumbulaway slu draken ar cheevable."

"Good," Moraden said. "Now you have the whole thing. Try it out and I'll wait here while you transport yourself through the gateway and back again. And hurry up; it's starting to rain."

As the dark clouds gathered above them, Randolph located the position to stand, focused his mind using the Sun chant, and spoke the password spell just as Moraden had taught him. Thunder rolled and the rain fell from the sky as Randolph took a step toward the shimmering granite rock face. He put his hand out in front of him and watched as his fingers, then his hand and his outstretched arm disappeared into the rock. He paused, fascinated by the fact he was passing through solid rock.

"Go on will you," Moraden called. "Hurry up; I'm getting drenched here."

As Randolph stepped forward into the rock, the rain became torrential, thunder boomed in the sky, and a bolt of lightning flashed as it crashed to earth somewhere the other side of Heartland's Mound.

Moraden waited but Randolph didn't come back.

❧᠁

Deep in a vault in the far reaches of the Caverns of Doom, Thrung stirred again. As the final shredded remnants of his slumbers left him, he became conscious of a need to reassert his power. His half-dreamed awareness of the intolerance of his ways by those now inhabiting the overworld left him seething with fury.

How dare they, mere mortals, presume to challenge the omnipotence of the mighty Thrung? he thought to himself. Raising himself to a materialistic form, Thrung roared his summons to his advisors. "Let it be known that preparations will be made for attack on the overworlders," he bellowed, as he shifted his enormous bulk in the confines of his vault.

Here he was vulnerable, here he was unable to move freely to counterattack. But his vault was itself protected by his army of evil beings and dark forces. His vulnerability when encased within the sepulcher walls was never a matter of concern to him because of the sheer inaccessibility of the vault itself. However, to communicate with material beings and to lead his attack on the mortal world, he had to take substantial form. He had to emerge from his protected environment in a guise capable of leading his armies. To use matter as a source of energy, he had to interact with the material world.

"Shallam shadung enfulment matrastical essentulasm," spoke Thrung as he engaged the language of his creation to provoke and prompt the universal powers to do his bidding.

His amorphous bulk shrank and solidified, converting energy to defined, structured matter as Thrung took a human-like form, and so emerged from the vault a seemingly human creature, formed to fool and confuse the senses. For while his appearance was that of a man, what was contained within that shell was of purest evil. And so began the third era of Thrung's impact and influence on the living universe. His senses told him, however, that there was a One and while that One continued to exist, his own dominance was threatened.

"The One must be sought and destroyed," he murmured as he made his way to the Cavern of Despair, the place where he and his chief advisors would determine their battle plans and select the objects of their attention.

Seated in the Cavern of Despair, attended by an entourage of groveling, scraping serfs, Scumfest and Beaktool, his twin lieutenants of devastation, prepared for the final stages of their master's waking demands.

"Master," they chorused as Thrung entered the chamber. "All salute and acclaim the master."

All present sank to their knees with downcast eyes. Thrung swept through the chamber, his flowing robes billowing in his wake as he strode to the high seat of power at the far end of the cavern. He signaled Scumfest and Beaktool to accompany him on to the raised dais and to take their places at his side. Once seated, he spoke to the assembled company.

"Go now and gather together all who labour in my domain. Bring them here that they may know of my completed reawakening and may pay homage to me. Let them also know of the re-domination of the world of humankind. Go now and return with speed. I await their due deference and respectful obedience."

Thrung gestured and the attendant serfs and slaves scurried to do their bidding, returning soon with many other creatures and beings until the Cavern of Despair was filled with a seething mass of grotesque slimy, slobbering bodies, each fighting selfishly for space. Some loyal to Thrung and his wicked obsessions came eagerly to hear their master speak. Others came unwillingly, driven by gang masters until the cavern was filled to capacity and beyond. Thrung, once again standing, raised his hand in a gesture indicating a demand for silence.

"I, Thrung, have risen from my slumbers and taken material form that I might command you. Hear now that each of you will do my bidding and that failure to comply with my wishes will result in your elimination, along with all those humankind and faerykind that will shortly provide the source of energy for my domination of all things living. It is just and proper that they should through my hand provide the source of power for their own annihilation. Total destruction, extermination of all that which fails to worship the power of darkness, is our aim. Until such time arrives, we will not rest. Let it be known that the creation of the universe was tainted by the introduction of weakness as we now see displayed in humankind and faerykind; their elimination and assimilation can be our only way forward."

Thrung paused as if undecided about what he might next tell those assembled. He drew breath suddenly, as if having made a decision to share his further thoughts publicly.

131

"I have become conscious of a One—a being of some uncommon power of goodness and light. One who seeks to serve only that which is weakness and humility, yet turn that power against me and my kind. He must be sought and destroyed, along with his followers. This task is of immediate and utmost priority."

Thrung raised his clenched fist in salute. "All power to the forces of darkness," he proclaimed. "Let us lay plans for the attack and conquering of that kingdom known as Alusia and open the gateway for our domination of all living things. Let us contrive a strategy whereby our forces and armies shall overthrow first the lands of humankind, and through them enter other worlds of faerykind. Let it be that all will ultimately pay homage to me."

He swept from the hall, followed by Scumfest and Beaktool, and the three disappeared down tunnels and corridors to little-known reaches of the Caverns of Doom, where their scheming and plotting for the location and elimination of the One and their overthrow and domination of Alusia might continue unhindered.

"The three subcenters of power are the Castles Tharla, Fortnum, and Dark, reported by our scouts as the homes of the armies of Alusia," Thrung said to his lieutenants. "They will be our focus and through them we will move on to the prime seat of power in the kingdom, to Castle Drent. Once they are all under our control, the peasants of the countryside will be at our mercy to enslave. They will have no choice but to do our bidding."

ॐ•ॐ

Moraden waited and waited. He got wetter and wetter.

"Where is that man," he grumbled to no one but Twig. "I'm standing here in this downpour with thunder and lightning crashing all around me and he's back in the Realm, basking in the evening sunshine. I bet he's met somebody on the other side of the gateway and he's having a chat. If he doesn't come back soon, I'm going through to get him."

And eventually that's what Moraden did. He picked up Randolph's pack, Twig, and the instruments Randolph had left in a heap by the rockface and went back through the gateway to the Realm. But, when he emerged into the spring evening, there was no sign of Randolph.

"Surely he hasn't gone back to the castle," Moraden said to no one in particular.

There was a group of young faeries standing chatting on the track leading from the gateway. Moraden recognized some of them as sons and daughters of the people of the court.

"Did you see anybody come from the gateway in the last ten minutes or so?" he asked them. "Blond, humankind man, about the same height as me, Randolph is his name; you might have seen him in the castle over the last couple of days."

"I know who you mean," said one of the youngsters. "I've not seen him pass this way, sir. Not in the last few minutes. Mind you we've only been here a few minutes; we could've missed him."

"The only person we've seen is the one they call Brock. He came from the direction of the gateway and we spoke with him. He was explaining to us the way the gateway works using different vibrations to change the pathways between worlds. But he went off back toward the castle," said another of the youngsters.

"Oh, it must have been him who dropped this pad of notes we found after he had gone. They seem to be written in some language unknown to us. Maybe you would return it to him sir," the first youngster said, and he handed the small parchment pad to Moraden.

"Strange," Moraden said, scratching his head and peering down the track toward the castle. "I can't think why Randolph would've gone back to the castle. Not without telling me; not just leaving me standing on the other side. Unless he felt ill. Come to think of it, he wasn't very well earlier and the gateway can make you feel a bit queasy sometimes; it's the vibrations. Thanks anyway lads. I'll go back down to the castle and find him."

Moraden set off, laden with both his own travel pack and Randolph's gear, happy not to be standing in the torrential rain of Alusia, but showing a little irritation with what he had described to the group of youngsters as "Randolph's undeclared sudden disappearance back to the castle."

At the castle gates, Moraden made a point of inquiring of the sentry, but he hadn't seen Randolph either. "Although I have only come on duty in the last while, sir. He may have come through while Adsam was still on guard. I think he's still in the guard-house, sir."

Moraden asked at the guardhouse but Adsam hadn't seen him either. "What is he playing at?" Moraden said to Adsam, now showing annoyance at Randolph's stupidity.

Moraden asked several others, but he wasn't in his room and nobody had seen him.

"Well I's beed 'ere allsalong," Stumple said, "and eese b'aint beed thisa ways."

Moraden's expression displayed irritation as he sought out his father, whom he found showing Galdore his link-word puzzle in the Great Hall. It appeared Galdore had completed it in about three minutes flat, much upsetting Brodika.

"What do you mean, you've lost him?" Galdore said. "You can't have just lost him. I mean he's big enough not to just mislay. And he wouldn't just wander off; he isn't stupid. But, on the other hand, he is Randolph. He brightened, "But, he's probably back on the other side of the gateway, in Alusia, wondering where you've got to. Come, we'll walk back up with you and have a look."

"Can I give you this notepad?" Moraden asked Galdore, "I think it belongs to Brock and he dropped it up by the gateway. Some of the youngsters from the court found it."

"Thanks," Galdore said, glancing down at the notes. "If he lost that, I don't know what he'd do. I'll give it to him when I see him."

Galdore was conscious of the worried expression Moraden wore and, in fact, he was just a little concerned himself, so the three of them went together through the gateway, but Randolph was nowhere to be found. The reason they couldn't find Randolph in the Realm was quite simply that he wasn't there. The reason they couldn't locate him on the other side of the gateway, in Alusia, was, again quite simply, that he wasn't there either.

"Well I don't know," Galdore said. "Is there any way he could be stuck between worlds? Could he still be inside the mound?"

"No," Brodika said. "That's not possible. But I tell you what could have happened."

Moraden and Galdore looked at Brodika, awaiting his thought. Brodika hummed and harrumphed a little, looked a bit doubtful, then held his finger up, raised his eyebrows and opened his mouth as if to speak; then he shook his head without saying anything. Finally, he pronounced his thought, sounding reasonably confident that he had worked out the solution to the puzzle.

"I . . . think . . .," he said slowly.

"Yes?" chorused Galdore and Moraden.

"I . . . think . . . the storm you were talking about, Moraden, might have caused a vortex of some sort in the mound and shot poor Randolph off on another pathway. This did happen once before, many, many years ago. Took us weeks to get the fellow back."

"We haven't got weeks." Galdore tugged impatiently at his beard. "We can't have him off on holiday around the worlds. There's urgent business to be attended here."

ৰু✦ঔ

Holiday was the last description Randolph would have chosen for his present plight, and all his head would do was compose and sing a song.

> *"I wake to find the mist around my mind's eye.*
> *I speak to find my voice a whispered thread.*
> *I listen hard but only hear the breeze blow.*
> *I am somewhere that a faery dream has led.*

> *I look about me, captured by the wonder,*
> *I try to make my thoughts come into time,*
> *With the beating of my heart that gives a rhythm,*
> *To the feeling that my being is in rhyme.*

> *I look behind, I see a golden gateway,*
> *Ahead I see an archway made of sand.*
> *All around are trees and sea and mountains,*
> *I hold the source of nature in my hand.*

135

I realize I've made a special journey,
To the place that's known by folk as Tir N-iall,
I've stepped beyond the world I had my home in,
To the place of which the ancient stories tell.

In between the here and ever after,
A land where elves and gnomes and faeries dwell,
I stand in neither one world nor another,
Encased in just this fragile mortal shell.

Now on again I'm traveling through that gateway,
I've landed with my feet upon earth's soil,
I've only been an instant in between lands,
I know I only stood there for a while.

Could it be the folk I knew are dead and gone now?
Have I been away a hundred years or more?
Encased in elven magic and enchantment,
Have I traveled far in time through faery lore?

Have I got to start my life again all over?
There's nothing here I recognize at all,
And however loud I shout to get assistance,
There's not one single faery answering my call."

He didn't know where he was. He didn't know whether he had traveled in time or space or both. He only knew that this land was neither the Alusia he had grown up in, nor was it the Faery Realm he had been introduced to just a few days previous. However, the snow-covered ground told him that it was winter, and so did his shivering knees.

"Hey buddy boy, if I'd known you weeerrrz a comin' I'da baked some fresh chestnuts," said a deep but friendly voice.

Randolph looked around, peering into the distance, but could see no sign of anybody that might belong to the voice.

Well, at least, wherever I am and me have baked chestnuts in common. I suppose that's a start, he thought.

Randolph was cold. He hadn't expected to be up to his knees in snow all of a sudden. Nor had he thought that he would be separated from his cloak, pack, Twig, and his lute and piccolo, which, as far as he knew, were all still wherever he had just come from. In fact, they weren't, because Moraden had just taken them back through the gateway to the Realm, but Randolph, surrounded by a Gnoma winter, had no way of knowing that.

"Aren't you cold buddy boy?" The disembodied voice spoke again.

Randolph repeated his visual scan of the area, but could still see nobody. Then the voice came for a third time, now in a lilting rhyme, starting slow and gathering pace line by line.

> *"They seek him but they find no trace*
> *They say he moves with stealth and grace,*
> *He's in the air, but cannot fly,*
> *Behind the voice there is a guy.*
> *Look up buddy, into the air,*
> *I'll peek-a-boo, you'll see me there,*
> *I'll be your friend if you'll be mine*
> *Come join me; it is time to dine."*

Randolph looked up into a grand old oak tree. The snow-laden branches were heavy with their load and seemed to shimmer against the rolling gray clouds and the swirling snowflakes that had started to descend. Peering into the upper branches, squinting against the snow that swirled into his eyes, Randolph could just make out a person. He looked to be all dressed in white fur and he had long flowing gray hair and beard.

"Hello," Randolph called up into the tree. "Who are you? My name's Randolph. Can you tell me where I am?"

The person in the tree seemed to find the question amusing and started to laugh. He laughed harder and louder until the branch onto which he had clamped himself shook and deposited large heaps of snow on the ground below. Randolph had to duck and dodge to avoid being hit by them.

"Can you come down?" Randolph called. "We could talk much easier if you could come down."

"Righty-ho buddy boy," came back the reply and a body tumbled from the branches, landing with a thud and disappearing into the knee-deep snow about four yards from where Randolph stood shivering.

"Are you all right?" Randolph called.

But the only thing that emerged from the hole in the snow was a deep chuckling noise. Randolph repeated the question and watched as a figure uncurled from the hollow and turned to face him, a huge grin spread from ear to ear. Randolph inspected the short stocky figure. His head was no higher than Randolph's chest and seemed to be marginally too large for his body. He had the most enormous shock of white-gray hair and beard that seemed to grow on every available inch of head and face, other than in the space around the eyes. These sparkled and shone with glee as he regarded Randolph.

"So, cut off me legs and call me shorty," laughed the figure. "Now you're a big one if ever day turned into night-time, and no mistaking the flies for bees."

"Pardon," Randolph said.

"What did you say yer handle was? Randolph? Guess y'er not from round these here parts, buddy boy."

The figure seemed to find some huge joke in his own words and disintegrated into further gales of laughter. Randolph didn't see what was funny. He thought he might have been more inclined to join in the laughter if he wasn't so freezing cold, but his feet were now going numb, his fingers had started to itch with the cold, and his ears felt like the were about to drop off.

"Grumbleweed's the name," the figure announced. "Come on buddy boy, better get you into the warm before yer doodangs drop off. What are you thinking, a comings out on a day likes today without yer 'at?"

More peels of laughter followed as the figure turned away and beckoned Randolph to follow. They had only gone a few paces, when looming through the now heavy snowfall Randolph saw a small thatched cottage a short way ahead. The windows glowed with a welcome light. A wisp of smoke curled from the chimney pot in a spiral, as if dodging the acrobatic flakes flying hither and thither in their effort to avoid being melted into oblivion on the hot stonework of the stack. They reached the door and Randolph had to duck low to get under the portal as he followed Grumbleweed into the cosy room. He straightened to find that he could just stand erect, with his hair brushing the ceiling of the room.

"My oh my, he's a big one," said a gentle female voice from a doorway on the other side of the room. "Where did you find him?"

A woman, slightly less tall even than Randolph's rescuer, appeared in the room and crossed to where Randolph stood. He felt as if he was taking up too much space in the already rather cramped surroundings.

"Come over by the fire luvvy, you look frozen," she said as she reached up and pulled him toward the blazing log filled grate. "Supper won't be long. D'you like stewed groodle?"

Randolph didn't know whether he liked stewed groodle or not. This was mainly on account of the fact that he didn't have a clue what a groodle was, even when it was unstewed.

"I expect I will," he said. "Although I've never had it before."

"Never had stewed groodle," the woman said in total amazement. "What sort of upbringing have you had if you've never had stewed groodle?"

She turned to the man.

"Never had stewed groodle," she informed him, although he was well within earshot of the information on its first airing. But just to make absolutely sure he knew she repeated, "Never had stewed groodle luvvy, he says he's never had stewed groodle."

"What is a groodle?" asked Randolph. "I mean," he added quickly so as not to offend, "I'm sure I'll like it, but I don't know what a groodle is. We don't have groodles where I come from. Is it like a sheep or a cow?"

He surveyed their stony faces, which gave away no clue as to whether a groodle was like a sheep or a cow.

"Or maybe a chicken?" he tried.

Bretti, for that was the gnome woman's name, exploded into laughter, joined almost immediately by Roody, for that was her husband's name. They laughed until the tears ran down their cheeks. They rolled on the floor clutching their sides, hooting with delight. Eventually, Bretti and Roody Grumbleweed recovered the power of speech and explained, with only one or two minor bursts back into merriment, that a groodle was a collection of various vegetables and fungi. Randolph, although he had been captured by their howling laughter and had had no choice but to join in, through the occasional returning splutter said that he didn't see why what he said was particularly funny. That started all three of them off again and, once more, they were weeping with mirth, until Bretti nearly wet herself and had to be excused. She returned more composed and able to answer some of Randolph's questions, while Roody sat by the fire and now only occasionally vibrated with mild chuckles.

"Well I never did," said Bretti, which was about as much as she had said several times in the last five minutes as Randolph had explained how he came to be standing close to their cottage in the snow. "Well I never did," she said again as Randolph went on to explain that, if this was Gnoma, then, as long as he hadn't shifted in time, he had visited three different worlds in the space of the last hour. "Well I never did."

As more information was sought and provided by each of them, Roody became more and more interested in what Randolph was saying and particularly in the fact that he had to get back very quickly, on a matter of very urgent and important business to either his own world or to the Faery Realm. Although he was careful not to mention anything about the Caverns of Doom, the rise of dark forces or Thrung.

"Well, you won't be a'going back thata way buddy boy," Roody said.

Randolph looked anxious and concerned at Roody's words.

"Nope, the gateway's bin broke for many years now; that's why I was surprised to see yer. Used ta be a lotta traffic thisaways years ago. But not fer many years now. Not since it's bin broke."

"Well how will I get back home?" Randolph's tone expressed his deep concern at the situation. "I've got to get back," he said. Deciding that he now had to demonstrate how vital was his return to his own world, he said, "My return to the world of humankind may be the only thing that can prevent the forces of darkness overthrowing my world, the Faery Realm, the Elven Kingdom, and even Gnoma."

Roody and Bretti looked at each other. Their laughing faces now transformed to serious expression. Roody leaned forward in his chair, bringing his face close to Randolph.

"What you say, is this really true?"

Randolph was unsure how much he should divulge. The way Roody had asked the question indicated to Randolph that this might not be the first time he had heard this information. However, he had to find some way of getting back through the gateway. He thought back to some of the things Galdore had said—how it was that his purity of decision was the important factor in defeating the evil power. There was nobody there to advise him, and even if the others had been present, he thought they would probably have declined to interfere or advise. It was clear they had to avoid the risk of contaminating his thought, particularly when he was placed in situations where the direction he chose was fundamental to their mission.

"Looks like I'm on my own with this decision," he said, speaking half to himself and half to Roody.

"Randolph," Bretti's tone was transformed to one of sober and solemn intent. "I'm not sure what you meant by that, but know this, know that when you're in the company of Professors Roody and Bretti Grumbleweed, you are never on your own, never alone."

Randolph couldn't help a smile. The thought that professors might really have the name Grumbleweed made it difficult to take this new information seriously. His reaction would have been the same, he thought, if Galdore had tried to tell him that the forces of darkness were commanded by someone called Lily Thistledown. Luckily, Bretti responded to his smile thinking that the support she had offered had made him feel more comfortable.

"There's better," she said, as if cooing at a baby gnome. "There's a little smile."

Randolph was just thankful that she didn't tickle him under the chin.

"Professors?" Randolph asked. "Do you mind me asking what you are professors of?"

"Of cosmos," Roody answered. "I study the balance of things; order, harmony, structure, organisation of nature, that sort of thing."

"Roody is one of the most respected gnomes on the subject of cosmos in the whole of Gnoma, luvvy," Bretti said. "I'm only a student by comparison with his work on Trignomeometry."

"Now come on dear," Roody said. "Don't underestimate yer own work. You're the one doing most of the moil on the creaturespeaker venture."

"Whoa, Whoa," Randolph said. "Slow down. Can we go back and start at the beginning? The main question is, can you help me get back?"

"No problem, buddy boy," Roody said. "No problem."

Over the rest of the evening they talked long and deep, Randolph deciding that Roody and Bretti should know as much as possible about Thrung and the threat to the humankind and faerykind worlds, and they, in turn, giving Randolph much comfort as he learned of the work Roody Grumbleweed and some of his fellow experimenters had been doing in linking up to other worlds through new and different gateways. He was also fascinated by Bretti's work on learning to speak the language of animals. She promised Randolph that she would teach him a bit about how to talk with creatures before he went back, but she explained, this was only because he "had a bit of magic in him, luvvy."

"There's not manya human I would show," she confessed with a little giggle. "But you seem a bit special."

"The trignomeometry's not perfected yet," Roody confessed, "But should be good enough to get you home, buddy boy."

Randolph began to relax a little. However, he still found it difficult to link the picture of Roody and Bretti rolling on the floor, heaving with laughter, with the fact that they were among respected scholars in their land.

But, he reminded himself, *I'm in a different world, where people behave differently. I must keep an open mind and accept whatever help I can get.*

"So, tomorrow, buddy boy," Roody cut across Randolph's thoughts. "Tomorrow we go to town, to Cosmic Lodge, and get you back home. It's no good going now 'cause the link can only be operated when the vibrations balance, and that's only well after sunrise. So, relax, we might as well enjoy the evening, and the spare room's all aready and await'n'. Bretti, we got any of that hooch left?"

More confident now than he had been earlier about getting back to Alusia relatively quickly, Randolph sank back into the chair, which seeing as it was a bit too small for him, was surprisingly comfortable. He gratefully accepted the mug of hooch Bretti gave him and for the first time since he had entered the room, studied some of the detail of a gnome home. The bright yellow walls gave the whole room a sunny perspective, even though out through the window Randolph could see the wind lashing the snow into a blizzard under the darkening sky. The roaring log fire, which Roody had now built up to mountainous proportions, gave out enough heat to toast bread at three paces and Randolph had to slide his chair back half way across the small room to avoid being roasted alive. Potted plants stood all around the room and happy drawings, artistic weavings, and murals adorned the walls, reminding Randolph of a child's room back in his own world. He spotted a ball lying partly hidden under the table, a straw doll sitting in an ungainly manner where she had been plopped on a chair, and a pile of shells on the hearth. He asked if there were any other members to the Grumbleweed family living there.

"Oh no," Bretti chuckled. "There's only the two've us now. Children are all grown and gone, most married themselves now."

These are nice people. They're different and their pleasures appear plain and simple, but they're nice gentle folk. They may be a different race from me, but they are still part of what I am being asked to stand for, Randolph thought to himself.

During the course of the evening, Randolph learned a lot about Gnoma from Roody and Bretti and the more he heard, the more he felt that, once again this lucky break was more than just an accidental happening. He felt there were more forces at work than even Galdore and the other Council of Worth members might appreciate. He felt his unexpected trip to Gnoma was not entirely accidental. The more hooch he drank with Roody and Bretti the more special he became and the greater the responsibility that he carried. Just before midnight, he carried it off to bed in the little room that Bretti had prepared for him for the night. The bed was at least half a leg too short for him. Randolph found that when he pulled the quilted bedspread up to his chin his feet stuck out at the bottom and when he covered his feet, half the top of his body was exposed to the cold air. He solved the problem by keeping his boots and shirt on and curling up in the bed. Considering this sleeping arrangement, he had quite a comfortable night and didn't wake until cock's crow the next morning. The hooch may well have contributed to the soundness of his sleep.

"Morning luvvy," was Bretti's cheery greeting as she laughed her way into the room, carrying a steaming bowl of oats and a mug of hot brew, which she deposited on the small table beside his bed and swept on out of the room again all in the space of one flowing movement and one long chuckle. "Best get yourself up soon," she called from the door. "Roody'll be ready to take you to town in 'bout an hour."

The mug contained chamomile and the smell took Randolph's mind way back to Galdore's marquee at the Northern Forest where they had rescued Sir Lionel Graceforth and destroyed the evil witch, Griselda. He now began to wonder if Griselda had been in the employ of Thrung and, if so, whether her destruction might not have gone unnoticed in the Caverns of Doom. He wondered whether he would ever make it back to Castle Drent and, once again enjoy the warmth of the welcome that he was offered there. His mind wandered on, to thoughts of Nick, Martha, Dragon, Sulaman, Twig, Walter, and the latest parts of his journey into the Caverns of Doom with Moraden and on to the Realm to meet Charmila, Brodika, Martha, Grafdun, Brock, and Galdore. He recalled the vision of Reeka silhouetted against his moonlit window and suddenly realized that it was only the previous night; it seemed many moons ago. His part in the battle of good against the forces of darkness was growing by the day. Responsibilities clung to him like bees to a sunflower and he saw himself grow in stature so not only gnomes, but all other people, human and faerykind alike, were smaller than him. He seemed to extend upward in a stretch that enabled him to look over the whole of existence to everlastingness, to see each of the worlds he had visited as small islands bobbing in a sea of eternity. The people in those worlds gazed up toward him as he dominated their sky and he saw them cower in fear; not in fear of the force of darkness, but in fear of him and his atrocious and terrible presence. A thought formed in his head that he was all-powerful; he knew he could reach down and crush them and he was suddenly conscious of power. He knew now that he was the One. More frightening was the fact that, somehow, Thrung might know as well. Suddenly, he was afraid. This was neither a fear of falling nor a fear generated through lack of confidence or experience; this was a fear that struck to the roots of his being and twisted his senses out of proportion. It wrenched at his very essence and he heard Thrung laugh at his vulnerability. Deep within his being he perceived himself torn from his purity, ripped from all he knew as right and good, corrupted by his own power to take what he wanted and scatter the crumbs of what remained for others to scrabble and fight over. He saw himself seated on the right hand of Thrung and he knew the power of the force of darkness.

"Ready buddy boy?" Roody's voice called from the other room.

Randolph looked down at himself as he stood, fully dressed, the bowl of oats empty and the mug drained.

"How did I do that?" he said to himself in amazement. "A second ago I was still in bed, and now, like magic, I'm ready to go."

Once again he heard, inside his head, the rumble of a low-pitched laugh. Randolph was still worried as he and Roody trudged through the crisp snow on the way to Cosmic Lodge. Bretti had promised to join them later in town. Randolph, swathed in woven blankets to protect against the cold, as nothing of Roody's would fit him, was silent and thoughtful.

"Brass button for them?" Roody said.

"Sorry?" Randolph said

"For your thoughts?" Roody said. "Brass button for your thoughts? You're miles away and you've got a bigger brow on you than that there hill."

"Sorry," Randolph said again, but this time as an apology for his mental absence.

"You look worried, buddy boy. Anything I can help with?"

"Actually," Randolph said, "you might be just the right person to help. What with all your study and knowledge on balance of nature and Cosm . . . Comolos . . . Colomosogy."

"Cosmology," Roody corrected.

"Yes that," Randolph said. "You said you understand about the balance of life, harmony of things, and all that sort of stuff. I'd ask Galdore if he was here, but he's not, and you might know."

"Try me buddy boy," Roody offered.

"Well, you remember all that I told you last night about Thrung and the rise of the forces of darkness, and Sulaman believing that I might be the One," Randolph said. "You know the one to lead the domination of good over evil?"

"Yep," Roody said. "Remember it plain as if it were yesterday."

He started to laugh at his own wit so, before he worked himself into a frenzy of mirth, Randolph went on quickly.

"Well, I'm afraid."

"Exactly what're you 'fraid of, buddy boy?" Roody asked, responding back in serious mood.

"I'm afraid," Randolph said, trying to find the right words to express his inner feeling of inadequacy. "Afraid that my power isn't anywhere near as strong as Thrung's and that he could easily . . . well . . . take me over."

Roody just looked at Randolph without saying anything, so Randolph went on.

"You see, maybe I am special in some way, maybe I am the best person to lead the resistance against the forces of darkness. In some ways, I feel I am. But then this morning something happened to me and I'm afraid it was Thrung showing me that he has complete control over me, that he can make things happen to me just . . . well . . . as if by magic."

Randolph explained to Roody what happened about having a sort of vision about becoming all-powerful and being on Thrung's side. Then suddenly being up, dressed, and finished with his breakfast without knowing how it happened.

"I know it sounds silly, but I think he was playing with my mind and I'm frightened that I can't resist him."

Roody thought for a long while as they continued on their way to the town. Randolph respected his thoughtful silence and watched him as he stroked his beard, scratched his head, pulled at his ears, and ahummed and aharred quite a bit. Eventually, as they were just on the outskirts of the town, he stopped and turned to Randolph.

"I've got one big cheese," he said. "You know, one of those great big round whole cheeses."

Randolph confirmed he knew about big cheeses, but he didn't see what it had to do with his problem.

"Hear me out, buddy boy," Roody said. "And I've also got a lot of smaller cheeses. When I put them in the cart to take them to market, I put the one big cheese on one side of the cart. But because I haven't got another big cheese, I have to load all the small cheeses on t'other side."

"Why?" Randolph said.

"Make it balance," Roody said. "Make it balance."

"But what's that got to do with me and Thrung?" Randolph asked. "We're not cheeses and we're not off to market."

"No," admitted Roody. "But principle's same. And that's where your purity of thought is going to work as well. When you've got a difficult problem of balance, think've it in simple terms, boil it down'ta basics, and you'll crack it easy."

"So, what you mean is that Thrung is like the big cheese and I and all the others working with me are like all the little cheeses that, together, are as heavy as the big cheese," Randolph said.

"Now you're getting the idea," Roody said. "And which would you choose to have, one big cheese or lots of smaller ones?"

"The smaller ones are, obviously, better," Randolph said. "They're easier to move around, they can be spread around different places, they can be stored easier and don't have to be used all at once. But, if you do use one up and want more, you can always start on another one."

"Brilliant," Roody said. "We'll make a Cosmos professor of you yet. Now, afore we go on to Cosmic Lodge, tell me why the big cheese might be trouble for the smaller cheeses?"

"I don't understand what you mean," Randolph said.

"If on the way to market, the track gets bumpy and the cheeses all start to roll about in the cart?" Roody asked.

"The big cheese might squash the little cheeses," Randolph said.

"Right on, buddy boy," Roody said as he turned and started off again into town. "Right on the button."

Now quite excited about the cheeses and how such a simple example could solve a difficult problem, Randolph said, "All I've got to do is avoid the bumpy parts of the track and the big cheese can't get me."

Randolph almost skipped in his excitement at finding a solution to his worry, but he tamed his gait to a just a bouncy walk as he hurried to catch Roody.

"Keep control of your head," Roody counseled. "Keep yer mind in order, keep yer eyes and ears in balance, and remember yer journey, however long, can only be taken one step at a time—just make sure each one's in a forward direction and that you don't trip over yer own feet."

They passed another gnome on his way to market. He was pulling a cart full of cheeses. There was one big one and several smaller ones. As they drew level, Randolph spotted a big hole on the track just ahead of the cart pulling gnome.

"Mind your cart wheel in the hole," he called to the gnome. "Don't want to squash your smaller cheeses."

The gnome waved thanks to Randolph and steered around the rut. Roody looked at Randolph, his grin stretched from ear to ear.

≈•≈

"What are we going to do?" Moraden asked his father and Galdore.

"I think we need to go back to the castle and talk with Martha, Grafdun, and Brock before any of them leave," Galdore said. "Randolph's disappearance will be certain to change our plans a little."

Once again they gathered up Randolph's pack and instruments and Twig, all of which they had brought in the expectation of finding Randolph somewhere around the gateway, and went back to the castle where they gathered in the Great Hall. However, this time King Brodika occupied the seat that had previously been allocated to Randolph. Dragon had completed the cat things she had gone off to do on arrival in the Realm and lay curled, as cats do, in a patch of warm evening sunlight close to Galdore's feet. Randolph's things they piled in a heap and Galdore stood Twig up in the corner as he remembered Brock's notepad and took it from the pocket of his cloak to return it to its rightful owner.

"Don't know why you keep so many notes about everything," Galdore teased Brock. "And all in some mysterious unreadable text. Some language of your own invention, I'll be bound."

He laughed as he handed the pad to Brock, who clutched it to him as if it were a lost child being returned to a distressed parent. Galdore explained the situation of Randolph's disappearance to the others and asked for ideas about how they might now proceed.

"Interesting turn of events," Brock mused. "I wonder how it happened and I wonder where he's gone." He stroked his beard thoughtfully and made some notes on his reclaimed parchment pad.

"How it happened is not as important at the moment as where he is and how we locate him and get him back," Martha said.

"I'm fairly sure he'll be in Gnoma," Brodika said. "Apart from the humankind world, the mound is gateway only to the Elven Kingdom and Gnoma, and if he'd gone to the Elven Kingdom, they would have sent him back by now, they're quite efficient. But the gateway to Gnoma doesn't work well these last years, with the increased drift, and even if the gnomes were of a mind to send him back immediately, they might not be able."

"If we're fairly sure that's where he is then Moraden will have to go through and try to find him," Galdore said. But first, we need to ensure that the gateway works so they can get back, and we will need to find somebody who knows the password to Gnoma. Do any of us know anything about the workings of the gateway?"

All the council members said they could offer no useful help in that direction, and so Brodika suggested Moraden seek out and talk immediately with those members of his court who might still have past knowledge necessary to repair and operate the gateway link to Gnoma.

"I'll take Randolph's things up to his room," Galdore said, "We'll meet back here first thing in the morning, hopefully with some information on how we can recover Randolph."

"What if we can't?" Brock asked. "If we can't get him back quickly, one of us will have to take on his responsibilities and go back into the Caverns of Doom to seek further knowledge of Thrung's intentions. I would be willing to take on that role."

"That is a noble offer and shows considerable bravery," Grafdun said. "You are a staunch member of our council, Brock, and I applaud you."

"And I can brief King Atha and prepare the bridgehead armies without him," Martha said. "It doesn't need two of us to do that. Brock could rejoin me later when we eventually get Randolph back."

"If we get Randolph back," Brodika corrected. "I can't guarantee we have the ability to get the gateway to Gnoma working again, and even if we do, we are not absolutely certain that is where Randolph has gone."

Galdore studied the faces of each of those seated at the table and said nothing.

"I'll come with you now and start to track down those from whom we need to seek advice," Moraden said to his father as they left the Great Hall.

"Martha and Grafdun, you must both continue the allocated responsibilities alone," Galdore said. "You will need to leave immediately after we meet again tomorrow morning. Brock and I will remain for the while and join you later or not as our task here unfolds. May good fortune go with you."

Galdore gathered up Randolph's belongings, called to Dragon, and left the hall, heading for Randolph's room. "There's more mice in the hayloft than you can see," Dragon said to Galdore when they were alone in the corridor.

"The same thought was forming in my head," Galdore replied.

"Excuse me sir," Twig's voice startled Galdore. "I apologize, sir, most humbly for the breach of ethics of one wizard's staff addressing another wizard."

Galdore harrumphed a bit. "This is most unusual, a total breach of protocol," he blustered.

Twig fell silent. He dare not speak again without the risk of being chopped up and discarded. Speaking to someone other than one's wizard master was unheard of for a staff, particularly to address another wizard. However, Galdore knew the risk that Twig had taken in talking to him and he knew that he would only have done so in the most extreme circumstances.

"I cannot allow you to speak with me," Galdore said to Twig, "It is a breach of the fundamental codes. However, if you were to speak to Dragon and I were to accidentally overhear you. Well that would be . . .," he left the sentence unfinished.

"Brock's parchment pad," Twig said to Dragon, "I caught sight of the notes as Galdore passed it to him in the Great Hall earlier. There are few that would recognize it, but the notes are made in Anciental text."

☙❧

Leaving the snowy landscape, Randolph followed Roody into the entrance porch of Cosmic Lodge. It was surprisingly warm inside the building, which Randolph thought looked more like a barn than a lodge. In fact, most of the buildings they had passed as they entered the town were of similar construction, like a large collection of farm and country dwellings that just happened to have been built close to each other, rather than a planned or laid out town. Two gnomes came from the other end of the huge room to greet them.

"Drimble Crowsfeet and Thirma Barleyfine," Roody introduced. "And this is Randolph Kettle. Stumbled through the old gateway by accident; some sorta freak vibration threw him off the pathway to the Faery Realm. We godda try and get him back there or to humankind world, a bit urgent."

Roody had asked Randolph not to divulge too much to others they met of the information they had shared about Thrung and the impending rise of the forces of darkness. He felt there was no point in worrying folk. As he had said, "Soon as we get you home buddy boy, you'll give that Thrung fella an old-fashioned wugwug, and that'll sort out the problem."

Drimble, Thirma, and Roody went off to some strange-looking devices and equipment laid out on the other side of the big room, leaving Randolph to investigate the workshop cum laboratory housed in Cosmic Lodge.

"Have a look around," Roody had said. "But don't touch things, some of the stuff is a mite delicate and fragile. And some of it might bite you!" he added with a laugh.

Randolph started on a tour investigating the shelves and paraphernalia arrayed around the room and Roody and his companions laughed themselves off to the far end of the huge room. Some of the equipment stacked around the place looked so old and battered that Randolph thought it might be left over farming tools from some previous life of the building. Other stuff was new and shiny, looking as if it had been polished hard with beeswax. He hadn't seen such a fascinating array of apparatus and strange devices and contraptions since the day he went into Galdore's study back in Castle Drent.

"What's this?" he called to Roody across the room, pointing to a small polished bucket on a shelf.

But Roody and the others where gathered around a bench, all leaning forward and concentrating in excited babble on some diagram or drawing they had spread before them. They didn't hear him. Randolph lifted the lid and peered inside. It was full of what looked and smelled like ordinary sea water. He peered closer. Suddenly a claw popped out of the water and grabbed him by the nose. He pranced and danced around the floor, the crab dangling from the firm attachment to his nose. He dare not pull it, at the risk of ripping his nose off and he couldn't pull the claw open, so he just danced and squealed. But the more he jiggled the crab around by his cavorting, the tighter it clamped his nose and the more it hurt. Roody, Drimble and Thirma came hurrying up the room when they heard the commotion, but when they saw Randolph hopping about with a crab hanging from his nose, they dissolved into hysterical fits of laughter and rolled on the ground with their legs in the air and tears streaming down their cheeks. It was fortunate, indeed a true lucky break for Randolph, that Bretti came through the door at that moment. It was also fortunate, given the gnome predisposition for folding into peels of laughter at the slightest catalyst, that she maintained sufficient presence of mind to talk to the crab. As soon as she explained to it that Randolph meant it no harm and, indeed, it was causing Randolph considerable pain, it released its grip and allowed Bretti to return it to its bucket.

"It says it's sorry," she reported to Randolph. "But it was dozing and you startled it."

"But it dearly bulled by dose off," squeaked Randolph, still hopping from one foot to the other and clutching at his nose.

"Roody," Bretti said, "didn't you warn him that I keep my animals here?"

"I told him not to touch things because he might get bitten," replied Roody still shaking with laughter.

"I dought you bwas joging," Randolph said who had stopped hopping and was now just slightly bobbing, but still firmly clasped his throbbing nose.

The whole scene looked like some form of ritual rural caper. Bodies pranced, gamboled, and frolicked about a central person as Bretti stood chastising Roody for his lack of warning, Randolph for his lack of care, and Drimble and Thirma struggled to regain their composure and wipe their eyes dry. When Bretti had finished giving out, she turned to Randolph, who had released his face and was inspecting his hand to ensure it didn't actually contain his nose.

"Now while they carry on sorting out your transport, I'm going to teach you how to talk to crabs," she said. "And one or two other animals," she added after a pause.

She looked at Randolph and the funny side of the situation struck her. It was a full ten minutes and two visits to the washroom before she was able to carry out her promise.

"We'll start with crabtalk," Bretti said. "Seeing as you've already formed a bit of a relationship there," she chuckled. "That'll give you a good idea of the language of most water-based creatures, crocodiles, fish, porpoise, whales. Then I'll give you a short introduction to crowchatter; most birds'll understand that. Then last, luvvy, I'll teach you a few phrases of Anispeak. That's a basic creaturespeak language that most land animals will understand. You probably won't understand much of what any of them say back to you, unless you can gett'em to say it real slow and simple. That'd take years of study and we only got a few hours."

Randolph found that the language of animals was as much to do with movement as sound, but he learned well.

"Good studier luvvy," Bretti praised. "Must be a bit of basic animal in you somewhere," and off she went into hoots of laughter again.

Glad I'm not a gnome. I'd spend most of the time with aching ribs, Randolph thought to himself.

Bretti and Randolph had just finished when Roody came over.

"Think we've cracked yer problem buddy boy," he boasted. "Can't get you back to the Faery Realm, but there's three points in humankind world that we reckon have enough natural vibration power to maintain a link for long enough to shoot you through it."

"Shoot me through?" Randolph queried. He didn't fancy being shot anywhere. "Do I have to be shot through? Can't I just stroll through the link?"

"'Fraid not, buddy boy," Roody said, "Speed'll be the important thing if you don't want to get stuck up the ether."

Getting stuck up the ether sounded far worse than being shot through the link, so Randolph resigned himself to the lesser of the two horrors, hitched up his breeches, and followed Roody down to the Cosmos end of the room. If this was his only option to get back quickly, then he had to risk it. Roody explained that at certain times of the day, the sun's rays were powerful enough to drive their vibrators to harmonize with the natural vibration of three points elsewhere, and this opened a vortex through which Randolph could pass. They knew he would emerge at some place roughly in the center of the three points, but they couldn't say exactly where it would be.

"So, where are the three points?" Randolph asked.

Roody unrolled an old map of Alusia and pointed out the three castles, Dark, Tharla, and Fortnum.

"We'll shoot yer somewhere in that triangle, but we can't be more precise than that, not till we done more work on fine toonin' the link. You're welcome to wait but could take four, maybe five moons, maybe longer."

"Other bit of good news," Drimble chimed in, "is that Thirma reckons she can get a scrap of a note back through the gateway if she times it right."

"That's right," Thirma said. "Only be a small single sheet, but enough to let your friends know that we've got you back somewhere."

"Yep, even if we can't tell 'em exactly where you are," Roody said.

Randolph took a deep breath and sighed. "I'll go," he said. "I'll go now."

❧❦

It was past midday when the Council of Worth reconvened in the Great Hall and Moraden reported that he had been unable to locate anyone with the ability to repair the gateway to Gnoma.

"I can't believe there's nobody at all," Brodika said. "But Moraden says he has asked everybody and none can help."

Martha looked very crestfallen, Grafdun looked his blackest and most terrible look, Brock's face gave little information on his thoughts, but Galdore was sure he detected a calculating look cross his face for an instant. The meeting was interrupted by a page, who brought a slip of parchment to Brodika.

"Hold everything," Brodika said as he cast his eyes over the writing.

"What is it Father?" Moraden asked.

"It's a message from Gnoma," the king said, and he read it out aloud. "Have linked with humankind world—Randolph Kettle to be sent back from Gnoma—expect arrival somewhere in triangle of three castles of Alusia later today—cannot be more precise. Roody Grumbleweed, Cosmos Professor of Trignome-ometry, Cosmic Lodge."

Martha smiled, Grafdun relaxed, Brock's face gave little information on his thoughts, but Galdore was sure he detected a narrowing of his eyes for an instant.

Chapter Seven
Escape to Merrytown

Root's Cottage

"MASTER," BEAKTOOL drooled. "Your orders have been obeyed. The swarm has been despatched. The defeat of the One is imminent."

The swarm to which Beaktool referred was of evil stinging black wasps created and born of the dark magic of Thrung. They moved as separate insects and either attacked as a mass of individuals or combined to form a single entity on confronting their foe. Their purpose—to locate and destroy the One and then move on into Alusia.

"Once the swarm traps him, they will certainly put an end to his interference," Scumfest whined. "It's a pity we can't have the bits brought back and put on display. They would make a pretty sight and be a warning to any who oppose you master."

"My information is that the One gathers strength and is abroad in the land of the gnome creatures," Thrung growled. "He must travel the ether to return to his own world."

Scumfest cackled. "That is when he will be alone and vulnerable; that is where he will encounter the swarm."

"He will enter the ether, never to be seen again," Beaktool squealed with delight.

"And he will be replaced with one of my choosing," Thrung added. "One who will do my bidding. One who will dominate and drain the life forces of the human and faerykind worlds to satisfy my growth. Be gone." Thrung waved Scumfest and Beaktool away. "Be gone to track and direct the swarm. They must enter the ether at exactly the right time to encounter and defeat the One."

The evil twins scurried away to carry out their orders. Over the Boglands of Thrung, a seething, swirling gathering of black wasps emerged from the shaft leading to the Caverns of Doom. They circled as they climbed high into the dark and stormy autumn sky of Alusia. Up they flew until they were hidden from view, far above the rolling clouds, where they turned northward for Heartland's Mound to enter the between world's space; the ether: to find and destroy the One. But, that was not Thrung's only preparation. In the boglands where the Gantwine and Condor bled into the marshes, there was a stirring. Tentacled, soft bodied, slimy creatures, one missing the end of a tentacle, wriggled and squirmed their way through the muddy ooze and slid unnoticed into the clear rippling waters of the river. The squirds slithered and swam their way up and down stream. The once-safe waters of Alusia became home for these evil creatures laying hidden, waiting only for command from Thrung to clutch and overpower all living things that came within their reach on the riverbanks.

"I am the all-powerful," Thrung stormed. "I alone command the forces that will dominate the whole of creation. I need no other, except to do my bidding. I reign supreme."

മ∞ഗ

"We must work together, combine our resources, and between us we might be able to locate him quickly," Galdore said. "But it's a big area we have to cover and we may need to carry out some physical search as well as using our thought powers."

"How might we best divide our efforts?" Brock asked. "Maybe we should all split up to cover more ground."

"No." Galdore's sharp response was emphatic. "We stay together. Our strength is together. We need to access the orb. It is to Castle Drent we must journey with haste."

"That makes sense," Grafdun agreed. "Castle Drent has my agreement."

"And it's probably the place Randolph will head for if he finds himself stranded," Martha added.

"Brock?" Galdore asked.

Brock finished scribbling something on his notepad and looked up.

"We don't know where he might materialize," Brock said. "Should not at least one of us travel south to Castle Tharla? I am happy to do so."

"If we are to base ourselves at Castle Drent, which we must do to access the orb, then I will need your special skills of analysis there," Galdore replied. "If it's thought necessary for one of us to go south, then Moraden, with his fleetness of foot, or Martha, with her command of the natural forces of the wind, would be more logical choices."

"Mmmm," Brock said thoughtfully. "On reflection, maybe Castle Drent is the right decision; maybe it is better that we remain together for the present."

"So, to Castle Drent we go," Galdore confirmed. "We leave within the hour? Moraden, take Randolph's belongings along with your own pack, will you?"

Moraden smiled and brayed like a donkey.

"I'll take that as a yes," Galdore said. "Come Dragon, we must pack."

"And I'll get the kitchen to organize provisions for us all for the journey, but you can all carry your own," Moraden said, as he went off, still braying and hehoring.

"I'll give you a hand," Brock said to Moraden. "I don't have your strength, but at least I can take his staff and some of the lighter pieces from his pack."

Just over an hour later, the group of five and Dragon left Heartland's Mound in the still-pouring Alusian rain and struck out for the River Westerling crossing and Castle Drent.

⊱⊰

Randolph said his farewells to the Grumbleweeds, Drimble, and Thirma. Bretti stood on a box to give him a big hug. "You go careful, luvvy," she counseled. "And when you get a minute come back and see us if you can find a way to get here."

Randolph promised he would and helped Bretti down from her pedestal. He shook Roody warmly by the hand and said goodbye and repeated thanks to them all as Drimble seated him in a slightly rickety wooden chair.

"The thing we need to do is to get the entry angle right." Drimble said. "Then we can pop you out the other end as close as possible to the center of the triangle between the castles. You see, where you enter the ether and the angle of entry will determine the exit point. Even two people entering at the same place at the same time might come out at different exit points, depending on their angle of entry."

"I see," Randolph said, who didn't really have a clue what Drimble was talking about.

"Now," Roody said to a rather nervous Randolph, "let me explain what you'll need to do, buddy boy."

"I thought you were going to do whatever needed doing," Randolph said. "I thought my part was just to be shot through the link." There was a noticeable quake in Randolph's voice.

"Don't be frightened luvvy," Bretti said. "Roody knows what he's doing."

As the words left her lips, Roody tripped over the box on which Bretti had been standing and fell forward. He grabbed the nearest thing to save himself, which was a lever. Under the lever, Randolph saw, was written just one word in big red letters. It said SHOOT. As all about him began disappearing into a misty haze, Randolph could hear gales of whooping laughter.

"I meant to ask when I arrived and first met you Roody, why were you up a tree?" he asked.

As he and the chair twirled and spun, faster and faster, he caught sight of four small figures rolling on the floor clutching their sides. As he whisked round and round, he saw them as they shook uncontrollably, tears of mirth streaming down their cheeks. He thought he heard Roody call back. "I was up there because . . ." Roody's voice trailed off into an unintelligible whisper speckled with laughter. Randolph's skin prickled just as it had done

160

coming through the gateway, his hair stood on end, he gripped the rickety chair tightly, and everything went black.

൭๏൭

"Now," Scumfest squawked. "He's gone in."

Beaktool peered into the black crystal and passed his hands in a massaging motion over its surface. Some distance away over Heartland's Mound, a swarm of black wasps dived from the sky and entered a small shaft in the top of the hill like a stream of black treacle being poured into a funnel.

൭๏൭

Blackness gave way to drifting blues and grays that mixed and swirled all around him like blueberry syrup being stirred into cream. Randolph's head swam as he floated in the nothingness of the mists of time and space. He felt that he was traveling forward quite fast, but there was nothing against which he could check the feeling, no markers by which he could determine his relative position. There was no wind, no smell, no noise, only swirling colors that now shifted through the whole spectrum of the rainbow and back again. Randolph didn't know if he was the right way up or upside down, but he clung to the rickety old chair for fear that he might fall off if he was upside down. He peered up ahead and saw what looked like a revolving tunnel. He remembered once falling by accident into the sea and watching the surface of the water disappear as he sank down into the rocky pool, his eyes wide open. He was conscious of his breath as he inhaled and exhaled and his eyes as they blinked open and closed to shield against now dazzling brilliant flashes of light that zoomed toward him, zinged passed, and flew swiftly into the reaches of space somewhere behind him. The rickety chair, on which he sat and to which he still clung firmly, started to vibrate and a distant noise like a buzzing swarm of bees started to reach his ears from somewhere in the void behind. It increased in volume slowly until Randolph felt that it was a swarm of bees, right behind him. He turned to face not bees but a mass of black wasps just a few hundred yards away and gaining on him as, perched on his rickety wooden chair, he flew at breakneck speed into the mouth of the revolving tunnel. He looked back to see the wasps follow and he felt the presence of Thrung. He watched in open-mouthed disbelief as they transformed from a swarm into a solid form with reaching clasping claw-like hands, sporting razor sharp, hooked nails that extended toward him, grasping and groping in their horrible enthusiasm to rip and tear his flesh.

"How do I make this chair go faster?" he shouted. "Chair, go faster," he commanded in the vague hope it was that easy. The chair accelerated to a speed faster than the advancing claw-handed devil just as it took a swipe at Randolph's head. He felt the waft of air and a sting as one of the nails grazed his cheek and blood trickled to the corner of his mouth. He drew his sword and slashed at the hand all in one smooth movement, severing it from the creature. The disembodied hand immediately turned into a cloud of black wasps flying beside the creature until they reformed and rejoined to the main body, with no sign of a wound. But the manoeuvre had distracted the creature from its task and it lost a little speed as it reconfigured, falling behind slightly before it started another acceleration in its attempt to catch Randolph.

"Chair, go even faster," he yelled in terror. "Chair, go as fast as possible."

He gripped his rickety carriage with all the strength he could muster as they screamed through the tunnel, the devil creature in hot pursuit, once more gaining on him. Randolph looked to the front again and could see a white glow up ahead.

"Could that be the tunnel end?" He prayed, "Please let that be the tunnel end."

He looked back at the black form that was almost on him as it pulled back its claw for another strike. Suddenly it was raining. Randolph had never been happier to sit in the rain, even in the middle of a forest clearing on a rickety old wooden chair. He looked up to dark clouds above as the soft droplets fell. They ran down his face like tears of happiness, turning pink from the wound on his cheek and staining his shirt, but he didn't care; he was back in Alusia. He could sense this was Alusian rain and he laughed out loud. There was no sign of swirling colors, revolving tunnels, or black creatures with long talons; just trees, grass, rain, and clouds.

"Thank you Roody Grumbleweed," he called to the clouds. "Thank you, Professor."

꙰

The river crossing was torrential. The rain-swollen waters tumbled and tossed the usually shallow ford in powerful bursts of current, making it too dangerous for the party to risk an unroped crossing on foot.

"Will you be able to sustain windfloat long enough to get us and all our kit across?" Galdore asked Martha.

"I don't think so," Martha replied. "I could probably get myself and two others over, and maybe a third, but certainly not a fourth or the packs as well."

"I could attempt a foot crossing," Grafdun offered.

"Brave, but too risky," Galdore said. "I think we camp here on the west bank tonight and hope the water recedes a little by tomorrow. The rain has lessened in the last few hours and the waters should start to calm if we have no more downpour before sunrise."

"I could go off and scout the bank up and down stream to search for an alternative crossing," Brock said.

"You seem very keen to go off by yourself lately," Grafdun laughed. "Don't you like to be with us anymore?"

Galdore didn't join the laughter of the others. Instead he busied himself conjuring shelter and fire to comfort them through the night. The rain had stopped now, and the dark clouds gave way to patches of starlit sky that jostled and barged across the expanse above the forest in their attempt to dominate the heavens. The moon graced them with her presence, shedding light on the trees and sparkling the river with twinkling stars, blessing all that she touched with the gift of silver. Galdore sat in deep thought, Dragon curled by his feet. The others lay in semi-sleep around the fire. Martha looked across at Galdore. One side of his face was lit by the orange glow of the fire, the other by a shaft of white moonlight. The contrast exaggerated the look of concern and doubt that sat heavily on his countenance. Martha raised herself on her elbow in a half-sitting position.

"Galdore," she whispered, so as not to disturb the others. "Should you not get some rest? We have much to occupy us tomorrow and a distance still to travel."

163

Instead of heeding Martha's suggestion, Galdore raised himself to standing. In the light of the dancing flames, he appeared to grow in stature as he stepped gently around the stones that bordered the fire and moved quietly to where Martha lay. He crouched beside her. None of the others stirred.

"Martha, come walk with me a while," he whispered.

Martha saw the deep furrows of concern on his brow and sensed his urgent need for counsel. She slipped soundlessly from the woven blanket that covered her and followed Galdore as he moved toward the riverbank, stepping onto the path that followed beside its course. They walked in silence for a short way until they were out of earshot of the rest of the party. They sat on a log and looked into the flowing waters of the Condor. The bright light of the moon now shone from an almost clear sky, bathing the river in a lustrous, gleaming cloak that tripped on the ripples of the cascading water. Somewhere in the forest, an owl called with a low hoot, receiving a distant reply. All was peaceful; the land slept. There was no hint of the dark forces that threatened to destroy the tranquility of Alusia and its people.

"Martha," Galdore finally broke his silence. "Martha, I am sorely troubled."

"As are we all, Galdore; we all share the burden of the task that we have to meet. Me, Randolph, Grafdun, Moraden, Brock, and many others. We stand together in the toil and effort that must be both shared and linked in defeat of the forces of darkness. You are not alone."

"Your words give me comfort," Galdore said. "And for that I thank you. But, there is one whom we have grown to trust, one who has shown us past purity of vision and in whom we have placed our faith, but who now fails to inspire me with confidence. I fear we may now be facing more than an army of evil creatures that will be stopped by the swords and arrows of our brave troops. I feel there is an enemy within. That our ranks have been breached by Thrung's power over mind as well as matter."

"I don't understand what you mean," Martha said. "If you're talking about Randolph's disappearance, then I do not believe he is master of his present fortune."

"It is that very thought that tugs at my heart and causes me grief," Galdore replied. "Who of us are master of our own present fortune? Who of us are to be trusted and who of us may have been penetrated by the might of Thrung? Who of us may have had our minds invaded and turned in the struggle of wills that may ultimately determine our world's destiny?"

"Why do you feel this way?" Martha asked. "What has transpired to bring doubt into your mind about the loyalty of Randolph?"

"It is not Randolph's loyalty or his present plight that troubles my mind," Galdore said. "I do not question Randolph's motives; I do not believe it is he who is the weak link. But, Thrung seems to be aware of our moves, informed of our plans, as if he were inside our thoughts and able to counter our moves. I fear we are all at risk and I speak with you now only because of my belief in a special bond between you and Randolph. He is the hub upon which our future may turn. Caution must be our standard bearer and unity our staff. I can say no more, for I know no more, only that I am troubled for the sake and safety of Randolph and, by that, for the whole of humankind. Guard him well, Martha."

Although Martha probed, Galdore would say no more of his thoughts and concerns. They returned to the camp to find Brock now awake and seated by the fire; Grafdun and Moraden slept.

"We should all rest while we can," Martha said, sliding back beneath her blanket.

"We should," Brock agreed, "Who knows what challenge tomorrow may bring?"

ॐ

Randolph assumed that the black creature or the swarm of wasps had been ejected from the ether at some distant point. If what Drimble had said was accurate about the exit point being relative to the entry point, then they could be anywhere. Although he was safe from them for the moment, Randolph didn't know how easily they might detect him and return to complete their work. Away to the left he could hear the sound of running water, a river he guessed, maybe even a waterfall.

If I make my way to the river, I might be able to get my bearings. I need to find some point of reference so that I can get back to either Heartland's Mound or Castle Drent, he thought to himself.

165

Saying goodbye to the rickety old chair, Randolph left the clearing and headed for the sound of the river. The thick undergrowth didn't make his way easy and in the end, he had to use his sword to slash through the brambles and vines that blocked his path, twisted around his ankles and threatened to trip him at every step. Slowly he made his way toward the sound of the rushing water and eventually he emerged, puffing, scratched, and bruised, into a clearing that bordered the river. As he looked upstream he could see, some way off, a waterfall that was the source of the noise for which he had been aiming. The recent rains had turned the falls and the river into a wild and turbulent flood, and Randolph was reluctant to approach too close for fear of the overhanging banks collapsing and sweeping him away downstream.

"I can only imagine those are Devilrock Falls," Randolph said to himself. "I know of no other waterfall with a reputation of that magnitude in Alusia."

He squatted on the damp grass and unrolled his map from the leather pouch on his belt. Orienting the map to the lie of the land, with the waterfall ahead of him and the river on his left, he figured out that, if he was correct and he was looking at Devilrock Falls, then Roody's accidental early shooting had landed him right on the edge of the triangle of castles, rather than in the center.

"I must be in the Western Forest, and Merrytown must be my nearest haven," he informed anything that was listening. "But not tonight."

The sun had set. Although the rain had now eased to a drizzle and the clouds had broken to reveal occasional shafts of moonlight, Randolph was not inclined to strike out for Merrytown through unknown country until he could see properly. He shook the water from his hair, sending droplets flying in all directions. Suddenly he was conscious of the chill wind, his aching feet, and tired legs. His empty stomach rumbled and misery descended on his person. There was little but berries to stave off his hunger and river water to quench his thirst. The wound on his cheek continued to ooze blood and had now become quite sore and swollen. He felt gray and battered. A little further upstream a fallen tree, close to a place where the riverbank appeared safe to approach, gave him some shelter from the breeze. He went to the river at that place and found a back eddy that allowed him to access the water. Bathing his throbbing cheek and drinking deeply of the cold water revived him a little and he resolved to go back into the skirt of the forest where brambleberries grew and the trees might give him some overnight shelter. As Randolph looked out over the moonlit rapids shimmering in the center of the river, he wondered where Martha might be. Had he known at that moment she was sitting with Galdore looking at the reflection of the same moon in the same river, but some three days' trek southward, then his spirits might have been lifted further. But he didn't, and he felt very alone.

"Oh Martha." He sighed across the flooded river. "Would that I could change this saga. Would that there were no forces of darkness and this torment was but a foul dream."

As he sat, lost in his own thoughts of Martha and Nick and the time that he had spent at the Black Swan back in Portalbion, something dark and slimy swam unseen into the backwater eddy by his feet. If he had not taken a sudden spurt of strength at the thought of an evening in the barroom of the Black Swan, Randolph might not have jumped to his feet and headed back to the forest when he did. Instead, he might have found his leg sheathed with a tentacle, maybe even a tentacle missing about half a yard from its end. He did not see the squird, but the squird saw him.

"Aaaaarrrrrgggghhhhh." Randolph yawned aloud and quite fearsome yawn as he stretched away the stiffness of the night. Early November was not the best month for sleeping rough. Even though the days could still be quite mild, the evenings and nights were invariably cold. *So, why am I not cold?* Randolph asked himself.

The early morning sun shone from a clear sky and already the probing heat of its rays lifted a mist across the clearing between Randolph's forest bed-chamber and the river. "But the sun is not the source of my warmth," Randolph said.

"Me," a voice growled. "Me you keep warm."

Randolph rolled onto his side to come nose to nose with a huge brown bear. "You make talk words," the bear said.

Randolph didn't know how it was working for him, but the creaturespeaker lesson he had had from Bretti enabled him to interpret the growls and grunts coming from the bear into an intelligible sentence.

"You make talk words in sleep," the bear said. "You say cold. Me you next sleep. Keep man warm night."

I wonder if I can talk to him? Now what did Bretti say? Just think the words in my head, keep thinking them over and over, and concentrate hard. Open my mouth and sort of groan, and it should come out so that animals can understand. But keep it simple, Randolph thought.

He tried what Bretti had taught him. "Thank you," he thought and groaned.

"No needing thanks," the bear growled. "Man help need, Brommel help give."

"Brommel?" Randolph said in Anispeak, "You Brommel?"

"Yes," came the bear's reply, "Me Brommel."

"Me Randolph."

"Nice meet."

"Nice meet too," Randolph said.

"We go river drink," Brommel said.

"Yes," Randolph said.

They crossed the clearing to the river, back to the spot where Randolph had been the previous evening. There was only space for one at a time to get down to the water. The bear stood back from the bank by the fallen tree, allowing Randolph first access to the pool.

"You strange," said the bear, as Randolph knelt down, splashing the water over his face and head and drinking from cupped hands. "Me no hear man talk before. You first one. Usual man just make noise, but no talk."

"I only just learned it a few days ago from a friend. Actually, now I think about it, it was only yesterday. I met her in a parallel world. She's a professor in creaturespeaker language. It was her husband, Roody, who sent me back here and I landed in the forest," Randolph said.

"Brommel no understand," said the bear, "Too many talks."

"Sorry," Randolph said. "Me learn from friend."

Randolph had turned to look away from the river as he spoke to Brommel. He didn't see the swirl that disturbed the surface, he just knew, suddenly, that he was sliding backward into the water. Brommel receded in his vision as Randolph flailed in the pool in a desperate attempt to keep his head above water, to fight against whatever was dragging him down. He broke surface and gulped a lungful of air, only to be dragged straight back under. Something had him, wrapped tightly around his legs, pinning them together. He could only use his hands to fight back toward the surface again. Randolph struck out for the bank in an attempt to grab the roots of the small trees lining the river. He thrashed and tried to kick at whatever held him back and dragged him down. He needed air. His head started to swim and a grayness descended on his mind. His one thought was air, air, air, and he clawed at the surface of the water in an attempt to grab handfuls and drag them down to his bursting lungs. The grayness turned to blackness, and Randolph was gone from consciousness as the cold water burned his throat and lungs, and his chest exploded into the river.

"Give me air," he called between coughing and spluttering. He lay on the grassy riverbank, panting and gasping, his water-filled lungs painful as he spluttered back to consciousness. Brommel stood over him like a wet rug, dripping, festooned with weeds, and caked in a layer of black mud: Reeds clung to his head like a bonnet and even in his traumatized state Randolph couldn't help be amused at the sight. He pulled himself up to a half-sitting position to see that beside Brommel lay a slimy, awesome tentacled creature. Its body twitched intermittently, but Randolph could see where its bulbous form had been gashed and ripped open, its internal organs spilling out, staining the fresh green grass with a blackness and a stench that made him retch.

"Me save man friend," Brommel growled in response to Randolph's smile. "Me kill big fish many arms and suck pads."

Randolph sank back on to the grass. "Thank you Brommel, Thank you friend," he groaned.

Brommel rolled in the rough meadow grass, removing the weed and mud from his coat. He dropped to all fours and shook himself violently to remove the water from his long fur. "Better," he announced at last.

By this time, Randolph had recovered sufficiently to stand, and he crossed to examine the remains of the creature that had attacked him. It had stopped its death-throw twitching now and lay still and deflated like an empty sack, with its contents strewn from a gaping tear, its huge lifeless eyes stared skyward, and its hooked beak sagged open. Randolph saw that one of its tentacles was partly missing from an old wound.

"Surely this couldn't be the same creature that attacked me in the boglands," Randolph murmured under his breath.

"What man talk?" Brommel queried.

"No matter," Randolph replied. He realized this was, indeed, the same creature he had encountered when Moraden had slipped and stunned himself in the boglands.

"How has it tracked me here?" he wondered.

He said nothing to Brommel of this realisation. It would be too difficult to explain and would confuse his new friend.

"Brommel see fish like this before?" Randolph asked.

"No," came the simple reply.

That knowledge made Randolph uneasy. The black swarm, which Randolph was sure had exited the ether somewhere nearby, and now this, brought an apprehension that Thrung's presence, or at least the presence of his army of evil beasts, was spreading fast throughout Alusia and was doing so in some planned, coherent way.

"Randolph must get to man town." He formed the thought and groaned it to Brommel.

The huge bear bent down, scooped Randolph up in his forepaws, and swung him gently onto his back as he dropped to his four legs and started off along the riverbank away from the falls.

"We go man town," he growled.

They traveled all day. The brambles that had caused Randolph's slow progress through the forest the day before snapped like twigs as Brommel crashed through the undergrowth. The river, although now tame in comparison to its powerful flood of the previous day, was still full and running wild, but Brommel crossed as if it were a mere trickle. Randolph, perching on the bear's broad back, clung to his fur like a giant burr, refusing to be dislodged by even the most violent shaking and jolting. It was dusk by the time they were about a mile from Merrytown. Brommel stopped on a rise looking down into the shallow valley where the lights of Merrytown twinkled through the evening haze.

"Me stop here," Brommel grunted, "Man see Brommel, man shoot arrows. Most man not same Randolph."

Randolph slid from Brommel's back, landing lightly on the track. He could see that it wound down the rise and through the forest to the town gates. "Brommel," Randolph turned to the bear, but for a moment, he couldn't find the right thoughts to project what he wanted to say. "Brommel," he tried again.

Brommel looked at Randolph, his head tilted to one side, a quizzical expression on his face. "Yes?" he growled.

"Me tell men not shoot arrow at Brommel," was the best he could do. "Me tell men Brommel Randolph friend."

He threw his arms around Brommel's neck and hugged the bear warmly. "Randolph thank Brommel."

"It fun talk man," Brommel replied. "Hope see Randolph again."

Randolph turned toward the lights of Merrytown. He looked back several times to see Brommel still sitting at the side of the track watching his progress toward the town. Then all of a sudden, Randolph turned and the bear wasn't there anymore. He wished he could have expressed his thanks better and he was sad at their parting.

I hope I see him again, Randolph thought, and he formulated a groany grunt to express himself, then suddenly, realizing he wasn't a bear, he laughed, a human laugh. "Thank you Brommel!" he shouted at the top of his voice. "Thank you!"

A roar came from the forest in reply.

It wasn't difficult to see where Merrytown got its name from. No sooner had Randolph crossed the boundary and entered the gates than he was surrounded by gaiety, laughter, dancing, and festival. There were street jugglers, fire-eaters, tumblers, entertainers, clowns, and jesters. Everybody laughed and smiled at him as he made his way through the narrow cobbled streets and colorful squares and places. Single stalls and arcades of traders abounded, selling everything imaginable, from fruit to boots, hats to bread. Randolph was dazzled by the spectacle of fun and joviality.

"Hello," said a voice close by. "Are you new in town? I've not seen you before."

The voice belonged to a stooped elderly man with a squint, who regarded Randolph from under a wide-brimmed pointed felt hat that also housed a mop of disheveled black hair sticking out in clumps and looking as if it hadn't seen a comb in a long, long time. His plump personage was wrapped tightly around with a long black cloak, from the bottom of which protruded two huge black boots.

"Hello," Randolph said, "I've just arrived."

The figure stuck out his hand. "Barkman," he said. "Leafy Barkman, but my friends call me Roots. Oaks, Willows, Chestnuts, Ash, Laurel, Holly, even brambles if you want. Just tell me what you need and we'll make it for you. We did most of the forest round here and large parts of the Northern Forest as well."

And so saying, he completed an ungainly twirl, tripped over his own feet, and collapsed in a crumpled heap on the ground. Randolph smiled a not-very-hidden smile, which then burst into an even-less-discreet spluttering laugh.

"I'm sorry," he said as he helped Leafy Barkman to his feet. "I didn't mean to be rude, but you looked very comical in a heap. What did you say your friends call you?"

"Roots."

"Well Roots, unfortunately I don't want any trees, and even if I did, I don't have any money. In fact, I'm hoping that I can persuade one of the tavern landlords here to swap me a room for an evening of songs and entertainment. That is if I can borrow a lute; I left mine behind by mistake."

Roots squinted even harder at Randolph.

"That's strange," he said. "Strange for an entertainer to leave something as important as his lute behind . . . by mistake. Left somewhere in a bit of a hurry, did we? Huh?"

He narrowed his eyes so hard that his whole face screwed up like a prune and his hat tipped forward over one eye.

"Well since you ask, I did leave my last stop in a bit of a hurry, but I'd already left my lute behind somewhere else." Randolph said. "Sort of took a wrong turn and couldn't get back to the mound where I left it."

The one visible eye now opened wide, and Roots thrust his face closer to Randolph.

"Mound?" he asked in hushed tones. "Heartland's Mound? You been at the mound? You been playing around with them pesky faeries?"

"What do you mean, pesky?" Randolph asked. "They're not pesky; they're my friends."

"Huh," Roots said. "You'll be telling me next you mix with wizards and gnomes."

"What if I do?" Randolph said. He was feeling a bit irritated by this intrusion into his privacy and the judgment of his friends by a total stranger. "What's it got to do with you who my friends are? It's none of your business who I mix with, and I'll thank you to keep your opinions to yourself. I bet you've never even met a wizard."

Randolph turned on his heel and started away from Roots.

"What, like Galdore, you mean?" Roots asked.

Randolph stopped sharply in his tracks, kicking a little cloud of dust up where he skidded to a standstill. He turned to look at Roots, who had pulled himself more erect, pushed his hat back into place, and completely lost his squint.

"You know Galdore?" Randolph asked.

"Bosom buddies," Roots declared.

"So why are you criticizing?" Randolph asked.

"Just testing," Roots said. "Can't be too careful, 'specially in these troubled times."

"So who are you then?" Randolph asked. "I mean, apart from being Leafy Barkman."

"A friend," Roots said. "Come with me."

And he strode off. Randolph followed as they went on into the center of the town and into the Copper Kettle Tavern. Roots stuck his hand up in the air, displaying two fingers to the barman as he crossed the room to the private snug in the far corner.

"Two pints of the best coming up, Mister Barkman," the barman called. "Bring 'em to you as soon as they've settled, sir."

Once seated and fidgeted into a comfortable position, Roots turned his attention to Randolph.

"Now young man, you'd better bring me up to date with what's happening. From what Galdore tells me, we need to act quickly to avoid a disaster."

Randolph's caution was evident in his hesitation in responding to Roots. Although he had a good feeling about the old man, he had no positive proof that this wasn't just a clever ruse by one of Thrung's spies to gather information. He decided to play Roots at his own game.

"So what tall stories has young Galdore been weaving?" Randolph said. "I tell you, him and that joker cat, Whiskers, they can spin a good yarn when they need to."

Roots half closed one eye and the hint of a squint returned to the other as he peered at Randolph across the table. "Not very good at this, are you?" he said, and his face burst into a grin. "But you're right to be cautious."

To prove his genuineness, Roots told Randolph of his knowledge of the situation. He related what he knew of Randolph's first meeting with Galdore, the story of the defeat of Griselda and of the meeting with Sulaman in the cave with Martha and Dragon. He concluded by saying that although Galdore would be flattered by Randolph's false description, he was, in fact, older than the hills and wiser than any other person in Alusia. Randolph was pretty much convinced that Roots was honest, but if he was as closely associated as he claimed with the Council of Worth members and the court and personalities at Castle Drent, one final test would confirm, beyond all doubt, that he was to be trusted.

"Who has the biggest nose and bakes the best bread in Alusia?" he asked Roots.

"Why, who else but old Walter Bottle," Roots said. "Haven't seen Walter for years. Not since we both left the court when good King Petre passed on. How is he? Ears still waggling? Still puffing away on the old baccyweed?" He laughed.

Randolph was now satisfied that Roots was who he said he was. He seemed well informed about the situation and was obviously an intimate friend of those united in the struggle against Thrung. Randolph shared his experiences of the last few days; how he got lost in Heartland's Mound, his visit to Gnoma, and the happenings of his meeting with Brommel. Throughout, Roots stroked and tugged at his chin and "hhmmd" and "hrrumphd" at the more alarming parts of the story.

"Something smacks of being not right," Roots said when Randolph had finished recounting his recent travels. "Thrung knows too much. More than he should and too soon. But that's another day's work. First thing is to get you back to Castle Drent and joined up with Galdore and the others again."

"Can you put me on the right path?" Randolph asked.

"Why can't you fly on the wind like you told me?" Roots asked.

"Can't be seen flying," Randolph replied. "And anyway, it's hard work balancing on the wind for too long. I can only do it for short bursts at a time. So, can you show me the right path?"

"More than that, my lad," Roots said. "But now we dine and sup. Tomorrow you meet the trees and start out for the castle. I'll send word ahead to Galdore that you're safe and will meet him at Drent in two days."

The food and ale was of the finest and, once again, reminded Randolph of his time back at the Black Swan in Portalbion. They ate and drank their fill and went off down the cobbled streets, through the town gates, and away up a narrow forest track to Roots' home and tree factory, some way out along the south bank of the river to the west of the town. As they went, Roots sang.

> *"They call me Roots; I got big Boots*
> *And they will tread a pathway.*
> *You follow me, then you see*
> *The way that is the right way.*
>
> *I build the trees, the ones you sees.*
> *When walking through the woodlands*
> *There's many a type, some raw some ripe,*
> *All made with clever craft-hands.*
>
> *So off we go, up high, down low.*
> *Make trees for hill and valley.*
> *We'll cut and saw; we'll drill and bore,*
> *No time to dilly dally.*
>
> *And when they're made, we'll take a spade,*
> *We'll plant them where they're needed.*
> *They'll fill the gaps; they overlaps*
> *With those that's natural seeded."*

"I always thought the trees in the forests and the woods were all naturally grown," Randolph said.

"'Course not," Roots said. "Can you imagine the confusion if they were allowed to just run wild? They'd grow in all the wrong places, at all the wrong times, to all the wrong sizes. You'd have willows where there should be oaks, brambles where there should be ferns, tall ones blocking out the sunlight, and short ones with branches interfering with pathways. 'Cooouuuurse not."

"Oh." Randolph had never really thought about this before.

"The forests have got to have leader trees, and that's what I make. The ones that control the natural breeders. See, my trees have a head on them; they've got brains and can organize what happens in the forests and the woods. The natural breeders . . ." Roots lowered his voice to a whisper and drew closer to Randolph's ear. "Well . . . how do I put it? . . . They're just interested in lumping and logging, know what I mean?" He winked at Randolph. "No sense above the seed line, see? Run rampant they would."

"Oh." Randolph had never associated trees with sex before. His mind drifted off as they walked, back to a few nights ago in his rooms in Brodika and Charmila's palace. But the vision took on a strange twist. The door to his room was now made of human planks, each with a face of its own. It creaked open as he lay log-like on a soft bed of fallen leaves. A young Reeka willow sapling slid quietly on dainty roots through the doorway. She stood silhouetted against the bright moonlit window of his room. The flimsy garment of new leaves she wore was transparent in the moonlight and her nakedness under it was revealed by the luminescence from the window. The soft curves of her stalks and stems were revealed as she swayed gently there beside him. He felt a stump harden on his trunk as he watched her move closer to his leafy bed and bend forward, her gentle leaves lightly brushing his rough bark. Her naked twigs kissed his boughs and he felt the sap rise as he extended a branch to caress her fronds.

"Nearly there," Roots announced, snapping Randolph back to reality. "Only another couple of hundred yards up the track."

"I'll never think of trees in the same way again," he said to Roots. "I didn't realize about them."

"There's not many folk do," Roots said. "Most just take them for granted, as part of what's around. Never give them a second thought."

"The trees you make, when you've planted them out there; I mean; do they move around; can they walk about?"

"Don't be daft," Roots scoffed. "Trees walk around? You've been listening to too many fantasy stories." He laughed out loud. "Trees, walk around?" he said to himself, laughing again as he lifted the latch on the cottage door, "What will they think of next? Huh!" He shook his head, tutting in amusement at the idea. "Trees walk around? Hah."

Inside the neat cottage, Randolph found all the wooden furniture exquisitely carved and crafted, and highly polished with beeswax, giving a fresh clean smell to the room. Roots took Randolph through to a small back room. "This is the spare room. You can sleep here tonight, and we'll get you back on the road in the morning."

That night Randolph dreamed of trees and bushes flying in swarms and doing battle with armies of black wasps and tentacled river creatures. The old rickety chair on which he had flown from Gnoma took root in the forest and grew to become King of the Trees, crushing Thrung and all the evil forces and creatures that attempted to infest Alusia with dark wickedness. The whole of creation was dominated by Lord Randolph and his trusty bear, who provided protection and friendship at all times.

"But why would I need protection?" Randolph asked.

"What's that you say?" Roots responded. He stood beside the bed, mug of herbal brew in one hand and plate of bread and honey in the other. "Having a bit of a waking ramble?"

Randolph rubbed his eyes as he struggled to balance the reality of the external morning with what appeared to be the equal reality of his internal slumber meanderings.

"I was dreaming," he said to Roots. The world started to come into focus and his memory of the events of yesterday returned to clarity. "Dreaming that I was in charge of the whole of creation and that I was lord of all living things."

Roots frowned.

"Do you have that sort of dream very often?" he asked.

"Only in the last few days," Randolph said. "I had a very strange experience a couple of nights ago where I thought that Thrung was getting to my mind and turning my thoughts to favor dark power."

"Mmmmh," Roots said. "I think the sooner we get you back to Galdore the better. He may need to put some cloak of thought protection around you. Help you sort the good power from the bad in your own head. If I was Thrung, one of the first things I'd do would be to try and get inside the heads of all of the Council of Worth members and, above all, you."

"That's what worried me the other day," Randolph said. "But the gnome I met said as long as we don't get divided we will be stronger than Thrung. He will only succeed if he can split us up."

"That's very wise and true," Roots agreed. "But how do you know if you're being separated? How would you know until it was too late?"

"I suppose you'd get the sort of feelings that we're talking about," Randolph suggested. "You know, like feelings of wanting power over others for your own benefit."

"Suppose you're right," Roots said, "But don't we all have those feelings anyway sometimes? Could we survive if we didn't put ourselves first?"

Randolph explained Roody Grumbleweed's cheese theory to Roots. "Makes it easy to understand how we can beat Thrung and also how dangerous he can be to each one of us," he said.

"Certainly does," Roots agreed. "But what I'm saying is the survival instinct of those small cheeses is, in itself, a selfish desire. Aren't we all basically selfish and doesn't that give Thrung a head start?"

"I don't think it's that simple," Randolph said. "To assume selfishness is a bad thing may not be the right approach."

"Do you know, apart from Galdore, you are the only other person I've ever heard say that," Roots said.

"I've thought a lot about this in the last few days," Randolph said. "And I don't believe it's the act of selfishness that's right or wrong, it's the way we achieve it and then what we do with it that determines whether it's good or bad."

"That sounds sensible," Roots agreed. "So, like my trees, if they can organize the forest in the way that they want it to be and, at the same time help the other trees to get what they want, then that's good. If they do it without helping the others or, worse still, at the expense of others, then it's bad."

"That's sort of what I mean," Randolph said. "But I think the right or wrong is done even before that."

"I don't understand," Roots said.

"I mean, bothering or not bothering to take time to think about what others might want or about how they might view something is the root of the positive or negative energy," Randolph replied.

Roots was quiet while he thought about what Randolph had said. In fact, he was so lost in thought that he went off, back to the kitchen, still clutching the mug and plate containing Randolph's breakfast. Randolph left his bed and followed.

"With the possible exception of when they do it unconsciously," he said, pointing at the brew and the bread.

They both laughed.

"You might be right," Roots said. "Talk to Galdore about it when you get back to Castle Drent. What you say might be a good foundation for a more powerful protection spell, and we're going to need to consider every option."

"I'll do that," Randolph said. "But we better get started. You know what they say; it's the first bird that gets the worm."

"Yes, but it's the second mouse that gets the cheese. We shouldn't rush into things too fast. In my business, we have a saying that 'Good forests aren't crafted in a week,' even if all the leader trees are planted," Roots retorted. "There's still a whole lot of lumping and logging to do!"

Before he put Randolph on the right path, Roots wanted him to see the workshop where the trees were produced and to understand something about the process that grew and controlled the forests. "Never know when being aware of what's happening and how things are done might come in useful," he told Randolph.

Thinking back to how learning to fly, become invisible, talk to animals had all helped him, Randolph could only but agree, and anyway, he was interested to see what Roots did. The tour of the workshop took most of the rest of the morning, and it wasn't until after lunch that they walked together out into the forest to join the track leading directly north to the river crossing, after which, Roots explained, Randolph would need to turn east and then just follow the path as it turned southeasterly and on toward Castle Drent.

"It'll take you a couple of days to get there," Roots said. "But as long as you stick to the track, you'll come to no harm; it's a safe enough journey on a well-used pathway."

What Roots didn't know was that as well as being well used by people, it had also recently become the new play place for the Ghost of Crumble Hills.

&~&

"Tiddle diddle fiddle widdle," Tinkerboo said to himself.

He wasn't a malevolent ghost, just mischievous. He enjoyed nothing more than leading folk on merry dances through the forest. He would never let them come to any real harm, but he did take pleasure in a good giggle at the expense of others. He justified this by telling himself this was a ghost's job, and he wasn't the sort of person in lifeliness or ghostliness to shirk his duty. Tinkerboo had been a boot-maker in the living world but one day had fallen from a cliff in a happy and relaxed state of inebriation. He didn't feel a thing as he hit the rocks below and didn't even know he'd been killed. That's why he still hung around the Northern Forest. He didn't know anything of Thrung or forces of darkness. Evil to Tinkerboo was something that only existed in people's imaginations. If he ever came to know the truth of the gathering doom, he would be mortified. If he hadn't already been dead, he would die of shock.

"Tiddle diddle fiddle widdle," he sang happily, as he sat on a large rock some way above the track, waiting for the sunset. Tinkerboo enjoyed the sunset and watched it every evening, every day of the year. It was his special time.

Randolph had said goodbye to Roots at the bridge spanning the River Westerling, north of Merrytown, to where they had walked together before Roots left him to his solitary journey.

"I'd have come all the way to Castle Drent with you to see Galdore," Roots had said. "But I've got a busy planting over the next few days, and I have to get that finished. Maybe I'll join you down there later."

Like Tinkerboo, Randolph now sat on a large rock beside the track watching the sunset and waiting for darkness. Roots had kitted Randolph out with a pack containing bedroll, food and drink, and a change of clothes. He had also given Randolph a new pair of boots that had stood in the corner of the workshop for years. They had been made to order from the local bootmaker by one of the tree crafters but hadn't fitted properly, and then the bootmaker had fallen from a cliff and been killed. The boots had been gathering dust ever since, but they fitted Randolph perfectly and so Roots had donated them to what he described as "this worthy cause."

Although both Randolph and Tinkerboo thought they were waiting for the sunset, each was unaware that he also waited to play a part in a major turn of events for the battle between good and evil in Alusia.

☙❦❧

Galdore stretched noisily, rolled onto his side, and threw a bolt of sparks at the fire, bursting it into life. He looked at the other mounds around the campfire made by the still-sleeping forms of the rest of the party.

Mmmm, there's one flat mound, Galdore thought.

He scratched his head, screwed up his face, and chastised himself.

"Stupid old man," he said to himself. "You're beginning to sound like Randolph. How can there be a flat mound?"

"It's a sign," one of the other mounds said.

"Sign?" Galdore said. "What's a sign? A sign of what?"

"Talking to yourself," the mound replied as it heaved, shuffled, and shifted, eventually transforming into Brock. He emerged from the pile of blankets and bed skins like a butterfly from a cocoon. He looked somehow different to Galdore, different from the Brock of yesterday. The analogy of a metamorphosis from a creeping caterpillar to a crusty chrysalis to an emerging butterfly was not lost on him. But before Galdore had time to dwell further on the matter, a grunting, farting, snorting Grafdun ejected from his sleeping pod like a bolt from a crossbow. This analogy was also not lost on Galdore as Grafdun stumbled around, rubbing eyes and making morning groaning noises until he trod on the still-sleeping form of Martha, who thought she was being at-tacked and with the speed of lightning had Grafdun pinned to the ground in a full body lock. Galdore watched the activity with interest until Moraden appeared from the surrounding trees with a bag of nuts and berries in one hand and more wood for the fire piled in the crook of his other arm, and some level of sanity re-turned to the group.

"Breakfast?" he asked the rest of the group.

"You're up early," Galdore said.

"Things to do," Moraden said. "It's the first bird that gets the worm."

"It's the second mouse that gets the cheese," Brock said.

Galdore looked from one to the other and back again, his expression a mixture of concern and confusion.

Chapter Eight
Shawadarg's Lair

The Draken Mountains

THE SUN was setting as Galdore and his party crossed the moat bridge and entered the gates of Castle Drent. They had been spotted earlier from the watchtower and Atha and some of the knights were waiting in the courtyard to greet them.

"Welcome home, Galdore," Atha said, and embraced the wizard warmly before turning to the others. "And welcome to you Prince Moraden, as always, our hospitality is yours. I look forward to hearing news of your mother and father and of the fortunes of the Realm. My dear Martha, it is good to see you again, and Brock, it is some time since we last had the pleasure of your wise company. Maybe we will find the time for you to tell me more of your studies of the ancient texts and dead languages."

"I didn't know you had been studying ancient texts," Galdore said to Brock.

"Have been for some time now," Brock replied. "Many of the modern languages are rooted in now-forgotten or rarely used tongues. Their study is important to interpretation and translation of old scriptures, tablets, and runic symbols, as well as gaining a greater understanding of the way animals communicate with each other."

Last, Atha turned to Grafdun, of whom he was always a little wary.

"Grafdun, my good fellow," he greeted. "Sir Nigel will be pleased to see you; he has new defense and battle plans to discuss for protection of the kingdom against the forces that threaten us."

"Do you have any word of Randolph?" Martha asked.

"We do," Atha replied. "Word arrived only yesterday that he has been safe in the hands of Leafy Barkman in Merrytown and, as we speak, journeys here. His arrival is expected tomorrow night."

Martha's look of relief was obvious.

"He's a tough one all right," Grafdun said. "With a little schooling in battle skills, I could make a fine warrior of him."

"That opportunity may yet be written in his fortune," Galdore said. "We have a long road ahead and much lies unseen around every corner."

"Maybe I should go out to meet him," Moraden suggested.

"I think that unwise," Brock said. "We have already agreed it is better that we remain together, and the road from Merrytown is not known as hazardous."

"Brock's counsel is, as always, wise," Atha agreed. "And you yourself are tired, Moraden. A good night in a comfortable bed will be of more value than another day's journeying. I will send out Graceforth with spare horse to locate Randolph and guide him home. Let Graceforth repay his debt of gratitude in kind."

And that was what was done. Good food and wine were provided for Galdore and his party as they recounted recent events to Atha and the Council of Knights. After dining, Sir Nigel and Grafdun went off together to discuss plans for defenses, but first Sir Nigel despatched Graceforth northward to meet with Randolph.

"And don't be getting sidetracked by any comely wenches on the road," called Sir Nigel to the figure now disappearing up the track.

Sir Nigel and Grafdun laughed as some unintelligible, but obviously derogatory reply drifted back. "He'll never live that down," Sir Nigel said. "Poor Graceforth."

Martha retired to a tub of hot water, Galdore to his study and spell-brewing, accompanied by Brock, who professed to have some new device for recording and cataloging information. Moraden remained in the Banquet Hall for a while, passing news of the Faery Realm to Atha before admitting to the weariness suggested earlier and excusing himself. Later that night, a lone figure walked the ramparts of the castle watching a swarm of black wasps circle high above before they headed, as if purposefully directed, northward.

While Galdore and his friends dined in the comfort of Castle Drent, Randolph made a fire with a small spell he had learned from the wizard and toasted some of the provisions from the pack Roots had given him. The sun had set and darkness had descended on the forest. To counter the feeling of loneliness Randolph sang, wishing that he had his lute with him and looking forward to being reunited with his friends and his belongings at Castle Drent. He thought back to the time he had first met Twig and how he had nearly chosen to throw the staff in the ditch. He smiled to himself as he realized how important his decisions were to his destiny and how easy it could be to make a wrong choice in haste. He missed Twig's company and his advice.

> *"Friends are those we trust and know,*
> *As through our life we choose and go*
> *Our way, to meet our destiny.*
> *But beware, careful, lest any*
> *Friend may turn into a foe.*
>
> *But listen here, and listen kind,*
> *The way of others you may find*
> *Is not what it appears to be;*
> *We often look and then we see*
> *Our foes to us as friends might bind.*

But careful needs, as careful be,
Some foes as friends we would not see,
For domination of our land
Is not to be by my own hand.
Such friends will shackle those now free.

My role in life is now quite plain.
The trust of others I must gain,
But never to abuse that trust
In selfishness, I never must
Indulge myself. Be proud, not vain."

Randolph's melodic ballad rang around the forest, and his voice brought quiet and tranquil feelings to the woodland creatures that stopped their nightly labours to listen to his song. But also, floating on the gentle breeze, attracted by the prospect of some merriment, a phantom drifted toward the sound and hovered, for the moment unseen, close by where Randolph lie snug in his bedroll.

"Tiddle diddle fiddle widdle," it said quietly to itself. "So it's music this one likes, eh? Well then, music shall be our ruse to tempt him. Tiddle diddle fiddle widdle, or my name's not Tinkerboo the cobbler." He chuckled.

Ghostly strains of magical music were conjured from the breeze by Tinkerboo as he orchestrated the forest sounds into a hypnotic charm of irresistible beauty and mystique. Like distant bells from a hilltop church on a summer day, the melody echoed and rang in Randolph's mind. At first he thought he was dreaming, but then, realizing he was still awake, he got to his feet and listened, his keen sense of hearing scanning the forest for the cause of the sound. Having determined the direction of the source of the music, he moved toward it, following as if tracking a sweet smell. It seemed to move and skip among the trees, darting first one way and then another, jumping from left to right, now louder, now quieter. Wherever it went, Randolph followed until he was hopelessly lost; then it stopped.

"Tiddle diddle fiddle widdle," Tinkerboo said, hiding his slightly luminous and ghostly form behind a large oak. "Who's there?" Randolph called. "Who is it? Was that you making that music?"

> *"Want to see me? Like my style?*
> *You'll have to make it worth my while.*
> *I'll only show myself to those*
> *Who sing a song or recite some prose.*
> *I've heard you have a pretty voice*
> *So, for you, I'll make the choice.*
> *Sing me a song and I promise you*
> *You'll get to see old Tinkerboo."*

"Tinkerboo?" Randolph said. "Is that your name? Where are you? Come on out, I won't hurt you. Don't be scared."

At that, Tinkerboo took umbrage.

"Don't be scared?" he blustered. "What do you mean, don't be scared? You're the one that's supposed to be scared. I'm the ghost; I'm doing the haunting around here."

Randolph laughed.

"Now you're laughing," Tinkerboo said. "That's not fair. How can I do my job properly if you're going to laugh at me?"

"But you're not scary," Randolph said. "Your music was beautiful, and I want to know how you made it."

"I'm not playing," Tinkerboo said. "If you're not going to be scared, I'm just not going to waste my time." He floated off in search of a more timid subject, leaving Randolph wondering who in Alusia he had been talking to.

Tinkerboo had gone off, leaving Randolph to find his own way back to his camp place. He wouldn't have done that had he thought Randolph might come to any harm. But then, Tinkerboo didn't know of the swarm of black wasps heading toward them and he knew nothing of Randolph's quest. In fact, he was so indignant at Randolph's failure to be scared, and so upset at his own incompetence that he decided there and then not to seek another playmate but to accept his mortal death and move on.

"The time has come for me to journey to the Great Cobbling Halls of the ever after," he announced to the forest. "Farewell brave hearts, may your boots lead you to good fortune."

And with that, he was gone. Never again did the Crumble Hills tinkle with his laughter or echo to the sweet sound of his music; some might say Alusia was a sadder place with his passing. Had Randolph not already faced the wrath of Thrung, he might have been a little more frightened of strange noises in the forest at night and Tinkerboo might not have felt the need to move on. Thrung's influence on all that was good and fun in Alusia was having an effect. However, whether that was to his benefit or his detriment was not yet clear. Certainly, Thrung was a threat to the gentle humour and natural forces of good in the land, but there was a combining of power against him. Randolph sensed that in his encounter with Tinkerboo, brief though it was, he had been involved in such a transformation, and his hatred of Thrung intensified.

"I don't know who or what you were Tinkerboo," he called into the forest. "But may the power of goodness go with you on your travels, and may the power you have bestowed on me ensure the forces of darkness wither and decline. I pledge my soul to upholding your memory. We are the One."

In that place, alone among the trees, a change happened in Randolph. He grew in mental stature and strength, he absorbed the might of the good that was Tinkerboo, he took on a power that was to bring him to the full consciousness of control over his destiny. He vowed to defend the good against all that was evil. Tinkerboo's passing had included a bequest of power. Humble cobbler that he was, had he lived, he too might have been the One. With his final passing, that potential was released to Randolph who knew now, for certain, he was the chosen one. He knelt and gave thanks to the unmet, unseen Tinkerboo, confident in his knowledge that this brief encounter had been more than a chance meeting, more than just a lucky break, much more.

In Castle Drent, Galdore witnessed a flaring of the orb in his study, Martha dreamed of Randolph. A lone figure on the ramparts felt a twinge of pain. All sensed the transformation in Randolph's power; all knew that the discord between good and evil had heightened.

ॐ•ॐ

Randolph awoke feeling refreshed. He felt stronger than ever before. At first, he could not understand where he was or how he had gotten there. His pack and bedroll were nowhere to be seen and although he searched for a distance in every direction, there was no sign of the path he had been following. Thick gray clouds and the forest canopy hid any clue to the sun's direction. As memory of the night's events drifted back, the urgency to move on seized Randolph and he took a best guess at the direction to travel.

If I can find the track again, all I need to do is turn left on it and Castle Drent is only a day away, he thought.

Some short while later, he was able to translate his thought into action as he stumbled from the undergrowth onto a track, turned left, and picked up a steady pace. Randolph still had the map Martha had left for him when he started out for the boglands and this indicated another track should join the path he was following from the left, about half way to the castle. After walking for most of the day between wooded hills, Randolph was delighted to find another track joined him on the left, confirming to him that he was on the right road. Also, he could hear the sound of water off to his left.

"That must be the Swallow," he told himself. "It can't be more than a few more hours to Castle Drent. If I keep up a good speed, I'll be there in time for supper."

He whistled as he walked and he sang out loud, with a, "fah la la and a hey nonnie no."

The dark, overcast sky threatened; rain and thunder rolled in the distance. After walking several hours, Randolph followed the track around the foot of a hill on his right, emerged from the forest, and some short while later came to a fork in the path with a view of mountains in the distance straight ahead of him.

"This can't be right," he said out loud. "There are no mountains of that magnitude near Castle Drent. They can only be the Draken Mountains, and they should be way behind me."

Examining the map again, Randolph worked out his mistake. After being lost in the forest to the southeast of the Crumble Hills, he had mistakenly found the track leading east from Basiltree to the hills and turned left on it toward Devilrock Falls. The track joining his path was that leading northwest from Merrytown. He had spent all day traveling in the wrong direction and was now just north of Devilrock Falls on the road leading from Dark Castle to Fortnum Castle.

"How could I have been so stupid?" He chastised himself. "I've wasted two days."

Evening was drawing in and travel on through the night was not a good option. Randolph needed shelter and from the map calculated that he was now closer to Dark Castle than Castle Drent. Turning right at the junction in the path would likely find him overnight shelter in the foothills of the Draken Mountains and put him within a day's journey of Dark Castle, whereas Castle Drent would more likely be a two-day hike. Grafdun would welcome him and send word to Castle Drent. He may even have Galdore and the others as his guests.

Castle Drent and Dark Castle are equally good options, Randolph thought as he rolled up the map and replaced it in his leather pouch. *My main concern is making contact with at least one member of the council as soon as possible.*

As Randolph uncoiled himself from where he had squatted to study the map, he heard a faint droning sound from somewhere to the south and knew that he needed to find cover quickly. Some half mile from the junction to his right, the path plunged back into the trees that festooned the foothills of the mountains on the left of the track and climbed up over the Crumble Hills to join the Western Forest on the right. Randolph surprised himself with his speed, as he sprinted the distance in less than a couple of minutes, conscious of the fact that he must be hidden before the swarm spotted him. No sooner had he entered the tree line and the cover of the forest when he heard the volume of the droning increase, as the swarm rounded the end of the Crumble Hills. As he looked back, the sun dropped below the western horizon, its last light filtered by the gray rolling clouds, provided a striking backdrop to the silhouetted swarm. The wasps flew in a drawn-out stream across the sky like a long arm and hand reaching, searching, clasping. Randolph was reminded of his close encounter and narrow escape in the ether and he shuddered. He moved further into the forest under the protection of the close growing fir trees, climbing into the foothills of the mountains as he went, seeking some secure nook or cranny in which he might spend the night hidden from the swarm.

❃

By the time Graceforth had reached the Crumble Hills, he could only assume he had somehow missed Randolph and he made his way back to Castle Drent. Shortly after he turned, he spotted something in the forest just off the track and discovered an empty bedroll and pack containing a day's supply of food and water, but there was no person to be seen anywhere. After searching the area for almost an hour, Graceforth strapped them to the saddle of the spare horse he was leading and continued his return.

"Well he's not here," Galdore said to Sir Lionel as he dismounted. "You definitely turned left at the junction and took the track leading up to Merrytown?"

"That's the way I went," Graceforth replied. "Not only did I not see Randolph, but I encountered not one single person on the whole trip, so I was unable to make any inquiries. All I found was this bedroll and pack. I have no idea who they belong to."

"And you went right up as far as the Crumble Hills?" Galdore asked.

"Right up to where they start," the knight said.

"Where's Randolph?" Martha asked as she came across the courtyard.

"We don't know. Sir Lionel can't find him," Galdore said. "All he discovered were these things." He indicated the items strapped to the saddle. "We don't know if they're Randolph's or not."

Martha unstrapped the bedroll held it in both hands and closed her eyes.

"I can sense Randolph from them," she said. "They were in his possession."

Dragon, who had joined the small group in the courtyard, sniffed at the bedroll. She looked at Galdore and, if cats could nod in agreement, that is exactly what she appeared to do.

"Then we must ride north to find him," Galdore said to Martha. "You and I will take the Merrytown road and Grafdun

191

and Brock can follow the path up to Dark Castle. Moraden must return to the Realm to report our lack of progress to his father. He must be kept informed of the increasing risk from Thrung."

"Atha." Galdore called to the king, who had just stepped out into the courtyard. "Can you arrange a party of men to search the Crumble Hills? We've lost Randolph."

"I'll call Sir Nigel now," Atha said and strode off to the armoury.

"Martha, will you find Grafdun, Moraden, and Brock and tell them what we're doing?" Galdore said.

In little more than an hour, the party was ready to leave. Atha led a dozen of his most trusted knights. He headed the group on his sleek black mare. Galdore took up a place at the rear. "Forward men, to the rescue of Randolph and a blow to the evil of Thrung," Atha called.

As he had done once before when a similar party rode to the aid of Graceforth, Atha raised a chainmailed fist above his head signaling for the castle gates to be opened and the rescue party to ride forward. However, this time Graceforth took the place previously occupied by Randolph, and Martha, Brock, and Grafdun were additions to their number. Evening was approaching as they departed the castle. They planned to ride through the night northward. The king and his knights, along with Martha and Galdore would fork left at the track toward Merrytown. Grafdun and Brock would continue due north, heading for Dark Castle to mobilize Grafdun's army. Moraden bid them farewell before making his own preparations to leave. Galdore had asked that he discuss plans with his father for putting the Faery Realm on alert. A few hours into the ride, the party approached the fork in the track where Grafdun and Brock were to separate from the main group. They halted for a while to rest both men and horses. Galdore drew Grafdun aside and spoke to him in low tones.

"All is not well and I am, indeed, troubled by events," Galdore said. "I feel a growing sense of darkness in our midst and, searching with the orb, I have become aware of the presence of creatures of darkness abroad in the kingdom. Our rivers and our skies are no longer safe places. I have seen eyes watching and detected ears listening, some too close for comfort. Go forward with caution, my friend."

Galdore searched deep into Grafdun's dark eyes for reaction to these words. He found nothing more than loyalty and trust, and a determination to protect the kingdom from all that threatened the power of good.

"I will, as always, heed your words of wisdom," Grafdun replied. He grasped Galdore's arm in a gesture of farewell. "And do so in the hope that they bear no deeper warning of treachery or skulduggery than a caution against the dark forces of Thrung."

"Times are not as we might wish or may have held dear in the past," Galdore said. "I can offer you no more advice than to follow your instincts and do whatever must be done."

Dragon, who usually avoided Grafdun, was suddenly at his feet. She nuzzled his ankles and looked up at him as if to say, "Farewell and may good fortune go with you."

"You know, I swear that cat can smile sometimes," Grafdun said, looking down at Dragon. "If only it could talk, we might find we had a lot in common."

Grafdun called for Brock to join him. They mounted and rode off on the path to Dark Castle without looking back again. Galdore stood for some time, alone, watching the space that had been occupied by the now-departed pair.

"I hope I am mistaken," he said quietly to himself.

He scooped up Dragon in his arms and returned to the main party, where Atha, Sir Nigel, Graceforth, and Martha were examining a map and discussing what they might best do to most efficiently cover the ground in their search for Randolph.

"Galdore, Atha thinks it best that we all go on up the track to where Sir Lionel discovered Randolph's pack and then consider our options," Martha said.

"We may find some clue there as to what happened to Randolph, or even what direction he may have taken," Sir Nigel added.

"That sounds sensible," Galdore said. "But we should keep close observation from here onward; we don't know how far along the way Randolph might have progressed."

The party remounted and started forward up the track. Graceforth now rode at the head of the party alongside Atha, seeking to identify the place where he had discovered the pack and bedroll. Two hours before dawn, Graceforth located the place and the party set up a temporary camp for a few hours' rest prior to beginning their search in earnest. Galdore, as usual, paced the ground, unable to relax when urgency played on his mind. Some time earlier, he had heard the drone of the black wasp swarm passing back and forth high overhead, confirming that Thrung's search for Randolph also continued.

"It must be that Randolph is still free from Thrung's clutches." he said to Atha. "We can delay no longer in starting our search. Martha and I will ride on past Devilrock Falls and join the track running to the north of the Crumble Hills. If you and your knights search the mid and westerly end of the hills, Grafdun and his troops will shortly join us to cover the easterly area and into the lower reaches of the Draken Mountains."

After Galdore had spent a short time sitting alone with Dragon, who then disappeared in the direction of Castle Drent, Martha and Galdore mounted and rode at speed through the remainder of the night. Dawn was breaking as they rounded the end of the hills and started along the track leading toward Dark Castle.

૱৵

Randolph stretched and yawned. The hollow in the rockface he had found the previous evening had not protected him from the dampness and chill of the night and his clothes clung to him with an uncomfortable wetness. He also felt a hunger and emerged cautiously, checking the sky and the surrounding area before starting on a collection of breakfast nuts and berries.

"I feel particularly well and strong this morning," Randolph announced to the forest. "In spite of my uncomfortable night. However, I think a small fire to warm myself and dry some of the dampness from my garments would be good."

Randolph summoned up the magic in his soul as Galdore had shown to create the fire spell; the same spell that Randolph had used the previous night to start his fire shortly before he met Tinkerboo. He pointed his finger at the small pile of twigs he had gathered and threw the spark-making energy and the incantation required.

"Alacasam and hulabaloo, make a spark and fire too."

Randolph reeled from the blast he created.

194

"Suffering serpents," he said to himself as he clambered back to his feet. He crossed to examine the small crater he had just blown in the ground. *How did I call up that much energy?*

And then he remembered the feeling after meeting Tinkerboo. And the sprint to the trees at unbelievable speed. And his feeling of strength and wellness this morning in spite of a chill, damp night. *Could it be? Could it be that my small powers have grown that much?*

He closed his eyes and focused his thoughts on Martha and he knew immediately that she and Galdore were close by. In his mind, he could see them approaching on horseback—Galdore astride his huge white stallion and Martha riding a dapple-gray mare. Randolph ran to the track and looked back in the direction of Devilrock Falls. He saw with his eyes exactly what he had visualized in his mind.

"Hello." He called down the track. "Nice to see you!" He waved frantically with both hands high in the air to attract their attention as they galloped toward him.

Galdore was off his horse almost before it had come to a stop, surprising Randolph with his agility. Martha was only seconds behind him, sliding from the saddle as fast as she could to greet Randolph.

"Are you all right?" She pushed passed Galdore in her eagerness to embrace Randolph. "My, you've grown," she said as she clasped him to her and felt the tautness of his strong muscles.

Martha eventually let Randolph go and allowed Galdore access to greet him. He placed his outstretched hands on Randolph's broad shoulders and looked him up and down.

"It is true then, you have taken on a greater power, you are indeed now confirmed as the One," he said. "I will help you bring the power under control."

"Thanks," Randolph replied. "I nearly blew myself up just now trying to light a fire."

Galdore couldn't avoid a wry smile at the thought of a singed and blackened Randolph standing in front of a small explosion with a look of total amazement on his face. He was pleased that Randolph had remained Randolph, even through the transformation to a more powerful being.

"This marks a day to celebrate," Galdore said. "We still have much to do and many bridges to cross but, at least we now have greater power available to defeat Thrung."

Galdore clapped his arm around Randolph's shoulders and steered him to a fallen tree at the side of the track. "Come," he said. "Tell us of your travels and adventures since you disappeared into Heartland's Mound; we must decide on our best course of action." They sat, all three, on the log, while Randolph narrated his experiences in Gnoma, his trauma in the ether with the swarm of black wasps, his landing in the forest, and conversations with Brommel.

"Dragon will be jealous," Martha said. "I wouldn't over-emphasize that bit of the story when we get back to Castle Drent."

Randolph went on to tell of his attack by the squird and his brief visit to Merrytown and Leafy Barkman.

"Ah, he is a good man, lucky you found him when you did," Galdore said at the mention of Leafy.

Finally, Randolph recounted the tale of his almost-meeting with Tinkerboo and how he seemed to take on a greater power and strength after the encounter. Galdore listened carefully and attentively to this part of the story and quizzed Randolph in considerable detail about exactly what was done and said.

"That explains much that Sulaman and I have pondered for several years," Galdore said. "We knew the One had not been finally chosen, and although you came along we were unable to identify the other contender. Now I understand that was because he was suspended in the half-life. That meeting was more important to our quest than you may realize."

∾∾

"Have you gobbin' got down there yet?" Spike's voice echoed menacingly around the cavernous domed ceiling of the old mine.

"Fink so," came Toady's reply. "Gob, my Candles just gobbin' gone out and I can't see a gobbin' fing down 'ere. It's like a coal cellar at midnight."

"Whaja expect?" Spike said, "We're nearly a fousand meters underground 'ere and at least two miles in from the front door."

"Look, you'll 'ave to come down wiv anuvver candle. I daren't move to find me pack wivout being able to see the edge, and it's a bit narrow 'ere."

Spike grabbed on to the hemp rope and swung his leg over the rim of the drop. He felt the stretch of the rope take the strain of his weight as he leaned back into darkness and stood on the face of the shaft wall. The light from his lamp stabbed at the pitch black below as he peered down, probing for the ledge on which Toady stood.

"Looks like we'll need to go down to the next level," Toady called.

He watched the bobbing candlelight above him as Spike edged his way down the shaft.

"How many more levels d'yer reckon we need to go? I fought this would be the place we'd find it," Spike said. He came over to stand beside Toady. "We need to 'ave anuvver look at the chart. Where's your gobbin' pack?"

"Just along the gobbin' ledge there," Toady said.

Spike turned to shine the light from his lamp in the direction Toady indicated. "Where?" Spike asked. "I don't see it."

"Don't be gobbin' stupid," Toady said. "I put it there only a couple of minutes ago, just before me light went out."

"Well it's not 'ere now. But it can't 'ave fallen we'd 'ave 'eard it."

As Spike's lamp dimmed and went out, they heard a shuffling sound along the ledge to their right. It seemed to come from the place where Toady had left his rucksack.

"Quick," Spike said, turning his back toward Toady. "Get the tinder box out the top of me pack."

Toady fumbled with the cord on Spike's pack as the shuffling drew nearer and stopped, it seemed, just a few paces from them. Now they caught the stench; a damp, musty, rotting vegetation smell that enveloped them; and a sort of wheezing, laboured, catarrhal breathing. At last the pack was open, and Toady pulled out the tinder box and struck a spark, relighting the candle. The eerie yellow fluorescence illuminated the ugliest, foulest creature imaginable. The slavering mouth dripped green mucus as it oozed between wrinkled gums; the wart-encrusted face resembled that of a semi-decomposed corpse, except for what looked liked open weeping, pus-filled sores covering the whole head, indicating that it was a living entity of some description. The rest of the stunted, misshapen body appeared to be smeared with a yellow slime.

"Dad?" Spike said. "What you doing down 'ere? I told you to wait up on the fifth level. You scared the gobbin' daylights out of us. We fought you was one of the Shawadarg Trolls."

The ugly mouth creased into an alarmingly wide grin, spraying green grunge over Spike and Toady. "Us goblins gotta stick together," Spike's dad said. "I told you there wuz an easier way down to the lower levels. All that crazy dangling on ropes never did nobody no good. If we wuz meant to go up and down rock faces we'd 'ave been born wiv claws—woodenwee."

"But it's much more gobbin' fun," Toady said. "Much more fun than just coming down the old tunnel road."

"And it avoids the old slime pit," Spike added. "Which you obviously didn't. It looks like you fell in 'ead first . . . and you're covered in slimy snails."

"Not so steady on me pins as I used t'be," the old goblin said. "And it's dark in the tunnel. Those cheap candles you got are no good. They keep goin' out."

"I know," Toady said. "Both our lamps 'ave given up on us as well. 'Ave you seen my backpack? I've got some good candles in there."

"Yez," Spike's dad replied. "Dragged it just into the tunnel mouth there; it wuz perched right on the edge."

The three goblins crouched in the tunnel mouth around Toady's rucksack and replaced and lit their lamp candles. The tunnel was suddenly illuminated like day.

"That's gobbin' better," Toady said.

Spike looked at his father. "I'm not sure about that," he said. "I fink 'e was better in the dark. Clean yourself up, Dad; you're gobbin' disgusting. And when you've done that, get a brew going, will yer? If y'er goin' to be 'ere, yer might as well make yerself useful. Toady and I are goin' to 'ave anuvver look at the chart."

Three hundred meters below them something stirred, and the mountain trembled.

꙰

An aeon had passed since anyone had disturbed Shawadarg. She was mistress of the eclectic doctrines of the evil Gnostics, practiced in the redemption of the soul from black matter through dark spiritual knowledge. Shawadarg guarded the secret of the birth of evil as it was first drawn from the original creation—to that extent Shawadarg was the guardian of Thrung's essence. Shawadarg's charge was the Talisman of Power, the runes that could be disclosed to no living creature. For the power of darkness to be understood by the living was forbidden by Thrung. Legend told of the talisman and of its location deep within the mountain, protected in the lair of a most fearsome creature. Some said it was so fearsome that even to gaze on its countenance brought instant death of a kind so horrible that the perpetrator would be banished to the fires of eternity; and the end of the world would be heralded, where all would be assimilated into evil. Shawadarg stirred and the mountain trembled.

Squatting in the tunnel of the ancient mine, Spike, Toady, and a now less gruesome Spike's dad felt a tremor. "Wazzat?" The old goblin spilled the contents of his mug into Toady's boot.

"Watch out," Toady shouted as he jumped up, shaking the scalding brew from his foot and cracking his head on the low ceiling of the tunnel.

Spike spun round at the commotion, knocking the chart into the candle that had just produced the hot beverage. It flamed in an instant and was gone into gray ash.

"You gobbin' fool," Spike yelled, "Look what you've gobbin' made me do."

"Me?" Toady shouted back, "It was gobbin' 'im."

"Wuzznt my fault," the old goblin retorted. "Wuz the mountain. It knows we'z cumin'."

A second tremor brought silence to the small group.

"It knows we'z cumin'," the old goblin repeated.

"It might know weeezzzz gobbin' cuumminnn, but wivout the gobbin' chart, we don't know where weeeezzzzz gobbin' gowwwin, do we?" Spike mocked the old goblin's speech.

"But we can't be far off," Toady said. "The chart seemed to show just anuvver level down straight below us. It was labelled 'Minus Level Six' or somefin' like that."

"I knowz the way."

Toady and Spike turned together to regard the old goblin.

"What did you say?" Spike asked.

"I knowz the way," his father repeated. "What Toady just said, 'Minus Level Six'. When I wuz workin' here in the mine as a lad, we wuzn't allowed near the door to 'Minus Level Six.' Always barred and bolted it wuz—dangerous; no air, we wuz told."

"Where's the gobbin' door?" Toady squealed.

"A bit up the tunnel 'ere," the old goblin said. "I'll show-zeee."

The big old black wooden door boasted heavy metal hinges fastened with huge bolts to the thick planks. Each of the three keyholes were nearly large enough to insert a clenched fist, and the iron bars clamped across the door and its frame were secured with strong padlocks and steel pins.

"That's no gobbin' good," Toady said. We'll never get fru there wivout the keys. I vote we go back to the ropes and down the gobbin' shaft."

"Could be our best choice," Spike agreed. "I can't see any gobbin' way were going to prise this open."

"I knowz where the keyz iz."

For the second time in just a few minutes, Spike and Toady turned in unison to face the old goblin, who produced a bunch of enormous keys from behind a rock. "Picked 'em up on the way down. Juzt in case."

The mountain shuddered again as Shawadarg turned uneasily.

෨෬

Shawadarg was angry. *Not since prelapsarian times had there been a threat to the talisman by living beings. Even during the goblin's mining activities, the lair containing the talisman had been protected. But now, what was all this noise and activity by the doorway to the steps of eternity? And jangling keys—could that be the sound of jangling keys?* Shawadarg turned uneasily and the mountain shuddered.

200

❧

The rusty locks turned with difficulty, and the heavy bars and steel pins took the strength of all three goblins to lift them clear of their fastenings. The hinges shrieked displeasure as the weighty door swung open, revealing a spiral of stairs, hewn from the bare rock, descending into the gloom below. Spike took the lead and moved forward through the doorway onto the first step. As he entered the chamber of the stairwell, he felt an unfamiliar weight on his shoulders. He felt his usual carefree mood disperse and, suddenly, he knew he was in the presence of wickedness that terrified even him. He turned to leave the chamber, to re-cross the threshold of the huge doorway, but he couldn't. He could only go on, drawn down to face the anger of Shawadarg.

❧

As Spike's dad and Toady watched, they saw Spike shimmer and disappear, as if transported by the portal of the doorway to some other place in time or space. They watched, transfixed, as the heavy door slowly swung closed, separating them from Spike, as he was gone to answer for the disturbance of Shawadarg.

❧

Spike felt as if he was floating. He looked down and found that he was indeed suspended in mid-air and all around him was, at the same time, both light and dark, both hot and cold, soft and hard, loud and quiet. He had a sense of being everywhere at the same instant in time; he felt as if he was one with the whole of existence—and through his mind went the silly thought: *And me an 'umble goblin of lowly breeding—I'm not even a goblin prince.*

"You're much more than a prince but also less than a lowly bred goblin," floated a voice that came from nowhere and went everywhere. "You are in the presence of Shawadarg—that makes you more than a prince. However, you have disturbed my slumber and that makes you a lowly worm."

"B . . . B . . . B . . . But," stammered Spike. "I don't want to be . . .," his voice trailed off as Shawadarg spoke again.

"WANT?" boomed the disembodied voice. "WANT?" And then continuing in a whisper: "What you want is of no consequence; you are but a token in the destiny of the universe."

"T . . . T . . . T . . . Token." Spike quaked. "W . . . W . . . W . . . What's . . . s . . . sort of t . . . t . . . t . . . token?"

"You are the meanest worm that ever crawled on any earth. You are unworthy, you are goblin, you are my servant, and you are master of nothing. Speak now, for your words are those by which you shall be judged."

"That, what you said," Spike stammered. "That's what I'd come to tell yer. I'm a worm, and . . . and . . . and . . . Thrung's awake. He's been getting' me and Toady to stir up trouble. And now . . . and now . . . he's sent us up 'ere to wake you."

Suddenly Spike found himself standing in the tunnel beside his dad and Toady. "Wherez you bin," his Dad asked. "It wuz very misty in there. You looked like you disappeared, and why'd you shut the door behind you?"

"Dunnow," Spike said. "But I think we need to gobbin' get outta 'ere quick. I fink yer was right about the gobbin' poison gas down there."

Toady and the old goblin looked at Spike but, before they could speak further, he swung his pack onto his back and rushed off up the tunnel. Shawadarg roared her evil amusement and the mountain trembled. Toady and the old goblin overtook Spike at speed.

෨✎ᡃ

"Anyway, we shouldn't sit around here. Time enough to talk more when we get to safety," Martha said. "I suggest we head toward Dark Castle, that's the nearest and Brock and Grafdun will be there by now."

"Yes," Galdore agreed. "That had been my thought also. We can send out word to Atha and the knights to join us there."

"Where's Moraden?" Randolph asked.

"He's gone back to the Realm to update his father on the danger," Martha replied.

"I've asked him to join us again in three days' time at Castle Drent," Galdore added.

The three mounted the horses, Randolph riding behind Galdore on the white stallion, and set off eastward for Dark Castle. A few miles on, they emerged from the thick forest that had hidden Randolph from the swarm and traveled for a while on the open track. Having left the forest curtain some miles behind, it was not a good time to hear the low drone of the swarm. Martha urged her horse forward. Galdore spoke a word to his mount and it responded immediately, gathering speed as they raced along the track, seeking a place to take cover, away from the probing eyes of the black wasps.

"The Old Goblin Mines!" Galdore shouted to Martha.

The rushing wind created by their speed grabbed his words and hurled them to Martha's ears.

"They start about a mile up the track. We can take cover there."

The noise of the swarm grew louder and as Randolph looked back, he saw the wasps transform into the creature that nearly caught him before. The claw-like hands and searing razor nails slashed at the empty air in practice as the creature dived from the sky toward them.

"Faster," he shrieked in Galdore's ear. "It's seen us."

As the creature plummeted down, they rounded a shallow bend in the track and saw an entrance to the old mines just ahead. The great solid wooden gates stood ajar and as they reached them, the three slid from their mounts and rushed inside the mine in a single, flowing movement as if they were performing a slow, elegant dance. Time seemed to slow for Randolph and he saw every detail of every motion in infinite detail.

"Closumos, colosumos!" Galdore yelled as he directed a stream of lightning bolts toward the doors. "Closumos, colosumos. Sealumos, sealoffumos!"

The old hinges groaned and creaked as they swung the lumbering door closed and sealed tightly. They were plunged into total darkness. Galdore waved his hands into the air and the walls emitted a low glow sufficient for them to see they were in a tunnel not much more than standing height and about an outstretched arm's span wide. From outside they heard a shriek of frustration as the creature reached the doors just too late to slide inside. Randolph felt the wound on his cheek throbbing and he raised his hand to find it hot to the touch. Galdore reached into his cloak and extracted a phial from which he shook a powder onto the wound.

"That will need more treatment than I can give here," Galdore said. "I think it will flare up whenever the creature comes close and will get slowly worse, rather than better, until I can counter the dark spell that it contains. That is the way of such evil wheals."

"What now?" Randolph asked. "We can't go back outside; the swarm or whatever that creature is, knows we're in here."

"And we can't stay here forever," Martha said.

"And we can't get out again even if we wanted to," Galdore said. "That sealing spell won't be breakable for years. Our only option is to follow the tunnels through the mines and seek another exit, preferably much closer to Dark Castle."

"Do you know the way through the mines?" Randolph asked.

"No," Galdore said. "I've never been in here before, but it shouldn't be difficult, I don't believe the tunnel system is likely to be complex. The goblins wouldn't have given any more labour to digging them than was absolutely necessary to reach the gold seams. If we're lucky there will be just one straight tunnel running all the way along the front of the mountain range and then just side tunnels off to each seam."

Randolph examined the map he had once again unrolled from his pouch. "As long as we stay on the main tunnel we should be able to get half way to Dark Castle without leaving the cover of the mine."

"Sounds like a plan," Martha said. "Let's go then."

The tunnel walls responded to the wizard's magic, glowing faintly as they approached each section, fading back into blackness behind them. Randolph used the narrowness of the tunnel as an excuse to stay close to Martha, brushing and touching her at every opportunity. She didn't seem to notice, her focus being ahead as she led the small party through the mine. Randolph resolved that when they reached Dark Castle he would ensure that he created an opportunity to spend time alone with Martha.

It seemed that Galdore had been right in his assumption about one long tunnel with subsidiary passages at intervals leading off into the depths of the mountain toward the old, now exhausted, gold veins. Until, that is, they reached a chamber off which led four tunnels of equal size. It was here they felt the tremor that, way below them, filled Toady's boot with hot brew.

"What the serpent's tail was that?" Randolph said.

"Don't know," Galdore replied. "But I sense it didn't come from a source likely to be favorable to us. On the other hand, probably only a mild earth tremor and nothing to be particularly worried about. These mines have stood for years; there's no reason they should fall down today."

They were silent as a second tremor shook the floor of the chamber. "Whatever it is, I don't want to hang around for too many more of them," Randolph said.

"But we can't just guess at which tunnel to take," Martha said. "We could get lost somewhere down in the inner mine, and who knows what lurks there. We have to choose the right passage to lead us toward Dark Castle or out onto the track."

"How are we going to do that?" Randolph asked as he turned to Galdore.

"If we use a bit of logic, examine each tunnel, and try a direction spell, we should be fairly certain to get the right one," Galdore replied, as if he did this sort of thing all the time. "If we combine your new strength of mind, my magic, and Martha's practical approach, we're sure to get the right result."

Galdore's confident words made Martha and Randolph feel a little better, but that was mainly because they couldn't see the crossed fingers on his hands as he held them clasped behind his back. Even wizards need the odd lucky break.

"Here," Randolph said. "I'll look at the map again; it might give us some general direction." He unfolded it onto the earth floor of the chamber.

"Martha and I will go about a hundred paces into each tunnel in turn while you do that. We'll see if we can get any clues about where they might lead."

Randolph bent to his map task, trying to calculate how far through the mountain they might already have walked. Galdore and Martha entered the first tunnel to their right, but soon re-emerged.

"That one's blocked only about twenty paces in," Martha said. "We'll try the second one."

Randolph worked out that by the number of paces they had taken since entering the mine and the time he estimated they had been walking, they had probably reached the point on the map that showed the greatest mass of mountain. Logically, he thought, this would be where there might be several tunnels going off to different seams in different directions. He also thought that the right-hand tunnel, which Martha and Galdore had found was now blocked, was probably originally a main entrance to the mine. He thought it likely that the third tunnel from the right; the one leading the most straight on; would be the best option. He stood, folded the map, and moved toward the second tunnel mouth to await the other's return. As he did so, there was a tremor and the mountain shuddered for a third time, but now more fiercely.

"Galdore," he called into the passage. His words were drowned by the crash of falling rock as the tunnel ceiling collapsed without warning, blowing him backward into the chamber, where he landed spread-eagled on his back, and for an instant, stunned by the force of the blow. Regaining his senses quickly, he leapt back to the tunnel mouth but his surroundings dimmed into pitch black as he reached the opening and the walls lost their magic glow.

"Galdore . . . Martha," he yelled, terrified. "Can you hear me? Galdore, are you there? Martha, are you all right? Can you hear me?"

His call was met only by silence. Randolph sank to his knees. He felt fear grip his stomach and his heart pounded, sending a gushing sound coursing through his temples. He curled, covering his head with his hands and cringed like an embryo, wrapping himself into a tight ball, unable to think, incapable of movement. Terror and panic seized him and he heard himself babbling. How long he remained in that position he did not know but, as he crouched there alone and afraid, he felt the mountain shudder again. He unwound himself to a sitting position and then, on all fours, felt his way forward into the tunnel. He was calmer now and managed, by feel, to establish that the rock fall had completely blocked the passage. His hope was that Galdore and Martha were well away from the other side of the collapse and that they had some means of escape to the outside. Randolph's feeling of dread had not been so much for himself; he still had two more tunnels as potential escape paths; Martha and Galdore had only the one.

I must get out, I must get to Dark Castle and get help from Grafdun, Randolph thought.

Feeling his way back to the chamber, he maintained contact with the wall and followed it around to the entrance into the next passageway. Once he had located it, he slid down the wall to a sitting position and called his brain to order in an attempt to orient himself and formulate some sort of plan.

Galdore and Martha entered the second tunnel and made their way forward.

"This looks more hopeful," Martha said. "There are dead leaves and twigs up ahead on the ground."

"Yes," Galdore said, shaking his right foot. "And I've just stepped in a small package that some friendly animal has left right in the middle of the passageway."

"That's good," Martha said.

"What do you mean good?" Galdore said. "It's not good. It's all squidged between my toes; it's horrible."

"I didn't mean good you trod in it," Martha giggled.

"Oh, well as long as you meant it's a good sign that this leads to an opening, then I'll forgive you," Galdore grumbled.

"Actually," Martha laughed. "I didn't mean that either. I meant it's good because I thought for a minute it was you making that nasty smell."

Martha had to stop for a minute as she shook with laughter at Galdore's ungainly cavortings in his effort to wipe his sandal and foot clean. Still grumbling, Galdore moved up along the tunnel to join Martha.

"Phew," Martha said. "Go on ahead will you, and stay at least ten paces away from me. I only hope this passage leads to some fresh air."

No sooner had Martha spoken than there was a crashing sound from behind and a blast threw her into Galdore's back. They struggled to their feet.

"The tunnel's collapsed right behind us!" Galdore shouted. "Quick run forward in case more of the roof caves in."

They moved quickly along the passage for about forty paces until they felt they were safe from the immediate danger.

"That was a close one," Martha said, wiping the sweat from her brow and streaking her face with dust. "We must go back and check if we can still get through to Randolph."

"Wait a moment," Galdore said. He grasped Martha's arm, restraining her from dashing back down the tunnel. "Let's just make sure the collapse has finished. We need to go carefully."

There came another tremor but no more rock fell. After a few minutes, they edged back down the tunnel checking the walls and roof as they went.

"It seems fairly sound," Galdore said. "But be ready to make a dash if there's any sign of more movement."

But the tunnel remained secure and they worked their way back to the fall, which they discovered completely blocked the passageway.

"This looks like a major collapse," Galdore said. "It's as if the whole side of the mountain has sat down. There's no way we're going back through there without a gang of miners and tools."

"But what about Randolph" Martha cried. "How will he get out. Randolph? Randolph, can you hear me?"

But only silence replied.

"Come," Galdore said. "Let's see if we can get out of here. We can't do anything to help him unless we can find an exit. We need to get to Dark Castle as quickly as we can."

They turned and retraced their footsteps. Well, almost; Galdore made a point of avoiding one particular step he had taken earlier. Suddenly Martha stopped.

"Sssshhh," she said. "Did you hear anything?"

"No," Galdore replied. "What was it?"

"Sounded like running feet," she said.

But all was silent.

"Must have imagined it," she said as a breeze of fresh air reached her nostrils and the chirruping of a bird caught the attention of her sensitive hearing.

Five hundred paces and several sharp twists and turns later, she and Galdore emerged into a watery evening sunlight. They narrowly missed seeing three goblins, running like the wind, who had popped from a hidden adjacent tunnel mouth a few minutes earlier and darted, like scared rabbits, across the track and up the bank opposite, away into the forest that adorned the Crumble Hills. They were still running when they blundered into a group of knights sporting the crest of the house of Dondrenton on their shields. Galdore whistled a shrill call and his white stallion appeared, galloping along the track, closely followed by Martha's dapple-gray mount.

꙰∘ଈ

Randolph was regaining his composure, but try as he might he could not visualize Martha and Galdore, something was blocking his thoughts.

Well, he thought to himself, *Let's look on the bright side. There's no way the black wasps can get me in here; I'm all in one piece; my choice of tunnel to follow has been reduced to two; and I'm closer to Dark Castle than I was this morning. Not a bad list of positives.*

Randolph's logic told him that the third tunnel; the one by which he now sat, was the best choice. He figured that the fourth led directly into the mountain, probably to one of the main seams. Suddenly he realized that being thrown into the chamber by the blast had torn his belt from his waist, and his sword and his leather pouch containing the map were somewhere in the darkness on the chamber floor.

I must find them before I go on, he thought. *But how can I be sure of getting back to this tunnel if I go off feeling all around the floor of the chamber in the pitch dark?*

His dilemma was soon solved as he felt the ground immediately around where he sat to find that it was covered with loose stones of various sizes.

If I build a trail of stones behind me, and search the floor in a pattern of squares I'll be able to find my way back easily, he thought. *And Galdore would be proud of the initiative!*

By the time Randolph located his belt and its attachments, he had built a network of small squares, lines, and arrows behind him giving a clear tactile indication of the route back to the third tunnel. He sat for a moment in what he judged to be about the center of the chamber, cross-legged and quite proud of himself. The mountain trembled as Shawadarg reared from her lair and roared a fearsome warning to any that might hear her. A second, more powerful bellow and the mountain quivered, as if itself in awe of her dark power. Randolph's carefully laid trail of stones vibrated, rolled, and shifted on the dusty floor of the chamber as it shook with the violence of Shawadarg's awakening. As he sat there in total darkness, now looking and feeling less smug about his cleverness, Randolph thought he could detect a very faint glow outlining the entrance to one of the tunnels. But, the harder he stared into the blackness, the more he was convinced that his eyes were playing tricks on him. In the end, he shut them and relaxed for a while, planning to look afresh in a moment or two. When he opened his eyes again, the faint outline still seemed to be there in the same place as before.

"It can only be daylight," he said to himself. "Nothing else down here would create a glow like that."

Walking slowly, hand extended in front of him, he shuffled toward the infinitesimal glimmer ahead and passed into the mouth of the passageway. Once inside the tunnel, he located the wall and felt his way gingerly along, happy to find that the faint glow increased a little as he progressed.

Strange though; it must surely be after sunset now. How can there still be a glow of daylight? he thought.

Randolph had mistaken the orange glow of Shawadarg's lair for the evening sun and was now progressing further and deeper into the bowels of the mountain along the fourth tunnel. With every step, he descended unknowingly further down toward what the goblin miners of the past had called Minus Level Six, into Shawadarg's bed-chamber, to the place where she lay guarding the Talisman of Power, into Shawadarg's lair. Randolph stopped to rest and to think about what he should now do. He felt cut off and alone. He wished he could reach out to Martha and Galdore but he knew that, although he was the One, he was also only one among many reaching hands. A song came into his head and he sang quietly to himself.

"Dark nights reach out, touching the shadows of minds.
Somewhere in the maze of blackness are feelings that resign
Themselves to the world and all that is good and bad.

Tangled webs of sorrow, mingle with sparkling times of
laughter,
And all are entwined in a lacework, patterns of joy and
disaster,
Heralded by the setting sun, portraying glory that is both
happy and sad.

Reach out to me dark night, and touch the way I am.
Let me understand how I, too, can be part of the shifting
sands
Of time and space, but still retain the dignity that I had.

I cry out in my weakness, in the darkness and the gloom,
I stretch my hand, I pray for sight, but still there is no
room
For me to find the peace, the quietness of soul, to make me
glad.

Then suddenly a crystal flashes, somewhere in the night.
The beams strike out, caress my eyes, and show me there is
light.
And in this glow, I see my place among other reaching
hands."

His words gave him strength and he could feel his path was the right path. But he also sensed immense danger. Standing determinedly, he drew his sword and started on down the tunnel to meet whatever lay ahead.

⋻

In her lair, Shawadarg sensed a presence.

It's not those stupid goblins, she thought to herself. *No, it's something more dangerous and threatening, and it comes closer. I must crush it now, before it grows too powerful.*

211

Shawadarg reared and took on substance, transforming into a monster of terrible proportions and there, in the arena of her cavernous lair, she crouched and waited, watching each of the entrances as she felt Randolph's presence grow closer. As he entered the lair and peered through the orange glow that filled the cavern, Randolph couldn't rid himself of a picture in his mind of gladiators at the ancient games. He carried only a sword rather than a three-pronged spear and a net, but he sensed a weakness in the embodiment of evil that faced him. If only he could find it.

Significantly vulnerable; a pussycat by comparison to Thrung, was the phrase that leapt into his mind.

But as Randolph stood there alone on the perimeter of the huge arena, he spotted Shawadarg crouching in the center of the cavern.

"Significantly more vulnerable, my arse," Randolph said to himself. "And if that's a pussycat, I'll eat my breeches."

Shawadarg eased herself into a standing position and unfurled her wings. The shimmering crest of head scales perched above the long snout, culminating in flared, steaming nostrils, making her, in Randolph's eyes, very dragon-like. A forked, snake tongue tasted the air, flicking droplets of blood-red saliva in a sunset shower onto the floor of the cavern. Her mouth parted slightly to reveal several rows of needle-sharp teeth with four dagger fangs standing like sentries at the gates to Hades. Each side of the crest sprouted rainbow horns about two feet long and sharpened to a fine point. Evil eyes reflected the light from the cavern's glow in silvered plates with black holes like centered tunnels leading to terrible darkness within. Shawadarg was glorious in her terror—a magnificent, petrifying spectacle of evil power and strength, but somehow incongruously beautiful in all her colorful splendor. Shawadarg roared and Randolph felt the hot, sticky wind of her foul breath flood over him. He called on all the powers of goodness and light for his safe deliverance. He cursed the forces of darkness. He prayed to any god who would listen as he felt the terror of death descend on his mind and freeze his body to the dusty ground beneath his feet. Shawadarg moved toward Randolph, displaying her feet and long talon claws. Even her tail was spined with thorn-like spikes designed to deal out instant death with a cavalier swish and lunge.

212

"There must be a weakness," Randolph said to himself as he stood transfixed with the terror of Shawadarg's seemingly slow but menacing approach.

And then he heard it. It sounded like Sulaman's voice.

"Soft spot, go for the soft spot."

"Sulaman?" Randolph called. "Is that you?"

But instantly he realized the voice was in his head.

Randolph snapped back to conscious attention.

"Third rib." He heard the voice sing out again in his head over the roar of Shawadarg. "Just behind the front leg; and mind the tail."

Randolph moved forward to meet the monster. They circled each other as if performing some terrible ritual mime; the dance of death. Randolph lapsed into the rhythm of a folk dance he had once learned as a young boy. Step, step, turn; bend, step, turn; one, two, three; step, step, turn; bend, two, three; step two, three; one, two, three; glide, turn, bend—and the mantra-like rhythm became hypnotic lullaby sounds, captivating Randolph's mind and calming his racing, pounding heart. As he moved, his gestures and steps flowed with the grace of a gliding swan. He started to hum quietly to himself, a tantalizing, deep murmur—a sound so rich that Shawadarg seemed entranced. The cavern resonated with the sound and amplified the base pitch until Randolph felt the very walls vibrate and shake with the magic of the sound. He felt strong again and fear had left his mind. He sang.

> *"The breeze and I were lovers once;*
> *The wind and I we kissed.*
> *But I grew old and the wind stayed young,*
> *My love I sorely missed.*
>
> *The trees and I, we were as one.*
> *The woods became my friend,*
> *I yearned to stay forever young,*
> *Our friendship not to end.*
>
> *Come stay with me, come be my love,*
> *Whispered nature to my ears.*
> *Our love will be forever true,*
> *However long the years."*

The wind came, even to that dark place, but it lifted only a part of him. Above the trance-like state that Randolph seemed to have induced for himself and beast alike, floated his own consciousness. He looked down from on high, observing from some detached platform, the scene below, as a man and a dragon engaged in a ballet of movement, circling and turning about each other in perfect harmony. As his mind flew on the wind, he realized the man below was himself. He was, somehow, separated from his body, watching as he and the dragon paced and circled each other. From somewhere in his head, the voice called again: "Watch out for the tail."

Too late, Randolph watched himself slip as he turned on the dusty floor of the cavern. He was conscious of a deep stabbing pain that penetrated his body, his very essence. He felt the shock of the tail spines as they touched his heart and stopped its life-giving beat. All went black in Randolph's mind down in the arena, but up above the gruesome scene, up high in the dome of the lair, was a perspective that he retained. He watched, awe-struck, as his body crumpled and slumped lifeless in the blood-soaked earth of the cavern floor.

Is that it? Randolph was conscious of thought. *Am I dead? Has the monster killed me?*

He could see his motionless body lying there below, but his mind floated somewhere in the cavern, suspended in mid-air, observing the scene below as Shawadarg pawed at the corpse as if playing with a rag doll. He watched as the evil creature obviously became satisfied at the completeness of the defeat, grew bored, and moved off to some other part of the lair.

Chapter Nine
The Baron of Dark Castle

The Entrance Gates
to Dark Castle

DARK CASTLE was a fortress. Its smooth stone exterior reflected the surrounding plain and the encircling moats and watercourses protected its raised position on a central mound. The four towers, positioned at each corner of the square construction, gave a symmetry that delivered a clear message of organisation and efficiency to any observer. In the center of the south-facing rampart, the portcullis shielded two enormous black wooden doors and at a high level the whole perimeter wall was peppered with arrow-slot windows. Dark Castle was built to be impenetrable and that's the way Grafdun liked it. In many ways, Grafdun was as impenetrable as his castle; until, that is, he had satisfied himself of the trustworthiness of a person and invited them into his inner circle of comrades. Grafdun was a leader respected by his men and friends alike. He was fair, honest, and loyal, giving them the best possible in return for their dependability. However, he was a hard taskmaster, treating laziness and weakness harshly. His men knew this and knew they were free to leave his service at any time, but none ever did.

"Serve me loyally, with a true heart and you shall just have reward," he would often say. "Serve me disloyally and with bad grace and you shall have just reward." This he would say with a deep growl of a laugh.

His hospitality and warmth of welcome to approved guests rivaled that of the king and Castle Drent, but guests were invited or known friends rather than speculative passersby. Two such known friends rode speedily toward the entrance, crossed the drawbridge, and reached the portcullis.

"Ring the bell will you?" Galdore said to Martha.

Martha hauled on the long rope that hung from the arch of the entrance and a gong-like bell echoed inside the castle walls.

A peep-hole slid open and eyes peered at Galdore and Martha.

"State your business and your names," said a voice that was obviously attached to the eyes. "Friend or foe?"

"Is that you, Theodore?" Galdore asked. "Stop pissing about and let us in, will you; we're in a hurry."

The voice laughed and one of the huge doors started to creak open. Galdore and Martha dismounted just inside as Theodore returned the door to its closed position and came over to greet them.

"Good morning and good to see you both up and about so early," he said. "Grafdun and Brock arrived last evening; I think you'll find them up in the Great Hall. I understand we might have a search on our hands."

"Yes," Martha replied. "But not the one you've heard about. We found Randolph once, but now we've lost him again in the Old Goblin Mines. There's been a rock fall and it's blocked the tunnel. Randolph's on the inside somewhere."

"Best get up to the hall then," Theodore said. "They're making plans to start searching the forest and the mountains. We'll catch up with news later. And remind Grafdun that we've got some old maps of the mines in the store. They'll be useful," he called after them as they crossed the courtyard and went into the central building that housed the stairs up to the Great Hall.

"Thanks," Galdore called back. "See you later."

As they entered the hall, Grafdun and Brock looked up from the long trestle table on which they had spread out many maps of the surrounding area.

"Brock's worked out a brilliant search pattern for the men to find Randolph in the shortest possible time," Grafdun said. "I think it's our best chance of . . .," his voice trailed off in response to Galdore's raised hand.

"We know where he is," Galdore said.

"Where?" Brock asked. He got up from the table and came over to greet Galdore with a warm handshake. "Where is he?"

"He's trapped in the Old Goblin Mines," Martha said. "We need to get to him quickly. There's been a collapse in the mine from some sort of earth tremor. He might be hurt. We've ridden through the night to get here."

Brock's look of concern was obviously sincere.

"Theodore said to remind you about the old maps in the store," Galdore said.

"I'll get them now," Grafdun replied. He hurried off, saying, "I'll be back in a few minutes."

"Tell me what happened," Brock said.

Galdore and Martha related the story of the last day as Brock listened intently, making several notes on his parchment pad. His face became more concerned as he listened.

"I know those mines well," he said. "I was involved in organizing the digging of the later tunnels. It was many, many years ago now, but the system isn't complicated and there are several entrances. As long as he wasn't hurt by the rock fall and as long as he doesn't wander to the lower depths, he'll come to no harm."

"What's in the lower depths?" Martha queried.

Brock looked nervously at Galdore.

"Go on," Galdore said. "Tell us."

"Well, I don't know if there's any truth in it but there was always a rumour that somewhere, in the innermost caverns, deep under the biggest mass of mountain, below the mine workings was where Shawadarg's Lair was located," Brock said.

"You're not telling that stupid story about Shawadarg's Lair being in the Draken Mountains are you?" Grafdun came back into the Hall. "That's just a tale invented by the goblin gangmasters to scare the new recruits."

"I'm not so sure about that," Brock replied. "I've got notes that I made many years ago of strange happenings in those mines. Things that have never been explained. I don't think we can be over-cautious."

"Well, I've been in there many times," Grafdun said. "And nothing's ever chased me."

"Anything you met in there would be more likely to run away from you than chase you," Martha laughed. "I bet the notes Brock has got about strange happenings are from people who have seen you in there."

Grafdun put on a hurt look and Martha gave him a hug.

"You can't help being scary," she said and laughed again.

"Look, stop your messing, both of you," Galdore said. "We've got work to do and I think Brock's counsel is wise. We can't be over-cautious; Randolph's life could be at stake."

"Come." Brock laid the mine maps out on the table. "Let's get ourselves organized."

Galdore crossed to the table and leaned on it opposite Brock. Brock looked up at Galdore and met his direct gaze. "It isn't you . . . is it?" Galdore said, combining statement and question in one phrase.

"No," Brock replied, drawing out the word and shaking his head. "It isn't me, but I don't know who it is yet. At one point I even thought it might be you, but I know now that isn't the case." He turned his attention back to the maps as Martha and Grafdun gathered around the table.

"I'm glad it's not you, my friend," Galdore said as he smiled at Brock. "I'm glad it's not you."

❧

Randolph floated for a while, staring down at his own body lying crumpled, broken, and bleeding in the center of Shawadarg's Lair. He could taste salt in the air. The wind had gone now, but he still flew above that grim scene below. He couldn't believe this was where it ended. He had never visualized his death. It was not something that had even crossed his mind. *I'm too young*, was all he could think. *I can't be dead. I haven't lived yet; and I haven't said goodbye to anybody. Martha, I can't leave now, I can't.*

As these thoughts repeated over and over in his mind, he felt himself drifting upward, up to the high-domed roof of the cavern, above what appeared to be his final resting place. *What a horrible place to die*, he thought. *Here in the lair of an evil, dark creature, alone and unattended. What will become of my body? I hope that foul serpent doesn't eat it.*

He drifted higher until he reached the rock ceiling, but he didn't stop there. He floated on through the stone, up through the rock and earth forming the mass of the mountain, and out into the air under the starlit sky. He hovered, no longer able to see back down through the mass of silt and boulders; he could no longer see the lair or his own bodily remains.

> *"Here . . . am . . . I*
> *Under the moon, up high in the cold night sky.*
> *Where . . . are . . . you?*
> *When you look up, can you see the same moon too?*
> *Where . . .are . . .we?*
> *Now we can't be together under the greenwood tree.*
>
> *So love, love me do,*
> *You know I love you,*
> *Your eyes are the only thing I see.*
>
> *Because, I was the storyteller, I came from here and there,*
> *I used to give you rhyme and rhythm, then go, I know not*
> *where.*
> *But now, my destiny is written; I've lost my true love's*
> *gentle hand,*
> *So now, I'll wait for you forever, in the distant afterland."*

"Martha," Randolph cried. "I don't want to leave you, I don't want to go."

He felt a warm tear trickle down his cheek and watched it fall, bursting into minute droplets as it splashed on the mountain peak below him.

"So sad," a voice beside him said. "And such a pretty song."

Randolph turned to face a floating figure. "You?" it said to him. "What are you doing here; I said I wasn't playing with you."

"Pardon?" Randolph asked. "Who are you?"

"Who was I, you mean," the figure sulkily said.

"All right," Randolph said. "Who were you?"

"Tinkerboo," the figure replied. "I was Tinkerboo . . . and now I'm nobody."

Randolph thought back to the forest and remembered.

"Sing me a song and I promise you, you'll get to see old Tinkerboo," he said.

Tinkerboo lost his sulk and a smile crept onto his face.

"You remember," he said. "But now you've sung the song and you've seen me, you're no better off. I've already given you my power and fulfilled my destiny of combining with you to make you the One."

"That may be so," Randolph replied. "But it's not going to be much good to me now; I think I've just been killed by an evil dragon."

"I wondered why you were floating around up here," Tinkerboo said. "Tell me what happened."

They sat together up on the mountaintop in the moonlight and Randolph told Tinkerboo of his journey through the mine, his encounter with Shawadarg, and his untimely death in the lair.

"I can't believe I'm dead," Randolph said. "I mean there was so much for me to do; who's going to be the One now? Who's going to defend Alusia against Thrung now? How can it be that fate has allowed me to die before even getting to tackle Thrung?"

"There may be one last thing I can do to help," Tinkerboo said.

"What do you mean?" Randolph asked. "What can you do to help a dead body?"

"Well, nothing, to help a dead body," Tinkerboo said. "But it might not actually be fully dead yet. You might be able to get back into it and revive it if we act quickly. I have one last gift for you before I leave for the everafter."

Tinkerboo reached out and took Randolph's hand between both of his own. Randolph felt an energy surge into him, and Tinkerboo grew fainter and more transparent.

"What's that?" Randolph asked. "What have you done to me?"

"I've bequeathed the remainder of my mortal life force to you," Tinkerboo said. "It's no good to me where I'm going, but combined with your own, it may just enable you to reenter and revive your body if you can get back to it quickly."

As Randolph watched, the moon extended its beam like a stairway and Tinkerboo climbed from the last stage of his mortal contact to the happiness of everafter, leaving Randolph floating there alone above the mountain. He looked down at the hand Tinkerboo had held and a radiant glow spread from the tips of his fingers, through his hand, up his arm, and enveloped his whole body. He felt a pulling, as if a rope was tugging him, dragging him back down through the fabric of the mountain. Suddenly, he was back floating near the roof in the cavern, looking again at the body lying below him in the dust. His eyes searched around the lair but there was no sign of Shawadarg in dragon or any other form. As he floated there, a silver cord extended out from his chest; it seemed to come from his heart and drift slowly down toward the still form below. As it touched the body, Randolph was suddenly back down on the ground, back inside his physical form—he felt pain, he felt terror, he felt a weakness the like of which he had never experienced before, a salty taste was once again in his mouth; but he knew he was alive.

I must get out of here before that creature returns! This overpowering thought screamed through his mind.

Randolph raised his head a little from the dusty floor and looked about him. There was still no sign of the dragon he had fought and he knew he had to escape immediately to stand any chance of regaining his freedom. Across the floor of the cavern, he spotted what appeared to be a huge wooden chest, beside which was the bottom of a stone stairway, hewn from the solid rock and spiraling to a ledge about halfway up the cavern wall. On the ledge, there looked to be a large wooden door. Randolph dragged his complaining frame across the floor to where the chest stood. For some reason, he felt it was important to look inside. He lifted the lid to find the chest was full of a white substance. It looked like salt. Randolph tasted it to discover that it was, as he thought, sea salt. He plunged his hands deep into the crisp salt to find the chest contained a smaller casket, buried near the bottom. In this, he found a gold medallion on which were inscribed runic symbols. "Some sort of amulet?" Randolph whispered to himself.

He picked it out of the casket and stuffed it into the leather map pouch on his belt, then slowly clawed his way up the stone stairway. His confused mind was torn between moving as fast as his broken body could be dragged forward and going slower to make as little noise as possible. Eventually he reached the ledge and crawled to the door: It stood open by only a fraction, an almost nonexistent crack down the side, just wide enough for Randolph to insert his fingers. He tugged with all the strength he could muster and the door creaked open sufficiently for him to drag himself through the gap. Once out of the lair, Randolph felt some small strength return to his muscles, and for the second time in just a few days he thanked Tinkerboo for power bestowed.

"I'll just have to follow the tunnel on the upward slope and hope it leads to an exit," Randolph babbled to himself. He set off, his attempts to keep his body upright causing him to zigzag his way along the uneven floor, tripping and stumbling, but gathering a little more strength the further he left the dark power of Shawadarg behind him. He didn't know it, but only a matter of hours earlier, the same tunnel had witnessed three terrified goblins running for all they were worth away from the door on which Randolph had now, very happily, turned his back. It was about midnight when he fell out onto the track, bathed in the same moonlight under which he had floated two hours earlier with Tinkerboo.

Dark Castle must be to my left, he thought as his consciousness came in waves, bursting on his mind like breakers on the shore. *But I wonder how far?* That thought echoed around his head, seeming to bounce off the inside of his skull and reverberate in his ears.

Had they waited, Galdore and Martha would have been there to welcome Randolph back from the dead. But by the time he emerged from the mine, they had covered half the distance to Dark Castle. In the hours to daybreak that it took Randolph to stagger a few miles along the track, they had completed their journey and were seated with Brock and Grafdun in the Great Hall, examining the mine maps.

Ǝ∽Ǝ

"There's little point us all going into the mine," Grafdun said. "Brock and I know the passages and tunnels, and the layout isn't complex. If we can get around the rock fall, then two of us can rescue him easier than four."

"You're right," Galdore agreed. "The time has now come for us to deploy our resources wisely. In fact, Brock, Martha, and I need to get back to Castle Drent along with Atha and the knights and continue our preparations for the assault on the Caverns of Doom. We can leave Randolph's rescue to you and your men."

"That's fine by me," Grafdun replied. "I can send word as soon as we've found him and brought him back here. Then, when he is able to travel, I can bring him down."

Brock said to Galdore, "I think it's important that we get back to Drent to meet with Moraden. We need to check his progress."

Galdore gave Brock a look that said, "Are you thinking what I'm thinking?" Brock's nod was imperceptible to the others, but Galdore caught the meaning.

Theodore entered the Great Hall.

"Baron," he said, "I'm sorry to disturb your discussions but thought you should know the lookout has spotted the king and some of his knights approaching the castle."

"Thank you, Theodore," Grafdun said. "Tend to their needs when they arrive and we will be down to join them."

Theodore went off to do Grafdun's bidding.

"Time is now important," Galdore said. "I feel the growing strength of the dark powers of Thrung and his armies. The urgency to act increases, even if we must start our plans without Randolph."

Grafdun said, "There is no more we can do here. Let us go down to join Atha and the knights and make ready for you to leave for Castle Drent immediately. I will arrange preparations for Randolph's rescue. Theodore!" Grafdun yelled as they walked swiftly down the corridor from the Great Hall: "Theodore, where are you?"

In the courtyard, Atha and the knights were dismounting and dragging three squirming sacks from the horses.

"What have we here?" Grafdun asked. He prodded one of the sacks and made it squeal as well as squirm.

"Three goblins blundered into us as we were searching the forest on the Crumble Hills," Atha said. "They keep babbling something about shaking and earth tremors in the Old Goblin Mines, but they need to be stuck with a roasting spit to get them to squeal a bit more."

"We know about that already," Grafdun replied. "There's been a rock fall in the mines and we need to go in to rescue Randolph. He's trapped. Galdore will fill you in on our plans." Grafdun called to Theodore, "Empty these sacks into the dungeon. We'll deal with them later; we need to get a group of men together to go into the mines to rescue Randolph. Get that organized, will you?"

"No sooner said than done," Theodore replied. He dragged the wriggling sacks off, calling instructions for the rescue preparations.

The courtyard came alive with men. Horses were brought from the stables, ropes and equipment were loaded, maps were folded and stowed in saddlebags, and supplies and provisions were packed. Amongst these activities, Atha, having been briefed by Galdore, Martha, and Brock, assembled his party of knights for immediate departure, ready to take the road south to Castle Drent.

❧

Randolph still staggered in a half-stupefied, fevered state, barely able to drag one foot after the other, as Atha and the knights, accompanied by Martha, Brock, and Galdore, forked left on the southbound track. Grafdun, Theodore, and a party of rescuers headed westward on the track below Dark Castle.

"May good fortune go with you," Grafdun called to Galdore. "See you in a few days at Castle Drent." He spurred his mount on, leading his men toward the Old Goblin Mines.

It was a day later that Grafdun and his rescue party returned to Dark Castle with the babbling, gibbering, rambling Randolph. His incoherent, uncontrolled, fever-driven mutterings and shouts were those of a mad man and Theodore, to the rear of whose horse they had lashed Randolph, feared for the recovery of his sanity. Once inside the safety of the castle walls, Randolph was tended by Theodore's wife, who was well practiced in the art of natural healing and medicinal potions. She sat with him for two days and two nights, tending his wounds, mopping his fevered brow, and listening to his apparently nonsensical babblings.

"I don't understand how he is alive," she had confessed to Theodore. "The severity of his wounds would have killed most men. He must have the constitution of an oxen and the will of a lion."

Randolph recovered his senses slowly, and his bodily strength increased a little each day. But he was still given to bursts of incoherent ramblings and sudden bouts of physical weakness, even two weeks later.

"I fear there is more than just flesh wounds and fever at work," Theodore's wife pronounced. "There is a dark force of evil present here that will need a wizard's hand if proper cure is to be found for Randolph. And even then, he may still not be fully mended. But he certainly will not be able to travel for many days yet."

Word of Randolph's rescue, his slow recovery, and Theodore's wife's prognosis was sent to Galdore at Castle Drent. He had replied that he would make the journey to Dark Castle as soon as he was able to leave the preparations for the defense of Alusia in safe hands.

"What does he mean, safe hands?" Grafdun grumbled. "There are many there who can be trusted."

"And, maybe some who cannot," Theodore had offered in response.

Grafdun looked at him as if to reply, but then chose to keep his counsel, preferring to grunt and walk off, stroking his chin in thoughtful manner.

"You may be right," he said over his shoulder. "You may well be right, my friend. These are strange times."

Randolph seemed to recover quicker after he started to move about more, and Grafdun took the opportunity to school him in the use of weapons.

"If you'd been more skilled with your sword, you may not have sustained such wounds from your battle with whatever it was you encountered in the mine," Grafdun said. "And I'm sure that won't be the last time you draw your sword in the days to come."

Randolph proved to be a good pupil and quickly became skilled in the techniques of personal defense against even the most aggressive attack. Grafdun was an excellent master and during the days of schooling in swordsmanship and battle tactics, the two became firm friends.

"You have done well," Grafdun said. "You have a natural ability with flowing movement that is vital to good swordplay."

"And I have benefited from tuition by the most excellent of sword masters," Randolph replied. "I thank you sincerely for giving me skills that may, one day, prove to be party to my survival."

They questioned the captured goblins together, and Grafdun soon discovered, to his amazement, that Brock's caution concerning the existence of Shawadarg bore a truth that was most worrying. Randolph discovered that evil beings like goblins were selfish creatures, interested only in their personal survival, with total disregard for any semblance of friendship or loyalty to others. All Roody Grumbleweed's words and his philosophy of the cheeses came flooding back to Randolph's mind. He grew to better understand how working together was the way to defeat the independent mights of Thrung and his evil sister Shawadarg. He also came to the realisation that, should the evil beings ever take it into their heads to work together, to trust each other, to develop a common purpose, or to become interdependent, then the battle to save Alusia from the dark power would become significantly more difficult. After they'd got as much out of the goblins as they could, they turned them loose.

"Harmless enough," Grafdun said. "Just a couple of dickheads and an old man who should know better than to mix with the likes of Thrung. I think they've learned their lesson."

"Gobbin' told yer 'e'd let us go if we squealed enough," Spike said as they hurried away from Dark Castle and headed south. "Gobbin' told yer."

"Poor misguided idiots," Randolph said. He and Grafdun watched from the battlements of the castle while the three goblins scurried off. "If they put half as much effort into helping people as they do into thieving and spying, they'd have a much easier life."

"Huh," was all Grafdun replied.

As Randolph regained strength over the days, the bouts of mental and physical weakness grew fewer and more infrequent. But night still bothered him, and on several occasions Theodore's wife or Theodore himself, for it was in their quarters that Randolph was still billeted, needed to wake him from fitful dreams.

"It's as if that monster was attacking me all over again," he told Theodore. "I feel the spines of the tail penetrate my body and I lose control of my mind as I float away to some distant place."

"Galdore will arrive soon," Theodore said encouragingly. "He will bring powerful magic to counteract the dark power left within you from your wounds."

Randolph was quite thoughtful about all that had happened and tried to balance in his mind why fate and destiny had chosen to direct him down the difficult path he had followed. He tried to understand why he had not been allowed an easier passage.

"I believe that what has happened to me has all been necessary to our ultimate success in the battle against the dark forces," he said to Grafdun one day, as they sat together.

"How do you mean?" Grafdun asked.

"Well, how do you know if your kitchen serves up good food?" Randolph asked.

"Because if they didn't, I'd whoop their hides." Grafdun bristled.

"No, no," Randolph said. "I don't mean how do you keep the quality high, and incidentally I don't believe that is how you do it, but that's another day's discussion; I mean when you taste it—how do you know if it's good or bad?"

Grafdun was a man of action, not a philosopher, and such a question caused his brow to furrow deeply. "I don't know," he said. "I suppose I just know it's good because it isn't bad. But what's that got to do with all that's happened to you and the saving of Alusia?"

"Have you ever tasted bad food before?" Randolph asked.

"You obviously never knew my mother," Grafdun said. "She was the best at boiling every bit of flavour out of anything edible. Sure, her meals kept you alive, but I always enjoyed staying with my aunt because her food tasted good."

"There; see what I mean?" Randolph asked.

"No," Grafdun replied. He completely failed to see any connection between the quest to save Alusia from evil and his mother's cooking.

"What I'm saying," Randolph said, "is that you can only know something is good if you've experienced something that isn't. It's all about balance. My success as the One; my training, if you want to call it that, to prepare me for when I ultimately have to face Thrung head on; my sincere belief in the power of good, can only exist if I've been visited by darkness and evil. My strength to build us all together as a united force that can overpower evil will only exist if I fully understand the weakness of independent action."

"Oh," Grafdun said, his brow still deeply furrowed. "What you mean is I wouldn't think of going into battle without the support of my well-trained men?"

"Yes, Randolph said. "Because you know that untrained or badly trained armies don't win. But you have to experience losing before that realisation is proven to you."

Grafdun was saved, for the moment, from further philosophical trauma and mind bending as the lookout heralded Galdore's approach. They went down to the courtyard to greet him. Theodore cranked up the portcullis and wound open the main door to allow Galdore immediate access to the castle.

"Greetings, friend," Grafdun called, as the white stallion slid to a halt in the courtyard and Galdore dismounted.

"Is it weight of the whole load or just the weight of the last straw that breaks the cart's axle?" Galdore said.

"Or is it neither of those things?" Randolph replied. "Is it the bumpy track that is the main culprit?"

"Look, will you two talk in some language that I might understand? Grafdun asked. "Or should I say, is it all the philosophers in the kingdom or just the last piece of gobbledegook that causes total confusion to the normal person?"

"That's very good," Randolph said, laughing. "We'll make an old sage of you yet."

"Take him away," Grafdun said to Galdore, "before he has me reading books or something."

The three laughed their way to the Great Hall where they gathered around the table and a more serious mood descended.

"It's good to see you in high spirits," Galdore said to Randolph. "Exposure to Grafdun's way of life and the care of Theodore's wife seem to have benefited you."

"They have," Randolph replied. "And I owe to each of them, and others here at Dark Castle, a debt of deep gratitude. But Galdore, I am still much troubled on occasion by a weakness and images of terror that capture and divert my mind. I know I am more vulnerable to Thrung's influence than is safe. Can you help me overcome these things before I go forward further on our quest?"

"I can," Galdore replied. "And that is my main purpose in coming here. That and to bring you and Grafdun news of our preparations and knowledge of Thrung and Shawadarg's activities. I must also share with you both some deep concern that I have already discussed with Brock and Martha. But, all that in due course. First, I am in need of sustenance and rest after my journey. Come Grafdun, where is that legendary hospitality?"

That evening was spent in friendly chat and enjoyment of good food and wine. Galdore brought wishes of goodwill and speedy recovery from Martha, Brock, and Dragon. Twig, who had passed on his good wishes through dragon, was looking forward to Randolph's quick return to Castle Drent and to their reunion.

"Moraden asked that I pass on his hope you will soon leave Dark Castle," Galdore said.

Grafdun, complaining, was subjected to more discussion about life and its meaning, although Randolph ventured a suggestion: "Grafdun, you seem to be more in tune with the tapestry of life and its rich pattern than you care to admit."

Grafdun just smiled. Randolph felt confident that Galdore would heal the weakness that still plagued him, and he was eager to start early the next morning on the business to which they had to attend. As the evening drew on, they prepared to retire but, just before they went to their separate rooms, Randolph asked Galdore about the concern he had mentioned earlier.

"That is a matter for later discussion," Galdore said. "But it will not have escaped your notice that my messages did not include overt wishes of personal goodwill from all you might have expected."

Galdore would say no more at this point, claiming that the matter was for discussion and examination, not for immediate judgment by himself or any one person. The next morning, they gathered again in the Great Hall. Galdore had asked that Theodore's wife join them to give details of Randolph's treatment so far and her opinion of his state of health.

"That is our first task," Galdore declared. "We must determine what is to be done to rid Randolph of the remaining effects of the wounding by creatures of the dark forces."

"The wounds I treated where deep and should have killed," Theodore's wife said. "And there is also that scar on Randolph's face, which I believe still harbours some magical blackness."

Until now, Randolph had not shared all the details of his battle with Shawadarg. He had not confessed to seeing the death of his own body, his second meeting with Tinkerboo, or his resurrection. But, with Galdore present, he told the whole story and related details. "Even now," he confessed, "I have difficulty distinguishing between what was reality and what might have been in my imagination."

"That's often the case," Grafdun said. "When you are battling against such strength of dark power, you may be tricked into seeing and believing things that are not real."

"But," Galdore said, "We have already heard that Randolph's wounds were of a severity that should have killed him. I am certain all Randolph experienced was, in fact, reality. We must prepare the potions and incantations that will draw the dark poison from his body and his mind, and I must consult the orb. Come." To Theodore's wife he said, "I will need help with preparation."

Galdore left Randolph with instructions to bathe in hot water with lavender incense, dress in loose robes, and prepare his body through relaxation and his mind through internal focus.

"Go with him, Grafdun," Galdore said. "Prepare his mind as if for battle and his body as if for fornication, and bring him to my quarters at midday."

And with that, Galdore and Theodore's wife went off together, already in discussion about the various merits of different remedies and potions.

"Right," Grafdun said, rubbing his hands together in mock glee. "Sounds like you're in for a bit of a strange session. Serves you right for trying to make me philosophical. This is where I get my own back. Hhmm, mind for battle and body for humping. Must make sure we don't get this the wrong way round!" He laughed heartily.

Randolph didn't see the humour in the situation and followed Grafdun meekly as they wound their way through the castle passageways to the aquaroom. This was one of Grafdun's pleasures in life; he had few indulgences, but those he did allow himself, he satisfied in a manner that others might perceive as obscene over-gratification. When the castle was renovated on his appointment to the baronage, he had designed the most spectacular and luxurious bathhouse; his aquaroom. It was a place where he invited special guests and, on rare occasions, held aquaparties. Today Randolph was to be treated to the pleasure of a few hours' exposure to the most lavish pampering in a pure ecstasy of pleasure, a rhapsody of relaxation of the mind and stimulation of the body.

"When I've finished with you, you'll be capable of copulating with a bucking horse and have the mind to do it," he announced to Randolph.

Through Randolph's head floated a vision of a rampaging mare with himself attached to its rear, firmly gripped by the genitalia and being thrown from side to side in a pageant of desperate mistreatment and abuse. Around him in a circle stood Grafdun, Galdore, and Theodore's wife, all taking bets on how long he could stay mounted. Then horror of horrors, his privy parts started to come loose and tear off. The more the horse bucked, the looser they became until eventually he fell from his copulatory perch and lay stunned on the ground while the mare galloped free in a display of equine gymnastics, sporting his now ex-organs, until they fell, discarded, in a little pile in the dust behind the beast. In his vision, he hobbled to them and picked them up, trying to reattach them to the now vacant space on his person, but they were too battered and misshapen. He could think of nothing more to do but hold them aloft in a gesture of defiant victory as Galdore, Grafdun, and Theodore's wife clapped, cheered, and hooted in bawdy appreciation of the entertainment he had provided.

"How hot would you like the water?" a soft and sensuous voice asked, dispelling the disturbing vision from Randolph's mind and replacing it with one of infinite beauty.

He gazed at the scantily clad form of a beautiful young woman as she started to remove his clothing in an expert fashion until he stood there, naked and exposed, with his mouth open in disbelief. He scratched his head and glanced quickly down to ensure that the horse episode had not been a reality. He was delighted to find himself intact. As his eyes drifted back to the maiden, his intactness became erectness.

"Now, now," she crooned, "get yourself under control; we're not here for that. I'm to relax you, not excite you. The baron has asked me to give you back to him in a state of ease of mind and physical peak. Are you ready to begin?"

Randolph didn't know if he was ready or not. However, as long as it didn't involve a bucking horse, he felt he could cope. He squeaked a positive response and nodded.

"Where's your voice gone?" whispered his nursemaid as she led him down the marble steps into the warm water of the pool.

"I'll see you later," called Grafdun. He had watched the whole performance with a smirk. "And shut your mouth when you get in the pool or you'll drown."

He went off laughing.

Randolph was treated to washing, massage, sweet music, relaxing herbal brew, and gentle exercises that triggered and stimulated muscles he didn't even know he had. By the time Grafdun returned to collect him, he was feeling in peak form and waiting, dressed in a long flowing robe of the finest silk. His skin tingled with freshness, and the scent of lavender followed him as he strolled contentedly around the aquaroom.

"Right! Lead me to that horse," he said to Grafdun, laughing.

"What?" Grafdun asked. "Smelling like a whore's bed chamber? You'd terrify a whole herd in that condition, and I'm not having my horses scared. No, I'm afraid it's Galdore's quarters for you."

As they entered the room, Randolph saw several steaming bowls and dishes set out on a long table. An alter-like construction had been arranged and draped in a soft pink fabric, on top of which burned two white and two black candles. A dagger and a long sword lay unsheathed on the pink cloth and the whole room was filled with an aroma of incense. The orb was floating between two multicolored candles just as Randolph had seen it when he first peered around Galdore's study back in Castle Drent. Galdore and Theodore's wife were robed in long garments, white all down the right-hand side and black on the left. These were adorned with silver images of moon and stars and other magic symbols Randolph recognized as similar to those he had seen on Galdore's spell machine and which decorated his own lute.

"Looks like a sacrificial ceremony," Randolph said.

"You're not too far wrong," Galdore replied. "The basis of destroying the dark poison is much the same as a sacrifice. We just have to make sure we don't get rid of you at the same time. But I'm fairly sure we've got it right."

"Fairly sure?" Randolph said, "What do you mean, fairly sure? I think I'll go back to the aquaroom until you're completely sure."

"Don't be such a milksop," Galdore said. "It'll be fine."

Randolph's mind went back to the last time Galdore had called him a milksop. It was in his tent on the mission to rescue Sir Lionel Graceforth, just before Galdore nearly blew Dragon up and before Randolph himself had come close to being on the wrong end of one of Griselda's lightning bolts.

"Will I be likely to need my lute?" Randolph asked, a sarcastic hint in his voice bringing a frown to Galdore's face.

Galdore chose not to reply but indicated Randolph should lie down on the alter-like arrangement. The steaming bowls and dishes were brought round and Galdore instructed Randolph not to speak once the spell chant was started, whatever happened.

"What will happen?" Randolph asked.

"Oh, the usual," Galdore replied, as if it was a stupid question.

Randolph had no idea what was usual and he had a suspicion that Galdore didn't actually know himself what might happen. "Will I feel anything?" he asked in a final attempt to get some clue.

"Hmmm," Galdore grunted. He started the chant, while Theodore's wife waved the incense burners around the room and over Randolph's body.

As he chanted, Galdore crossed to the orb and passed his hands over the surface, causing a rich glow to fill the room. Randolph felt a stirring in his chest and felt a floating sensation. He watched as a misty form left his body and hovered just above him, connected by a silver cord. The entity was horrible in the extreme. The ugly, misshapen form exuded the stench of death, enveloping Randolph and bringing the taste of bile to his throat. In a swift movement, Galdore picked up the sword and slashed the silver cord joining the entity to Randolph. A scream of pain rent the air and the room was filled with a hot green mist that seemed to vie with the orb's orange glow for domination of the space around Randolph. Theodore's wife dipped her hands in each of the bowls in turn and splashed the liquid contents over Randolph. He felt warmth from the anointing, and it seemed that his breath now came easier than it had done since his encounters with the black swarm and Shawadarg. The orange glow became the predominant color in the room, and slowly the green mist was disbursed.

"That looked easy enough," Grafdun said. He had sat quietly in the corner throughout.

"It wasn't too bad, but you can never tell how that sort of spell might go until you get started," Galdore said. "It depends on the power and the type of the poison, which obviously you don't know until you start to pull it out."

"Obviously," Grafdun said, not thinking it was obvious at all. "How do you feel?" he asked Randolph in an uncommon show of concern.

But Randolph was fast asleep and stayed that way for the rest of the day and all the next night, by which time Galdore had left for Castle Drent and placed Randolph, once again, in the care of Theodore's wife.

"Discuss with Randolph what is to be done," Galdore said to Grafdun as he made ready to leave. "Now that he is recovered and strong again, we must follow his intuition. I must return urgently to Castle Drent. Important business awaits my attention. Join me there with Randolph as soon as you can."

And with that he was gone, riding like the wind on his white stallion, his gray hair and beard streaming behind him as he made haste for Castle Drent and whatever business required his urgent attention.

തൗര്

Thrung's roar was loud and terrifying. His foul, hot breath made even Scumfest and Beaktool reel as he berated them for their inefficiency. "Lost him," he bellowed. "What do mean you've lost him? You'll pay for this!" He lashed out, sending Beaktool lurching to the corner of the cavern.

Scumfest dropped to his knees before Thrung, petrified that the wrath might also be directed at him. "We'll find him again soon, Master," he whimpered. "It's just that he got out of the ether a fraction before the swarm caught up to him. But he's wounded. We got the dark poison into him."

That news seemed to pacify Thrung, and his rage quietened a little.

"When will you find him? Be gone and locate the slime; ensure his demise and report it to me soon." Thrung waved a dismissal to the evil twins, and they scurried off like frightened rabbits to carry out his orders. Delays in his preparations for the overthrow of those holding power and influence in the overworld did not please the impatient Thrung. Randolph was still at large, his strength building. The black wasp swarm was unsuccessful in its attempts to eliminate him and the squird leader was killed.

However, word that Randolph was in the Old Goblin Mines and within striking distance of Shawadarg eased Thrung's impatience. Shawadarg, at least, was terrible in her venomous hatred of all opponents of the dark forces. Thrung was confident she would vent her revulsion in a way that would suit his needs and culminate in Randolph's death.

"And then," Thrung roared, "the One, the True One, my Dark One will be free to represent my needs and do my bidding in all overworld domains. He, at least, continues my work undetected by those who might frustrate my plans."

Away in a back chamber of the Caverns of Doom, Scumfest and Beaktool made contact with the goblins Spike and Toady.

"Take your miserable hides to the Draken Mountains," Beaktool growled. "Awaken Shawadarg and inform her of the need to be active in our campaign of domination. Thrung requires her presence in the battle against the False One. She has slept too long, and the time has arrived for her active participation."

It was several days later that news of the goblins' capture reached the evil twins, but with it came news from Shawadarg of the death of Randolph and that his broken body lie crumpled in her lair, stabbed to the heart.

"Stuff the goblins." Thrung's roar of delight at the news of Randolph's demise shook the caverns. "They are but irrelevant pawns in the scheme of my dominance of the overworld; they are expendable."

"We are pleased to have played a small part in his death," Scumfest and Beaktool whined.

"Yes, you have, at last, done well," Thrung bellowed. "You both deserve to live a little longer in my service. Now, start the plans for installing the Dark One. Send word he is to come to the caverns to receive his instructions. I will meet with him person-ally and instruct him in my demands."

"Yes Master," Beaktool squeaked. "I'll see to it immediately."

"And you, Scumfest," Thrung growled.

"Yes Master?" Scumfest groveled. "What is your desire?"

"Send out word that the swarm and the squirds are to pre-pare to intensify their terrorisation of the overworld, as soon as I give the word they are to commence open attack, they will soon no longer need to remain hidden."

"Immediately Master, immediately."

Scumfest and Beaktool bowed low as they scraped their way backward from the Cavern of Despair.

"We seem to be back in favor for a while," Scumfest wheezed to Beaktool, as a little green goblin messenger ran up and passed a scribbled parchment to Beaktool.

Beaktool paled from his already gray-white complexion to a hint of bluish green as he read the Anciental text from the parch-ment.

"What is it?" Scumfest squealed. He could see the terror cross Beaktool's face.

"It is word from the Dark One, from Thrung's One to be. It would seem the false One may not, after all, be exterminated. It is reported here that Shawadarg returned to her lair to find the body gone."

"That doesn't mean he's still alive," Scumfest said. "The body could have been eaten by the trolls, or even removed by friends of the false One; you know the stupidity of the overworlders about decent burial and all that nonsense. Pull yourself together; dead bodies don't get up and walk away." Scumfest attempted a feeble laugh.

"Well it looks like this one did," Beaktool said. "But that's not the bad news."

"What do you mean?"

"The talisman is gone," Beaktool said. "Shawadarg reports it missing."

Scumfest's face turned the color of his twin brother as the consequences of bringing this news to Thrung dawned on him. "We must find out more before we inform the Master," Scumfest said. They scurried off together to find some course of action that would not result in their demise.

"We need to summon Thrung's One to come here anyway, as Thrung has instructed. We must meet him first; he may know more," Beaktool said.

The worried duo made their way to the orb and, using its power, contacted the Dark One, summoning him to the Caverns of Doom to meet with Thrung who, at this point, believed his plans to be working well.

"Make sure he comes to us first," Scumfest said. "We need to find out more before we face Thrung."

Later that night, a figure slid quietly and unseen over the parapet of the main shaft leading down to the Caverns of Doom and followed the tunnel leading to the quarters where Scumfest and Beaktool lived and worked. If the first figure was quiet and unseen, the cat tracing the steps of the figure was silent and invisible. Tail held high, like the pole of a regimental banner, the sleek black body moved with the stealth of an evening breeze in the treetops, darting and pausing, gliding and hiding, eyes and ears alert to the smallest movement or sound. Dragon had been following Moraden all the way from Castle Drent. She had much to report to Galdore.

Chapter Ten
A Sea Trip to Gospot

The Mindy Lou

RANDOLPH WOKE refreshed, feeling stronger than he had at any time since his encounter with Shawadarg. "Whatever you and Galdore did seems to have worked well; I feel good," he said to Theodore's wife as she placed the tray of steaming oats, pumpkin, and sunflower seeds beside his bed.

"That's as may be," she said. "But there's to be no rushing about for a few days. Rest will make the cure stronger, you mark my words."

"Yes Mum," Randolph jested.

"And don't call me Mum," came the indignant reply. "I'm old enough to be your grandmother." Theodore's wife stopped to review the stupidity of what she had just said and laughed. "Look," she said. "You've got me all in a tizzy now; eat your breakfast will you."

"Yes Granny," Randolph said, as she left the room in a swirl of mock embarrassment. "Hey, what is your name? Everybody refers to you as Theodore's wife, but if I'm to do what I'm told and stay here resting for a few days, I need to know your name."

Theodore's wife's head reappeared around the frame of the door for an instant. "Lydanalandermeraida," she said. "That's why people refer to me as Theodore's wife. But my friends call me Lydie." And off she went, singing as she tackled the daily chores.

Randolph's thoughts flooded back to his childhood. He hadn't thought about his sister Lydie in recent weeks. "What was it Sulaman said?" Randolph murmured to himself. "I do know that she is entwined with your destiny in some mysterious and yet-to-be-discovered manner. What does that mean I wonder? Where are you, Lydie?" Randolph called as if his sister might hear and come running to sit with him as she used to.

"Yes?" came the response from the next room. Theodore's wife appeared, framed in the doorway. "What do you want?"

"Nothing Granny, I was just talking to myself."

Lydanalandermeraida balled up the damp rag she had been using to clean the table and threw it at Randolph's head. "Come on you lazy bugger; when I said a couple of days rest, I didn't mean lounging in bed all the livelong day. You can get up and help me wash the vegetables for the stew."

"All right," Randolph said, smiling. "I'll show you how to make stewed groodle if you like."

"What's a groodle?" Theodore's wife asked.

"Never had stewed groodle?" Randolph teased. "What sort of upbringing have you had if you've never had stewed groodle?" His carefully aimed damp rag hit Lydanalandermeraida square in the back of the head.

"Yes," she said, turning and laughing. "You're nearly better."

As Randolph cleaned the vegetables, he and Theodore's wife sang an old Alusian folk song together.

> *"Down where the folk are country bred,*
> *There's time to find some space in your head,*
> *There's time to laugh and time to live,*
> *And time to care and time to give.*
> *With a fah la la and a fah la la la la*
> *With a fah la-la ha and a hey-ey nonnie no.*

I'd give the world if I could stay,
Down on the farm, live the country way,
I'd milk the cows and tend the sheep,
I'd gather eggs from the hens I'd keep.
With a fah la la and a fah la la la la
With a fah la-la ha and a hey-ey nonnie no.

They'd come from the town and the villages too,
They'd come to laugh the whole day through,
And when the time to go came by,
To tarry a while they all would try.
With a fah la la and a fah la la la la
With a fah la-la ha and a hey-ey nonnie no.

Down where the folk are country bred,
There's time to find some space in your head,
There's time to laugh and time to live,
And time to care and time to give.
With a fah la la and a fah la la la la
With a fah la-la ha and a hey-ey nonnie no."

That evening, Randolph sat with Theodore and his wife, discussing what was to be done next.

"Well, you'll be fully recovered and ready to travel in another two days," Theodore's wife said.

"I think the time has come to unfold the map again." Randolph got up and crossed to his room, where he picked up the leather pouch that had hung on the end of his bed since his arrival at Dark Castle.

"This feels heavier than I remember," he said, as he came back into the room and resumed his seat by the log fire. Randolph unstudded the pouch and pulled out the folded map. There was a clanging and a clattering as something fell from the pouch to the slate tiles on the floor. All three of them stared at the bright gold medallion and the chain that lay there on the floor at Randolph's feet. It sparkled and danced reflections of the fire's flames, spraying the room with speckles and dots of shimmering golden brilliance.

"What's that?" Theodore asked.

"Don't know what . . .," Randolph's words trailed off as memory flooded back. "Oh my blessed old breeches," he said. "I'd completely forgotten about finding this. It was inside a casket, inside a wooden chest, inside Shawadarg's lair."

"Surely it couldn't be?" Theodore's wife said.

"Couldn't be what?" Randolph queried

"Couldn't be the Talisman of Power," Lydanalandermeraida said with a nervous laugh. "Sure, that's only a legend." She repeated the nervous laugh.

"But there's many who believed Shawadarg was only a legend until a couple of weeks ago," Theodore said. "Until Randolph stumbled into her lair."

Randolph felt a shudder up his back at the thought of the lair and the piercing memory of Shawadarg's tail spines probing his heart. He leaned forward and picked up the medallion and chain.

"It's got strange symbols and runes carved on it," he said. "I wonder what they mean?"

"I think Grafdun should see this," Theodore said. "There's no saying it is the Talisman of Power but, if it is, he should be aware it is in our possession. Shawadarg and Thrung, once he knows of its loss, will stop at nothing to retrieve it. Although I cannot read the runes and symbols, they are reputed to hold the key to the existence of evil and, by that, of Thrung himself. If we can interpret them, they may tell of the way in which Thrung can be defeated."

"Jumping jackrabbits," Randolph said and let out a long, low, between-the-teeth whistle. "This could be the lucky break we've been waiting for."

"I'll go and fetch Grafdun," Theodore said. "Best he comes here to see it rather than us parading it about the castle; you never know who might be watching in these troubled times."

Theodore went off into the night air to fetch Grafdun, while Randolph and Theodore's wife examined the medallion and chain to see if they could gain any clue as to whether it might be the Talisman of Power.

"From what I know of the Anciental runes," Lydanalandermeraida said, "there seems to be two separate stories or messages, one on each side of the medallion."

"What, like one side for the dark powers and one for good?" Randolph asked.

"Something like that, but more complex and entwined than a simple good side and bad side. But I don't really know enough to be certain."

At that point, Theodore and Grafdun came back into the room.

"That was quick," Randolph said.

"Yes," Theodore said, "I found him just outside in the court-yard gazing up into the night sky, talking to the clouds and the birds."

"I was not talking to the clouds," Grafdun said indignantly. "I thought I spotted a large flock of birds, or maybe a swarm of large insects way up in the sky. They seemed to be circling round and round, almost as if they were searching for something. I was concerned that it might be Randolph's swarm of black wasps."

"They're not my swarm," Randolph retorted. "In fact, I never want to see them again . . . but, I don't suppose I'll be that lucky."

"Anyway, enough chatter about black swarms," Grafdun said. "It seems we have more immediate business to attend."

"Yes," Randolph said. He handed the talisman to him. "What do you make of this? I stole it on my way from Shawadarg's lair and only just remembered it when I went to get my map out."

Grafdun took the medallion and examined it, turning it over and over in his hand. "If you'd shown me this a few weeks ago and told me it was the Talisman of Power, I'd have told you to go and boil your head," he said. "But then I'd have done the same if you told me Shawadarg's lair really existed deep under the Old Goblin Mines. If there is such a thing as the Talisman of Power, this could be it."

"Do you know what any of the runes mean?" Randolph asked. "Lydie is fairly sure they are Anciental runes, but she doesn't know enough to read them properly."

"They don't mean anything to me," Grafdun said. "We need to show it to Galdore, or better still to Brock or Moraden, I know they both have a special knowledge of the Anciental text and runes."

"I knew Brock studied the old languages," Theodore said. "But I didn't know Moraden was also a scholar of the runes."

"Oh yes," Grafdun said. "I once found him buried in the old rune books in the vaults of his father's palace. He asked me not to tell others of his interest, as he was completing some private study. But that was many years ago now. I'd forgotten about it until this moment, and I'm certain it's no longer a secret."

"Is there no one here in Dark Castle who may have knowledge of the Anciental text and is to be trusted?" Randolph asked.

"What about old man Drimage?" Theodore's wife asked. "I know he's two boars heads short of a feast, but he may have some knowledge that we could extract from him; he does have sane moments between his mad ramblings. Also, if he did repeat what he'd seen to anybody, they would just take it as one of his mad mumblings."

"It's worth a try," Theodore said. "We may not get any sense from him, but he is the only one in the castle that might be able to read the medallion."

"Where is he?" Randolph asked.

"He has a room at the very top of one of the towers," Grafdun said. "He likes to be up there so he can talk to the birds." He flicked his eyes skyward in a gesture of incredulity. "Come, we best go see him now, before midnight arrives and he turns into a turnip or something. We'll never get any sense out of him then."

Randolph put the talisman back into the map pouch and slid it onto his belt. The four of them left Theodore's quarters and crossed the courtyard to the northwest tower. They looked up to the top window and saw flickering candlelight.

"His light still burns," Lydanalandermeraida said. "He is not yet sleeping."

"We might get more sense out of him if he was," Grafdun scoffed.

They climbed the spiral stone steps that wound their way up the tower, getting narrower and steeper as they went. Grafdun led the way with Lydanalandermeraida behind him and then Randolph followed by Theodore. All four puffed a little from the climb as they stood in a line, one behind the other in front of the wooden door that blocked the end of the stairway. Grafdun knocked.

"Drimage, are you there?" called Grafdun through the door.

"No," came the emphatic reply. "I'm away for a while; bugger off."

Grafdun turned to the others. "He's in one of his difficult moods," he said. "I can't cope with that."

"Here," Lydanalandermeraida said. She squeezed past Grafdun to the door and produced a small flask from somewhere beneath her voluminous skirts and aprons. "Let me try. He usually listens to me."

"That's cheating," Grafdun said as he nodded toward the flask.

"There's more than one way to catch a rabbit," Lydanalandermeraida said. "Oh Drimage, come and see what Lydie has for you."

At the name Lydie, Randolph felt a sharp jabbing pain run through his body and then it was gone immediately. "Ouch," he said.

"What's the matter?" Theodore asked.

"Nothing," Randolph said. "Only a twinge; it's gone now."

Lydanalandermeraida was still crouched, calling softly through the keyhole, enticing Drimage to come and let them in. There was a shuffling sound from the room and a clanking of keys, like the sound of a gaoler doing his evening rounds. A key was inserted in the far side of the lock and it turned noisily. The door creaked open a fraction, and an eye peered through the slit.

"Hello Drimage," Lydanalandermeraida said in a dreamy, soothing tone. "Look what I brought you." She held up the flask. "And I've brought some friends to see you as well. Are you going to let us in?"

There was a grunt, like the sound of a pig at its trough, and the door creaked open wider. "As long as there's no bear's or wolves with them, then they can come in," a voice said from the gloom.

"Anybody got bears or wolves with them?" Lydanalandermeraida asked.

A chorus of no's seemed to satisfy Drimage, and the door opened further to allow them access. Randolph looked around the small circular chamber. It contained a bed and a table and some chairs, several cupboards and a whole host of knickknacks, bottles, and books. Candles burned and flickered, making the room and all its contents jump and wobble like a jelly. Drimage reached for the flask, but Theodore's wife pulled it away.

"Not yet," she said gently. "There's some things we need you to help us with first. Then you can have the flask."

Drimage scurried of to a chair by his bed and sat in it, pulling his legs up under him, wide-eyed and eager to please in the expectation of reward for good behavior. Randolph was reminded of an obedient dog, and he felt sorry for Drimage. The four of them sat around the table, turning their chairs to face Drimage.

"This is Randolph," Lydanalandermeraida said. "He has found something and wants to ask you about it."

"Show him the medallion," Theodore said.

Randolph unbuttoned the leather pouch and drew out the chain, followed by the medallion, which sparkled and glittered as it reflected the candlelight. Drimage took one look at the twisting medallion, covered his eyes, curled himself into a ball, and buried his face in the back of the chair. His muffled voice sounded hollow in the small stone-walled room.

"Dangerous," he cried. "Dangerous to have this. Randolph in danger."

"Drimage." Randolph got up, crossed the room to the cringing figure and knelt beside the chair. "I'm not in danger yet, but I may be if you don't help me. I need to know what the runes and symbols on the medallion say."

"Drimage cannot tell," he said, his face still buried. "Drimage not allowed to say."

Randolph placed his hands on the old man's shoulders and gently turned him back to face the room. He looked deep into sad and tormented eyes and he saw into Drimage's mind. A confused and turbulent mind, driven crazy by powerful knowledge and insufficient experience or ability to deal with it. Through the mists of conscious and unconscious thought, into the patterns of recollection and tapestry of long and jumbled perception Randolph probed, until at last he found the one piece of memory he sought.

"I have what we need," Randolph said as he stood to face the three figures sitting silently around the table.

"What did you do?" Grafdun asked.

"Oh, only a simple mind probe," Randolph said, as if it was an everyday activity.

"You sound like Galdore when you say things like that," Theodore said.

"Theodore, if the three of you go back to your quarters, I'll join you in a while. There's something I must do to repay Drimage for his help."

"I've got his reward here," Lydanalandermeraida said.

"There's something else I can do to help him more," Randolph said as the others filed out through the narrow door and down the stone stairway. "I won't be long." He closed the door behind them and carefully replaced the talisman in the leather pouch on his belt. He turned back to Drimage and, once again, knelt beside the old man, placing his hands on his shoulders and looking deep into those forlorn eyes. He probed into Drimage's mind, seeking the point in his memory where contact with the power of darkness had driven him mad.

> *"In time and space,*
> *In greed and grace,*
> *Let all that once belonged to you*
> *Return to challenge and defend*
> *The mind, the thoughts, the person who*
> *Once lived inside this troubled shell,*
> *Who used to know just how to tell*
> *Good from bad and dark from light.*
> *Let weakness turn to strength once more*
> *Though madness still, like day and night*
> *Will always now*
> *Be part of how*
> *You face the world that comes to you,*
> *But torment will not burden, so*
> *I grant you peace, contentment too."*

"Thank you old man, you have served life well and given me a chance to defend our world against the might of Thrung. In return, I have given you all that my powers will allow. May you live out your life in a little more harmony than you have been able to enjoy these past years. Be at peace with your soul. I will go forward for both of us." Randolph turned to the door.

"Thank you," Drimage said. "May your strength be greater than mine. May you bear the responsibility better than I was able. May they, this time, have chosen more wisely. May you succeed where I failed. My thoughts go with you on your journey. You know now that you must go south to solve the riddle of the runes."

Randolph walked slowly back to Theodore's quarters where Grafdun, Theodore, and his wife waited. In Drimage's mind, Randolph had seen much that raised questions, but found few answers. He knew now that the medallion was, indeed, the Talisman of Power, but that the message written in the runes only provided direction, and not solution. What he had seen through the confusion of madness was that Drimage, many years past, had been selected by Sulaman and those who formed the Council of Worth at that time as a possible One. Although he had bravely followed the trail to counter the threatening growth of evil, he had failed to achieve his goal.

However, he had viewed the talisman and even possessed it for a short while. From those who knew the runic symbols, he had discovered the secret to Thrung's strength and weakness lay somewhere to the south. He had also discovered the talisman had its own energy. However, this could not be realized until it was rejoined with the Master Orb, which had been hidden for many millennia by the first high wizard, Mithrip, in an attempt to prevent the forces of darkness from ever rising. The secret of the Master Orb's whereabouts had died with Mithrip.

"There are many loose ends unexplained," Randolph said to the others. He recounted, as best he could, his contact with Drimage's mind. "And much of what I learned was just a sense of things rather than distinct or certain fact."

"Do you know what is to happen next?" Grafdun asked. "Galdore advised before he left that on your recovery, we would once again need to rely on your instincts to move forward."

"That responsibility weighs heavy on my shoulders," Randolph said. "But I know it is so, and I must choose paths that we all shall tread. I will journey south, but I must go alone, quietly and undetected. The talisman must be hidden and protected, for it will become vital to our later resistance against the dark forces."

"So," Grafdun said, "How should we proceed?"

"You must journey to Castle Drent," Randolph said. "Take the talisman to Galdore and tell him of the need to hide it well. Also, inform him that I have journeyed south in search of Mithrip. He will understand. Tell him I feel that there is a connection with the Salt Lakes and that is where I am bound."

"How will you travel undetected through the whole length of the kingdom?" Theodore asked.

Randolph turned to Grafdun to seek advice. "You are much traveled in these lands," he said. "How would you reach the southern parts of Alusia quickly and without raising interest from swarms of black wasps, squirds, goblins and other spies and servants of Thrung?"

"Haggerty," Grafdun replied, without hesitation. "Captain Haggerty's our man."

"He is a good man," Theodore's wife confirmed. "A true and trusted friend. You can be in no safer hands, and his mouth is not large and loose where gossip is concerned. Your business with him will be no business of others. Although he is a man of action and will demand what he considers right. You will find him over-ready to speak his mind at times."

"He will be at Basiltree Harbour, at the fish market two days from now," Theodore said. "He never misses a month."

"Then that is settled," Randolph said. "Tomorrow I go to Basiltree, under cover, although it must appear to all observers that I leave with Grafdun for Castle Drent, but for tonight we must rest; there are busy times ahead."

☙❧

Martha and Brock were at the gates of Castle Drent awaiting Galdore's return. The lookout had spotted his approach and, as instructed, informed them immediately. Dragon also had followed them down from the hall and purred and nuzzled around Brock's feet while they waited.

"Dragon knows something more," Brock said. "I am sure of it."

Galdore slid from his mount to greet them.

"Welcome back," Martha said. "How is Randolph?"

"Much improved," Galdore replied. "He is almost ready to continue. Another few days' rest and he will be fully recovered."

Martha's face beamed.

"Well done," she said to Galdore. "You saved his life with your cure."

"Let us hope I did not save it for the purpose of him losing it a little later," Galdore said. "But what is it that is so urgent, requiring my immediate return?"

"It's Moraden," Brock said. "We are certain now that it is he who is in league with Thrung. He has disappeared. We don't know where and we don't know why. Neither do we know whether he is a willing participant in Thrung's plans or if his unwilling mind has been turned in some way by the force of evil."

"Dragon has followed Moraden and returned, but will tell us nothing of what she has discovered. Although I believe she has information for your ears."

Galdore bent low and took Dragon into his arms.

"You can speak openly," Galdore said to Dragon. "Tell us all that you have observed and heard."

Dragon purred her words gently, telling them how, as Galdore had requested, she had followed Moraden in the castle for the last while, watching for any indication that he might be passing information to Thrung.

"Initially there was nothing definite," she said. "But then, over the last few days, since you have been away in Dark Castle, I saw him using the orb and heard him speaking Anciental tongue; I saw him at night directing the black swarm as they circled on high; I heard him as he slept, dream-talking of the time to come when he would be all-powerful and rule the overworlds. I followed him as he left the castle and went to the Caverns of Doom. He entered the main shaft and, obviously, knew his way as he hurried off into the tunnels. I dared not follow further for fear of detection and so returned here."

"So, I fear we may now be only four," Galdore said. "This is a sad time."

"We are not four," Brock said. "There is Randolph, making our number back to five. As lord high wizard, you have the authority to adopt him as a member of the Council of Worth."

"You are right my friend, I do have that power, but let us not be too hasty in our judgment of Moraden. Do we not owe him the loyalty to try and recover him to the path of the light? Is that not our way? It may be he has been taken from us rather than chosen of his own free will to follow the course of darkness."

"But you just said yourself that we are now four," Martha said.

"No," Galdore said, "I said I fear we may now be four. Although I also fear it may be too late, but let us not be panicked into hasty accusations by the pressure of Thrung's wickedness. If we forfeit our way for that of his, are we not our enemy's best friend?"

Dragon purred and nodded approval at Galdore's wisdom.

"What can we do to save Moraden then?" Brock asked.

"We may not be able to recover him," Galdore said. "We can only try, we can only hold out the option, but we cannot make his decision for him. However, should the option be declined, then we must consider him our enemy, and we must prepare ourselves for that eventuality."

"Randolph and Grafdun must be told of the situation," Brock said.

"I have asked Grafdun to join us here with Randolph as soon as he can. I would expect their arrival in no more than two days."

༒

Theodore loaded the wagon with the empty barrels as he did every month for the trip to Basiltree fish market.

"I'll take the lid off as soon as we get a way down the track," he whispered through a knothole in one of the largest barrels.

"I'm going to stink of fish for weeks," the barrel replied.

"Well, you said you wanted to travel alone on the journey south." Theodore laughed. "That should ensure it for you."

"Bog off," the barrel said.

"Quiet now, I'm going to open the barn doors onto the courtyard and hitch up the horses; then we'll be off."

Randolph, dressed in the clothing of a crew member of a merchant coastal vessel, sat in silent stinkiness and listened to the rattle of the harness being fitted. A few moments later, he felt the cart rumble over the cobbles and heard Theodore call.

251

"Goodbye Grafdun, bye Randolph, have a good trip to Drent; see you soon."

Randolph couldn't see out of the barrel but he could visualize the scene with Grafdun and the cloaked and hooded dummy mounted together in the courtyard. It had been agreed they would all leave at the same time. Grafdun and the dummy heading south, and Theodore, with the real Randolph secreted in one of his fish barrels, heading east to Basiltree to meet with Captain Haggerty and secure a covert passage to Gospot on the *Mindy Lou*. Randolph heard the portcullis lift and the main gates creak open as the cart trundled forward and across the drawbridge, closely followed by the sound of the two horses behind them, their hooves beating a tattoo on the wooden planking.

"May the lord high wizard preserve us," Randolph said quietly to himself. "I'll never eat fish again." He closed his eyes in a vain attempt to shut out the overpowering stench of fish that now seemed to have crept into every pore and crevice of his person. There was further calling and wishing of good journeys as Grafdun and the dummy Randolph took the southward track and Theodore steered the cart left to follow the easterly road. After what he judged to be several miles of bumping along the track, Randolph called to Theodore.

"It must be your turn in the barrel by now."

"Ssshhhh," came the whispered reply. "You'll have to stay in there; there's too many people on the road to let you out yet."

"Hello, Theo," called a voice from somewhere on the track close beside the cart.

"Hello, Thomas," Randolph heard Theodore reply.

"Are you off to Basiltree?" the voice asked.

"Sure am," Theodore said.

"Give us a ride then will yer?" the voice said. "I'm going to the market."

"Hop on," Theodore said.

What else could he say? Randolph thought. *Just when I need a lucky break, I don't get one.*

Randolph sighed a silent, fishy sigh and resigned himself to the smelly barrel for the duration of the journey.

If I had to face Thrung now, he'd give up without a fight, as long as I promised never to come within a hundred yards of him. He chuckled to himself quietly, surprised that he was able to find any humour in the task that lay ahead. *But you have to keep smiling, I suppose. That's part of what I'm defending. . . . But, saints alive, it's smelly in here.*

The journey to Basiltree took all day, and when at last they arrived, Theodore bid farewell to his passenger, Thomas, and pulled the cart into the stable yard barn. Randolph had to be tipped out of the cramped barrel and straightened out by Theodore's brute strength. It was several minutes before he could stand unaided.

"It could have been worse," Theodore said to a hobbling Randolph.

"You wouldn't say that if you'd been in the barrel," he replied.

"It could have been," Theodore insisted. "It could have been a hot summer day instead of a chilly December one."

"Balls," Randolph said.

Once Randolph was able to perform basic walking maneuvers, they left the barn and headed for the Ship Inn, where Theodore was certain they would find Captain Haggerty propping up the bar.

"Can you smell that dead fish aroma?" Theodore said.

"Smell it?" Randolph said, "I am it."

"Well, would you mind walking downwind a bit?" Theodore asked. "And a couple of paces away? People might think it's me."

Randolph put his arm around Theodore's shoulder. "Not likely buddy," he said. "We're in this together. Where you go, I go. Where I smell, you smell."

The Ship Inn was crowded, as it always was on the eve of the market.

"Go over and stand by that small table in the far corner will you," Theodore said to Randolph. "The one with the three chairs around it. I have a feeling the people using it might be leaving soon. You grab the table when they go. I'll find Haggerty and bring him over, but introduce yourself as someone other than Randolph until we've filled him in on a few details. He can be a bit loud sometimes, and he'll have a few pints of ale inside him by now."

"But, they don't look as if they're ready to leave yet," Randolph said as he looked over to the corner.

"Just go and stand there before anybody else gets the table," Theodore said. "Trust me, I'm a fortune teller."

Randolph went and stood by the table. After a moment, the three occupants of the chairs got up and went to lean on the bar, muttering and glancing back repeatedly toward him. Randolph sat down at the table as Theodore and Captain Haggerty came over.

"Haggerty," said the captain as he stuck out his hand to Randolph.

"Fishman," Randolph said, shaking Haggerty's ham-like hand.

"Saints! What is that awful smell?" Haggerty asked.

"Drains," Theodore said, in an attempt to protect Randolph's dignity. "They must be blocked again. Always happens when the bar gets this crowded," he said, winking at Randolph.

"Landlord, do something about the drains, will you?" Haggerty shouted across the barroom. "The stench over here is enough to rot the stitchin' on yer main sail."

Randolph tried to shrink into the corner, as everyone looked over to Haggerty. Not only was he conscious that on closer inspection he would be found to be the source of the drain smell, but he didn't want attention of any sort drawn to his presence.

"SSsshh," Theodore said. "We don't need attention, and we need somewhere we can talk in private."

"Follow me," Haggerty said. He got up and made for the door. "We need to get away from that drain smell anyway."

Theodore and the drain smell got up and followed him. Once in the open air, Randolph could position himself downwind and a little distance from Haggerty to avoid being discovered as the source of the aroma.

"Here," Haggerty said. He opened a door and led them into a barn-like structure where fish of all kinds lay on slabs among piles of ice. "This'll do; no-one will be in here until the market starts in the morning. Smells a bit fishy, but it's better than those drains."

Disguised by blending into the fishy atmosphere, Randolph relaxed a little, as Theodore explained to Haggerty the urgent need to travel south undetected. Theodore confessed that Randolph's name was not Fishman at all but that he was using it on the trip in case his true identity was overheard in conversation by those who need not know of his whereabouts just now. The deal was struck and Randolph was enrolled as a temporary cook, a new crew-member on the *Mindy Lou*, the regular cook being allowed a much-overdue shore leave.

"That's good," Theodore said. "You'll be down in the galley for most of the time. It'll avoid too many questions that don't have watertight answers."

"Where will we find the *Mindy Lou*?" Randolph asked.

"You can't miss her," Haggerty boasted. "Best looking boat in the harbour. We sail at daybreak, day after tomorrow. See you there. I'm back off to the Ship Inn, see if that drain smell's gone yet."

"Well that all seemed quite easy," Randolph said, as they watched Haggerty's bulky form disappear through the doorway.

"Haggerty's a good man once he knows what's what. So it's best to keep him informed, otherwise, as you've seen, he can draw attention without meaning to."

"A bit like me at the moment," Randolph said. "Where are we staying? I need to get cleaned up."

"Come on then; I've got a couple of rooms arranged at the Piggery Tavern. That's where I always stay when I come to the market; it's down on the quay."

"Hope it doesn't smell like one," Randolph said.

"Look who's talking!" Theodore laughed as they made their way down to the harbour and the Piggery.

"Is that the *Mindy Lou*?" Randolph asked. He pointed as they stopped outside the tavern door and looked toward the harbour.

"That's her, all right," Theodore said.

She was, as Haggerty had said, the finest looking craft in the harbour. Triple-masted and with sleek lines, she looked as if she could make a fair turn of speed. Randolph felt positive about the way things were going and he wondered how Grafdun and the dummy were progressing on their way to Castle Drent.

"Uneventful," Grafdun said to Galdore as he dismounted in the courtyard of Castle Drent. "Randolph hasn't said a word all the way."

Martha, who had just crossed the courtyard to welcome Grafdun and Randolph, went straight over to where the dummy still sat motionless in the saddle.

"Watch this," Grafdun whispered to Galdore, and winked.

"Randolph," Martha said. "How good to see you again."

The dummy sat, still and silent.

"Randolph?" Martha's tone changed to a mixture of concern and chastisement. "Aren't you pleased to see me?"

The figure maintained its aloof air, giving no indication that it had even heard Martha's question.

"Randolph!" Martha's voice now took on an irritated tone, and she reached up and grabbed the figure's leg. It came off in her hand and she squealed. Turning to Grafdun, she hit him with the leg. He dissolved into peels of laughter, and even Galdore chuckled a little.

"Pig," she said. But then seeing the joke, she smiled. "Where is he?"

"He's fine," Grafdun said. "He sends messages of goodwill as well his instructions. He's gone south. There is much to tell and much to do. But first let me wash the dust of travel from my face."

"We also have important news to share. Shall we meet in the Council Chamber as soon as you have freshened yourself?" Galdore asked. "Come, Martha; we will collect Brock and Atha."

Before an hour had passed, the five of them sat around the table.

"Where is Moraden?" Grafdun asked .

"He is the subject of some of our information," Galdore replied. "But all that in good time. Tell us first of Randolph and his whereabouts."

Grafdun related the details of the talisman, which he produced and handed to Galdore for safekeeping, and of the meeting between Randolph and Drimage.

"It is good that he is now recovered and proceeding well with his instinctive choice of action," Brock said. "This bodes well for us. His decision to travel by sea is wise, and we must support his actions by setting up a pretence that he is here at Castle Drent."

"I will pass word that his quarters are to be prepared," Atha said. "And I'll give instruction that he is not to be disturbed."

"But what of your news?" Grafdun said. "Tell me, what word of Moraden's progress?"

"It is grave tidings, I fear," Galdore replied. "We now believe he is in the employ of Thrung, but whether by his own will or by capture of his mind is unknown."

"In any event," Martha said, "it is important that Randolph is made aware of the situation."

"It's probably too risky to try and reach him now at Basiltree before the *Mindy Lou* sets sail," Grafdun said. "But I know Haggerty will call at Seaville on his way down the coast. A ride direct across the Weald starting at first light tomorrow would be in plenty of time to catch Randolph there."

Galdore looked at Martha, the unspoken question producing an immediate response. "I'll leave with the sun," she said.

"He's bound to need equipment and supplies," Atha said. "I'll give you a letter of authority for him to charge what he needs to the court account from our general suppliers in Portalbion."

As day broke and the golden orb of the winter sun heralded a new day, Martha rode hard across the grassy plains of the Weald toward Seaville. She was eager to see Randolph, and had missed him much since they had become separated in the Old Goblin Mines. She reflected on their first meeting in the autumn just gone and mused on where their destiny might lie.

"Are we meant to be together?" she asked herself. "Would it be a happy alliance or do our ways plough different furrows through the field of life? Maybe the answer will be found if we allow a closer union to develop. We shall see what may transpire."

૭∾૭

It was late in the afternoon that Haggerty steered the sleek boat into Seaville harbour. Martha had been in the village for almost a whole day and was relieved to see the *Mindy Lou* glide gently into her berth at the quay. She had rented a room at the Lute and Flute Tavern for that evening, someplace that she and Randolph could talk unobserved and not be overheard by flapping ears that resided in every harbour town in recent days.

257

"Gone are the times when you could mind your own business in a public place," the landlord said as he took her reservation. "There's too many folk too interested in others activities these days. Come to a pretty pass when you need to rent a private room to do your trading; that's what I says anyways. But can't complain too much. It's all money for the coffers and no mistake."

Martha had just smiled politely and nodded. She didn't want to get into any more conversation than absolutely necessary. She now had to work out a way to get Randolph's attention and get him to come to the room. She didn't want to be seen talking to him. Thrung's hired ears and eyes could be anywhere and by now, he was certain to know of the missing talisman. She watched the *Mindy Lou* dock and then hurried back to the room she had rented.

☙❧

"Secure for'ard," shouted a crew member as he tied off the mooring rope.

"Secure aft," came another shout from the stern.

"Secure your place at the bar!" Haggerty shouted with a laugh as he dismissed his crew for a few hours ashore. "Back by two hours after sundown," he called. "And don't be pissed; we got loading to do to be ready for early cast-off tomorrow."

"Aye, aye Cap'n," chorused the crew as they fought to be first down the gangplank and into the tavern bar.

"'Bout as much chance of them not being pissed as fish walking," Haggerty said to himself as he descended the ladder to the galley. "Well done matey," he said to Randolph, "That were a mighty fine beef stew you cooked up for the men today. But what's that fishy smell down here? Can't understand a fishy smell when it was beef we had."

"Don't know," Randolph said. "That's probably the fish for supper," he quickly added, making a mental note to get fish out for supper and wash himself and his clothes yet again in an attempt to rid himself of the aroma still haunting him and all those who came within sniffing distance.

"Not going with the others?" Haggerty asked.

"No," Randolph said. "Best I stay hidden here, don't want to tempt fate."

"Right you are," Haggerty said. "I'm ashore for a while then. You're in charge of the *Mindy Lou*." And with that, he was gone.

Randolph sat back, balanced the chair on its two back legs, and put his hands behind his head. "In charge of the *Mindy Lou*," he said to himself. "Hhhmmmm."

In his mind, Randolph became captain of the *Mindy Lou*, the most feared pirate vessel that had ever roamed the waters of the Alusian coastline. He stood, proud at the wheel, a patch over one eye and a parrot sitting on his left shoulder. Away on the horizon, the lookout had spotted a trader sailing northward and called the information down from the crow's nest, perched high on the for'ard mast. Captain Randolph barked orders to go hard t'port and let go the mains'l, which billowed in the sharp wind as the *Mindy Lou* lurched forward and picked up speed in pursuit of her prey.

"Shiver me timbers and splice the main brace," Randolph called out aloud, without having a clue what timbers were or even less idea where he'd find a main brace.

"What?" Martha's voice said, jerking him back to reality as he toppled off the chair and landed in a heap on the cabin floor.

Watching from the window of her rented room in the Lute and Flute, Martha had seen the crew leave the *Mindy Lou* and a little later observed Haggerty swagger down the gangplank. She had rightly guessed that Randolph had stayed on board to remain hidden and thought this would probably be her best opportunity to get to talk to him or, at least pass a quick message for him to come to talk with her at the Lute and Flute.

"Martha," Randolph said, scrabbling to his feet. "What are you doing here?" He crossed the cabin to embrace her and plant a fishy kiss on her lips.

"Yuk," Martha said. "You stink of fish; get off me."

Randolph cursed Theodore quietly.

"Haggerty might be back at any time," Randolph said. "He didn't say how long he'd be gone."

"Look then," Martha said. "I've got important news. As soon as he gets back, tell him you need to go ashore for a while and come to meet me at the Lute and Flute tavern. It's right on the quayside. Come up to the last room on the left on the first floor. We can talk then."

There was a noise up on deck, and Haggerty's voice boomed down the hatchway.

"Got any food on the go Rand . . . Fishman? I'm starving hungry; that stew's got all me juices working." His bulky posterior followed his legs down the ladder.

"There's someone here to see you," Randolph called, thinking quickly how he might explain Martha's presence. "She's inquiring after a passage down to Gospot. I said she'd have to wait till you came back."

Although Haggerty knew something of Randolph's quest and, Randolph was sure, could generally be trusted, he was a bit loud and forthright sometimes, and the less he knew the safer Randolph felt.

"Passage . . . Gospot . . . she . . ." Haggerty said while descending. "No, don't think we have space," he said as he reached the bottom of the ladder. He turned to see Martha. "But on the other hand, I'm sure we could squeeze her in. What's yer name, love?"

"Mandy," Randolph said.

"April," Martha said.

Haggerty looked from one to the other.

"Mandy-April," Martha quickly said. "I need to get down to Gospot to see my sister; she's having a baby."

Randolph covered his eyes and massaged his face as he turned to the galley to disguise his amusement at the developing farce.

"I'll put on a brew for three and get something for you to eat, while Mandy-April negotiates her passage with you," he said to Haggerty.

"Would you like anything to eat, love," he asked Martha, emulating Haggerty's style of speech.

"No thanks, ducks" she replied. "I've just had a mess of potage."

"Nice lad, Fishman," Haggerty said, gesturing toward Randolph's back as he left the cabin. "Makes a good stew, but there's a bit of a fishy smell that follows him around. Anyways, if he doesn't mind, you can have his cabin. It's good and private and away from the other quarters, and he can transfer his stuff to the bunk in the galley. I'm sure he won't mind, and we don't want to disappoint your sister, do we?"

Randolph returned with three mugs and a wad of cheese and bread for Haggerty.

"I've said that if you don't mind moving to the galley bunk, Mandy-April can have your cabin," Haggerty said.

"Fine by me," Randolph said.

"Right then; get your stuff and bring it on board," Haggerty said to Martha. "Fishman here will help you get bunked down." He went off to his cabin, nursing his mug and plate of bread and cheese.

When he had gone, Randolph and Martha looked at each other and fell to the floor, completely disabled with laughter. "Sister. . .," Randolph chortled. "Having a baby!"

"Fishman. . .," Martha burbled. "Where did you get a name like Fishman? Is that because of the way you smell?" She burst into an uncontrollable fit of mirth.

"Well, fate seems to have dictated that we travel to Gospot together," Randolph said when they had recovered sufficiently to speak coherently. "And my instincts tell me that is right."

"I'll get my pack and come back on board straight away," Martha said. Suddenly, she became serious. "There are important developments that you should know about; we can talk later."

Martha was soon back with her pack and, not long after, the crew appeared in dribs and drabs to complete the loading of boxes and other goods that had resulted from Haggerty's trading negotiations with merchants he had met on the quays. While the loading was going on, Haggerty came down to the galley area to see if Fishman had gotten Mandy-April bunked down.

Randolph and Martha had discussed the matter and decided it would be best to confide a little more in Haggerty. If they wanted his help, it was important he felt they trusted him.

"Captain, if you can spare a few moments, there's a few things Mandy-April and I need to tell you in addition to what Theodore has already said. In strict confidence though."

"You can trust Haggerty with yer business," he said. "It'll go no further."

They told Haggerty of their work together and said that while they would both maintain their false identities during the voyage, they thought it was important for him to know who they really were and that they were on a secret mission on behalf of Galdore and the king. They told him it was vital that their movements were undetected by forces that were working against the king and against the good folk of Alusia. Haggerty listened intently, and when they had finished, he touched the side of his nose with a podgy index finger and winked.

"Silence is golden," he said, and winked again. "Now that you'se finished your yarn, I must tell 'ee there was a mighty shifty looking character on the quay asking if I was carrying any passengers.

"No, I told him, only the crew and a friend of mine going to tend her pregnant sister. He seemed satisfied with that and went off asking questions of others from other vessels."

"Well done," Randolph said. "That was almost certainly one of the spies from the ranks of the king's enemies."

"Anyone against the king is an enemy of mine," Haggerty said. "Your secret's safe with me and the crew know nothing. They number you among themselves and I've told them I have a lady friend of mine joined us for the trip down to Gospot to see her sister, so they'se been warned to mind their manners. But it'd do no 'arm to mix with them a bit more."

"Good thinking," Randolph said. "I'll do a few songs for them after the meal tonight. The singing galley slave."

"You could borrow my lute if you know how to play one," Haggerty said.

"Thanks," Randolph said. "I do play a bit."

"And one or two of the men play the whistle. We'll have a bit of a sing song tonight and then break harbour for Portalbion in the morning."

"Right," Randolph said. "I'd better get the grub started; they'll be hungry after the loading."

"Oh, there's one other thing," Haggerty said.

"What's that?" Randolph asked.

"D'yer think you'd manage to get rid of that fishy smell before the sing song?"

"I'll sort him out," Martha said. "That'll be my contribution to the evening."

"And a great big one it'll be; he smells like his spent a day in an old fish barrel," Haggerty said. The ladder shook with his laughter as his ample posterior and then his legs were lost to view on deck.

Martha made Randolph do the meal preparation dressed in nothing but his cook's hat and apron while she took his clothes and tied them to the end of a rope, which she then doused off the side of the *Mindy Lou*.

I'll give them a good soaking and then dry them in the oven, she thought.

Unfortunately, when she pulled the rope back on board, Randolph's clothes were nowhere to be seen. Randolph's apron had no back, so he spent the whole evening either sitting down or with his back to the wall until he dropped a spoon and, forgetting his state of dress, turned his back on the assembled crew and bent down to recover it. The applause was deafening, and everybody thought it was a stunt he had devised on purpose.

"I know I said mix with them a bit more," Haggerty said quietly to Randolph. "But I wouldn't get too familiar. I'd do the songs now if I were you and keep facing north."

Randolph sang a shanty he had composed while he was preparing the meal.

> *"I'm friggin' in the riggin' and I'm dancing on the deck,*
> *I've got a seaman's jumper and a lanyard round my neck,*
> *I've scrubbed and cleaned the figurehead,*
> *I've rubbed and polished brass,*
> *And now I've done a hard day's graft,*
> *I'm resting on me arse.*
>
> *With a yo ho ho and a fiddle diddle dee,*
> *We're all a goin' a sailing on the sea,*
> *With me and you and all the crew,*
> *And good ol' Cap'n Haggerty.*

We're sailing down to Gospot where I lived when but a lad,
But on the way we'll call and see some good ol' friends
      we've had,
In Seaville and Portalbion,
We'll spend some time ashore,
But when cap'n wants us back on board,
We'll hurry for the door.

With a yo ho ho and a fiddle diddle dee,
We're all a goin' a sailing on the sea,
With me and you and all the crew,
And good ol' Cap'n Haggerty.

And when we mount the gangplank and we're welcomed
      back on board,
We can see we've all been missed a bit; it's just that we're
      adored,
By our cap'n, well without us,
He'd have to do it on is own,
And while he's quite a good ol' lad,
He can't sail it all alone.

With a yo ho ho and a fiddle diddle dee,
We're all a goin' a sailing on the sea,
With me and you and all the crew,
And good ol' Cap'n Haggerty."

The song was a great success and the crew made Randolph sing it three times while they all joined, with raucous voices, in the chorus and the two men who Haggerty had said played the whistle, picked up the tune and made it sparkle. Then, after they'd all sung some traditional Alusian shanties and other folk songs, there was a polite call, respecting Haggerty's instruction to "mind yer manners, there's a lady on board," for a song from Mandy-April.

"Yes," Randolph said. "Come on Mandy-April, I heard you singing in your cabin earlier; you've a sweet voice."

The men cheered and whistled, and Martha stepped forward.

"The Green Leaves of Summer," she said to Randolph.

Randolph played the introduction to the well-known ballad and silence fell on the assembled company as Martha's magical voice rang out with the gentlest tones ever heard on board the *Mindy Lou*.

> *"Oh, the green leaves of summer,*
> *Are like my heart's desires,*
> *They're fresh and clean, they shine and sheen*
> *Across our homeland's shires.*
> *They bob and play, the livelong day,*
> *They dance there in the sun.*
> *Remind me of the love I have,*
> *Remind me of my one."*

Stunned silence hung in the air for a moment after Martha had finished her song and then the crew exploded in applause, whistles, and cheers. They insisted Mandy-April sang several more songs before they were prepared to let her go. Randolph finished off with his usual storyteller song and Haggerty announced bunk time as they had an early call to catch the tide. The men drifted off to their various quarters, leaving only Randolph, Martha, and Haggerty in the dining cabin.

"I'm going to station myself here tonight," Haggerty announced, stretching himself out on the long bench against the cabin wall. "Make sure we don't get any unwelcome visitors coming to snoop around during the night. I promised Theo I'd get you safe to Gospot," he said to Randolph, "And that's what I'll do. And now we have a lady on board, we wouldn't want any of the crew coming back for a private performance durin' the night, would we?"

"Thanks," Randolph said gloomily, aware that this cut off his access from the galley bunk to Martha's cabin. "Good night Captain; Good night, Martha, and thanks," he said again turning to leave for his galley bunk and inadvertently exposing his bare rear end to Haggerty.

"I think I might have preferred the fishy smell," Haggerty said, and laughed loudly.

The next morning, Randolph woke early to prepare breakfast for the men. Haggerty was just stretching and yawning in the dining area and there were shufflings and scufflings up on deck, as the crew started their morning routine. Randolph still didn't have any clothes to wear, and after the crew had been fed and the *Mindy Lou* was underway, he knocked on Martha's door to seek help in obtaining something to put on other than his cook's apron and hat.

Haggerty had told Randolph that they would be docking at Portalbion shortly after lunch and would then leave the port in the early evening for an overnight run down to Gospot, arriving there about sunrise the next day. Randolph planned to go with Martha to see Nick briefly at the Black Swan and get some clothes from his friend.

"But I can't go swaggering around the town with my bum hanging out," he said.

"We'll need to be careful you're not seen by any of Thrung's spies," Martha said. "Portalbion is a busy place, and you're know there as well."

"I must see Nick. As well as getting some clothes, I need him to make some arrangements with local suppliers in Portalbion and Gospot to get me some equipment. I can't do it myself for fear of being spotted by Thrung's cronies and it would look odd if you were to order the stuff I need."

"I've just had a brilliant idea," Martha chirped. "Brilliant idea."

"If we get you dressed up in some of my spare clothes, we can go to see Nick with you disguised as a woman. Thrung's spies won't be looking for a woman, and it will solve the problem of you not drawing attention by exposing your arse to the world." She giggled.

Randolph wasn't sure about parading himself through the streets of Portalbion in a skirt, blouse, and bonnet, but as Martha pointed out, nobody would know who he was and if she did a job on his hair and powdered down his face a bit, they could hurry along and nobody would be any the wiser.

"Well, I suppose you're right; it'll be a good disguise, but Haggerty and the crew musn't see me. I'd never live it down and they'd talk about it in the local tavern and destroy the purpose of the disguise," Randolph said somewhat apprehensively.

"We'll wait until they've all gone ashore and then I'll get you kitted out," Martha said. In the meantime, go and shave that stubble off your face; as close as you can; I'm not walking through the town with a bearded lady."

After docking at the quay in Portalbion harbour, Haggerty and the crew were soon ashore to complete various deals and trades or to spend a couple of hours with friends in the quayside taverns.

"Need to get yerself ashore, if y'can," Haggerty advised Randolph. "Need to stretch your legs a bit."

"We're going up to see a friend at the Black Swan," Randolph said.

"Be back down before sunset," Haggerty said. "We sail on the night tide."

Even with his fidgeting and complaining, it took Martha only a short while to arrange Randolph's golden curls in a very flattering style under the frilled bonnet that she produced from her pack. A little powder and rouge on his cheeks along with a patterned skirt, white blouse, and shawl, disguised Randolph so that he wouldn't even have recognized himself in a busy street. This was also the first opportunity that Martha had had to bring Randolph up to date with the events surrounding Moraden's defection or capture. He was shocked to hear that his friend had turned to evil, whether by choice, persuasion, or subjugation, and his first thought was to launch a campaign to save him.

"Take off that map pouch and sword," an exasperated Martha said as Randolph buckled his belt. "And try and walk a little more refined. Waggle your hips a bit. Women don't stomp like gorillas."

Randolph felt very self-conscious as they hurried through the town, but nobody gave them a second glance, and they were soon entering the porch of the Black Swan as the old mechanical timepiece chimed three times.

"Afternoon ladies," said fat Ham, who was passing through the entrance area. "How can we help you?"

And then he recognized Martha. "Oh, it's you, Martha. 'Aven't seen yerself for a while. And who's this pretty young friend you've gotten with you?" he said, winking at Randolph.

But before Martha could reply, Ham was off. "I'll be callin' master Nick and let 'im know y'er 'ere," he called over his shoulder. "Make yerselves comfy in the bar there."

Randolph and Martha went and sat down at one of the tables. "Put your knees together, will you," Martha said. "Young ladies don't sit like that."

Randolph found himself blushing at the thought of somebody looking up his skirt, and then told himself not to be so stupid, but he quickly put his knees together as Ham came back.

"Master Nick'll be right down to sees 'ee. I'll goes'n makes a good brew," he said, as he went off to the kitchen.

Randolph's back was to the door through which Nick soon came in.

"Hello Martha. Great to see you. Have you been away? I've not seen you around for some time."

"Yes," Martha replied. "And we're only here on a flying visit now. We need to be back to the boat before sunset or we'll miss the sailing."

"We?" Nick said, gesturing with a nod at the back of Randolph's bonnet.

"Oh, sorry," Martha said. "Let me introduce you to a friend of mine. Randolphia, this is Nick Freedom."

Randolph stood and turned toward Nick. "Saints alive," Nick said, looking startled. "I'm sorry," he added apologetically. "I didn't mean to be rude, but you are the image of a friend of mine, or you would be if he was a woman. I mean if you were a man. . . . No, I don't mean you look like a man. Marthaaaaaa . . . help, dig me out."

Randolph couldn't keep up the pretence any longer and burst into laughter.

"You bastard," Nick said. "You really had me going there for a moment. What are you playing at, you fool; surely you didn't come through the town dressed like that?"

"Well it was either like this or with my arse hanging out, and this seemed the better option. But there's another reason as well. Nobody must know I'm here, not even Ham, so if he comes back in you must keep up the pretence. It's very important."

"Right," Nick said. "But what's going on? Explain."

Ham delivered the pot of fresh brew while Nick talked briefly about nothing in particular. Once he had left, Martha and Randolph told Nick of the events since Randolph had last been at the Black Swan in the autumn. At first, Nick's total disbelief in things magical and mystical made him scoff at their story, but as they went on, he could see this was no joke and both his concern for his friend and his amazement at the tale they related grew enormously.

"So this Thrung character is out to get you, then," Nick said, "I'm not having that; nobody threatens my mates without answering to me." He puffed up much larger than his normal size. "If he wants a piece of you, he'll have to climb over me first."

"I'm glad you feel that way, and I thank you for your loyalty to me," Randolph said. "But this isn't a tough guy you can just poke on the nose; this is the dark forces of evil that have been in existence since the creation of all things. But I am going to need your help."

"It's yours for the asking; you know that," Nick said. "I'll do whatever you need."

Randolph was sure that Nick hadn't really truly understood the seriousness of the matter, but his willingness to help was very welcome. Apart from getting a bundle of clothes, which they took back to the *Mindy Lou*, Randolph left Nick with a list of equipment he needed from the suppliers to the court, plus Atha's letter of authority to charge, and a request for him to load up the cart and bring it all down and meet them at the Mucky Duck tavern in Gospot at noon in two days' time. Saying a hasty farewell, Martha and Nick hurried back to the *Mindy Lou* to get on board before Haggerty and the crew returned.

Randolphia was keen to get turned back into a man and wanted to talk more with Martha about the Moraden situation and his plans for when they reached Gospot. By the time the *Mindy Lou* set sail, Randolph was feeling more secure in the knowledge that he could face the world in any direction, and he no longer needed to waggle his hips when he walked or keep his knees together when he sat down.

The crew worked the night through. Randolph responded to constant calls for hot beverages and food from the crew. Shortly after sunrise the next day, they dropped anchor in the southerly stretch of Condor Basin awaiting high tide for their entry into Gospot harbour. After breakfast, Randolph and Martha went up on deck and looked out over the waves toward the shoreline.

"This is where I spent most of my childhood," Randolph said. "Directly inshore from us, at the south end of the bay there, that's where I last saw my sister, Lydie."

At the thought of Lydie, Randolph became sad. The twenty-plus years that she had been gone had not lessened his love for his sister. He could still see her smiling face as she ran to him when she needed to share her joy and hear her sobs when she needed comfort or reassurance. He could still hear her screams as the boat was pulled out further and further by the strong current. He could still see her waving frantically as she stood alone in that small craft. He still blamed himself for not attempting to save her.

"Is this where you were born then?" Martha asked.

"No," Randolph replied. "Lydie and I were born in Riversend, but we were sent to live with our Aunt Margreta on her farm here in Gospot when our parents were killed in an accident. We were only two years old, and I don't really remember either my mother or my father. Aunt Greta brought us up; she's a dear soul and looked after us well. She's sold most of the farm now and lives alone in one of the old cottages. She's about sixty, and I still go and stay with her whenever I'm down this way. The old hayloft is sort of my home now."

"Why didn't you stay and work the farm for her?" Martha asked. "There's a good living to be made in farming."

"That's what she wanted," Randolph said. "She didn't have any children of her own and after Lydie was lost, I was the only one she had to pass on the farm to. We talked about it, but I wasn't born to be a farmer. However, it's only in the last few months that the real truth of that has been proved to me."

"So, how long did you live in Gospot?" Martha asked, interested to find out more about Randolph's background.

"When I was fifteen, I took to the road to make my fortune and travel Alusia, and maybe the whole of the Western Realm. Things were a bit strained between Aunt Greta and me for several years. It's only since she sold the farm and settled down to a gracious retirement that we've grown together again. She'll be delighted to see us, and particularly if I'm with you. She always tells me recently that I should get a nice young woman and settle down. She mustn't know anything of the truth of our quest or that I am destined to be the One."

"Nick's from Gospot as well, isn't he?" Martha said.

"Yes," Randolph said. "Nick, Lydie, and I were inseparable as young children. His parents ran the farm down the lane from Aunt Greta's. They still do, although they're getting on a bit now. Nick was with me when Lydie was swept out to sea, and it was through saving him from the water that I wasn't fast enough to catch her boat as the current dragged it out."

"But Sulaman seemed certain Lydie is alive somewhere," Martha said.

"Yes," Randolph said. "And that our destinies would bring us together again. Will you come with me down to that place when we get ashore? I always go there first when I come to Gospot. I know it's silly, but I still expect to see that boat washed back to shore with Lydie safe and sound."

"Of course I will," Martha said. she gave Randolph a hug, "And then we'll go up and meet your aunt; I'll be your girl, and she will be happy."

"Thanks," Randolph said and kissed Martha tenderly.

She responded. He felt her sink into him as the softness of her body folded into his own. "Tonight," she whispered.

The sound of Haggerty puffing up the ladder from his cabin below separated them. They didn't want others to know of any deeper feelings than friendship. In these troubled times, such emotions, if known, might prove powerful to the enemy. Randolph reflected for a moment on that thought. Until now, he had not viewed Thrung as the enemy; his focus had been on defending Alusia and the power of good against an attack by the forces of darkness. But now, suddenly he felt his mind changing. Thrung was now the enemy; he was a force that must be swept from the land. He was a power against which Randolph must plan an attack. He could not sit and wait for Thrung to infiltrate the overworld, to cause more damage, to enlist, enroll, and kidnap more decent folk. The loss of his friend, Moraden, weighed heavily on Randolph's mind. He hoped above all else that Moraden could be saved, but he knew Thrung and his evil cohorts must be crushed; if fate dictated that included Moraden, then so be it. But, it wouldn't stop him trying a rescue.

"Then so be it," Randolph said out loud.

"So be what?" Martha asked, as Haggerty stomped up to them.

"Tell you later," Randolph said.

"Mornin'," Haggerty said, "We'll be alongside in an hour, so I'm glad I've caught y'ere now. Just wanted to say good luck, and if there's any service I can be in the fight against the king's enemies, then you can always rely on Haggerty and the *Mindy Lou.*"

"You've done more than your share," Randolph said. "And I thank you for your kindness and your loyalty to the crown. When I get back to Castle Drent, Galdore and King Atha will know of your support. You're a good man, Captain, but the best service you can now give is to forget I made this trip. I was never here."

"Who said that?" Haggerty asked, looking around in mock amazement as if Randolph's voice had come out of thin air.

The three of them laughed together until the first mate shouted from the poop deck. "Tides up Cap'n; we can weigh anchor and make for harbour."

"Make it so," Haggerty called in reply. "Make it so." He shook Randolph and Martha by their hands, and his rolling gait took him off down the deck to command of his ship.

The *Mindy Lou* was soon docked and, once ashore, Randolph took Martha up the coast a little to the place he always visited in memory of Lydie. They stood together, Randolph gazing out across the ocean, Martha silent and respectful of the feelings that Randolph exhumed from the childhood he had briefly described to her.

"I know now that Sulaman is right," Randolph said, breaking the silence. "I know she is out there somewhere; I can feel her presence in the world, but something isn't right. I don't know what, but something is different about her."

"Well, it's bound to be," Martha said. "Your memories are from more than twenty years ago. She will have lived a life for those years in a place far away from here. She will be different; she may even have a family of her own. She may be rich, she may be poor; we don't know her fortune. But one thing we do know.

She is no longer a six-year-old child. You must get used to that thought."

"You're right," Randolph sighed. "I will just have to wait until destiny finds us together again." He turned to leave the shore and Martha followed. At the top of the track from the rocky coastline, Randolph stopped and looked back once more to the sea.

"I wish I knew, Lydie," he said. "I wish I knew where you were."

Chapter Eleven
The Salt Lake Skeleton

The Black Swarm

"RANDOLPH!" GRETA squealed as she enveloped him in a smothering embrace of the sort that is the special reserve of aunts for their nephews.

Randolph extracted himself from her ample bosom like a pearl diver coming up for air. "Hello Aunt Greta," he said. "Got a room for a poor wandering minstrel and his friend for a couple of nights?"

"Come on in," Greta said, tousling his hair affectionately as if he were still ten years old. "And who's your little friend here?"

They all went through to the comfortable country kitchen at the rear of the cottage. The smell of fresh-baked buns, stew, and herbs filled the air, and Randolph felt the saliva flow in his mouth at the thought of his aunt's delicious cooking.

"This is my friend Martha," Randolph said by way of introduction.

"Well, come on in Martha," Greta said. "Any friend of Randolph's is welcome here, especially one as fine looking as you, my dear. What a lovely couple you make."

Martha smiled at the fact she had already been marked as Randolph's mate, but flattered by Aunt Greta's overwhelmingly warm welcome. This was the sort of home where you immediately felt one of the family, as soon as you crossed the threshold. She could see from where Randolph had learned his caring attitude for others and his love of people. Martha felt it a pity that his destiny had been chosen to prevent him staying with his aunt and running her farm. She silently cursed the forces of evil and Thrung for all the harm and destruction they brought to the lives of good people like Aunt Greta.

"So where are your wanderings taking you now?" Greta asked Randolph. "How long will you be able to stay? Is Nick with you? How are you? Surely you're not expecting this lovely young lady to stay in a hayloft?"

"Whoa, whoa," Randolph said. "One question at a time."

"And the hayloft will be fine," Martha laughed. "I'm a country girl myself and haylofts are one my favorite places."

Randolph's mind was off on a private adventure in anticipation of the coming night. At last a whole night alone with Martha, with no distraction and no disturbances. He visualized the dark barn, the warmth of the hay, the sliver of moonlight as it tumbled through the high window and fell gently on Martha standing there before him, soft and expectant. Her black hair, streaked with the silver of the moon's blessing, cascaded down over her bare shoulders. He reached out and pulled gently at the lace that fastened the front of her tunic, releasing it to reveal the fitted white cotton blouse beneath, hugging the curvaceous lines of her spectacular body. His hands caressed her bare shoulders, pushing down to the line of her blouse further to feel the curve of her firm breasts, which he cupped gently in his massaging hands. He saw the look of ecstasy on her face as her pursed lips invited him to come closer, her own hands griping him by the waist, drawing him toward her and sliding down, down, across his stomach, reaching for the hardness that bulged between them.

"Rabbit stew all right?" Greta asked. "For supper later tonight, I mean."

"Yes." Randolph groaned with delight, as he swung his legs round and pulled his chair up closer to the table, suddenly conscious of the ballooned lump in the lap of his breeches. "Yes," he repeated, his voice reflecting the erotic fantasy that his now hidden groin confirmed.

"Coo!" his aunt said. "Sounds like you haven't had rabbit stew for a long time, but no need to have some sort of orgasm over it; it's only an ordinary rabbit stew."

Randolph coughed and recovered his composure, hoping that Greta had not seen his excited, pulsating trousers.

"You might want to freshen up a bit from your journey, my dear," Greta said to Martha. "The washroom's out back, and there's hot water boilin' in the tub out there. I know the place is small, but when I sold the farm there was plenty to have all the best installed in the cottage here. It's a pity we only have the one bedroom, otherwise you could be more comfortable. Randolph's used to the hayloft."

"And so am I Greta," Martha said, as she picked up her pack and made her way out to the washroom. "The hayloft will suit me fine."

And me too, thought Randolph to himself, as he felt his breeches stir again.

"Now," Randolph's aunt said, turning to him. "You didn't answer my questions. Tell me the news and where you're off to. And I want to know all about Martha." She grinned and rubbed her hands with glee at the thought that Randolph might at last be on the verge of being tamed.

"Well, I've been chosen as the best person to fight the forces of darkness and to destroy the evil that has existed since time began. So, I'm off on a quest to find the source of the master power and turn it against the Lord of Wickedness. In the last couple of months, I've learned how to fly, how to make myself invisible, talk to animals, and I've been killed and resurrected. I've fallen madly in love with Martha and when I've completed my quest to save the Western Realm, then I'm going to move in with her and have lots of babies."

"Stop talking nonsense," Greta said, giggling at Randolph's stupid answer. "You never change. I don't think you've ever given me a straight answer to what you've been up to. Tell me what you're really doing."

"Oh, if you insist," Randolph said. "Martha is a friend of mine I met when I was staying up with Nick in Portalbion. He's coming down to join us tomorrow and we're going off on a visit to the Salt Lakes."

"You be careful when you go there," Greta said. "You make sure you wrap up warm or you'll catch your death. And you look after Martha. I think she fancies you, by the way she looks at you. I can tell these things."

"You think so?" Randolph teased. "Do you think I'll be safe in the hayloft with her tonight; she won't abuse me in the night will she?"

"Now you stop that sort of talk," Greta said. "You're a rude boy. I can see that she might fancy you a bit, but I can see she's a respectable girl too. Don't you be sayin' things like that about her, or the cat'll get your tongue."

Martha returned refreshed from the washhouse.

"That was great," she said. "A good soak in a hot tub was just what I needed. Your turn now Randolph; there's still a faint aroma of fish hanging around you. This is your chance to get rid of it completely."

As Randolph crossed the yard to the washhouse, he failed to notice the two pairs of eyes that spied on him from behind the high fence.

"It's gobbin' 'im," said a voice attached to one pair of eyes.

"Well ain't we gobbin' done well," the other said.

"Weasel, gobbin' weasel. I'm gonna get 'im back," Toady said.

"We need to wait for night, 'fore we try anyfink. If we do somefink while it's light, we might gobbin' get caught again," Spike said.

"Right," Toady said. "Let's find somewhere to 'ide."

"Down 'ere'll do," Spike said. "Down 'ere in this old barn, under the 'ay lorft."

∂∽⌒

The rabbit stew was as delicious as Randolph remembered of Aunt Greta's cooking, and it was dark by the time they'd eaten their fill and decided to make for the hayloft.

You can leave all your stuff here in the kitchen," Greta said. "Just take what you need for the night over to the hayloft."

Randolph was almost hopping with excitement in anticipation of his forthcoming undisturbed night with Martha. As they left the back door of the cottage and crossed the yard in the chill night air, Randolph took Martha's hand and pulled her along toward the barn.

"There's no need to rush," Martha said. "We've got all night, and anticipation is half the fun."

"Not when it's been going on for months and months," Randolph said.

Once in the loft, Randolph pulled up the ladder and closed the trap door. The smell of the hay took him back to his childhood days when he, Lydie, and Nick would build a hideout up in the loft and play games of secret and mystery as they tunneled through the mounds of dried grass and climbed and rolled among the bales. It was also the place where Randolph had brought one or two of the village girls in the early days of his sexual explorations, but tonight was different. Tonight was to be his first encounter with someone for whom he felt true love. Martha stood, as in Randolph's earlier vision and the moon was on cue, shimmering white light falling like stardust through the high window. Randolph followed his vision's script and gazed longingly into Martha's dark eyes as he reached out and released the lacing on her tunic. Their hands explored each other freely as they sank slowly to their knees and rolled themselves into the warm hay. Their lips met, just as the smell of smoke and the crackle of burning timbers reached their senses and two stooped figures ran unseen up the track away from the barn.

"That'll gobbin' sort 'im," sang one of the figures. "That place'll go up like a torch."

"Yeh," said the other. "A beacon to warn others not to mess with Spike and Toady." He cackled. "We'll be the golden bollocks when Frung 'ears our gobbin' story. Whaja fink?"

They hurried on past the farm owned by Nick's parent and increased their speed considerably as two large dogs detected their presence and gave chase.

"I'll 'ave to steal some new breeches now," Spike said. "We can't go all the gobbin' way to the boglands wiv me arse 'anging out."

"Is that all y'er gobbin' worried about?" Toady asked. "I reckon I'll need to steal a new arse." He felt the bruised and bitten flesh of his bleeding buttocks.

Two self-satisfied dogs sat in the middle of the track, worrying lumps of material that used to fit in the holes in the goblins' breeches. By this time, Randolph and Martha had easily escaped the now-blazing barn through the rear, by sliding down the hoist rope used to haul the bales into the loft. They and several of the neighbours formed a chain to throw buckets of water onto the burning building.

"No, it's gone too far," Greta said as she supervised operations from inside an enormous nightshirt. "We'll not save that now; all we can do is make sure that sparks don't start other fires around."

Randolph stood drenched to the skin with splashing from the buckets, his ardor considerably cooled, as the chill night air enhanced the effect of the cold water on his skin. He shivered as the blaze finally died down and the small group of smoke-blackened firefighters relaxed a little.

"I'll make up a bed for you on the floor in my room," Greta said to Martha.

"And we've got a spare bed you can have for a couple of nights, Randolph," Benjy said. "Mum and Dad will be pleased to see you for a few days."

"But before we do anything else, all back into my kitchen for a hot brew," Greta said. "And thanks to everybody for your help."

It was warm in Greta's kitchen, and soon the five neighbours, Martha, Greta, and Randolph recovered from the trauma of fighting the blaze. It was still well before midnight, as Randolph and Martha had gone to the hayloft to get an early night and nobody was inclined to hurry away.

"So, what brings you down Gospot way, Randolph?" Benjy asked.

Benjy was one of Randolph's boyhood acquaintances, son of the local smithy. Already nearly as skilled as his father, he was destined to take on the trade in the years to come when his father eventually admitted it was time to retire from the world of work and succumb to support from his son. Benjy was a man of about the same age as Randolph, fit and strong, tanned and cheerful, he also held the local record for the fastest time to down a pint of ale.

"Well, Martha and I are on a sort of expedition," Randolph said.

"Expedition?" Benjy said. "That sounds interesting."

"We'll leave you lads to chat for a while," Greta said. "Come on Martha, come and help me make up that bed and then we'll see you boys in the morning. Don't stay up too late Randolph; you know you need your sleep."

"Yes, Auntie," Randolph said, as she kissed him on the top of the head and led the way up the creaky stairs, leaving Martha to follow.

"Night," Martha said, as she kissed Randolph, "And remember, anticipation . . ." She left the whispered sentence unfinished. "See you in the morning."

Martha closed the kitchen door on her way upstairs, leaving Randolph, Benjy, and the four other neighbours sitting around the table sipping hot mugs of herbal brew.

"Are you and Martha . . . you know . . .," Gumbold said, waggling his head from side to side as if he had a rubber neck.

Gumbold was another of Randolph's chums from the past, but unlike Benjy, his apprenticeship to the town tailor had robbed him of the exercise that other more physically demanding work might have provided. While he wasn't what you would call fat, he was comfortably proportioned and still sweating a little from the earlier exertion. Gumbold, like all those seated around the table, was an affable fellow and known by his friends for his good humour.

"Well sort of," Randolph said. "Best say I'm working on it."

"Tell us more about your expedition," Benjy said. "You've whetted my appetite."

"I didn't want to say anything while my Aunt Greta was here," Randolph said. "She'd only get worried. I was going to get you all together tomorrow. Fact is, I need some help from a few people I can trust, but as we're all here now, I'll give you the background and you can sleep on it."

Sitting around the table as Randolph related his tale, Benjy bristled with a mixture of indignation and pride at the way his friend had been treated, but then at the way he had handled himself: Gumbold's eyes grew larger and larger in what would have been disbelief if anybody but Randolph had been relating the

281

story. Fernando, the baker, looked increasingly scared. Mendaph, a fisherman, chin in cupped hands and elbows on knees, became increasingly captivated, leaning further and further forward until he nearly fell off his chair. Torridian, who was not the adventurous kind at all, was soon fast asleep and snoring loudly in the corner. There were, of course, streams of questions from all but Torridian, who continued his slumbers, blissfully unaware of the excitement Randolph had generated among his colleagues.

"Tomorrow, I'll answer all your questions tomorrow, Randolph insisted. "But just be aware, all I have related is true and if you agree to join me, I cannot guarantee your safety, the length of absence from home, or anything about what may happen. However, I can say that if I fail in my quest, Alusia and the Western Realm will be in great danger."

The assembled company fell silent and took their leave one by one. A meeting in the Mucky Duck tavern had been agreed upon for midday tomorrow. Torridian was woken and he, Randolph, and Benjy left together—Torridian turning up the road to his home with a promise to see them all at the tavern at noon, and Randolph and Benjy turning down the road to the Old Forge cottage.

"I really appreciate this Benjy," Randolph said.

"No problem," Benjy said. "What are friends for? You always were the one to fall on your feet. I remember we all used to call you Lucky Break Kettle."

"I have a feeling this was more than just a lucky break; that fire in the barn was written into destiny. I don't know who started it, but in some ways I think it did me a favor." Randolph paused thoughtfully.

"How do you mean?" Benjy said.

"Bringing the very people together I was planning on talking to tomorrow. Almost like a practice run. Although, on the other hand there was one part of it that wasn't right and didn't do me any favor at all."

"What do mean?" Benjy asked, looking a bit puzzled.

"Oh, never mind," Randolph said. "It's just that the fire was an hour too early."

Benjy remained puzzled, but Randolph wouldn't elaborate and was saved from further probing questions by a faint buzzing sound that grew in intensity as they stood staring up at the northern sky.

"Quick," Randolph said. "Inside."

They ducked through Benjy's porch and into the cottage as the bright moon silhouetted what appeared to be a fast-moving cloud, heading south along the coastline. It seemed to be weaving from right to left, as if searching for something.

"What the smithy's furnace is that?" Benjy asked.

"That is the black swarm I told you about," Randolph said. "Searching for me, I expect. It may be I've been spotted on my journey down from the north and word has got back to Thrung."

They watched from a small window as the swarm flew on past, and the buzzing faded slowly until they could hear it no longer.

"Well, it doesn't seem like they know your exact location," Benjy said.

"Maybe not, but even knowing I'm in the south is too close for comfort. I'm going to have to stay hidden tomorrow. Can we get all those that were meeting us at the Mucky Duck to come here instead?"

"Yes," Benjy said. "I can go up there at noon and get them to come down."

"And Nick will be there too," Randolph said. "Hopefully with a cart load of supplies."

"I must confess that I had some doubts about your sanity when you told us of your adventures so far, but seeing the swarm has dispelled those. Father can still manage the smithy well enough; I, at least, will accompany you on the next part of your journey."

"I thank you for that," Randolph said. "And your support will be of great comfort to me. Much danger lies ahead. But now, we must rest. Tomorrow, I and those that will join me must leave Gospot for the Salt Lakes and the search for Mithrip's resting place."

"I don't pretend to understand the importance of Mithrip's tomb, and it may be that such detail is best left unshared for the present. But if that is our quest then that is where I am bound."

Benjy took Randolph's hand in his in a bond of friendship and felt the power that flowed from Randolph. He suddenly knew that his boyhood friend had taken on all that he had told. There was no question of his sanity but there was a burning urgency to find and destroy the source of the growing forces of darkness that threatened their world.

"I am with you Randolph," he said. "I am with you to the end, whatever and wherever that may be."

ॐ

The next morning, Benjy awakened Randolph. "Martha is here to speak with you urgently."

Randolph got up quickly, if a little reluctantly, from the warm and comfortable bed and his overnight travels back to the times of his youth in Gospot. He hurried down the stairs to where Martha waited in the kitchen.

"Randolph, I must return to Castle Drent," she said. "Galdore requires my presence for a meeting of the council and decisions that must be made concerning the defense of Alusia. It would seem that Thrung's campaign intensifies, and open, random attacks have now begun on the people of the kingdom. Goblins have become commonly seen in greater number. The rivers and waterways of the land appear infested with evil creatures, and the black wasp swarm roams the land destroying anything that opposes it or stands in its path."

"There are reports of animals fleeing their natural habitats in the area," Benjy added. "And the townsfolk are stirred to deep concern over their safety by the feeling of oppression that hangs in the air."

"Then you must not delay," Randolph said. "Fly on the wind, but keep careful watch for the swarm."

Martha gave Randolph a hug and kissed him before she turned to the door, already starting the melodic chant that would summon the wind as her chariot and bear her swiftly to Castle Drent. They followed Martha outside into the yard behind the smithy's cottage, where the wind gusted and twirled, raising spirals of dust. Benjy watched in amazement as Martha was lifted from the ground. He rubbed his eyes in disbelief as she flew higher and higher, turning to the northwest and waving a farewell as she disappeared beyond their view.

"I must show Martha the invisibility spell," Randolph said, half to himself and half to Benjy. "It'll mean she can fly easier without risk of being seen by people."

Benjy was speechless and followed Randolph quietly back into the cottage, where his mother and father had prepared steaming bowls of oats, unaware of the magic that their son had just observed.

"Hello Randolph," they said. "How nice to see you," Benjy's father said.

"Randolph stayed last night," Benjy said. "We had a bit of a problem with his aunt's barn burning down, and then he had nowhere to sleep."

"Hhmm. I'm afraid you've chosen to visit Gospot at a time when we seem to have some local disturbances," Benjy's father said. "There's a feeling of gloom sitting over our usually happy community and a few strange happenings over the last few weeks."

"Yes," his wife added. "Something very strange appears to be passing through our town. Greta's barn burning down? That's just another one to add to the list. First, there was all the dead fish in the river, then several farms had fields of crops just flattened. The landlord of the Mucky Duck had a load of barrels of ale disappear overnight. Strange happenings."

Randolph greeted the couple warmly but made no comment concerning their fears.

"Father, will you be able to spare me for a few days?" Benjy asked. "I'm hoping to travel with Randolph and a few of our friends . . . on a sort of . . . a short holiday."

"That's fine," his father replied. "Business will be slack now until the New Year, and you've worked hard. Yes, a good plan; a short break with friends will refresh you."

Benjy looked at Randolph, as if to seek confirmation that his father's words might hold even a glimmer of truth. The almost imperceptible shake of Randolph's head went unobserved by the others, but Benjy already knew the seriousness of their mission.

"Thanks," he said to his father. "We'll do our best to have a good time. Is it all right if we use the barn for a meeting of those who might want to come? About midday, if that's not a problem."

"Fine," his father said. "There's no horses in for shoeing today. So I'll be in the forge."

"I'll see you later, then," Randolph said. "I must go over and talk to my aunt. You'll gather up the others, will you?" he asked Benjy.

"Leave it to me," he said. "See you in the barn at midday."

Randolph left the smithy's cottage and headed for his aunt's home. All the while, he watched the sky carefully and studied the hedgerows and walls, making sure he was unobserved. Aunt Greta was in the cottage kitchen, preparing vegetables for a stew.

"Bit of an excitement last night," she said as Randolph came into the kitchen. "Did Martha find you? She said she had an urgent message to go off to meet somebody. Falgore, or some such name."

"Yes," Randolph replied. "It's Galdore actually. He's a friend of ours, lives at Castle Drent."

"It's nice you've got so many friends," Greta said. "I'm pleased for you. And now I suppose you're off on your next little adventure. I can't keep up with you youngsters and your games. Where did you say you were going, the Salt Lakes?"

"Yes." Randolph smiled. "A few of us are planning to leave this afternoon for a few days and then, who knows? We might go on up to Riversend."

"Ah," Greta said. "Back to where you and Lydie were born. Funny how people always like to go back to their birthplace, but I don't imagine you know anybody there now, do you?"

"No," Randolph said. "We were far too young to have any real memories. Our lives seemed to start here with you."

"Bless your dear mother and father," Greta said. They would be so proud to see you now, and with such a lovely young lady friend like Martha."

"Stop fishing Auntie," Randolph said. He laughed and gave her a hug. "You'll be the first to know when there's any serious romance in the air."

"Now, off with you and find your friends," Greta said. "But make sure you come by and see me before you go on your travels to the Salt Lakes." She shooed him out of the kitchen like a small boy being sent to play.

Randolph went over to the still-smoldering ruins of the barn.

"I wonder what started that fire?" he asked himself as he concentrated his mind on the scene in front of him. His vision blurred a little as pictures came into his head. He saw himself and Martha as they entered the barn the previous evening; he watched as they climbed into the hayloft. Suddenly there was a movement in the barn below them, and Randolph focused his mind on that spot that was in reality now no more than a charred piece of ground. His senses brought him pictures and sounds from last night; he heard a voice in his head.

"Give me the gobbin' flint, will yer?"

Randolph was instantly aware that his exact location would now be known to Thrung. Even if the goblins thought they had killed him in the fire, Thrung would not be about to believe a couple of bungling idiots like them without checking. He turned quickly and hurried back to the smithy, still watching the sky and the surrounding area carefully. He found Benjy in the barn, pulling bales of straw into a rough circle so that those coming to the midday meeting would have somewhere to sit.

"We need to move faster than I thought," Randolph said. "That fire last night was no accident and by now Thrung will know where I am. We need to get away from here quickly."

As if responding to a cue, they heard a low droning noise that increased slowly in volume as the swarm of black wasps arrived to circle close by over the village.

"I've got to get away from here or you'll all be in danger," Randolph said. "But I've got to say goodbye to Aunt Greta." He rushed out of the barn and sprinted up the narrow road with Benjy hot on his heels.

Coming toward them, driving a laden cart was Nick. From behind them, the noise of the swarm increased to a loud buzzing as the wasps scanned the neat rows of cottages, paths, and roadways below. They had not yet detected Randolph, but they were only seconds away from spotting him.

"Quick," Benjy said, "under the cart cover." He lifted the tarpaulin with one hand, picked Randolph up with the other, and threw him bodily into the back of the cart. He swung himself up onto the seat beside a startled Nick.

"Don't do anything suspicious," Benjy gabbled at Nick. "Just drive on normally, straight through the town and on toward the Salt Lakes," he added in a calmer voice.

Nick opened his mouth to speak, but shut it again in response to Benjy's shaking head and drove on, picking up the tune that he had been whistling earlier.

The swarm passed overhead, weaving from side to side, circling around the smoking remains of the barn and on, following the edge of the town. Randolph lay silent and still under the tarpaulin, hardly daring to breath. After several minutes, the noise of the swarm had almost gone. Benjy turned to Nick. "Hello mate," he said. "I must say, your timing was good."

"Good to see you," Nick said. "Was that a Randolph I saw you throw in the back of the cart?"

"It was," Benjy confirmed. "And that's the best place for a Randolph at this moment. He'll have to stay there until we're well out of the town; that swarm you just saw, it's after him."

"I'm glad I'm not a Randolph, then," Nick said.

The noise of a tongue vibrating on wet lips came from somewhere in the back of the cart.

"Did the horse fart, or was that something come loose in the cart?" Nick asked.

"Didn't hear a thing," Benjy said, as the noise repeated. "Probably just a small rut or something."

They trundled on through the center of the town, Benjy directing Nick as he steered the horse onto the track heading south and into the woods that lined the way to the Salt Lakes. Once hidden in the trees that formed the outskirts of Salty Woods, Nick reined in the horse, and he and Benjy lifted the tarpaulin back to let Randolph out.

"That was a close one," Randolph said to Benjy. "Thanks for your quick thinking."

"Hello," Nick said, shaking Randolph's hand firmly. "I see things have taken a turn for the interesting."

"They certainly have," Randolph said. "I nearly got burned down last night and . . . well, you saw the swarm. I can't go back into town now. I'll just have to go on to the Salt Lakes alone."

"You might not be able to go back and see the others, but you're not going on alone," Benjy said.

"And you don't think I'm leaving you two scoundrels to go on without supervision, do you?" Nick asked. "You've got to have someone with some brains to look out for you."

Randolph felt that it was unfair to drag Benjy and Nick into the situation but, despite his warnings of danger and his excuses about letting the others and his aunt know he had left in a hurry, his friends wouldn't hear of going back. Reluctantly, Randolph accepted their help after more protestations about the danger involved and the unknown forces they might face. In truth, he was very relieved they had chosen to come with him, but he felt there were many more details they should know about his quest—what had happened to him so far and about some of the powers he seemed to have acquired, before they finally decided to offer their help. The three of them sat cross-legged on the soft turf down beside the wagon while Randolph talked for a long while about all that had happened and of what he knew of the way ahead.

"Which isn't very much," he admitted. "I have no real idea what we are looking for in the Salt Lakes other than that we need to find the tomb of the legendary Mithrip, and I have no clue what horrors Thrung may have in store for me. Even with the three of us, we stand no chance against the swarm if it locates us. It can transform into some kind of solid entity as well. Then there are the goblin armies he will surely be directing into Alusia, and the many other wicked creatures, witches, trolls, the squirds I told you about, and other forms at his command, to say nothing of Shawadarg and her evilness."

"Sounds like fun," Nick said nonchalantly.

"Yes," Benjy said. "Piece of pudden and cream."

"Look," Randolph said. "This is not something you can just dismiss with a wave of the hand and a healthy disbelief in things mystical and magical. We are all targets if we travel together, targets to be killed. Thrung will be after our blood, because I am the only thing that stands in his way. I am the One."

Randolph's seriousness and the tone of his voice brought Nick and Benjy down to earth.

"All right," he went on. "I'll really welcome your support, but don't underestimate the danger or what it is we are facing."

The three clasped their hands together, making a three-strutted pyramid shape between them.

"I'm with you," Nick said. "Whatever it takes."

"Me too," Benjy confirmed.

"Thanks," Randolph said. "Now then, we best make some form of plan." He unrolled the map.

"The road is under cover of the trees all the way to the bend, where it turns right toward Hightown. If we're heading for the lakes and then on to the caves, we'll need to leave the track here," Benjy said, pointing to the bend on the map just above the northernmost lake. "Then we'll have no cover until we get down to South Wood and Silouhilou Caves."

"How long will it take us to cross the plain from Salty Wood to South Wood?" Randolph asked.

With the cart. Mmmmh, Benjy thought. "About three hours I'd say. You see there's only a very rough track. People don't go that way often; it doesn't lead anywhere."

"Except to . . . what did you say his name was?" Nick asked. "Milthroop's tomb?"

"Mithrip," Randolph corrected. "But I don't know its location. We've got to find it. In fact, I don't have any real proof that it's near the Salt Lakes at all; it's just a sense that that's where we'll find it."

"Well, as I say, it wouldn't need to be very well hidden to stay secret," Benjy said. "People just don't go to the Salt Lakes. Mainly because there's nothing there, but also, it's dangerous. The ground isn't very solid, and you could easily get swallowed up."

"I feel much better knowing that," Nick said, and he pulled a fearful face at Benjy.

"So we should reach the south edge of Salty Wood about dusk. There's a full moon tonight and there doesn't seem to be much cloud. We might have to use the invisibility spell to cross the plain," Randolph said. "I wonder if I can make it cover all of us and the horse and wagon?"

"Invisibility spell," Nick said. "That takes the cream, that does. You can make us invisible? What a load of tosh."

"Yes," Randolph confirmed. "And once and for all, it'll prove to you the truth of such things. I'll have you chanting from the book of spells yet."

"Pah!" Nick scoffed. "If you can make us invisible, I'll eat my breeches."

"I was hoping you'd brought something tastier in the cart," Randolph said.

"Pah!"

While this good-natured banter was being exchanged, Benjy had been studying the map in detail. "From what I know of the area, and it's mostly hearsay, the caves are down past the southernmost lake," he said. "If we're headed there, it could take us another three or four hours once we get under cover of the South Woods."

"That's where we need to go," Randolph said with an air of certainty that invited no question.

Sunset saw the small party at the edge of Salty Wood, as Randolph had predicted, and they settled down to have a welcome meal, gathered close to the wagon. Another hour would determine whether they might risk the next stage of their journey under cover of darkness, or whether Randolph needed to invoke the invisibility spell to hide them from the probing view of the swarm. They had heard the low drone of the searching swarm in the distance several times during the afternoon, and it was evident to Randolph that his general location was known to Thrung. However, the thick woods had hidden their travel and kept them from detection. As the last light of the now-absent sun paled, the glow from the moon transformed the view across the Salt Lakes' plains into a silver bath of shimmering mystery. The three friends stood at the edge of the wood and surveyed the scene before them.

"It's beautiful," Benjy said. "It looks like fairyland, like another place not belonging to our world."

Randolph felt a chill run up his spine, and he shivered at Benjy's words. His mind sped back to his visit to the Faery Realm and then on to a vision of the kingdom, the whole of the Western Realm, the Faery Realm, and Gnoma all becoming lost to Thrung's world. He shook his head to rid himself of the thought. "I sense we are short of time. I sense Thrung's increasing dominance over our world. Listen."

They stood like three silent statues—gray figures, barely visible under the skirt of the canopy of trees.

"I don't hear anything," Nick said at last.

"Nor do I," Benjy agreed.

"That's exactly what I mean," Randolph said. "Where are the noises of the night? Where are the badgers and the foxes? Where are the last callings of the birds as they settle down to rest? Where are the hoots of the owls as they pass information from tree-top perches? There is only silence, a black silence that contrasts with the beauty of the silver scene before us; a silence that threatens an impending disaster for humankind. The scene we view may be beautiful in its glistening white light, but it bodes danger in its quiet and its potential to shift into blackness."

Randolph's words reached the hearts and minds of his colleagues and they knew, abruptly, the enormity of their quest. No longer was this an adventure with a few friends. Certainly, they had already experienced danger and potential attack by the swarm of black wasps, but as yet, they had not had their senses touched by the mystery of the forces of darkness. They now felt the weight of their responsibility to Randolph and all that he was tasked to achieve. There were no words to express their feeling, but as Randolph turned his gaze toward them, he could see in their faces the solemnity of their thoughts. But he saw no fear.

"I am proud to be in the company of two such true friends," he said, and the depth of his meaning was not lost on his comrades.

They stood quietly together for some while, as if cementing a silent pact of protection for each other. In that time, they grew from boyhood friends to compatriots, from pals playing together to men fighting side by side, fully aware that their destiny might separate them, but each pledging, until that time, to protect the others with his life. Nick broke the silence.

"It looks like the moon is against us tonight, Randolph. You'd best teach us about being invisible."

They turned and faded into the dark protection of the trees.

༄•᷍

Martha landed gently and unseen in a clearing in the forest, just south of Castle Drent. She listened and was conscious of the silence. The usual hubbub of the business of the undergrowth was absent. She made her way quickly to the castle to join Galdore, Grafdun, and Brock. Soon, seated around the circular table of the Council Chamber, they were in deep discussion concerning the defense of the kingdom.

"Thrung has mobilized his initial forces," Galdore said. "But we have only seen the tip of his strength. I fear there will be many terrible and horrible armies and evil forces yet to be unleashed in his attack."

"What support can we give to Randolph?" Martha asked.

"Randolph is not now our first concern," Galdore replied. "He has moved beyond our immediate ability to help him in his task. We knew at the start this time would come; that is why he has been chosen as the One. His quest is not, at this moment, within our power to support. His initiative and vision will lead him to his destiny and, hence, determine the fate of our land."

"All we can do, is to delay the attack by Thrung's forces," Brock added. "All we can hope for is to give Randolph as much time as possible and divert as much of Thrung's attention as we can away from him."

"We have prepared our armies from Drent, Tharla, Fortnum, and Dark Castle," Grafdun said. "Already we are moving to gather forces around the Boglands, to scour the rivers and protect villages and towns from raids by bands of goblins and trolls. Thrung will not find us easy prey."

"However, without the Master Orb and without joining it to the talisman, we cannot create the power to finally defeat Thrung's force." Galdore said. "We may hold him at bay, we may even win battles, but the war against the forces of his darkness, the final destruction of evil, cannot be completed without the orb, and locating and recovering that is Randolph's present task."

❧

"You will demonstrate my power in the overworlds," Thrung cried. "You will show no mercy to the weakness of good. You will be granted power unimaginable to serve my needs. You will be the One."

"I wish only to use such greatness in the service of my Lord Thrung," Moraden said. "Give me that power and send me forth. I will show no mercy to any who stand in my way."

"But patience." Thrung's voice dropped to a whisper. "You must have patience. I will not have my ultimate success thwarted

293

by impatience." His voice rose slowly to a crescendo. "You will go when I am ready to send you, when those bungling fools have tracked and defeated the False One. When there is no threat to your way or to my supreme and absolute domination. You will wait until I am ready."

Moraden scowled but dare not offend Thrung. He was conscious of his present vulnerability. Until he was granted the full power, he could not stand up in his own right and dominate eternity. He could not yet challenge Thrung.

"As you demand, Master." Moraden spoke through clenched teeth.

"Even my own sister has failed me through impatience," Thrung growled. "She had the false One in her grasp, and he slipped through her claws like sand through the hourglass of time. He still lives and grows stronger."

Beaktool and Scumfest scurried into the chamber, bowing and scraping as low as they could while still managing to walk. They had had to confess Randolph's escape from Shawadarg's lair and Thrung had punished them accordingly. Their bruised and battered forms now groveled at his feet. Moraden crossed to where they lay prostrate on the ground and aimed a kick at Scumfest's head. "Incompetent scum." He spat his words with venom.

"And let that be a warning to all," Thrung roared.

అండ

"Now come to me you mists of time,
Now come and listen to my rhyme,
I command that all 'round me,
A cloak is made that folk can't see.

Make it tough and make it strong,
Make it wide and make it long,
It needs to hide us from the world,
Around us gather, around us fold.

Cover us, shield our forms from view,
Cover us, secret and invisible, to
All the eyes that look our way,
We go unseen by night and day.

And now I command the powers that be,
To work this spell, so that we
Will take your charm, will take it fast,
Three hours the magic spell will last."

Randolph had made Benjy and Nick join hands with him in a part circle as far around the horse and the wagon as they could stretch. He hoped his power would be strong enough to weave a spell that would cloak them all. He had also explained to the others the after-effects of the invisibility; that it might give them some aching heads for a while and, in answer to a question from Nick about why they didn't just stay invisible until it was all over, that they had to be sparing with the use of the magic for fear of becoming permanently invisible. As they watched each other, they faded away to transparency until the only thing that remained was a slight shimmer covering the area where they stood, imperceptible to all but the keenest eye concentrating carefully.

"That's brilliant," Nick said. "Just think of the fun we could have back at home with being invisible."

"No," Randolph said. "This isn't a fun thing. This is a serious power with huge responsibility that I carry."

"Sorry," Nick said. "I didn't mean to treat it lightly. It's just that I've never been invisible before, it's . . . it's . . . well, it's just incredible. I'd never have believed it if I hadn't seen it happen."

"Maybe that can be the last of our arguments over whether or not magic exists," Randolph said.

"From now on, I'm a believer," Nick said. "But how are we going to stay together and do things like find the horse's reins, get up on the cart and make sure we don't lose anything if everything is invisible?"

"By being careful," Randolph said. "And keeping contact by talking and by touch. We're only invisible, not disappeared."

Benjy joined the conversation. Until then, he had been silent in his amazement at not being able to see his own hand in front of his face. "I never really thought about the difference between being invisible and disappeared. To me, the two have always been the same. If I can't see it, it's not there."

"Yes," Nick said. "That's always been my argument. But now it's different, 'cause I can't even see me, and I know I'm here."

"Right," Randolph said. "Let that be a lesson to us all. We're going into a situation where there will be powers even greater than mine. Let's be aware that all we see may not be there and all that is there may not be visible to us."

Nick and Benjy nodded invisibly. And suddenly, realizing they couldn't be seen, both confirmed the lesson verbally.

"We only have three hours to cross the open area and reach the South Woods before we become visible again," Randolph said. "Nick, will you drive the wagon? The horse is used to your touch. Benjy, you can sit up alongside Nick and navigate a safe path through the soft sands; you know the area best of all of us. I'll get in the back with the supplies."

They all felt their way to their respective places and clambered aboard the cart.

"All right?" Nick said. "All aboard?"

"Yes," came the chorused reply.

The horse let out a gentle whinny as Nick tapped her rump with the reins and steered her out of the woods across the open stretch of grassland before them.

They chatted of past times and boyhood adventures as the cart jerked and bounced across the uneven ground and, with Benjy's careful direction, they made steady progress toward the fringe of South Wood. The trees loomed larger and larger as the remaining distance of their trek diminished and their feeling of exposure grew less. They were still some half-mile from the protective covering of the woods, trundling along under the bright moonlight when the drone of the swarm sounded, like a low hum in the distance.

"Stop the wagon," Randolph said. Nick reined in the horse to a standstill. "We need to be absolutely silent and completely still until the swarm has passed."

There, in the stillness of the night, they waited as the drone quickly increased in volume, faded a little, and then increased again steadily as the black cloud, silhouetted against the moonlight sky, headed across the open plain searching this way and that for any sign of Randolph.

Randolph looked out over the grassland. He thought of the days of his youth when often, on a clear night like this, he and some friends would go walking. They would meander in silence, listening for the night noises, marveling at the silver and gray landscape. Randolph remembered he had always been dazzled on those walks by the number of different shades of silver and gray that could exist; and here they were again, painted in all their glory, a memory on which his eyes could feast. The silence of their waiting enhanced his wonderment of the scene as his mind wandered through those youthful night walks, picking out some of the special times, like when his boots had a hole and the dew on the grass had soaked his feet. Another time, when he had been terrified as he disturbed a nesting partridge and it had flapped away into the night sky, missing his head by a feathers breadth; when they had all decided to spend the night sleeping up a tree and Nick had fallen out. Those were happy times, when what he had now become would not even have been a possibility in his wildest imagination.

He was suddenly comforted by the closeness of his two friends and he thought that, even given the option, he would change nothing of his life. He was concerned by the situation he now faced, he was worried about the responsibility he carried, he was frightened at the prospects, but he would change nothing. He smiled to himself and felt warm with the comfort of his own spirit. He realized he had always enjoyed that comfort, and he was glad to be Randolph Kettle.

The noise of the drone dragged his mind back to the present, as it intensified and zigzagged across the sky toward them. "Absolute silence," he whispered to the others.

The swarm seemed to head straight for them, as if it had spotted something. Randolph held his breath. Then, suddenly it veered, distracted by a movement off to their left as a hare sped away into the distance, pursued for a while by the searching wasps.

"Sssshhh." Randolph let out his breath, using it to confirm the need to remain silent and still.

A ferocious farting noise tore the air as the horse chose the worst possible moment to evacuate a cloud of noxious fumes, enveloping the two figures sitting like statues on the cart's seat. Randolph heard their sudden intake of breath as they gasped, seeking air to enable them to maintain their silent stillness. The swarm swung round at the sound and headed straight for the cart but, seeing nothing, circled higher directly above them, probing the night with a thousand eyes. Randolph looked in horror as his foot flashed into view for an instant and then took on a faint shimmering outline as it started to return to visibility. The swarm still circled, as Randolph became aware that other parts of his body had become faintly outlined. A cloud crossed the moon, plunging the grassy plain into midnight darkness, and thunder rolled in the distant hills toward Riversend. The swarm, distracted by this far-off sound, swooped away to investigate.

As soon as he judged it safe to move, Randolph turned to Nick and Benjy, who were beginning to show faint signs of visibility. "Quick as you can, but as quiet as you can, head for the trees," he said to Nick.

The moon held her cloak of cloud as the wagon lurched the last yards into the tree line and the now visible party dismounted from their various perches. "I've never liked horses," Benjy said. "They always do that on me. That's why I shoe them in the yard. For some reason, Dad doesn't attract that behavior and he can do them in the barn."

"Well next time, you can drive then," Nick said. "I'm going in the back with Randolph."

South Wood stretched inland from the sea some three quarters of the distance to Castle Tharla. Southward, it spread across the border into the kingdom of Rú, over which lands ruled King Jute, a good and loyal friend of King Atha and the Alusian people. King Jute was an old and frail man and, while he retained his monarchy, the practical duties of state now fell to the hands of his son, Prince Armel. The prince, like his father before him, was a just man and well respected by Atha and Galdore. Randolph knew that should Thrung's evil spread beyond the Alusian borders, Armel could be relied upon for support. However, the trees of South Wood grew close together, providing a dense barrier between the lands of Alusia and Rú for many miles in from the coast. Any travel between the two lands was conducted via the road south from Castle Tharla. The soft soil of the Salt Lakes' basin had, in much earlier times, been the province of the sea. These now-dangerous, shifting sands that Randolph and his friends had crossed were surrounded by granite cliffs, against which the sea once used to crash and break in mountains of white foam. To the north, the ancient cliffs were topped by the upper part of the town of Gospot. To the west, they provided naught but a firm foundation for the woods and thick undergrowth that stretched inland, but to the south they housed the legendary caves of Silouhilou.

In the past, many had searched for treasures that legend told were buried in the caves. However, for many hundreds of years now the overgrown woods, the difficulty of the location, and the unexciting few tunnels that formed the caves provided no incentive for even adventurous youths to explore.

The fables surrounding Mithrip, the first lord high wizard of Alusia, and the legends of his tussles with the darker forces of earlier times were no more than faery tales and bedtime stories for the present children of Alusia. It was said that discovery of the tomb of Mithrip would unleash the ultimate powers of darkness that had been so long restrained by his work. Randolph now saw something more than faery tale in the stories. His encounter with Shawadarg, his discovery of the Talisman of Power, and his mind probe with old man Drimage had pulled together pieces of the puzzle, all pointing to the existence of the Master Orb. He was certain in his own mind that the tomb they sought was also the location of the Master Orb and that finding it was the way to invoke the next stage of the encounter with the forces of darkness.

In essence, Randolph felt that neither could win nor lose until the orb had been located and fitted with the talisman. He somehow knew that until the source of the ultimate power could be found and controlled, until such time as the balance of power could be decided, both were locked in an eternal struggle. He had become aware that, throughout time, the ability of each was only to attack and counter-attack, one never capable of full defeat, or total victory. It seemed to Randolph that possession of the Master Orb and the talisman would enable a step to be taken toward a conclusion in this, so far, interminable struggle.

"We'll never get the wagon through the woods," Nick said. "It's far too dense and there's no sign of a path or track."

"I'm not sure we'll even get the horse through more than just the fringe," Benjy said. "We may have to pitch camp and operate on foot with whatever equipment we can carry."

"Any idea how far it is from here to the caves?" Randolph asked.

"On foot, through this undergrowth and dense wood . . ." Benjy paused for thought and calculation. "Well, if your map is accurate, I'd say about two days and that's being optimistic."

"We'll unload the wagon and set up a base camp here then," Randolph said. "We can hide the cart and leave the horse on a long tether to graze."

"I've got some packs with shoulder straps in the supplies," Nick said. "So we can load up some essential equipment like ropes and climbing hooks and enough food for a week's trek. Between the three of us, we can carry that easily."

"Right," Benjy said. "I can get some breakfast organized and sort out the horse while you two unload the supplies and set up the camp."

"Sounds good to me," Randolph said. "But we best not risk a fire; the smoke will be visible for miles, and I don't really want to invite the black wasps to a meal."

Benjy smiled as he started to prepare some oat cakes, fruit, and cured ham for the three of them. He tethered the horse so that it could roam over a wide area of grass on the edge of the woodland and then helped Nick and Randolph unload the remainder of the supplies and equipment from the cart.

"These look useful," Benjy said as he inspected some well-made swords.

"I asked Nick to get those, because I have no idea what we might face from here on," Randolph said. "Both of you should carry one and a dagger each as well. Also, I think it will be wise for us each to arm ourselves with a bow and a good supply of arrows."

"The packs are large enough for us each to carry a rope and our own food supply, plus some bits and pieces like tinder box and leather thongs," Nick said. "We can stack the spare equipment under the cart and camouflage it with branches."

"Good," Randolph said. "Then, while we have some food, we can look over the map, and plan a route and a search pattern to find the caves. If we grab ourselves a few hours' sleep, we can aim to start out about midday."

The early afternoon saw them leaving their base camp behind as they set out in an easterly direction, following the ridge of the old cliffs. They made their way toward the sea and the Silouhilou Caves and, they hoped, the swift discovery of Mithrip's tomb. The swords they carried proved essential, not at this point to defend themselves, but as weapons to attack the tangle of briars and other undergrowth that blocked the floor of the woods. Any pathway that might have previously existed was lost to the ownership of the knotted mass of thick vegetation and bramble-weed stretching before them. Their going was slow, and their arms soon ached from the constant slashing and cutting necessary to clear a passage. After several hours, they had covered no more than a few miles, and Randolph called a halt.

"No wonder nobody goes to the caves any more," he said. "It'll take us weeks to get through to the coast at this rate. Let's look at the map again and see if there's any other way we might try."

The party gathered round as Randolph spread the map on a fallen tree trunk.

"The only other option we have is to go down the old cliff face and make our way along the Salt Lakes' basin floor," Benjy suggested. "But the way is dangerous there, with soft ground and quicksand. Although it's firmer toward the back of the basin where we came across in the wagon, the closer we move to the coast, the more hazardous it becomes."

"Have you ever tried it before?" Nick asked.

"No," Benjy said. "And I don't know anybody who has, well not anybody who ever came back. There was a man I heard of some years ago, Dimidge or something was his name. He set off to try and access the caves, but he was never seen again. It was assumed he was lost to the quicksands."

"Dimidge?" Randolph said. "Did you say his name was Dimidge?"

"Yes," Benjy said. "Something like that Dimidge, or Dimage, or Damage." He laughed. "Yes, Damage would have been appropriate."

"Might it have been Drimage?" Randolph asked.

"Yes," Benjy said, snapping his fingers in instant memory. "That was it, Drimage. How did you know?"

"Never mind how," Randolph said. "But I've met Drimage. He was the old man I told you about earlier; he was the one who directed me down here to the Salt Lakes. Drimage must have been here many years ago, but he didn't perish, he survived."

"If only to be driven mad by whatever he discovered," Nick added.

"That may be," Randolph said. "But he must have got through the sands, and we're going much better prepared and informed than he was. It's down the cliff we go. But we'll be on view to the sky, so we can only travel at night and we'll have to rest up during the day."

"It'll be dark in a few hours," Benjy said. "So let's rest now and prepare for climbing down the cliffs as soon as the sun sets."

"There's a heavy cloud cover as well," Randolph said, looking up to the sky. "So the moon will be well hidden tonight."

"But the rain won't," Nick said. The weather seemed to take its cue from Randolph's upward gaze and unleashed a deluge on the earth below.

The three huddled under their cloaks and withdrew a little into the woods to shelter from the storm and await nightfall. It descended eventually on a damp and miserable trio. The ceaseless rain pummeled their faces and doubled the weight of their cloaks as they prepared ropes to descend the old cliff. Benjy, who was well practiced at ropecraft and climbing, gave instruction on how they should hold and feed the ropes around their bodies as they lowered themselves down the rock face. He constructed a special knot to allow him to release the rope from its fastening from the bottom, which he did once he had lowered the packs and followed the others to the sandy ground at the foot of the drop.

"Now, I think for safety, we should rope together, and I'll take the lead," Benjy said.

"Fine," agreed Randolph. He was glad to have somebody else take a little of the responsibility for a while. "How long do you think it'll take us to reach the caves this way?" he said.

"Much quicker," Benjy replied. "As long as we don't meet any quicksand bogs or get washed away by the rain, we should do it easily in a night and a half. But, we mustn't get careless; the shifting sands in the basin here are known to be very danger-ous, and this pounding rain is just the sort of weather to get them slithering and sliding."

They set off, tied together like a string of sausages, slipping and stumbling along the base of the cliff, some footfalls meeting soft sand that gave way under their tread, others encountering protruding rocks and stones that jarred in contact with the soles of their boots. The way was slow, but considerably faster than hacking through the tangled undergrowth of the woods, now way above them, decorating the cliff-top like sugar latticework icing on a birthday cake. The torrential rain hammered on them, and the wind veered to blow with increasing strength from the north, swirling around the Salt Lakes' basin and collaborating with the rain to chill them to the bone. But they soldiered on, thankful for the dark cloud cover hiding the moon. In the deep shadow of the cliffs, they were as invisible to the sky as they would have been under the cloak of Walter Bottle's spell. The safety of the darkness and their slightly faster progress gave Randolph renewed confi-dence and, in low tones, he sang.

> *"When troubles dawn*
> *And the way gets hard,*
> *When life seems dark,*
> *Deals the joker card,*
> *Get your spirits high and let your heart roam free,*
> *From the dusky mountains to the rolling sea.*
>
> *If your way gets weary,*
> *If your hopes are dashed,*
> *Let your mind lead onward,*
> *Leave behind what's crashed,*
> *Get your spirits high and let your heart roam free,*
> *From the dusky mountains to the rolling sea.*

You can lean on friendship,
Get support from trust.
Go ever forward,
'Cause you know you must
Get your spirits high and let your heart roam free,
From the dusky mountains to the rolling sea."

Randolph repeated the song, Benjy and Nick joining where they caught the words, and bringing harmony with their humming where they didn't. They trudged through the night until a faint glow on the eastern horizon heralded the waking dawn, and soon the sun shot radiant beams from behind the dark storm clouds that littered the morning sky. They had made good progress in spite of the difficult going, and were almost level with where they judged the Silouhilou Caves might start.

"I think the time has come to look for some place to hiiiiiiiiii . . ." Benjy's voice trailed off as he disappeared from view, followed by an avalanche of sand and small rocks into a gapping hole just a few feet from where Randolph stood, transfixed by Benjy's sudden departure.

The rope around Randolph's waist went tight as the full weight of Benjy's muscular form hung suspended from the edge of the crevice that he had stepped into. Randolph leaned back, digging his heel into the slippery soil as he felt himself being dragged forward by Benjy's weight.

"Pull," Randolph yelled to Nick. "Pull backward."

They both leaned into the task until they were almost horizontal, but the soft, sandy soil, made into slushy puddles by the still-pounding rain, gave their feet no grip at all. Randolph was just on the point of following Benjy's dive into the fissure when his foot slithered up against a buried rock and he jolted to a stop. Nick scrabbled to his feet while Randolph took the strain and then, lying flat on his stomach, crawled toward the edge of the gapping hole and, somehow, managed to drag Benjy back up to safety.

"Phew," Benjy said. He wiped his mud-spattered face, revealing two large, surprised-looking white eyes in a sea of filth. "That was close. Thanks."

The three slid carefully to the edge of the chasm and peered down into the darkness. As they did, the clouds parted and a stream of morning sunlight lit the gloom around them.

"As I was just saying, I think we need to find somewhere to hide for the daylight hours. And it seems that Providence was listening," Benjy said. "But I wish she'd given me just a little more warning."

"If it's not too deep," Nick said. "I can't see the bottom."

"If we get one of the ropes and tie a rock to the end, we can lower it over the edge and find out how deep it is," Randolph suggested.

"Good idea," Benjy said. "And there's plenty of large rocks here for us to tie a rope to so that we can lower ourselves down and then climb out again when it gets dark."

They discovered bottom at about twenty feet from the edge and Benjy quickly secured a rope to lower them all down into the pit.

"Couldn't be better," Randolph said to the others as he touched the floor of the cavern and released his grip on the rope. "We're out of the wind and rain, we've enough light to see by, and we're hidden from view of anything in the sky or on the plain. Well done, Benjy." He smiled.

"Right," Nick said. "If this is to be our home for the day, let's see if we can make ourselves a bit comfortable."

"We could start with some food," Randolph said. "I'm starving."

"And look." Benjy approached a large flat slab of rock raised up in the center of the cavern. "I've even organized a table for you."

The three of them crossed to the slab and heaved their packs onto its surface.

"This is a strange rock to find standing all alone in the middle of a cavern like this. It's almost as if it was placed here on purpose," Nick said.

Randolph stepped back and peered through the gloom at the slab.

"Is that just the shape of the rock, or is there something carved on the side of it?" he said.

The trio knelt and squinted at the sides of the stone.

"It's a whole line of carved symbols," Nick said.

"And if I'm not mistaken, they are the same runic symbols as I saw on the talisman that I discovered in Shawadarg's Lair."

"Surely this can't be what we have come here to search for," Benjy said. "It's too much of a coincidence that we should just fall into a hole that contains the hidden tomb of Mithrip."

"Or just a lucky break?" Nick asked, looking at Randolph.

The three exchanged glances. Randolph shrugged.

"Don't look at me," he said. "I wasn't the one who fell down the hole. But it does seem we might have been favored by fate, although that makes me uneasy. If fate has brought us this quickly to our path, is it treating Thrung with the same generosity?"

As if in answer to Randolph's question, there was a terrific crash of thunder from above them, and the sound of the rain beating on the ground increased to that of a waterfall from the sky. The flashing lightning penetrated the cavern, illuminating the three figures who knelt, in a seeming attitude of prayer, before the stone coffin of Mithrip, first lord high wizard of Alusia. A rumbling sound drew their eyes back toward the stone slab that formed the lid of the sarcophagus, and they watched transfixed as it slid aside and a white skeleton slowly raised itself to a standing position from inside the now-open tomb. Before their gaze, the skeleton glowed with a brilliance that made them shield their faces. They stared through half-closed eyes as the bare white bones took on a cloak of magical flesh and flowing robes. A long white beard manifested itself around a countenance that viewed them with smiling eyes.

"Greetings," the apparition said. "You come at last. I hope not too late. Many years have I awaited your attendance, and in the name of all that is good and loving, I grant you your one chance at choosing. You stand at the crossroads of destiny. Should you go ahead and pay no heed to the pathways right and left? Should you disregard the straightforward path and veer to the right? Should you select that which lies to your left? I can offer you no guidance in this decision, only tell you that one way leads to possession of the Master Orb, other ways return you either to continued future struggle and torment in the battle between dark and light, or to a future where the power of evil dominates all things."

Benjy and Nick turned their eyes toward Randolph.

"Your colleagues look to you for guidance, Randolph. The weight of decision rests heavy on your shoulders for you are the One; you have been chosen."

"But I d . . . d . . . don't know what to do." Randolph stammered a little and lowered his eyes to the ground.

"Have you come this far to face defeat?" Mithrip asked. "Surely the power that lies within you, the combined force of your own existence and birthright, joined with that of others who came before you but failed to reach this point, surely that has not been for naught?"

"Randolph," Benjy whispered. "Randolph, you must . . ."

Nick placed his hand on Randolph's shoulder.

"You have but one day to decide," the apparition said. "Use that time wisely, my One. I will hear your words and open the door to the destiny that will reflect your chosen way as the sun seeks rest this night."

Randolph raised his head and looked at the figure standing proud and erect before him.

"Mithrip," he said, "I will speak my chosen way at sunset, as you request, but give me the benefit of your wisdom, aid me in my decision; I know not what is required of me, I am but a child in comparison to your understanding."

"That is why you are chosen," Mithrip replied. "It is your purity of heart, your natural balance of the force of life, your instinct for good over evil. These are the things that have brought you here to meet with me; these are the jewels that adorn your crown. My wisdom, and all that of my forebears and lineage, pales beneath your clarity of vision. Knowledge is of use only in its application; it is an impotent burden in isolation. This is all the guidance I might offer."

The vision faded and was gone. Randolph got to his feet and peered into the stone coffin. There lay the skeleton, an inanimate pile of white bones, the skull staring back at him with empty eyes. He walked, dreamlike, to the center of the cavern and raised his gaze to the opening in the roof through which they had entered. He saw the raging storm above, heard the thunder, and felt the splash of the cold rain as it spattered his upturned face.

"I must leave you for a while," he said to his two friends. "I will be back. Wait for me here."

Nick and Benjy watched as Randolph sang. The wind came and lifted him, slowly at first and then, in a rush he was gone, spiraling into the sky, up through the clouds and away.

Chapter Twelve
A Calling to Evil

The Boglands of Thrung

WINGED CREATURES, the like of which had never before been seen in the overworlds, streamed from the center of the boglands. Like mini-dragons they soared and swooped, belching gushes of fiery breath over anything that challenged them or blocked their way. Songbirds and doves fell smoking from the sky, archers blazed in screaming terror, rolling wildly on the dusty ground while colleagues beat at the flames in vain attempts to save their comrades. Horned beasts crept stealthily along the narrow tracks between the foul pools of stagnant bogland slime as it oozed and bubbled, an immense cauldron of dark evil. In that watery filth, wriggled tentacled reptilian animals making their way to the rivers and waterways that would give them passage to the hinterlands of the Alusian kingdom. Armies of goblins and trolls stood ready to swarm up from the Caverns of Doom and wreak havoc among the towns and villages, claiming prisoners to drag back to Thrung's realm and be put to work in hard labour. Others would be drained of their life force, feeding the growing energy needs of Thrung, Shawadarg, and the dark forces that sought to assert victory over all that represented goodness, peace, and harmony. He stood, proud and fearless, in the Cavern of Despair, arms folded in defiance of all around him. Greed, in anticipation of ultimate power, evaporated from every pore of Moraden's body.

"Let all that follow me and the master, Thrung, be blessed with the power to overthrow our enemies," he cried. "Make ready the armies for their advance."

Scumfest, his head still sporting bruises from his last encounter with Moraden's boot, hurried from the cavern and down the tunnels leading to the huge area below the main shaft. The commanders of Thrung's forces were to be put on standby, awaiting their orders to advance to the overworld and commence their combat. Moraden knew they would not have things all their own way. He knew Galdore would put up enormous, well-planned resistance; he knew Grafdun and his armies would battle against all odds to crush any invaders. Atha's troops would resist to the last man and the other Council of Worth members would employ both overt and covert means to destroy the power source and the physical entities that threatened their world. But his chief concern centered around Randolph.

"Why have we not yet found Randolph?" He yelled at Beaktool. "We must destroy the False One to enable me to take my rightful place." He aimed a fist at Beaktool's ugly face, catching his large nose a glancing blow and bringing a glazed expression to his eyes. "Answer me."

"Bwell Marsthdder," Beaktool said, clutching his throbbing nose. "Bweell gedd 'imb thoon."

"Get him NOW," screamed Moraden, as he lashed out at Beaktool again. "NOW. And send word to Shawadarg in the north; Thrung demands her presence here to give support to the attack."

"Yedth, Marsthdder." Beaktool scurried off.

"Where is he?" Moraden said to himself. "Where is he?"

ॐॐ

Maybe I could just stay up here forever, he thought to himself. *Spend the rest of my life floating gently on the breeze. But no, I can't sing forever without stopping.*

He raised the volume and the tempo of his song and the wind took him higher and higher, until looking down, he could see the whole of Alusia and the lands stretching across the borders of the kingdom into Rú, Obor, and even as far north as Lanah. He could see the storm over the Salt Lakes extending up to Portalbion, across to Heartland's Mound and down again into the Western Hills, Riversend, Castle Tharla, and Hightown Village. It centered over the Boglands of Thrung, and he knew that the Caverns of Doom harboured the forces that fed the dark weather. As he looked down, Randolph saw winged creatures flying in amongst the clouds, and he sensed the evil that exuded from the bogland area. He knew that Thrung had stepped up his attack. He knew that he was running out of time. He knew that although Galdore, Grafdun, Atha, and the others would hold off the dark forces for a while, he didn't have long. Mithrip needed his decision, but he still didn't know what to say; he didn't understand what he had to do to make the choice.

What did he mean, Randolph wondered to himself. *What are the crossroads? How do I choose which is the right path? And even if I make a choice, how do I follow a hypothetical way? I don't know what it means to go straight on or to turn right or left.*

He sang louder and harder, and the wind raised him higher. He closed his eyes and filled his mind with song. He felt himself floating further and further into the sky, and in his mind he flew into the heavens, past the moon and the sun, out among the stars and away to a land he had never seen before. Here he heard the sound of peace, he listened as silence enveloped him and he attended to the tone of wisdom as it encircled and surrounded his mind. He tried to open his eyes but a voice inside his head said,

> *"No Randolph,*
> *Burden not your eyes with what surrounds you,*
> *Listen to things that you have found.*
> *The answer you seek is here before you,*
> *By the choice you make, your destiny bound.*
> *Who knows what path that you will travel,*
> *And without sight, you must rely 'pon sound.*
> *What has passed will hold the answer,*
> *Through your journey here, the way ahead is wound."*

"Through my journey here, my way ahead is wound," Randolph repeated to himself. "Do I begin to understand? Could it be that there is no answer? Other than that, I am who I am. Is it that each way is the right way and yet each way is also wrong? Is it only that all I have been told about positiveness, goodness, harmony, and doing right by others is the key? Is it only that selfishness, arrogance, jealousy, and hate, none of which can be seen, but all of which I have heard, are the forces that will destroy me? Is the only wrong answer not to make a choice; because any path I choose will be made into the right path if I follow my way?"

Randolph lowered his voice and sang softly now, and with his quieting and the tranquility that surrounded him he was transported back past the stars, through the sun's halo, and around the sheen that shrouded the moon. He was lowered back toward the storm below. Opening his eyes, he watched the swirling mass as the dark clouds blurred his sight and he felt the rain kiss his face. Slowly he floated down and landed quietly beside his sleeping friends on the dusty floor of the cavern that was Mithrip's resting place. He lay down and fell into a dreamless slumber.

"Randolph." Nick's voice cut a swath through the quiet. "Randolph, are you awake?"

"I am now," he replied.

"How long have you been back?" Nick asked. "Benjy and I sat up most of the morning waiting for you to come, but I suppose we must have dozed off. It looks like the light's fading outside, so I thought I'd best wake you. Mithrip will be looking for your decision; he said until sunset and that's about now."

"I don't know how long I was away," Randolph said. "It didn't seem all that long and I feel quite rested, so I assume I've been asleep for quite a while."

Benjy stirred at the sound of conversation and sat up, yawning and stretching. "Hello Randolph. You're back," he said, stating the obvious. "Have you made a choice for Mithrip?"

"Yes, I have," he said. "Whether it's the right answer or not I don't know, but I have an answer. It's not so much a choice of direction as an answer to a much bigger puzzle."

Benjy and Nick exchanged glances. "But don't you have to choose a way to go?" Nick said. "Isn't that what this whole thing is about? Mithrip said about crossroads and the straight path and turning right or left. I didn't understand what he meant but, you'll have to make a choice."

"I didn't understand either," Randolph said. "I was confused because I thought he was offering me three options of already defined destinies and I had to select the right one using some mystical power or something."

"That's what I thought too," Benjy said.

The cavern was filled with a soft hum, like a choir of children's voices, and the three of them turned toward the stone coffin. As it had done earlier, the slab of rock covering the coffin slid aside, and the apparition they had previously witnessed appeared. Randolph stood up and walked toward Mithrip. Benjy and Nick flanked him, a pace behind. The vision of Mithrip smiled warmly at Randolph, and he returned the expression with confidence. The scene reminded him of his meeting with Sulaman many months ago, and he knew that Mithrip was not here to trick or delude him. They were together, Mithrip, Galdore, Sulaman, the members of the Council of Worth (past and present), the kings of Alusia, and all those who now or previously enjoyed the power of good in the Western Realm. Randolph knew that he was the focus of all this energy and light. He knew the way, and that made the path he chose irrelevant. His way would bring him to the triumph of good over evil, for he did not stand alone.

"Roody Grumbleweed's cheese," Randolph said to Mithrip. The apparition's smile broke into a broad grin, for Mithrip now knew that Randolph had unraveled the enigma of paths and ways. Wisdom was indeed the true way forward, and Randolph had found that way. There was hope for the goodness in creation, and Mithrip could now rest. He had passed the responsibility he carried all these years, in death just as he had in life, and he could reveal the location of the Master Orb.

"Riversend," was all that Mithrip said before his form started to fade.

Randolph extended his hand toward the old man in a gesture of thanks. "Until we meet again in the everafter," he said to the fading figure, "Rest in peace, and trust in me, I will not fail you."

Thunder raged and lightning flashed as the anger of the storm grew more terrible across the land, heralding Thrung's advance. Randolph smiled to himself, as he looked down into the now-empty coffin.

"He has gone," he said to Benjy and Nick. "But he has completed the job he set out to do so long ago. He has passed on his knowledge and his wisdom, and he has given me the strength and the power to understand and to face those who would turn the magic of creation to dark purpose. Come, we also must be gone. There is no time to lose."

"But what happened?" Benjy asked. "What was all that about cheese?"

"And who, in the name of the kingdom, is Roody Grumbleweed?" Nick asked, for Randolph, in recounting his travels, had omitted many names of those he had met.

"What happened to Mithrip?" Benjy added. "Where did he go? Why did he go?"

"I'll explain on the way," Randolph said, wondering where to start his account so that his friends might understand the exchange that had taken place, what he had been told on his flight above the clouds, and how he had now been directed in his understanding of the way forward.

Nightfall made small difference to the darkness that now seemed constant below the black storm clouds, as the three comrades climbed from the cavern and retraced their footsteps toward their base camp.

"If this storm is manufactured by Thrung, then he has served us well," Randolph said to the others. "The black wasps cannot hope to fly through the turbulence, and even if they could, the gloom gives cover that will make it difficult for them to see us under the cliff face, even if we have to travel through day time hours."

"What you're saying is that Thrung has poisoned his own soup bowl by not working together with others?" Nick asked.

Randolph looked at Nick in surprise; he was impressed at the understanding Nick showed for the reasoning behind the way forward. "Yes," he said. "You've hit the mark with your first arrow. That is exactly the thinking that will give us a chance to defeat the dark powers. The selfishness, the hate for all but their own importance, the demand for sole power, the aggression and meanness with which they act are the very things that will give us strength over them."

Randolph explained to them further by using Roody Grumbleweed's analogy of the small and large cheeses, and then they could see what he had offered Mithrip. They began to understand how the way forward was different from choosing a predetermined path.

"Silly arseholes," Nick summarized when Randolph had finished his explanation.

Randolph smiled to himself at Nick's earthy interpretation of the delicate balance existing between the powers of good and evil, between the forces that had existed since the time of creation; of the struggle between darkness and light and the strength that surrounded the essence of support for one another. But then he remembered something else Roody Grumbleweed had said. He remembered the reason behind the cheese theory; to boil all things down to a simple idea and apply that to the situation.

"Yes," he said to Nick. "Your wisdom will yet qualify you as a sage. Thrung and his cohorts—they're just a bunch of independent arseholes."

"And what will make it worse for them?" Benjy questioned.

Nick and Randolph looked at him blankly.

"We'll feed them a diet that'll make them all constipated," he said.

The three of them laughed together, something Randolph noted they had not done for a while, and he felt good to know they could still do so, even in such times of danger as they now faced. Their steps lightened from the damp trudging they had fallen to and their pace quickened with their laughter.

"I bet arseholes can't laugh together like us," Benjy said.

The journey through the night passed quickly. The three friends joked and recounted memories of their youthful exploits, where their friendship and the care for each other had pulled them through many a scrape. The foul weather paled into insignificance with their high spirits, and they were soon back at the base camp with several hours of the night unused.

"So what now?" asked Nick as he swung his pack from his shoulders and dumped it on the cart.

The others followed his example and relieved themselves of their loads.

"Food," Benjy said, verbalizing the thoughts of all three.

Bellies full and feeling strong and confident, they grouped around the map Randolph had unfolded and examined their options.

"The choices," Randolph said, "are either to leave the horse and cart here and strike out westward through the forest to Hightown Village, or trek back northward across the Salt Lakes' basin with the wagon to the road."

"If we go the road way, we'll have all our supplies with us and we'll be able to travel faster," Benjy said.

"Yes. But even with the storm still raging, we can still only risk moving at night, whereas through the woods we can travel by day without any chance of being spotted. Remember, Randolph told us about those other flying creatures he'd seen when he was up above the clouds. I don't fancy those much," Nick said.

"I wonder how dense the undergrowth is in the woods further inland," Randolph said.

Their discussion continued for some time on the merits of each option. In the end, it was decided that going through the woods on foot would take them twice as long as crossing the Salt Lakes' flats and approaching Hightown Village by road. It would also mean starting out immediately to arrive at the same time as resting for the daylight hours and taking the slightly riskier road option. However, the final persuading factor that swayed Randolph in favor of the road was that the wagon with all the supplies would be with them.

"And, if it comes to the worst, we know the invisibility spell can cover the whole party; we'll go by road with the cart," he finally decided.

The decision made, they settled down to rest until evening, and soon all three were snoring, unaware of the large brown bear that watched over their slumber.

☙❧

The armies from all four castles had been mustered and through weight of numbers as well as the battle skills of Grafdun, Atha, and Sir Nigel, aided and abetted by the magic of Galdore,

they were causing the commanders of the dark forces some unexpected misery. The fire-breathing winged creatures had proved
to be impervious to the arrows of the archers, but had succumbed
to water jets sprayed from magical canons employed by Galdore. Goblins and trolls were found to be no more than flesh and
blood, with significantly less strategic battle skill than the armies
of Alusia. Certainly, they claimed some victories and had inflict-
ed much pain and suffering on unprotected towns and villages,
but at each appearance of Alusian troops they now fled for their
lives, increasing Thrung's bad humour as he roared abuse at his
commanders for their incompetence. Thrung's personal attention
was, more and more, diverted from his peripheral terrors and focused keenly on his central advance. The terrible storms he had
generated abated, and the weather improvement further favored
the Alusian armies. Shawadarg's arrival in the Caverns of Doom
created more distraction for Thrung, as her often-conflicting demands sent Scumfest and Beaktool into spirals of confusion and
they suffered much abuse and punishment from Thrung for fail-
ing to carry out his orders swiftly. Moraden watched with silent
amusement, his power growing and his knowledge of the dark
forces becoming stronger by the day. He awaited enough distraction to direct matters to his own benefit. His understanding and
knowledge of the overworlds gave him substantial advantage
over Thrung in his selfish cause to wrestle power from the creator
of evil.

࿐

"Good," Galdore said in response to Grafdun's report of
their successes in routing the goblins and trolls. "But even one life
lost to their raids is too many. Is there more we can do to prevent
their attacks?"

"We have the boglands surrounded by my armies to the
north and those from Tharla and Fortnum to the south and west.
Atha is preparing a strike into the Caverns of Doom with his
troops that are, as we speak, moving down from Castle Drent
through the Southern Forest toward Rivermeet."

"Good," Galdore said again. "I've sent Brommel down to
watch over Randolph and his two friends; he can move undetected through the woods and even if he is spotted, a wild bear will

draw no interest or attention from Thrung and his forces. Martha located them from one of her observation flights. They are down in South Wood by the Salt Lakes and appear to be heading back inland, but where they are bound, we do not know. We must not now interfere for risk of swaying Randolph's purity of thought and judgment, but we must give him what protection and indirect support we can. If we can keep Thrung occupied and his attention distracted, Randolph will have his best chance."

"Have you seen Brock?" Grafdun asked.

"He is working in my study, preparing some plans to discover Moraden's intent and for an attempt to rescue him if we are not too late to save his soul," Galdore replied.

"I will speak with him before returning to the boglands," Grafdun said. Bidding farewell and good fortune to Galdore, he made his way to the study, where he found Brock in earnest conversation with Dragon.

"Do you think you can get into the caverns and discover Moraden's location there without being detected?" Brock asked.

"And get out again?" Grafdun added as he entered the room and picked up the theme of their discussion.

Brock and Dragon looked up and greeted him. Brock shook him warmly by the hand; Dragon purred around his feet, nuzzling his ankles. Dragon had lately shown quite an affection toward Grafdun and seemed to hold him in high regard.

"How are things progressing on the battlefront?" Brock asked.

"As well as we could hope for at the moment. But I'm sure we've not yet seen the full might of Thrung's armies and whatever other evil creatures he might be manufacturing down in his lair. What of your plans regarding Moraden? Do you think there may be hope for his rescue?"

"The first matter is to discover his intent," Brock said. "If he is a willing supporter of Thrung, for whatever reason or purpose, then we have no hope. However, if he has been enticed away through some evil magic that has captured and twisted his sense of values, then we will attempt to rescue him. Dragon is prepared to investigate the position by creeping undetected into the Caverns of Doom."

"If we are to attempt recovery of Moraden, we must act fast," Grafdun advised. "Thrung's advance is now well underway and Moraden's calling to evil will only get stronger. Even if he was initially enticed into disloyalty to the overworlds, his recovery will quickly become impossible. His conversion to support of the dark forces will not be left uncompleted by Thrung."

"Your words are wise. We had drawn the same conclusion ourselves, and Dragon was to leave immediately. If you are riding back to the boglands, maybe she could accompany you."

"I'd be delighted to give you a lift, my little friend," Grafdun said. He leaned down, scooped up the cat, and placed her on his shoulder. "Come Dragon, you can ride with me." They said good-bye to Brock and off they went, Dragon perched like a precarious parrot beside Grafdun's left ear. Down to the stables they walked, mounted Grafdun's powerful stallion, and rode south on the still-warm trail of Atha and his troops. They soon caught the army of men, each battalion commanded by a knight of the kingdom, and all led by Atha, himself riding proudly at the head of his fearless fighting force. They stopped briefly to appraise Atha of Dragon's mission and to agree a time limit for Galdore's familiar to complete her objective before the assault on the Cavern's of Doom commenced. Then they sped onward with the dawn, Grafdun trying to get Dragon as close as possible to the cavern's entrance.

"I think this is about as far as I can take you, Dragon," Grafdun said. "The main shaft is but a mile further, and you will move much faster than my mount on these narrow and uncertain paths through the swamp. Goodbye, my brave friend, and may good fortune go your way. Do what you can and return safely."

He dismounted and gently lifted the cat to the ground, stroking her head as he placed her on the soft watery soil. She looked up at him and smiled. There was something incongruous about the fearless professional soldier and the gentle, silky soft cat. He watched as Dragon hurried away, stopping only once and looking back before she disappeared in the swirling mists.

"That's some cat," Grafdun told his horse. "I think we're going to be friends. Good friends."

The horse neighed in response.

"Sssssshhh," Grafdun said. He mounted and encouraged the stallion back along the path out of the mire.

Dragon moved quickly and quietly to the shaft, jumped the low wall that surrounded the rim and made her way down among the various platforms and steps to the caverns below. All seemed still.

Where are the troops and the many evil creatures of doom? Why is everything so silent? she wondered. Making her way stealthily along the main tunnel, she sniffed and listened with her cat senses, heightened now by the curiosity the stillness had created in her. Some few minutes' trot along the dark and damp corridor, she sensed a presence. She stopped and listened, her nose raised in an attitude of poised anticipation, but the dank musty smell masked any indication of what might have caused the feeling. As she snuck forward, the suspicion of an unannounced companion grew stronger until she rounded a corner and stopped suddenly only yards from a figure crouching over a bleeding body.

"And that's all you deserve, you troll," the bending figure said. "You and your brother are a waste of space; I have no place for you in my court, and now that you are in your rightful place of death, I will seek out your twin and invite him to join you. But you surprise me, Scumfest. I am amazed you managed to die so efficiently, when all else you attempt is riddled with the plague of incompetence. I wonder, will your brother, Beaktool, be so obliging?"

The figure stood and turned to reveal Moraden's scowling countenance. More accurately, his countenance resembled the Moraden that Dragon remembered, but he had changed. "Moraden looks so evil," Dragon whispered to herself. She moved slowly backward, melting into the darkness of an overhanging wall. She watched as Moraden continued to address the corpse.

"In some ways I pity you," he said. "You will not see my rise to power. You will miss my triumph. But you deserve no better, scum. And now I must away; I must counteract the stupidity of Thrung and his orders to suspend the attack and regroup. This quieting is madness when we should be increasing our show of strength. His caution comes of old age and lack of confidence. Randolph is no threat to me; he is but a small pawn in the path to my ultimate victory over all things."

Moraden swiveled on his heel, turned his back on the still form, and strode off along the passageway down which Dragon had just come. "I will go to the surface and assess the position before issuing my orders to resume the attack," he announced to the empty darkness.

Dragon followed, staying out of sight as they went up the levels in the shaft and emerged into the gray light bathing the kingdom. Moraden set off along one of the tracks leading eastward, his eyes probing the sky and the land, seeking information on the state of the forces that challenged the might of Thrung and his evil empire. Suddenly, looming out of the swirling mist, a phantom-like figure appeared. Grafdun stood tall and proud, his drawn sword at the ready as he moved slowly forward. Moraden stopped and drew his own weapon.

"Grafdun," he spat the name. "You trespass."

"If I trespass, then I am on the wrong world," Grafdun retorted. "But that may be the case, for in my world, traitors do not walk free."

"Ignorant filth; you are weak and insignificant in my domain. You are a ridiculous waste of time and energy. I do not have the need for you."

"That may be so," Grafdun said, "but there are others who do. My current mission is for the protection of a cat that is more worthy than a thousand of you."

Moraden turned to leave the scene and regain the safety of the caverns for, in spite of his words, he knew that in one-to-one combat he was no match for Grafdun. In doing so, he came face to face with Dragon and, with a sweep of his sword, all but cleaved the cat in two before he raced away into the mist.

"Dragon!" Grafdun yelled. He leapt forward and dropped to his knees beside the twitching furry form. Bright red blood mingled with the soft black fur and the tears that ran down Grafdun's cheeks as they dripped freely onto the gaping wound.

"Dragon," Grafdun sobbed. "What has he done to you? You cannot be gone. You cannot die."

"Grafdun?" said a voice from the mist.

He turned to see Randolph standing there on the track behind him. "Randolph, Moraden has killed Dragon."

Randolph moved quickly to Grafdun's side and knelt on the damp soil. He saw the mortal wound, and he knew then there was no hope of regaining the loyalty and friendship of the faery prince. He knew his friend was lost for all time. He looked down at the small, lifeless body before him and thought of Galdore and the time in the tent when Dragon had nearly got in the way of the demonstration lightning bolt. He thought of the time he had left Castle Drent after Sir Graceforth's rescue and how it was Dragon who had been there to see him off. He thought about the first time Dragon had spoken to him in Sulaman's Cave. Randolph extended his hands and gently stroked his friend's blood-encrusted fur. He placed both palms over the ugly wound and raised his eyes skyward.

"In the name of all that is right, I call on the spirit of the Lord of Creation and all the power that is granted to me as the rightful One. I command the return of the life that has been taken from this creature. I decree that my authority in this matter be ultimate and that for the sake of goodness and light in the world, this resurrection be deemed completed." He removed his hands to reveal the wound healed and the life returned to Dragon.

Grafdun looked at Randolph in amazement. "How in the name of the lord high wizard did you do that?"

Randolph seemed dazed as he replied. "I'm not sure; it just seemed to come to me. It seemed like the natural thing to do."

"But it's incredible," Grafdun said. "You've just brought a dead body to life."

"No," Randolph said, recovering his senses a little. "I restored the life that once inhabited the body back to its rightful place. That's different from bringing something to life."

"Well, whatever you call it, it's saved Dragon, and for that I thank you and so will Galdore and Dragon herself."

"Take her to Galdore." Randolph gently lifted the sleeping cat into Grafdun's arms. "She will need tender care for many days if she is to recover fully. I know this; I too have experienced that which she now faces."

"But what about you?" Grafdun asked. "Where are you going? How did you get here? Where are the two companions Galdore said were traveling with you?"

"Whoa. One question at a time. Nick and Benjy, they're my friends, and I were on the road from Hightown Village to Riversend. We met several of your troops of men at the junction, so we knew you were mounting a defense at the main shaft. Then a bear called Brommel came and told me my help would be needed here. I don't know how he found me or knew anything about this, but I trust Brommel and he brought me to this spot. I wonder where he is now?"

Randolph looked around but could see no sign of the bear.

"Where are your colleagues, then?" Grafdun asked.

"They are waiting on the road with some of your men," Randolph said. "At the junction to Riversend. I must get back to them and continue our journey. Time grows short now, and there is still much to do to secure our position."

As he spoke, there was a loud roar and a rush of air as winged horned creatures emerged from the shaft and spiraled upward into the dark sky.

"See—the black forces do not rest."

"Come, share my mount back to the road." Grafdun said. "I will then arrange for Dragon to be taken back to Castle Drent, and you can go west to rejoin your friends and whatever awaits you at Riversend. I will resume command of the troops and defend as best we can against the onslaught. However, it would seem our efforts are only buying time for you. Galdore's words are that it is your mission that holds the key to our destiny."

"Come then. Let us waste no more time; let us be gone."

And with that they rode as quickly as the track would allow, followed by an unseen shaggy brown protector. Back at the road, Grafdun blew a piercing note on his hunting horn and a small group of his men appeared from along the track. Grafdun instructed them to return the still-sleeping Dragon to Castle Drent.

"Tell Galdore that Dragon has been wounded and that Randolph has attended her. Tell him that life has been restored to her. He will understand those words and know how to care for her. Tell him also that Prince Moraden is lost to us."

"Aye, Baron," the leader of the troop said. "We will make due haste."

Grafdun reined his horse around and with Randolph clinging on behind him, they galloped west along the road to where Benjy and Nick waited with the cart. It was not too long before they met with the small group of Grafdun's men who waited as guardians with Randolph's colleagues. After a brief introduction to Nick and Benjy, Grafdun called his men to him and they rode off swiftly back toward the boglands, leaving the three friends to make their way to the Western Hills and the town of Riversend, nestling in the valley.

"All right then, are you ready to go?" Benjy asked Randolph.

"All set," Randolph said from the back of the wagon.

"Hang on a moment," Nick said. "I'm not riding up front again if Benjy's driving. You know what that horse thinks of him, and I don't want to be poisoned." He swung himself up on the planks of the cart floor beside Randolph, his legs dangling over the back.

Randolph looked at Nick and smiled. "Just like old times," he said.

Nick blew a raspberry and they laughed. "All right Benjy, get those wheels turning."

Off they trundled along the bumpy track. Randolph felt a strange sense of excitement at the thought of returning to his birthplace, and even though he remembered nothing of the first years of his life in the town of Riversend, he sensed a belonging, a certain familiarity. He somehow knew he would recognize the place when they arrived. He was sure he knew where they had to go, and he felt certain there was a challenge ahead.

"Randolph's challenge," he said quietly to himself.

"What?" Nick asked.

"Oh nothing, just talking to myself," he said.

Chapter Thirteen
Birthplace and Battlefield

The Banquet Hall
at Fortnum Castle

RIVERSEND, ALTHOUGH several thousand feet above sea level, was, in relation to its immediate surroundings, located in a valley. From the churchyard where Randolph stood, the view in all directions was of high hills, their green-velvet-covered slopes now bathed in a strange orange glow from the fires of Thrung's attacks, as if sunset had become a permanent fixture in the land. He marveled at the sight before him, his feelings of affinity for the village rewarded by the sight of the cliffs and peaks that called for him to save them from the horrors they now faced at Thrung's hands. He looked down again at the gravestone beside him.

"In loving memory of Brona and Thraper Kettle," he read aloud. "Taken from this world in a storm of personal violence. Their memory held dear by Randolph and Lydie and all who knew and loved them."

He was upset that he didn't have any recollection of his mother and father. The little he knew of their lives and their ways was what his Aunt Greta had told him. However, that didn't stop him from having a great respect for their memory and for the fact they had granted him and Lydie the gift of life.

"And where are you now, my sister?" he asked the headstone. "Don't worry Mum; don't worry Dad—I'll find her again. We will be reunited. It is written in the destiny that I will choose."

Randolph turned and started back toward the wagon where Nick and Benjy waited in respectful silence. As he reached the gateway to the enclosure of the churchyard, he turned and took one last lingering look at his parent's resting place. "Trust in me," he said. "For I will not fail you or all those that hold your memory dear. I go now to protect your resting place for all time from the ravages of the power of darkness."

A strange glow sat over the place where the remains of Randolph's parents lay, and he felt the warmth of their love as it flooded to him from wherever they now watched. He heard a distant drone and looked to the sky to see a far-off black cloud. He turned and ran toward the wagon.

"The swarm," he called to his friends. "Quick, we must find a place to take cover."

Nick and Benjy shook themselves into consciousness from the distance of their daydreams and Benjy grabbed the reins up from where they lay on the seat beside him. Nick grasped the back of Randolph's tunic as he hurled himself into the back of the wagon, and Benjy jolted the lazy horse into motion.

"Got you," Nick cried. "Make for the tavern down the street, Benjy. I saw they had a covered yard as we came past earlier. We can pull straight in there and nothing will see us from the air."

The horse's hooves drummed loudly on the cobbled roadway and the metal-clad wheels clattered with a noise sufficient to wake the whole village. And that was what happened. Heads appeared at windows and shouts between confused neighbours added to the din as the wagon trundled along the narrow street. The drone increased to a roar as the black swarm dived toward the village and angry heads turned away from the rattling, clanking cart to attend to the more serious matter of fear. Benjy hauled on the reins as he steered the horse in through the archway to the tavern yard, the cart sliding as it veered sideways in complaint at the rough treatment, but able only to follow where the horse led. Nick and Randolph rolled about in the back of the cart like two marbles in a swinging bucket, tossed and bounced unmercifully until they finally came to rest in a tangled heap in the corner of the wagon. The drone of the swarm changed to a growl as the wasps transformed into the black creature of doom that had chased Randolph in the ether. Like a phantom of terror, the thing lurched down the main street of the village, swiping at any heads still brave enough to protrude from windows and doorways. Window boxes, handcarts left outside houses, howling dogs, and screeching cats were all hurled aside or crushed beneath the rolling blackness that consumed the street. But the swarm passed the tavern yard unaware of the close proximity of its target. At the end of the street, the swarm reformed and flew high above the village, circling twice before resuming the hunt for its intended prey in the valley.

People started to emerge from their houses, some jabbering excitedly, others calling for a defense force to be formed.

"It's another attack," Randolph heard one of them shout. "It's time we did something to protect ourselves. Call for the mayor."

Pitchforks were wielded and those who possessed swords or bows hurried back to their houses to retrieve them before rejoining the growing number of villagers milling in and around the tavern as they waited for the mayor's arrival.

"Randolph, you'll have to take charge," Benjy said. "If they try to meet the swarm head on, they'll be massacred. And in a way it's our fault; we're the target, not the villagers."

As he spoke, the mayor, a ruddy-faced barrel of a man, arrived. First, the crowd's chattering rose, then quieted in anticipation. Without so much as a by your leave, the mayor, ably assisted by two groaning, puffing helpers, heaved his bulky form onto the back of the wagon and, trampling Nick and Randolph under huge black boots, hitched his thumbs into the front of his braces and took on an air of pompous importance as he addressed the villagers.

"Friends." He always started his public addresses with that word. "Friends, be not afraid. We are strong in both spirit and number. Whatever is threatening the peace and tranquility of our village will feel the sharp end of our wrath."

"Do something Randolph," Nick whispered. "He'll get them all killed."

Randolph untangled himself from the heap of equipment under which he had finished his rolling and bouncing and stood up behind the mayor. However, the man's bulbous body obscured Randolph from the crowd's view and his booming voice filled the yard with pomposity. Randolph had to bang a tin pan with a wooden spoon to get attention.

"What's up with you, lad?" the mayor boomed as he rounded on Randolph. "What's the meaning of interrupting me? Have you no manners? Don't you understand the danger we're in?"

"With due respect, sir," Randolph said, dropping into a style of address that emulated the mayor's approach. "I think I understand the danger better than anybody here, and unless we all work together to overthrow the evil that creeps through our kingdom, we will, as you rightly point out, find the peace and tranquility of our homeland shattered. But, be assured, this is no local threat. I am here as a representative of the king and of Lord High Wizard Galdore to lead the citizens of Alusia in a joint effort to protect our heritage."

The mayor looked a bit deflated, his authority usurped, but at the mention of Atha and Galdore, he had little choice other than to submit to the intervention. However, being a man of immense ingenuity, he quickly recovered his composure and proceeded to take full advantage of the situation.

"Friends, listen to us," he said. He pulled Randolph to the front of his makeshift rostrum. "We bring you word from the king." He gave Randolph a gentle nudge forward, nearly toppling him from the cart. "Come, tell the people what must be done."

The mayor was, secretly, greatly relieved by the distraction created by the interruption. Of course, at this moment, he had no idea whether Randolph was indeed who he had just announced himself to be or whether he was some sort of crank. But, it took the spotlight off him and offered some thinking time. If Randolph did turn out to be a crank, then he would be quickly discredited and the mayor could regain the stage, pretending he had been humouring him. On the other hand, if he did prove to be a royal representative, then the mayor wanted to be included in whatever solution was to be found to the terrible attacks. Importance was important to the mayor.

"You must return to your homes," Randolph announced. "The force we face is greater than anything against which pitchforks and swords might protect us. There may shortly come a time when you will be called to arms in defense of our land, but that time is not now. There is first a mission for me and my colleagues here to accomplish, and in that I will need the advice and guidance of your elders."

Randolph turned to the mayor. "Sir, is there a council of village elders with whom we might meet and seek direction in our quest?"

The mayor seemed to think this was a good plan, and Randolph's confident approach to the crowd had brought credibility to his story. "Friends, do as we bid you and return to your homes for the present. The council of elders is to meet at the hall immediately. Gather here again at noon, and we will bring you news of our progress."

He looked at Randolph for confirmation; he nodded his approval and the deal was done.

"Follow me," the mayor said to Randolph. His helpers once again puffed and struggled to lower his substantial frame to ground level.

"Looks like you've got their attention," Benjy said.

"Come then," Nick added as the mayor and his entourage disappeared through the archway and into the main street. "Let's go with them and see if we can find out what we need to know." He turned to Randolph. "What do we need to know?"

"I don't know," Randolph said. The three hurried off in pursuit of the mayor. They caught up at the entrance to the village hall and followed him and what they assumed to be the council of elders into a long, low wooden building. Tables and benches were erected quickly and a huge carved wooden seat was brought and placed at the head of the table for the mayor. The council members arranged themselves around the table, and the mayor indicated that Randolph, Benjy, and Nick should come and occupy the three empty seats next to him. Once all were seated and the mayor had harrumphed and shuffled a bit, he stood and opened the meeting.

"Friends, we welcome the king's representatives to our village and wait to hear of the actions we might take to protect ourselves against this terrible threat."

Randolph stood and told the elders something of their mission to locate the Master Orb and that they had been directed to Riversend in their quest. He also told them of his family heritage and that he was, indeed, a native of their town. Many remembered his mother and father and their respect and trust for Randolph grew in the light of this new knowledge concerning his parentage. There was much nodding and exchange of whispered comments as Randolph revealed the details of his needs. When he had finished his account of matters, he sat down and waited.

"Well, the request is clear," the mayor said. "Do any of us have information that might lead our friend Randolph and his brave companions to discovery of a secret place where such a treasure as the Master Orb might have lain hidden all these years?"

Silence fell on the hall and the council members looked from one to another shaking their heads. Such an idea, to them, seemed nonsensical. How, they thought, could such an important artifact lay hidden in close proximity to their village for so long without there being some information, or even rumour, concerning its presence? It was some while before anybody spoke but, at last, one by one the council of elders confessed a lack of any knowledge. Members got to their feet, bid Randolph and his companions good fortune, and made their different ways homeward.

Last to remain seated at the table was an old man called Artimus. He got to his feet slowly, as if to follow the others. "It may be of no value," he said. "But there is the story of the old man of the mountain; the tale of the Chair of Petre. That is the only story around in which a legend of hidden treasure and strange power exists. It may hold a clue, but it says nothing of an orb."

"Can you tell us the tale?" Randolph asked.

"I certainly can," Artimus said. "Come with me to my home and I will entertain you while I relate the tale of which I speak. I was closely associated with your parents, and I would feel it my duty to offer all support and assistance to their progeny."

"I thank you," Randolph said. "Your guidance will be much needed and much appreciated."

"Though none here may be aware, your mother and father entrusted us with your spiritual guidance and morale conduct in the early years of your life, and Lydie's too. I believe they had some premonition of your quest and knew in their hearts you would be chosen for some vital role. I am your godfather, Randolph, and while it may be that I have appeared to neglect that responsibility over the years, I sensed my part would be one of later involvement in some chapter of your life. That time has now arrived. My home is yours for as long as you may wish to avail yourself of my hospitality and help."

Before leaving with Artimus, the trio bid a temporary goodbye to the mayor. Randolph had appealed to his sense of importance by suggesting he report back to the villagers at noon. It was agreed he should tell them of the possible discovery of information, but that it would be some days before any certain course of action could be determined. He was to advise the villagers to remain hidden in their homes and to send a messenger to locate Grafdun, requesting a contingent of men to be sent to protect Riversend from any ground-based invasion by Thrung's forces. Randolph was concerned that his presence in the village would not go undetected for long, and he would attract an unwelcome level of attention for his birthplace and its inhabitants.

"Here we are," Artimus said. They had stopped outside a neat whitewashed house on a side lane close to the center of the village. "You are welcome to my humble abode." They entered the house and Artimus took them to his kitchen, where two benches and a table were arranged in the middle of the room. A cooking range and cupboards occupied the far wall and several small tables bore ornaments and articles of varying types and styles. Randolph noted that many of these items did not seem to be of Alusian origin.

"You have traveled much in your life?" he asked the old man.

"Much," was the simple reply.

Artimus indicated that the three should take their places at the table. He produced a selection of bowls and platters containing fruit, bread, and a variety of salted meats. A large jug of ale complemented the food.

"This is most welcome," Nick said.

"Yes, your hospitality is most generous," Benjy said.

"Eat and drink your fill, and I will relate the tale of the Chair of Petre."

The three sat entranced as the old man's voice captured their minds and hearts and the low tones of his speech painted pictures as vivid as reality. This is the story he told:

"This is the story of Petre's Chair. Petre flopped down on the moss-covered earth among the long evening shadows. It had been a tiring climb. He must have fallen asleep immediately, because the next thing he was conscious of was gazing wide-eyed, up into the clear, star-spangled night sky. The full moon rained down its sparkling silver light; shining so that the mountain around him was almost as bright as day. Petre stood up and glanced downhill to the river in the valley. The sky was reflected in the smooth waters and, along side it, the broken images of the mountain peaks looked more threatening than ever. Cadair—the chair, the Chair of Petre—a legend that included his own name. Petre, the guardian of the mountain. It was a high semi-circular mountain ridge, flanked on either side by slightly lower ridges forming the arms of the chair. Petre smiled to himself as he thought about the legend and the superstition, still believed by many locals, that if you sleep on Cadair Petre you wake up either mad or a poet. On a night like this, with that eerie silver light bathing the whole mountain, it would not be difficult to imagine that Petre the guardian was there, enforcing the ancient rules, protecting the secret of the mountain."

Artimus fell silent for a moment, gathered his thoughts, and then he went on. "As if to prove that he was neither a poet, nor mad, Petre shouted at the top of his voice,

> *'Mary had a little lamb,*
> *Its fleece was white as snow,*
> *And everywhere that Mary went,*
> *That lamb was sure to . . .'*

The last word never left his lips. It was late the next morning when they found him. His face, twisted into a grimace of fear, was ashen. He shook uncontrollably as they tried to coax him from his hiding place between the rocks. He spoke in a gibberish language, a sort of cross between his native Alusian tongue and unintelligible, demonic howls. They took him to the alchemist in the valley and within hours to the asylum, where he spent most of his time alone in a room, babbling incoherently. It was only after the intervention of a wise man, spell-caster Thoma, many years later, that Petre started to have bouts of lucid, coherent interaction, first with his own consciousness and then, eventually, with others. Thoma was a regular visitor to the asylum, where he brought peace and support to many of the residents. He would hold spiritual meetings there for those who were more able to conduct at least a semi-reasonable relationship with life."

Artimus paused again and drew breath. He looked at Randolph, Nick, and Benjy before continuing.

"Of course Petre never attended these gatherings; he was not capable of that level of interaction. One day, by chance, as Thoma made his way through the corridors of the asylum, Petre was ranting wildly, screaming from the small window of his lonely room, 'Cadair Petre, Petre you giant, Petre soul snatcher.' It appeared that the spell-caster, who had lived for most of his life at the foot of the mountain, was himself prone to dozing quietly through part or all of the night on the moonlit slopes. He was well acquainted with the legend and with the ways of the mountain. He was also well known locally for his poetic prowess, and it was his poetry that he used to calm the savage mind that inhabited Petre's head. The more poetry he read to Petre, the more frequent and longer became the periods of sanity he enjoyed. When Thoma eventually introduced Petre to writing his own poetry, there was a significant improvement in his mental state, although Petre never fully returned from a condition that most of us would describe as verging on lunacy. However, it was through that poetic vehicle that Petre managed to tell something of what happened to him. Did he meet his namesake, Petre the guardian? Was he stricken with a sudden mystic madness? Did he fall and crack his skull? Did some other mental disease cause this sudden condition? You must judge for yourself, for here is what Petre wrote shortly before he left the asylum and disappeared, without a trace:

'That lamb was sure to . . . PAIN, PAIN—let me shout.
Head turning—inside out,
Screaming purple darts at me.
My eyes are blind—cannot see
The treasure here, can't let it be
Known to any, good or bad.
Blood will flow and float
On high and golden ball.
Goodbye.

World—in turmoil—big man—crush me.
Don't hurt us—now please let us go.
Please don't make us feel so
Weak and . . . PAIN, no not more PAIN!
Why you do this—hurt us again?

And then the gentle pastel hue
Shrouding me and shrouding you,
So we can be together here
And rise above our human fear.

But sharpened daggers to the brain
Tear our flesh, return the PAIN—PAIN, go away,
Come again another day;
Little Petre wants to play.

Eyes on the inside, burning bright.
Keep me safe by day and night, night, night by day and
     night.
No not the night,
With moon so bright,
I see you coming for me to chew my flesh and grind my
     bones, you demon thing—
GET AWAY. GET AWAY FROM ME.

Yet surely, how can this be fair?
I see you there,
Your flaxen hair,
Flowing down to match the babbling brook's
Sweet music; Oh I love your look.
Your silken touch
And gentlest coaxing hath me hooked.

Yes, I will come down with you,
We will journey, just we two
And leave this worthless husk behind.
We'll leave it dead of soul and blind
To all the beauty we can see.
I am not it; it is not me.

Bury me deep in the mountain , oh wise one.
Bury me deep in your heart.
I am the chosen one truly, oh wise one;
I was your heir from the start.

I'll guard and protect your honor, oh wise one.
Your glory will always be told.
I am the one who will follow, oh wise one—
The secret of Cadair I'll hold.

I'll find us another to follow, oh wise one.
Another, so when I move on
To join you in ultimate glory, oh wise one,
We'll still have our own mortal son.

I see him already in mind's eye, oh wise one—
He's tall and he's handsome and fair.
He'll linger one night on Cadair, oh wise one
I promise you; I will be there.'"

And that," Artimus said, "is the story as it has been handed down. However, in recent times there has been an added ending. Some who travel on the mountain have seen a figure. Some say it is mad Petre, others say it is the best poet in the world. He is rarely seen, but on occasions, usually around a full moon, he can be spotted. A distant, lone figure, silhouetted in the moonlight, trudging along the mountain ridge, gesturing to the sky and searching, searching the whole mountainside. Locals say that his name is Petre, but they aren't too clear about when he came there or where he came from. It seems that all generations tell of a very old man called Petre living a hermit-like existence on that same remote mountainside. Not too long ago, there was a local lad. Petra was his name. Tall, handsome, and fair, he loved the mountain and often climbed high up to the rocky ridge. One day he had gone up higher than he originally intended, in fact further along the ridge than he had ever been before. It was as if the mountain was calling him, beckoning him on. But he became tired. He flopped down on the moss-covered earth among the long evening shadows. It had been a tiring climb. . . . It was late the next morning when they found him. His face, twisted into a grimace of fear, was ashen. He shook uncontrollably as they tried to coax him from his hiding place between the rocks. He spoke in gibberish, a sort of cross between his native Alusian tongue and unintelligible, demonic howls. Nobody noticed a wizened figure watching from the distant ridge. Well there you have it all," Artimus said. "That's the story as it has been handed down through generations plus the more recent addition. I don't know if it has any basis in fact or if it is in any way connected with your quest. It may hold the key to your needs and our salvation, but it is not a clear indication of who or what might inhabit the mountain."

"Do you know if the old man of the mountain might really exist and, if he does, can he be consulted?" Benjy asked.

"He may exist, for I have, on rare occasions, seen what appears to me to be a figure while on my meditations in the mountains. He sometimes darts and ducks among the trees on the lower slopes and other times he may be observed perched high on the uppermost peaks as he watches and waits," Artimus said. "I believe the most likely place for him to be found is in the caves on the high pass, but I cannot be certain and what I have seen may be no more than shadows and tricks of the light or may be the creatures of the mountain as they go about their natural business. However, if he is to be found and of that I can offer no certainty, the way in which he is to be consulted must be something for you to determine, Randolph. It may be he anticipates this moment. It may be he will be secretive and obscure. If he does exist and is the protector of destiny in some way, he is unlikely to simply hand out the information you seek without satisfying himself that you are the chosen One. What proof you might offer is something you should consider."

"When could we go to try and meet with him?" Nick asked. "And where should we go?"

"I will lead you," Artimus said. "And we can go as soon as you wish. However, the journey to the caves where I believe Petre resides will take a day in each direction, and we may need some time to locate him."

"Then, we must not delay, for the days grow short and snow will soon be seen on the peaks," Randolph said.

"That is wise. Already I have observed a creeping white blanket topping the highest masses in early morning, signaling heavy snowfall will soon cover them for the winter," Artimus said. "If we are to find Petre before the spring, we must not linger here."

"Then let us make ready to leave," Benjy said. "Our equipment in the wagon will be needed, so I will fetch it now and bring the cart down to your house. The mayor will need to find a new rostrum for his meeting at noon."

"Then you need to hurry," Nick said. "Noon approaches, and the mayor will soon be clambering over the cart. I'll come with you, in case he is already installed and we need to dislodge him."

Benjy and Nick hurried off to the tavern yard, leaving Randolph and Artimus seated together at the table. "Now that we are alone, let me tell you something of the pledge I made to your father," Artimus said.

"Pledge?"

"Your mother and father were unusual people, even by the standards of the wise elders and sages that have graced the history of our ancient village. Riversend is home to the ancestors of many of the soothsayers and visionaries now spread far and wide throughout the Western Realm. You and your sister, Lydie, are descended from a long line of magicians and spell-casters, and the powers you have inherited will be strong."

"I have found my abilities over recent months," Randolph said. "I have learned to employ capabilities that would have featured in only the wildest dreams of my yesteryears."

"You have explored but a small corner of your potential," Artimus said. "There is much yet for you to discover and many secrets of ancient enchantment for you to unfold."

"You spoke of a pledge just now. Tell me more of that?"

"It would seem your father had some ancient knowledge of the struggle between good and evil, and he was aware of the balance of all things supernatural. I promised him . . . promised him."

Artimus hesitated, as if he struggled to find the necessary words. Randolph waited, silent in expectation of some secret to be revealed to him, aware only of his breathing and a quiet that floated around him and the old man sitting gazing, with tired eyes, into his own. It was as if Artimus sought to unburden himself, to shed a heavy load he had carried for many years.

"Oh," he eventually continued, "the shackles of responsibility are weighty, and although I have worn them all these years, my release does not come happily. I am old, and whether I wear the bond of silence or no is of little consequence to the heart of an old man. But you are young and already bear more than your fair share of influence on the balance of all things."

"But your pledge?"

"Yes," Artimus replied. "You must be told. I promised your father."

"Then tell me, old friend," Randolph said. "Share with me your burden and pass to me my father's wisdom."

"I did not know whether it would be you or Lydie who returned to sit here now before me. Your father was not able to foresee that choice. But what he did know was that the One who came would, as you have done, seek to discover a secret for use in a struggle of light over the dark powers. His message to you is that your twin carries the same potential as yourself but, as in all that is balanced in life, her path will be contrary to yours."

"Are you telling me," Randolph said, "that Lydie may be a supporter of the powers of darkness?"

"Whether that is the correct interpretation and whether what is to be has already come to pass or whether it is the truth of the future is not known to me. All that can be told is that balance will be the stuff of nature, and nature will be the foundation of your destiny."

"As in all that is balanced in life, her path will be contrary to mine," Randolph repeated.

"Those were your father's words, and I have delivered the message. What you make of it must be by your own judgment."

"If I find Lydie quickly, the balance might be something I can shift. But if I don't find her, then I can have no control over what happens."

"That indeed may be the intention of the message," Artimus said. "Or it may hold deeper meaning. You must interpret your father's words as you think fit, Randolph. I have passed them as your father spoke them to me on his deathbed."

The noise of horse's hooves and trundling wagon wheels prevented further discussion, and soon a still-thoughtful Randolph and his two colleagues had the whole contents of the cart unloaded and piled in Artimus' kitchen.

"I think what we'll do, is make up supplies to last the four of us for four days," Benjy said. "But we'll only make up three packs. I don't think we should ask Artimus to carry a heavy load. He has been good enough to offer to accompany and guide us on our hike up the mountain, but we are young and strong like pack-horses. He is more frail and journeys with us for his wisdom, not his muscle."

"I'm bringing my wisdom too," Randolph said, eyeing the quantity of the equipment.

"You're also bringing a pack," Benjy said.

Mid-afternoon saw four figures slip quickly and quietly from the village outskirts and set a course northwestward for the foothills of the Western Mountains. The weather did not appear to be in league with them, and Benjy eyed the sky distrustfully.

"I don't like the look of those clouds. I wouldn't be surprised if we see snowfall before night time, and I don't mean just on the peaks."

With his words came the first solitary flake. It drifted silently downward to land on the tip of Randolph's nose, marking him as the target for many companions who quickly followed, increasing in size and number until a steady flow of petals of ice started to turn the landscape white. The echoing silence that accompanies a heavy snowfall wrapped the land in its blanket of quiet, and the features of the path blended into a haze of lacework, as if brushed by the hand of some celestial artist.

"Will we still be able to find our way?" Nick asked.

"We can navigate by the general outline shape of the range to the area that Artimus has indicated," Benjy said. "However, this weather will slow our progress and once we get up to the high pass where the caves are located, it will do nothing to aid our search for the entrance."

Benjy turned to Artimus, his expression seeking confirmation of his view and questioning the wisdom of continuing their journey in these conditions. Before Artimus could reply, Randolph pointed through the swirling clouds of snow. "What's that up ahead?" he asked. "I'm sure I saw a figure on the track."

The four peered into the gloom of the late afternoon and the graying blanket that was now the flat water-colored vista surrounding them.

"I don't see anything," Nick said.

"Yes . . . there," Randolph said, drawing his sword and using it as a pointer.

Nick and Benjy followed suit. Their weapons slid smoothly from well-greased sheaths as they stepped forward and flanked Randolph in a protective stance.

"There's two of them," Artimus said. "I can see two figures, and one of them is huge."

"They can be as big as they like," Nick said. "But they'll have to be larger than the mountain there if they want a piece of Randolph."

"Hold our position," Randolph said. "They're coming forward. Artimus, get behind us and stay well back."

"You jest, of course," Artimus said. He drew a shining blade from beneath his cloak and stepped, small and frail beside the others, into the line beside Benjy.

"Thanks," Randolph said. He turned again to face the two figures who were now clearly silhouetted against the darkening sky.

"Artimus," Randolph said, conscious of the old man's lack of physical ability for such an encounter. "You and Nick mark the small scrawny one on the left. Benjy, you and I will go for the big one on the right. Be ready, but do not make the first move; we know not yet who they are or what may be their purpose here."

"What do you mean, small scrawny one?" an indignant voice said.

"Galdore?" Randolph said, lowering his sword and stepping forward. "Is that you, Galdore? What are you doing here?"

"Me and Brommel thought you might appreciate a hand."

"Paw," Brommel growled. He had learned to recognize a few human words, although he obviously couldn't speak them. "Me no have hand."

Randolph laughed.

"What are you laughing at?" Nick said. "This is no laughing matter—that's a bear; it just growled at us."

"And I suppose you're thinking you don't need the services of a small scrawny one either," Galdore retorted.

"You said it," Nick replied.

Galdore suddenly loomed large, glowing and orange, towering above the whole party assembled in the snowy glen.

"All right," Nick said. "You'll do for me!" He joined Randolph's laughter, in relief rather than humour, as he realized this was indeed the wizard of whom Randolph had told him and Benjy so much, and that the bear could be no other than Brommel.

"What are you doing here?" Randolph asked again.

"Martha has been keeping a check on you from above when a quick flight has been safe enough," Galdore said. "And Brommel has been tracking your movements from the ground. When they both reported your start out toward the Western Mountains and the likely weather conditions, I decided that the time had arrived when it was safe enough for me to lend support without influencing your judgment."

"Well, I'm pleased to see you both," Randolph said.

He turned to Brommel and groaned a greeting. "Randolph pleased see Brommel."

"Brommel help friend," came the growled reply. He scooped Randolph up and embraced him.

Nick, Benjy, and Artimus stood wide-eyed and open-mouthed at the scene. "What the . . . what the?" It seemed to be all Nick could say.

Brommel lowered Randolph to the ground.

"Did you speak to the bear?" Benjy asked.

"And did he speak to you?" Artimus asked. "I've heard of the possibility of a language between mankind and animals, but I've never seen or heard it used before. So it really does exist?"

"Yes it does," Randolph said. "And without it, I wouldn't be here now. I owe my life to Brommel."

"And so does Dragon," Galdore said to Randolph. "I'm not sure how you did it, Randolph, but you saved her life, thanks to Brommel's intervention, taking you to the boglands. I've spoken with Grafdun earlier today, and he has told me of your help for her. I thank you from the bottom of my heart."

"I don't know how I did it, either," Randolph confessed. "There was some power on which I just seemed to draw and some unknown sense that seemed to direct my actions."

"Anyhow, the time and place to examine such matters is neither now nor here," Galdore said. "We will have opportunity for such once we have completed our present mission. But first, introductions are in order and then, tell me Randolph, what are your instincts for the way forward? How must we now proceed in our defense against Thrung and his evil forces?"

After each had been introduced to the other and confirmed allegiance and support for the kingdom, as is the correct way in Alusian custom, and a rather embarrassed Nick and Benjy had been persuaded to grunt a bit in an unsuccessful attempt to talk with Brommel, Randolph gave Galdore a brief outline of his plans.

"With Artimus' guidance, we are seeking the old man of the Western Mountains who, according to local legend, may hold the only key to the secret location of the Master Orb. Once that is in our possession and that fact known to Thrung, we will be faced with the battle of all battles as he attempts to recover it and the talisman for his own use to achieve total victory in the over-worlds."

"Then we must send word for the talisman to be brought here to Riversend," Galdore said. "It and the orb must be joined if they are to give us the power necessary to counter Thrung."

"Now that you are with us, Galdore, maybe Artimus could be spared the trauma of the journey up the mountains in this foul weather," Nick said. "Could he return to Riversend and send word for the talisman to be brought?"

"That sounds like a good idea," Benjy said. "We now know the location of the caves, and with due respect to Artimus, we can travel much faster through these conditions than he will be able."

Galdore turned to Randolph seeking his judgment. "That sounds sensible to me," Randolph said. "If Brommel takes Artimus back to the village and then returns to join us, Artimus can arrange for word to be sent to Grafdun, Martha and Brock. They can bring the talisman to a place and, with luck, arrive at about the same time as we return from the mountain with the orb."

"And where is that place?" Nick asked.

"And then?" Benjy asked.

"The place is Fortnum Castle," Randolph said. "And then we must prepare for a confrontation with Thrung, Shawadarg, Moraden, and the forces they command. Once Thrung knows we have the Talisman of Power and the Master Orb together, he will mount a full attack to gain possession of them. It is my feeling that our best chance will be in an area of open plain, but we will need a base from which to operate. Fortnum Castle seems an obvious choice."

Randolph looked to each of the others in turn, seeking their agreement. Each nodded to signal acceptance.

"I'll tell Brommel of the decision," Galdore said. "As you will see, Randolph, Brock has instructed me in creaturespeak. Artimus, if you come with me, I will also brief you on the messages to be sent to the council members."

Once Artimus had given Benjy final information about the route and pointed out the location of the high pass, he and Galdore went over to where Brommel sat quietly waiting. Soon the old man was perched, rather precariously, on the back of the bear, and they started off back toward Riversend. Randolph, Nick, and Benjy were hunched over the now rather-battered map when Galdore came over to them. "Brommel will return as soon as possible, and I have sent word with Artimus for the others to join us at Fortnum Castle in five days' time."

"We have a path planned based on what Artimus has told of the tracks and paths that lead to the higher passes and the caves where we might seek Petre," Benjy said.

"Then let us tarry no longer," Randolph said.

The thickening snow lay crisp beneath their feet as the party trudged toward the lower slopes of the mountain towering ominously above them. Benjy led; his skill at navigation had proved invaluable to their progress during the last few days. Randolph walked second in line, with Nick behind him and Galdore bringing up the rear. As they made their way forward in silence, Randolph fell to thinking once again about what Artimus had said concerning Lydie.

How could it be, he mused, *that my sister might be tempted to follow the path of darkness just because I have been chosen to champion the way of light?*

Randolph vowed that when this imminent battle was fought and Thrung and his cohorts dispatched, he would spend time to find and protect Lydie from whatever might threaten her. The words of his father, passed on by Artimus, still worried Randolph, because he failed to understand them clearly—"As in all that is balanced in life, her path will be contrary to yours."

What does that mean? he asked himself. He searched the depths of his memory for all the times that, as children, he and Lydie had played together. He could not find it in his heart to believe their paths were anything but parallel. Maybe the meaning was in their separation and the contrary path was no more than them each taking a different route to their reunion.

"Yes!" he said out loud. "That's it!"

"What's it?" Nick asked.

"Oh, nothing," Randolph said. "I was just working something out in my mind, but I've solved it now . . . I think."

"Well, how about us trying to solve the problem of the icicles that are starting to hang from my ears," Nick said. "Don't you think we should consider resting up for the night? It'll be dark soon and even though I have total faith in Benjy's navigation, some food and shelter would do us all good for a few hours."

"What do you think about a break for a while and some food?" Randolph asked Benjy.

"There's some woods a short way ahead. We can camp there."

The howling wind now swirled the snow into drifts and the fast-fading light turned the whole landscape into a backdrop of dappled gray. The silence shouted its presence at Randolph, and he felt an eeriness about the place. He wondered about the legend of Petre.

I wonder—are we following the right path? Randolph asked himself. *Or are we just off on a wild rabbit chase because I'm clutching at the wind? Artimus was right; the shackles of responsibility are weighty indeed.*

"Here we are," Benjy said. "We can shelter in the wood, have some food, and maybe a few hours sleep before we start the main climb to the high pass and the caves."

Randolph looked up to the point where Artimus had indicated the pass. It looked a long way and the storm showed no sign of abating. If anything, the giant white flakes now fell heavier and the blanket of snow seemed to deepen as he watched. But without the Master Orb, they would struggle to summon the power to defeat the forces of Thrung; they had to go on; they had to follow whatever clue destiny provided. Further into the woods, the thickness of the trees provided shelter from both the wind and the snow. The party huddled together under an overhanging rock, wrapped in blankets taken from their packs, as they ate some of the rations they had packed. It was not long before all four fell asleep.

Randolph woke with a start. He was aware of a faint light, an eerie glow that bathed the area where they were camped, but he was unable to pinpoint its source. He slipped out from beneath his blanket, drawn by a feeling that something or somebody was calling him, beckoning him, inviting him to follow. The faint illumination seemed to fall on the area where he stood and as he moved, it moved with him. He couldn't tell whether he was following the light or it was following him. And then he saw the figure—it darted between two trees some way off, deeper into the woods. Randolph followed, straining his eyes to make out who or what he was seeing. Suddenly he was in a clearing. There were no trees overhead, but no snow fell. In fact, he felt a warm breeze kiss his cheek, and daylight streamed down from above. The trees all around him were cloaked in green leaves and birds sang merry tunes as they hopped on green grass and among a sea of wildflowers that bobbed and swayed in the gentle wind.

"How can this be?" Randolph asked out loud. "It's like a summer afternoon and yet I know it's a freezing cold night in the middle of winter."

Then, walking slowly from under the canopy of the surrounding trees came a boy. He was dressed in bright colors, and his shining blue eyes twinkled like pools under the golden curls framing his smiling face. "Hello. I'm Petre. Welcome to my world. I've been expecting you."

"But, I don't understand," Randolph said. "Petre is supposed to be an old man, and how am I suddenly standing in sunshine? Where am I?"

"You're in the orb," the boy said.

"In the orb?"

"Yes, the Master Orb you seek, the all powerful orb, that which was secret to Mithrip, that which he left in my charge until the time of the meeting of the powers of dark and light."

"But you're only a boy."

"We are all but children in our own minds if that is our desire. I am Petre the boy or Petre the old man if I so wish." And with that, the boy changed form until he appeared to Randolph as a tall and elegant man of mature years, his silver-gray hair and long beard gracefully tossed by the soft breeze. He was Mithrip. And then a cloud of smoke and he was again a boy, but now they stood facing each other on the mountain top, looking down to the snow-covered valley below, where Randolph's companions lie sleeping in a cold wood.

"How?" Randolph asked.

"Did I do that?" the boy finished his sentence. "The Master Orb is powerful, even without the talisman. It can be entrusted to no other than the One. Are you the One, Randolph? Are you capable of wearing the shackles of responsibility of which Artimus spoke? They are indeed weighty."

"Are you Artimus as well?" Randolph asked.

"Indeed I am," the boy said. "Although he knows it not in his waking state, and his time now is almost spent. His journey to the everafter will soon be started, as will it be for all those who have protected the orb along with me for all this time."

"And you are Mithrip as well?" Randolph asked.

"I have been known by that name. It is my many forms that have been tagged as Petre in the legend you were told. All those who have been and gone, they have all been me, as I have drawn on the power of the orb to protect the balance."

"And now that task falls to me?" Randolph asked.

"If you show the wisdom," the boy replied. "If you demonstrate your willingness and your ability to bear the burden of truth. Can you be so mighty and yet so humble that such power as may be generated by the joining of the Talisman of Power and the Master Orb will not corrupt? Can you rise to the final challenge? Can you really be the One?"

"I have faced many challenges on my journey," Randolph said.

"There is a story told of a wise man. It is said that in his journey through life, he came upon a fork in his path. One way led down to darkness, the other to the source of all that was good. But which led to where he could not tell. The paths were guarded by twins, one of whom was good and always told the truth; the other was bad and always told a lie. But which twin was which, the wise man could not tell."

"So he had two choices to make? Between the right and wrong path and the good and bad twin?"

"No," the boy said. "He was required to make only one choice and that was which path to follow."

"Well that's easy." Randolph said he would chose the path leading to the source of all that was good. And by asking several questions of each of the twins, he could work out who was telling the truth and who was telling lies. Then he could find out from them which was the right path.

"If life were that generous, then we could all be wise," the boy said. "We could all draw on the knowledge of others to choose the right path. No, the wise man was allowed only one question on which to base his decision."

"So what was the question?" Randolph asked.

The boy just smiled but said nothing. Randolph knew he had to provide the answer if he was to be given the knowledge to gain access to the Master Orb. He thought back over all that had happened to him and over how it was he had come to be chosen as the One. He remembered an occasion when Galdore had explained that others who were apparently wiser could not bear the responsibility of being the One because they did not possess the purity of their own thought; they would be influenced by others and might not follow their own way.

But, all my decisions arise through what others might do or say, he thought to himself.

And then he saw the beginning of a solution to the puzzle. It was part of all he had learned about why Thrung could not succeed. "I must work with others but follow my own way," he said to the boy, who continued to smile but still said nothing. "That is the wisdom of balance."

Randolph thought also of Moraden and of why he had chosen the wrong path. Although they had talked much about many things; laughed together, faced danger together, been sad together, they had never discussed the question of the right path. Moraden had never asked the right question. He had listened only to Thrung and followed only Thrung's words. He had failed to seek the views of others before deciding on his path.

"And so your question? What, Randolph is the one question that will enable you to chose the right path?"

"I must ask either twin what I would be told if I asked the other twin which was the path to the source of goodness."

"And then?" the boy said.

"I should take the opposite path. Not the one indicated."

"You show an understanding of the complexity of life," the boy said.

Suddenly, Randolph was cold. He stood beside his sleeping companions in the wood. Gone was the clearing and the warm sun. Gone was the mountaintop where he had stood moments earlier. The boy was nowhere to be seen. Randolph looked down to something resting gently in his cupped hands. He found himself holding a round, golden ball. He held the Master Orb.

Galdore stirred and turned as he awoke. "Randolph, is it time to start out up the mountain already?" he asked.

"No, it is time for us to face our destiny."

He knelt beside Galdore and held out the orb. He had never heard a wizard's whistle before, but the one that escaped Galdore's lips was so shrill that Nick and Benjy were on their feet, swords drawn, within seconds.

"What was that noise?" Benjy asked.

"Are we under attack? Nick asked.

"Relax," Randolph said. "Everything's all right. In fact, it seems it's better than all right. I've got the orb." He described what had happened to him as they gathered around the golden globe and examined it.

"This is most certainly the prize we sought," Galdore said. "You see this here?" He pointed to a star-shaped indentation at what appeared to be the top of the orb. "This is where the talisman fits. Once they are joined, we can access every one of the other orbs that still exist. We can read their contents, see their histories, and look into the minds of the users. The Master Orb controls all the others."

"How many orbs exist?" Randolph asked.

"I'm not sure," Galdore said. "There's mine. Thrung has at least one; Griselda had one, but we destroyed that when Graceforth was rescued. I'm sure there are still others surviving from the original ten that were created, but I don't know where they are or who controls them. However, with the Master Orb that question will soon be answered for you."

"For us," Randolph corrected. "The might of the orb is not mine; it belongs to all that stand fast in the face of the dark power."

And so it was that the battle of battles between goodness and the dark power was set to commence. Randolph, Galdore, Nick, and Benjy struck out, with the Master Orb, north on the track through the lower pass of the Western Mountains, on route for Fortnum Castle. Martha and Brock, carrying the Talisman of Power, made their way from Castle Drent, and Grafdun, King Atha and the other barons and knights of Alusia, along with all troops and fighting men that could be mustered, gathered on the plains around Fortnum Castle. They awaited Thrung's attack with trepidation, for both his sister power Shawadarg and the quisling Moraden threatened with their own might and evil intentions, fighting in unison even in their selfish disharmony. Spring was almost on them by the time forces of the opposing armies had gathered.

"Thrung will not make his move until the weather has turned for the better," Grafdun predicted. "If he attacks before then, we have the advantage of the protection of the castle and its shelter. No, he will wait, and we must bide our time."

And so it was that preparations for battle continued. It was not known to Galdore what strength of number and wicked creatures might be spirited up by Thrung and his cohorts in their desperate attempt to gain control of the overworlds and capture the Master Orb and talisman. The foul winter weather that had seemed set on dispiriting the troops who met to defend the kingdom finally abated, and the commanders and leaders of the armies gathered in the Great Hall at Fortnum Castle where King Atha, Grafdun, Randolph, and Galdore addressed them. It was Galdore who spoke first.

"Even as we stand here, my brave companions, Thrung's forces gather on the plains in preparation for attack."

A murmur ran round the room, half expectation, half concern. The commanders knew that the groups of fighters waiting in the area surrounding the castle were eager to hear what was expected of them. They already knew they were defending the kingdom from a powerful and dark force that threatened the existence of their families. In the past months and particularly in the last few weeks, they had experienced the ambushes, the sudden attacks on their villages, the fire-breathing monsters that dominated the sky. They had suffered the plague of foul creatures that occupied their rivers and streams, the forays by troops of goblins and trolls, the emergence of practitioners of the black arts, and the transformation of their once safe and pleasant land into a place of danger and threat. They were in no mood to cower and hide; they sought revenge for the deaths and kidnapping of their friends and kinfolk. They were determined to restore the peace and tranquility of their land. But they were at a loss to know how to deal with this black and mysterious force that bred creatures of the dark places and monsters of their nightmares. Black magical forces did not succumb to the lances, slings, swords, and arrows of their defenses. They waited to hear what Galdore would say, seeking solace from their belief in his wisdom, and security and reassurance from their trust in his mystical powers. The defense of Alusia and the Western Realm could be in no better hands.

"We have an advantage," Galdore continued. "Thanks to Randolph, we have the Master Orb and the Talisman of Power, and while that gives us the strength to withstand Thrung's advances and even bring about a final defeat of the forces of darkness, it also makes us vulnerable. Thrung will not rest short of the last breath of the last of his troops in an attempt to secure that prize for his own evil purposes."

"Does he know we have it?" called a voice from the crowd filling the Great Hall.

"He will certainly be aware that the Master Orb has been activated and joined with the talisman. His own orb will have registered the fact to him, and he knows the talisman disappeared from Shawadarg's lair with Randolph. He will be certain both are now in our possession and he will also know they will be located within my reach. Yes my friend, he will know that if he takes Fortnum Castle, then he will posses the prize he so urgently seeks."

"So, we must protect the castle at all cost?" came another question from the assembled commanders.

"At all cost," Galdore said. "I will employ my most powerful magic, enhanced by the power of the Master Orb and directed by the intuition and vision of Randolph. We will throw up shields of energy and positive thought to counter the dark mystical powers and malevolence that will be thrown at us. But to you my friends, under the command of Grafdun and the king, will fall the task of beating off the physical attack that will be hurled on our number. We will be the target for attack from Thrung, Shawadarg, and now also, it would appear, our once-venerated friend but now declared enemy, Moraden, prince of darkness. Whether their advances be coordinated or conducted independently will not lessen the vast numbers facing our troops nor the spiteful and venomous aggression of their attack. We may find ourselves fighting three battles rather than one, and that may be the downfall of their advance for, working together, our might can be multiplied. Unified in victory, separate in defeat will be our battle cry."

And the cry went up from all those present.

"Unified in victory, separate in defeat," was heard by the men outside the castle walls, and they took up the cry until the whole army, massed around the castle, chanted in unison. That battle cry was heard by the distant armies of Thrung, by Shawadarg's forces, and by troops now loyal to Moraden. Their arrogant confidence was dented. Even though they failed to understand the concept of mutual support, they trembled at its manifestation, and in their ignorance they became vulnerable.

"And now," Galdore said. He held up his hands for silence to be restored. "Listen to the words of Randolph before you each go to your respective general for battle orders. Listen and hear, for Randolph is the One. He is the chosen One in whose hands our destiny is held, the one on whom our future relies."

Randolph stepped forward, and a cheer went up that made the rafters of the Great Hall ring and vibrate with the anticipation of victory to come.

"Follow your battle orders," Randolph said. "But equally important, follow your hearts. Our victory will not be in the ultimate elimination of evil but in the preservation of good. For without evil there can be no good. I have learned that balance is the ultimate power and if that is to be achieved, it is not by total destruction of that which threatens, but through domination by what we know is right. If we exterminate this evil, then another will grow to take its place, but if we maintain the balance of good over evil then peace and goodwill will be the driving force in our land. In the long day of the future, our way must be to favor peace over war. We must avoid fighting."

"But if we don't fight, if we don't eliminate the attackers, we will be overrun," a voice cried.

Randolph continued. "We must never be the instigators of war." He paused while the assembled company absorbed his words. "But if we are forced to fight by the hand of another, if we are given no choice but to defend ourselves—then we must win."

Randolph raised his hands above his head as if reaching for the sky. "Unified in victory, separate in defeat." Once again, the chant spread throughout the assembled troops until it rang on the plains and in the hills and valleys of Alusia. Grafdun came forward and raised his hands for silence.

"Good folk," he said, "You command troops that are loyal and brave, but before we go into battle let us be aware that blood will be spilled. Let it not be wasted. Let us join together in confirming our allegiance to the king and to the kingdom of Alusia."

He raised his right fist high above his head.

"For king and kingdom," he cried. "We stand unified in victory."

"And separate in defeat," came back the call from the crowd.

"I give you your king," shouted Grafdun. Atha took center stage and indicated his command for quiet with an almost imperceptible gesture.

"We go now in defense of our land and our ways. Our enemy has given us no choice. We go into a battle the like of which we have never known in the whole history of our kingdom. We face the truth of which my father spoke many years ago at his last meeting of the Council of Kings. It has been long in the coming but it is now upon us, and our strength is to be tested. Return to your commands. Tell your men of what you learned here from those who have spoken; go and await your orders. Go with strong will, the anticipation of victory in your hearts, and dedication to our cause. We fight for Alusia, but also for humankind. Go well my loyal subjects; go with the strength of right on your side."

The Great Hall slowly emptied. The commanders bid each other good fortune but knew that some would not return, each vowing to do whatever necessary to protect the balance of good over the dark forces that threatened the land.

Battle was terrible and fierce. Men fought bravely; men died bravely. Many lay wounded and dying on the plains, side by side with their foes. Red blood flowed and mingled with the black blood of the trolls and the green of the goblins. Swords bit deep into flesh of terrible creatures of evil, and fangs sliced through men as a hot knife through butter. Randolph and Galdore worked with the Master Orb, constructing spells and magical energy that they projected into the battlefield. Martha rode the wind above the terrible scene, dodging swooping dragon-like creatures, directing operations on the ground through Grafdun and Atha as they fought side by side in the thickest and fiercest encounters. Brock aided Galdore and Randolph, fetching carrying and calculating as the battle swung first in favor of the dark forces, back to the benefit of the Alusian armies, again to the forces of Thrung and finally, in a last desperate onslaught led by Grafdun, in defeat of the remaining troops that had streamed from the southeast of the plains.

"We must go into the battlefield," Galdore said to Randolph. "It seems the worst is now over and we have victory within our grasp, but we have yet to face Thrung, Shawadarg, and Moraden.

They cannot be left to regroup and go to ground. We must ensure they are powerless to threaten further attacks. I see through the orb that Grass Hills is their base. It is from there they have been directing their attack."

Leaving Brock to continue projection of positive energy to the battlefield through the orb, Galdore and Randolph made their way from the castle through the exhibition of destruction and death that littered the plains. Galdore mounted on his fine white steed and Randolph astride a black stallion, they made an imposing picture as they rode swiftly out across the plain toward Grass Hills. Some way out from the castle, they joined Grafdun and a troop of his men.

"Where are you going?" Grafdun asked.

"To Grass Hills, to deal with Thrung, Shawadrag, and Moraden," Galdore said.

"Then I will ride with you."

"But not with troops," Galdore said. "This is not a battle of physical strength. The troops will be better employed back toward the castle to ensure remaining raiding parties are kept at bay."

"So be it." Grafdun shouted orders to his lieutenants to return to the defense of the castle as he reined his horse around and galloped after Randolph and Galdore.

"Have you seen Martha?" Randolph asked Grafdun as he drew level with him.

"Not for a while. She was up above the main battle in amongst those flying dragon-type creatures. She was giving them a good whacking, but there were a lot of them. They went up into the clouds and I never saw her after that."

"I hope she's safe," Randolph said. "I asked her to stay inside the castle, but she wouldn't listen."

They rode on past several groups of Alusian defenders. Some were clearing up their dead, others were beating the brush to flush out the remaining goblins who had escaped their wrath and taken to hiding in the scrub. They passed Sir Lionel Graceforth who, with lance poised, galloped on the odd escapee troll or goblin with a, "Tally ho and off we go," as he spiked their ugly bodies with his weapon.

As they approached the low slopes of Grass Hills, they slowed to a canter. Randolph's keen eyesight scoured the hillside for any trace of Thrung, Shawadarg, or Moraden. Before long, he settled on a rocky outcrop some thousand yards from where they had come to a slow walk.

"There's movement up there," he said, indicating the promontory with his drawn sword.

"Let's ride toward it," Grafdun said. "If anything breaks cover and runs, I'll go after it. You both stay focused on the point from which it comes."

Nobody questioned his tactics, and slowly they rode forward. As Grafdun had predicted, a creature rushed from the hiding place and made for the open plain. Grafdun urged his mount into pursuit and, standing in his stirrups, reached for an arrow from the quill on his back, loaded it to his bow, and let fly, seemingly all in one deft movement. The arrow found its mark in the spine of the creature Randolph recognized as Shawadarg, and it fell to the ground on its scaly knees, paralysed by the dart that pierced its main nerve stem. Grafdun's horse sped forward to the writhing creature, and with one swift blow, the baron severed its head from its body.

No sooner had the creature completed its death throes than another movement from the rocky outcrop attracted their attention. A figure Randolph thought could only be the physical manifestation of Thrung appeared on a flat platform of stone. Galdore slid from his white charger and took a stance in direct confrontation. A bolt of yellow light burned toward him and with a simple movement, he produced a small shining mirror. Raising his hand, he reflected the bolt back to its source. The figure seemed to explode in a fireball of light and, suddenly, was gone.

"Over there," called Galdore to Randolph. He pointed some five hundred yards to their left.

Randolph encouraged the stallion forward and reined him to the left. As he galloped forward, two figures appeared high on the hillside—Moraden and a flaxen-haired woman, hand in hand, ran toward a cave mouth in the rock face. They reached the opening long before Randolph got close enough to loose an arrow, and as they turned in a gesture of defiance, Randolph went cold.

"Lydie?" he cried, as a pain of anguish struck him numb. The couple, still clasping hands, dived into the mouth of the cave, which closed slowly behind them, leaving only the bare rock face to view.

Chapter Fourteen
A Journey Home

Castle Drent viewed from the
southeast

"I CAN'T be certain," Randolph said to Galdore as they sat together at the long banquet table. "No, I can't be sure it was Lydie."

"So it could have been anybody?"

"I don't know." Randolph's voice indicated his rising irritation. He got up from his seat and stomped to the window overlooking the now quiet battlefield.

Bodies still lay strewn across the plain. For all the world, they could be the sleeping forms of tired, exhausted revelers, slumbering where they had dropped after dancing the night away. Randolph studied the scene in mock concentration, his eyes staring blankly into the night, his mind seeing nothing other than his thoughts. He was occupied with only one vision, the picture of Moraden and a flaxen-haired woman who, Randolph sensed with every fibre of his body, was his sister, Lydie.

Galdore crossed the room and stood behind Randolph. He placed his hand gently on his shoulder but said nothing, joining him in his wistful vigil over the darkness outside.

357

"I'm sorry." Randolph turned to Galdore. "I didn't mean to snap at you. It's just that I'm so angry with myself. If that was Lydie, then I should have sought her and rescued her many years ago. With that and . . . well, Martha missing and all . . . that's my fault as well. I should have been firmer with her. I should have insisted she stayed safe here in the castle. Flying in combat with those dragon creatures; what was she thinking of? What was I thinking of allowing her to do it? At least I should have been up there with her; I have the power."

Galdore tightened his grip on Randolph's shoulder and looked into his eyes. "Randolph, my son, for that is how I now think of you. You might be the One, but you are still cursed with the frailty of humankind. You are only a man and a young one at that. You cannot yet foresee the future clearly, nor can you be in two places at once. The journey through life you have so far made is incredible. You have achieved more in your short time on this earth than ten fully mature men could have expected to complete between them in a double lifespan. You have grown in power and strength and will grow still further. If that was Lydie, and of that we have no proof, you may yet be capable of saving her. As for Martha, I'm sure she will be safe. The battlefield has been searched and there is no sign of her; she is capable of much and often shrouds her actions in mystery. She will be safe, I am certain. She may simply have gone home for a while to feed her cat or off to arrange some after-battle necessities—that is Martha and you will not change her. She'll probably join us at Drent tomorrow or the day after. Certainly you cannot blame yourself for not making her stay in the castle. It would take more than the One to tell Martha to do anything." He chuckled. "She will be safe, trust me. I am, after all, a wizard."

"Thank you Galdore." Randolph clasped the old wizard's hand. "You truly are father to me, but let's hope you do not grow to regret the role, for I am no model son."

"You're not too old to have a good spanking," Galdore laughed. "Now come, let us return to our places; the victory speeches are about to start."

Arms around each other's shoulders, they walked back to their seats at the top of the long table just as Atha rose and Sir Lionel Graceforth banged his glass with a spoon to call for silence. The glass shattered into a million pieces and the uproar of laughter and shouts of "Can't bang anything properly" and "Bum move, Sir Lionel" rang around the hall.

Eventually order was restored and Atha raised his glass. "I toast you all; every last person here has given of their best this day. Many have suffered losses and personal wounds, some have even given their lives that the rest of us may live. But we have triumphed over the dark power that threatened our land. We can celebrate our victory in the knowledge that those who have died have not done so in vain. Yes, we are sad at their loss but we salute them in their bravery and we thank them for the ultimate sacrifice they have made to ensure our safety and continued freedom from the curse of the dark power. We thank them for restoration of the balance."

Nods, mumblings of approval and agreement, and some tearful sobs echoed around the hall as those present gave support to the king's words, each in their own way. Many had lost fathers, sons, lovers, brothers, and sisters but all present knew they had paid that ultimate price in the course of fighting for what was right. Their honor would be the stuff of legends, their memory would be the cornerstone of the restoration of peace, tranquility, and good in the kingdom of Alusia.

"I raise my glass in humble respect to those we have lost today, and ask you all to stand and give silent thanks for our salvation through their sacrifice," Atha said.

They stood and silence fell on that Great Hall, which was filled with the good people of Alusia. Randolph surveyed the faces in the crowd. His heart went out to them all and particularly to those he knew were suffering loss at this time of triumphant celebration. He spotted Benjy and Nick as they stood together a short way down the table from him, and he smiled as he caught their eyes. He owed them much and he would see to it that they were rewarded for the parts they had played and the support they had given him. They were, indeed, true friends. His thoughts turned again, in that silent reflection, to Martha.

Where are you Martha; what has happened to you? I sense your life force; I know Galdore is right in saying that you did not perish in battle, but where are you? Why are you not here? Why are we not standing together in victory?

And then his thoughts drifted to the vision of Moraden and that woman. Just as he sensed Martha's life force, he sensed, once again, that the woman was, indeed, his sister, Lydie. Randolph knew he had to try to save her, and he knew that to do so he would need to develop his power. While Shawadarg had been killed in battle, Moraden had escaped with his life, and it was unclear what had happened to Thrung. Much weakened and, he assessed, no longer a threat to Alusia or to the Western Realm, Moraden and maybe Thrung had retreated to their private domain of filth and treachery. However, he also knew his path would once again cross with theirs in their ongoing struggle to dominate the world with the dark force. He had the Master Orb and the Talisman of Power. Now Moraden and Thrung, even if he was alive, no longer posed a major or immediate threat to the forces of good and light. But in some ways, that caused him concern, for now they would work underground, now they would seek private revenge for what he had visited on them. It was possible that Alusia's victory heralded Randolph's private challenge to protect himself from their wrath and keep them suppressed so that they might never again rise to challenge the forces of good in the overworlds.

"Brass button for them?" said a voice from behind him.

He turned to meet the upturned, beaming face of Roody Grumbleweed. "Roody!" He bent down and embraced the gnome. "What, how? Why? Where? I mean when, when did you arrive?"

"Just now," Roody said. He turned and indicated a rickety old wooden chair that stood forlornly in the middle of the Great Hall. "Just this moment, buddy boy. We've improved our Trigno-meometry link and we can shoot through with quite a high level of accuracy now." He lowered his voice in confession. "Mind you, getting right into the room here was a bit of luck, I'll tell yer, buddy boy." He collapsed into a fit of raucous laughter.

Randolph couldn't avoid joining in the mirth, although he didn't really have a clue what he was laughing about. Nick and Benjy came over to see what was causing all the fun, and it wasn't long before all four of them were splitting their sides, rocking with laughter and rolling on the ground, stricken with irrepressible hoots and wails of delight.

"What's all the hilarity?" Brock asked as he joined them, standing over the rolling figures.

"I don't know," Randolph wailed as he managed to raise himself to a kneeling position at Brock's feet. "I always have this problem when I meet Roody."

"Is this Roody Grumbleweed then?" Brock asked.

"Yes, this is Roody Grumbleweed." He pointed toward the squirming, writhing, tear-stained figure on the floor beside him.

Randolph recovered himself enough to drag the incapable figure to Brock's feet, where he made halting introductions between bursts of giggles and guffaws.

"Thanks . . . for . . . the . . . invitation," Roody managed.

"Come on then," Brock said. He started to be infected by the humour and broke into the first broad grin that Randolph had ever seen on his face. "Come on, I'll show you to your room Professor, and then we can get down to business."

Randolph looked quizzically at Brock.

"Oh, I hadn't got round to mentioning it to you yet. After what you told me about Roody's work, I invited him over to see if we might help fine tune the Trignomeometry device and open up communications with Gnoma again. Now we have the Master Orb and the talisman, we can probably get it working properly."

Brock escorted the chuckling Roody off down the corridor leading to the castle bedrooms, and many minutes later Randolph could still hear whoops echoing from somewhere in the distance. He even thought he heard Brock's deep tones raised in overt laughter.

"That'll be a challenge for Brock," Randolph said to Nick and Benjy. "But a good laugh won't do him any harm. He's always far too serious."

"How about a song, Randolph?" Nick said. "You haven't played properly for ages."

"Yes, a victory song to celebrate our triumph over Thrung and his bully boys," Benjy said.

"In a while," Randolph said. "I must speak first with Galdore, and then I must find a lute and tune it. Mine still awaits my return somewhere in Castle Drent. Enjoy the rest of the evening; I think there are several young ladies queuing up to dance with the heroes. I'll talk with you both later."

Randolph went to find Galdore, for something the wizard had said earlier played on his mind. It was about going to Castle Drent tomorrow or the day after. Randolph had made no firm plans for what he would do now, where he would go, who he would go with. Atha had invited him to join the court at Drent, but his mind was in turmoil as many thoughts flooded into his head. Could he not just go back to being Randolph the Minstrel? Would he not pick up his journeying existence from where he had left off? Maybe go back to the Black Swan and stay with Nick for a while, or spend time wooing Martha; and he had to find Lydie.

"Oh where are you Martha?" he sighed to himself. "Why are you not here? What are you doing? And Lydie, my dear sister. What have they done to you?"

His thoughts drifted to the many things vying for his attention. There was Castle Drent and Galdore, there were all those he had met who had helped him in his quest. Many had invited him to return and visit them when peace reigned again in Alusia, people like Walter Bottle, Roody's wife, Bretti, in Gnoma, and even Rumble at the Traveler's Rest. There was Haggerty and crew, and he had to go in search of Brommel and thank him properly. In fact, he had to fulfill his promise to protect Brommel from the arrows of the hunters. Then there was The Faery Realm, where he had a permanent home if he wished. And Moraden; how would he face King Brodika, Queen Charmila, and Reeka? Supposing they blamed him for what had happened to Moraden? There was also Aunt Greta; he had to go to see her and explain his fast disappearance without saying goodbye. He was lost, deep in private thought and no little confusion, as he wandered unseeing down the corridors in search of Galdore.

Turning a corner, he almost bumped into Grafdun standing alone, gazing out of a tall window that overlooked the surrounding plains and the carnage of the battlefield that lay before him.

"Hello, Randolph." Grafdun's voice brought him suddenly back to the reality of the present time.

"Oh, hello Grafdun," Randolph said. "Not joining the party?"

"No, I've come up for air for a while," Grafdun replied. "And time to think," he added after a pause. "A lot has happened in the last few months and I need to consider what I should do now. I guess I'll return to Dark Castle and pick up my life from where I left off, although Atha has asked me if I'd consider taking on the supreme commandership of the Armies of Alusia."

"Congratulations," Randolph said. He assumed that Grafdun had accepted the role. "You'll do a brilliant job and none is better qualified or more deserving of the title."

"Hey, not so fast," Grafdun said. "I haven't accepted yet."

"But you will do," Randolph said. "You will."

"I don't know," Grafdun replied. "I've so much to attend to, so many people to see, so many places to go, so much to do."

"Being Supreme Commander doesn't mean you can't still attend to all those things," Randolph said. "If you don't accept, you'll still be lord of Dark Castle and member of the Council of Worth. You managed all the things that you had to do before the quest without having to give up being lord of Dark Castle. Don't confuse being what you are with who you are."

"That's good advice," Grafdun said. "Don't confuse being what I am with who I am. Thank you Randolph. But what of you; why do you not continue the revelry at the party? Why are you wandering the corridors alone?"

"I was looking for Galdore," Randolph said. "I, like you, have choices to make. Galdore and Atha want me to come back to live at Castle Drent. They say I am now an important member of the court. Atha wants me to become chief minstrel and master of entertainment at the castle and also to study under Galdore as apprentice court wizard, although Galdore says there are one or two things I might be able to teach him."

"So what's the problem?" Grafdun asked. "It sounds like a pretty good offer to me."

"But I've got so much that I need to attend to. There's the problem of my sister, there's Martha, there's all those I need to visit, there's Gnoma, the Faery Realm, there's all the friends I've made to go and see."

"Stop right there," Grafdun said. "Look out of the window. What do you see?"

"I see death and destruction," Randolph said. "I see the pain and suffering of battle."

"If you are to prevent that in the future, are you more likely to be able to do it as a wandering minstrel or as an important and honored member of the king's court? And another thing. I think you should confuse what you are with who you are. Well, maybe not confuse them, but you can't separate them. You are a combination of what you are and who you are. However, if they are both powerful, then you stand twice as much chance of succeeding as if you are only one or the other."

Randolph looked at Grafdun with his mouth open.

"And don't stand around with your mouth open; you'll catch flies," Grafdun said. "Now you stand here and think about that. I'm off to see Atha to accept his offer. I'll see you at Castle Drent in a few days, Mr. Apprentice Wizard."

"Warrior philosopher," Randolph said to himself as he watched Grafdun's back disappear down the corridor. He looked out again over the battlefield and saw the spirits of all those who lay still and unmoving. They stood shoulder to shoulder, good and bad united in a brotherhood of the future. He heard them speak with one voice.

"Minstrel wizard," they called to him, and he knew his way.

ॐ∘ॐ

"In my dreams, I hold the whole world in my hands.
In my thoughts, I roam these green and pleasant lands.
But the only way for me,
Yes, the truth is plain to see,
Oh, the only way for me, is to go home.

There are many friends I must look up, and so
There's a long and winding road for me to go.
On my journey to their doorways,
I will tread my path, but always
Having seen them, I will seek the path back home.

As I roam through fields and paddle in clear streams,
As I find and visit places from my dreams,
There will always be the feeling,
If I get bruised and I need healing,
That I've got a place to go that's called, back home.

Who I am is part of what I'm going to be,
And it's clear and plain for all around to see,
That I'm going to be a wizard.
Whether sunshine or a blizzard,
And I'll do it in a place I call back home.

But above it all, I know the course to plan,
The way I'll go is somewhere that I can
Know for certain that I'll be,
The one that will be me,
And the place I'll do it best will be back home."

It was the first time in many weeks, in fact the first time since he had sung bare-arsed to Captain Haggerty and the crew of the *Mindy Lou* that Randolph had picked up a lute. The thought of that evening on the ship amused him and he smiled, but it also brought Martha to his mind again and he wished she was with him. The applause from the assembled company reminded him of the time he had played at the Black Swan and of his first meeting with Martha all those months ago. The promise of spring was now just around the corner and threatened the dark winter months that had been supported in their gloom by Thrung's wickedness. Randolph gave a thought for those who had died on the battlefield.

"Spring is not a good time to die," he said quietly to himself.

"What was that?" Galdore said. He had crossed the hall to where Randolph sat on the small raised dais that had been his stage.

"I was just saying to myself that spring is not a good time to die," he repeated. "Those heroes lying on the field will not see the buds as they burst or the leaves as they fill and turn the landscape green. They won't see the blossom and feel the warmth of the sun."

"No," Galdore said. "But they will become those leaves and that blossom. They are the spring that we will enjoy, and the summer that will follow. Always remember, Randolph, life is not a once-off thing, it is a continuous cycle." Changing the subject, he went on. "So, I take it from your song that you've decided to come and accept Atha's offer. I'm pleased."

"So am I," Randolph said. "It was some wise words from Grafdun that helped me see the right path. We need to watch him, Galdore."

"Why so?" Galdore replied, looking a little concerned.

"I think he might be turning into a philosopher." Randolph smiled and Galdore's face broke into a considered grin.

"He'll be all right," Galdore said. "I'll have a word with Theodore. He'll sort him out and stop him getting too tied up with theories. A day's hunting followed by a night on the town, and he'll soon remember how to be a warrior chief and live life as a Grafdun."

"Galdore." Randolph's face took on a serious expression.

"What is it?" Galdore was immediately sensitive to Randolph's change of mood.

"I know I've chosen wisely in accepting Atha's offer, and I do believe that it will only help me in all that I feel I must now go on to achieve in life."

"Yes, but I feel a but coming on."

"But," Randolph said, "I must take one last journey as a minstrel. I must journey alone, on foot, back to Castle Drent. I'll leave first thing in the morning and see you back there in a few weeks' time."

"A wise decision," was all Galdore said.

"Will you explain to all the others? I mean to Nick and Benjy, and Brock, and Roody, and Grafdun—to all of them. It's not that I don't want to be with them or travel with them, but . . ."

"But you need to say goodbye to Randolph the wandering minstrel."

"Yes, that's exactly it," Randolph said. "That and . . . to the road and the springtime, and the . . . well, to it all really."

"Go, my son. Go and do what you must. Leave the explaining to me."

๛

To take the northern route up through the western forest, Merrytown, the Crumble Hills, and then touching the Northern Forest, and on down to Castle Drent was Randolph's chosen route. The other option would have been back through Riversend, past the Boglands of Thrung, and into Rivermeet before striking north toward Drent. He had no desire to see the boglands yet, and he wanted to spend his last journey as a wanderer in the place where this adventure had begun for him, in the Crumble Hills, gazing down into the valley. He wanted to see again that green and pleasant vista where Sir Lionel Graceforth had unwittingly been the catalyst for all that had happened.

Fortnum Castle was no more than a speck in the distance across the plain as Randolph's path reached the bubbling spring that was the source of the River Westerling. He had slipped out quietly that morning, leaving Galdore to explain his absence and had managed to get away without any goodbyes. Dressed in his old minstrel clothing, with pack on his back and borrowed lute and piccolo slung across his shoulder, he strode forth in the sunshine and went on his merry way, whistling and composing a ditty, with a "fah la la and a hey nonnie no."

He carried no sword, which, along with the leather map pouch and any other non-minstrel possessions, he had left with Galdore for transport to Castle Drent on the caravan that would be departing later that day.

> *"As I was walking out one day,*
> *Among the hills so green oh,*
> *I looked down on the valley track,*
> *Where proud Sir Knight did go.*
> *With a fah la la and a fah la la la la*
> *With a fah la la and a hey-ey nonnie no."*

Randolph stopped singing as he spied a figure ahead of him sitting on a log at the side of the track, his horse tethered beside him contentedly munching at the fresh green spring grass on the verge. As he drew closer, he recognized Sir Lionel Graceforth.

"Well, well," Randolph said cheerily. "Sir Lionel Graceforth of Dondrenton, I'll be bound. Good morrow and a hey nonnie no to you, good Sir Knight."

But Sir Lionel remained seated, chin in hands and a glum expression on his face. "Morning Randolph," he grunted.

"What ails thee, Sir Knight?" Randolph chirruped. "You have the sunshine on this fine spring morn to cheer your soul, and yet you sit forlorn, as if the weight of the world rested on your shoulders. Why are you this way?"

"Because I'm stupid," said Sir Lionel.

"Stupid? How so? You are a knight of the realm. You are honored in battle, cousin to the king, and a trusted friend to all at court. How is that stupid?"

"Well, maybe not stupid," Sir Lionel admitted. "But clumsy. I'm so clumsy that I can't get a lady friend. I'm always doing things like spilling wine on their ball gowns, treading on their feet, tripping over my own sword, and breaking things. You know, I finally enticed a young lady of the court, one of whom I have sought favor for many a year, to visit me in my rooms last night after the celebrations. But, while she prepared in the washroom for our night of passion, I fell out of the window into the moat. By the time I had struggled back to my quarters, covered in green slime and moat weed, my young sparrow had flown the nest and I was alone again. No, my first statement was right; I am but a stupid fellow."

Randolph suppressed the laughter that rumbled inside him and sat down on the log beside Sir Lionel. He had a regard for Graceforth and, while he knew the knight was right in much of what he said about his clumsy relationship with life, he didn't like to see him so despondent. Sir Lionel was one of the characters of the court at Castle Drent and, at heart, a good man. He was deserving of recognition rather than the ridicule that Randolph knew was so often heaped on him.

"You are strong," Randolph said, turning to look deep into Sir Lionel's eyes. "You are confident in your manner and caring in your demeanor. You are a brave and honored member of the court of the kingdom of Alusia. Go forth and behave as such." And some strange words came to Randolph. "Strongulatum performatus timeliorus amourlionus," he said as he touched Sir Lionel's forehead with his two thumbs.

Sir Lionel stood, a look of happy contentment spreading across his countenance. He mounted his horse with grace and competence instead of his usual stumbling, heaving attempts to get astride the beast. Sitting proud and erect, he raised his hand in a gesture of parting and turned his mount toward Fortnum Castle.

"Farewell for the present, good minstrel friend," he said. "I have business at the castle. My king and fellow knights await me, for I have important tasks to perform, and the hand of a fair maiden to win."

As Sir Lionel rode off, Randolph sat and gazed at his hands in wonderment. *What did I just do? Did I just weave a spell for Sir Lionel to give him the confidence he needs to better face the trauma of life? Am I already a wizard? Am I not just a simple minstrel again?*

A voice echoed in the quiet stillness of the spring morning that surrounded Randolph. He recognized the speech of Sulaman. "Your guise may be that of a minstrel, Randolph, but simple you are not. You have proved to have the eyes of wisdom and the heart of a lion that I saw when we first met many moons ago. But you now have the strength of the One, your hands can heal, and your mind can influence others. What you have just done for Sir Lionel is but stardust in the galaxy of power that will become your inheritance. Use that power wisely, Randolph, use it only for good. Go forth and, with this and all future spring times, grow and bloom into the summers of maturity, the autumns of reflection and the winters of understanding that will one day see me proud to sit on your right hand. Know now, Randolph, your choice to journey alone to Drent is not only to say goodbye to your life of before. The more important purpose is to say hello to your new life; to meet nature as you have never seen her before and touch hands with the powers that will be yours. Spend the journey well and learn, for there is much for you to find on the road ahead."

Randolph sat, bemused, still staring at his hands, his mouth open in awe.

"Oh, and don't sit there with your mouth open like that, it's not a very becoming pose for the One. And another thing, if you think it's been tough so far . . . well, it hasn't."

A popping sound in Randolph's head brought him to full consciousness as the reality of the birdsong, the bubbling of the brook behind him, and the rustling of the trees in the gentle breeze proclaimed him as minstrel wizard. Randolph scratched his head, stood up, adjusted his breeches to a more comfortable angle, and stepped forward into the first day of the rest of his life. As he walked beside the small stream, he was aware of birds flying with him. They would rush on ahead, land and wait for him to catch up; then, off again another fifty yards and, once again wait for him. The sun followed him as well. Although there were clouds playing tag across the sky, Randolph always walked in the sunshine. The light wind swirled around his ankles, seemingly offering its services of flight if Randolph wished to avail of them. But he didn't. Today, and in fact the whole of the journey he had planned to Castle Drent, would be, as far as he could make it, a non-mystical, wizardless, free-from-magic experience. He wanted to feel like a simple minstrel for the last time, before taking up his new role at court. He knew he was different now, he was aware of his powers and his potential, but for the next two weeks, in spite of what Sulaman's voice had said, he planned to pretend they didn't exist, at least for the moment. To recover and capture the essence of his being and relive some of the feelings he remembered from wandering unbothered and untethered in the sunny mornings, long carefree days and rich red sunsets of an Alusian springtime, was all Randolph wanted right now. He would heed Sulaman's words and touch hands with his new world, but not for a few days yet. He whistled happily as he sauntered along.

"It's gobbin' 'im again," whispered a voice from the forest skirt.

"Nahh, carn't be," said another. "'e must 'ave been dun for in that fire we lit in the barn. And even if 'e weren't 'e must 'ave got 'is comeuppance in the battle we saw goin' on. Surely 'e can't still be gobbin' alive. Surely gobbin' not?"

"Well," the first voice said. "Certainly looks like 'im; 'ere 'ave a gander."

"Stuff me breeches wiv ferrets if I'm not seeing the trooff. Y'er right Spike, 'tis 'im. Let's get 'im proper this time."

"Now 'old yer gobbin' 'orses a moment Toady." Spike's voice whispered in a taking charge tone. "This fella might only be a minstrel at 'eart but 'e seems to 'ave a bit of a charmed life about 'im. We need to gobbin' box clever if we wanna get 'im proper."

"So," Toady said, "whatja finkin'? My arse is still bruised and it says we should gobbin' give 'im an old-fashioned wug-wug. It don't look like 'e's got that gobbin' stick wiv 'im and 'e's all alone."

"I fink we track 'im for the day from in the woods 'ere. 'E's gotta camp up tonight and we can get 'im while 'e's gobbin' asleep. Know what I mean? Use our 'eads for once 'stead of just chargin' in. I mean, 'aven't yer learned nuffink, yer gobbin' moron?"

"Who yer gobbin' callin a gobbin' moron, yer gobbin' dog's turd."

"Don't yer gobbin' call me a gobbin' dog's turd," Spike said, raising his voice to a level for all to hear and taking a swipe at Toady's head.

"I'll kick yer nuts," was Toady unambiguous reply.

"Ssssshhh, 'e'll 'ear yer," Spike said. He clamped a hand over Toady's mouth.

"Gob off," Toady said after biting the hand and causing Spike to squeal like a stuck pig. "You're the one making all the gobbin' racket."

The two goblins subsided into whispered abuse and quiet stabs at each other's personal body parts, but too late. Randolph had heard them and recognized the voices and the style of speech. He smiled to himself, knowing that these two ruffians were no match for the fighting skills he had been taught by Grafdun, let alone the powers he now possessed. He stooped to pick up a stout stick from the side of the track and kept a careful eye on the trees beside the path.

Maybe I'll just call on a few of my new powers, he thought to himself. *Grafdun was right; I can't separate what I am from who I am.*

Throughout the day, he was conscious of the clumsy rustlings of the goblins in the undergrowth of the woods as they followed his progress.

Obviously waiting for me to settle down for the night, Randolph thought. *We'll have a bit of fun later then.* He chuckled as he plotted to give the goblins a scare they would never forget.

This time last year, I'd have been really worried and intimidated by a couple of characters like these. But now, well it just makes me realize how much has changed about me. And I'm not even going to hurt them, just have a bit of fun and . . . well . . . maybe frighten them a bit.

The bright sunny spring day passed relatively uneventfully, considering the happenings of the recent past. Randolph wandered the track slowly, savouring nature, examining the personality of each tree as he recalled his brief meeting with Roots, musing on the benefits of being a pebble in the now broadening stream that ran beside the track as he thought about when he crossed the bridge all those months ago on his way to meet the Council of Worth members at the Leaping Horse in Rivermeet. He thought of Martha and a forlorn, lost, alone feeling took hold of him for an instant. That led his mind to his first outing with Twig, how he had almost thrown him in the ditch and how they had become firm friends through dealing with that adversity in a positive way. His mind soared with the birds up into the clouds, visualizing, as he could now from personal experience, the wide view they commanded from on high, realizing how their perspective on life gave them much information not available to ground-based creatures. He thought about the way in which that information could be used for good or bad and that it was only of real benefit if it was combined with wisdom gained from experience. He whistled and sang his way down the dusty road, glad to have the opportunity once again to enjoy the simple pleasures of life, even though he now did so with a much enlightened vision. His musing were accompanied by the crashings and stumblings of the two goblins in the undergrowth as they kept their ignorant vigil over his meanderings.

Toward the late afternoon, Randolph became aware of another presence following his progress, watching from further back in the woods. He smiled as he sensed the attention of Brommel and an idea of introducing the huge brown bear to the goblins started to form in his mind. Randolph chuckled to himself as he looked for a place to pitch camp for the night and sent Anispeak mind-messages to Brommel to hide himself in the woods close by until a little later.

Randolph soon found a suitable hillock with a vertical side against which he built a lean-to shelter of branches and covered it with fronds and ferns to roof the bivouac structure. He crawled inside, set out his bedroll, and unpacked the bag he carried containing food and a few personal minstrel-like trinkets. He invoked the invisibility spell and, unknown to the watching goblins, left the shelter to find Brommel.

"Hello Randolph," came the deep voice of the bear as Randolph tuned his mind to the animal language.

"Brommel," he growled in reply. "Good see you."

"Good see you too," Brommel said.

"We have job to do. If you help me, that is?" Randolph formed the words in his mind and relaxed his voice as they grumbled into Anispeak.

"Randolph ask—Brommel help," came the predictable reply.

They sat down together under the canopy of a huge pine tree, and Randolph explained his plan to finally rid himself of the attention of the two irritating goblins. It was later that evening, after the goblins had seen Randolph apparently prepare for sleep and crawl into his shelter that they decided to strike.

"It's dark enough now," Spike whispered. "Even if the little shite is still awake 'e won't see us comin'. As long as you can keep gobbin' quiet, that is."

"Don't gobbin' start on me again," Toady said. "Or I'll gobbin' fump yer."

A'right, all right, all right. Just shut it, will yer. Follow me," Spike said as he started to creep forward. "I'll rip the roof off the shelter, pull back the bedroll, and you stick 'im wiv the gobbin' knife. And do it 'ard and proper."

Toady's eyes and teeth flashed in the moonlight, as he drooled his reply. "Good and 'ard, right in the gobbin' gizzard."

Randolph watched the proceedings from high in the trees where he had climbed invisibly a little earlier, shortly after Brommel, also under the temporary cloak of the invisibility spell, had swapped places with him in the shelter.

"You ready?" Spike hissed through clenched teeth, as the two goblins crouched close to the ground outside the bivouac.

"Go for it," Toady spat back.

Spike stood and leaning forward, grabbed the ferns, twigs, and branches that formed the roof of the shelter, dragging them aside and exposing Randolph's bedroll containing his apparently sleeping form.

"'E looks gobbin' 'uge in this light," Toady squawked, as he lunged forward with the dagger.

But the knife fell harmlessly from his hand, clanking on a stone on the ground, as he threw his hands aloft in horror at the sight rearing before him. "EEEKK 'e's changed into a gobbin' bear! Stuff me wiv a broadsword, Spike, 'e's transmogrified into a gobbin' 'uge gobbin' brown gobbin' hairy gobbin' bear. 'E mus be a gobbin' wizard or sumfink."

As Randolph and Brommel shook with laughter and fell to the ground in mirth-induced weakness, they could still hear the wailings and hootings of the arguing goblins, now a mile away and still running as if their lives depended on it.

"Next time you gobbin' spot 'im, you gobbin' tell me, and I'm gobbin' goin' the uvver way," were the last distinct words they heard from Toady.

"Gobbin' after me," came the clipped reply. "I'll gobbin fump yer, if yer push in fronta me. Gob orf, will yer?"

In the morning, Randolph said goodbye to Brommel, who had indicated a need to be at an animeet in another part of the forest. After packing up his bundle, Randolph swung it onto his shoulder and started along the track toward Merrytown. He was conscious of the sense of calm that sat gently on the surrounding countryside. The tension and feeling of gloom that had pervaded the atmosphere over the last few months was gone.

Randolph's footsteps fell lightly on the track, so lightly at times that he felt he was floating and once or twice, when he looked down, he found that he was.

"And without singing the flying song," he mused. "The wind seems to have taken it upon itself to help me on my way."

The sun shone with an early spring warmth that made Randolph think of the summer days to come and he was glad that Alusia had, for the moment at least, been restored to a land where peace and tranquility prevailed. He was glad also that he had chosen to take these few days to wander by himself, sucking in the natural surroundings, coming to terms with his new relationship with life.

"Time to think is important," he said to himself. "I resolve that when I take up residence in Castle Drent, when I take on my new responsibilities and my new role, I will find time each day to tune into nature and think."

The late afternoon sun wistfully eyed her horizon bed as Randolph came over a small rise, rounded a corner between the trees of a small copse, and saw ahead the outskirts of Merrytown. The shallow valley was beautiful in the soft golden evening light that played on the misty haze rising from the river ahead. The lights of Merrytown sparked into life one at a time as Randolph made his way toward the town. He remembered his last visit, when Brommel had rescued him from the river up by Devilrock Falls and taken him to the northern outskirts of the town. But this time his approach was from the south, the side of the river on which Roots had his cottage, a short distance out to the west from the main river crossing. Randolph had planned to skirt the town to his left and head straight for Roots' cottage.

Although it's quite likely that Roots will be in town for the evening, probably in the Copper Kettle. Maybe I should go there first, he thought.

So, plan revised, Randolph followed the track straight into town, his target, the Copper Kettle. His memory of the gaiety and jollification that greeted him on his last visit was different only this time in that it had increased threefold. The lifting of the threat and suppression of the forces of darkness had thrown Merrytown into festive spirit, and celebrations and jubilation were rife in the community. Everybody laughed, dancing down the streets, singing at the tops of their voices. The atmosphere was electric, and Randolph felt good.

He hurried through the town and found the Copper Kettle bedecked with flags, streamers, and banners proclaiming a return to a life of peace and goodwill. Folk jostled in and out of the tavern door, and Randolph found it difficult to get to the bar. Particularly, when people saw he carried a lute and piccolo, he was accosted many times with demands for song and music.

"In a moment." He laughed. "In a moment folk, but first I must find my friend Roots; I thought he might be here."

"Roots?" replied a voice from the crowd. "Leafy Barkman?"

"Yes," Randolph said. "Leafy. Have you seen him?"

"You haven't heard?" the voice asked.

"Haven't heard what?" Randolph shouted over the noise.

"Roots is dead," the man replied. "'is funeral was a few weeks ago. We buried 'im out in the forest on the edge of town near his cottage. 'e took sick one day and was dead the next."

The noise of the festivities paled into the background as Randolph's full attention focused on the owner of the voice, and the elation drained from his mind. "Roots, dead? He can't be,"

Randolph said, guiding the man to a corner of the room where they could talk easier. "Tell me what happened."

"Like I said, 'e was in 'ere one evening, laughing and joking about. He complained of a pain as 'e was leaving, went home, and died. Doc said is was 'is 'eart—just gave up working."

"Can you take me?" Randolph asked. "To where he's laid."

"Easy 'nuff to find," the man said. "Almost next to 'is cottage. Just to the right as you face the doorway. You don't need me to show you, but I'll come if you want."

"No, no," Randolph said. "Thank you, but I'll find it myself."

"I'm sorry to have to give you the news," the man said. "Was you a close friend?"

"Yes," Randolph said. "No, I mean no. What I mean to say is I only met him once before but he helped me. I've come back to say thanks."

"That's Roots, always offering an 'elping 'and to anyone and everyone."

"Thanks again," Randolph said. "I'll go out there now and pay my respects."

Randolph left the Copper Kettle sadly. He glanced back at the table where he and Roots had once sat together. He felt empty, sapped of emotion, as he dragged his feet toward the door, ignoring the repeated pleas for songs and music, his face displaying the sadness that his heart felt.

He followed the path out of the town that he and Roots had taken those many weeks ago. He looked down at the boots he wore and remembered it was Roots who had given them to him. "Why?" he said to himself. "Why?"

He made his way to Roots' cottage and, just like the man had told him, there to the right where a little clearing had been made in the forest, stood a gravestone. Randolph walked over to it and read the inscription carved into the wood.

> *In memory of a man who knew more than the trees*
> *Would it be that more were like him*
> *Leafy 'Roots' Barkman*

Randolph stood in silence and remembered. Then he sang softly.

"They called him Roots, he had big boots,
And they have trod a pathway.
I'll follow thee, then I might see
The way that is the right way."

The trees around rustled even though the air was still, and Randolph felt a sense of oneness with the land.

"My day spent with you was but a brief moment in time," Randolph said. "But it touched my soul and in me you will forever live on. That is the way of things. Thank you Roots, thank you."

Randolph turned and left the grave. He had learned another lesson in life. He saw the clarity of mortality, he knew that even good men must die, and he saw the importance of making every living moment count. He saw the wisdom of his journey and knew the value of his chosen way. Above all, he realized that all questions might not have answers.

ॐ∞ॐ

It was ten days later, after visiting Tinkerboo's old haunts, journeying through the Crumble Hills and the edge of the Northern Forest, revisiting the valley where he first encountered Sir Lionel Graceforth, and making his way slowly down past the Swallow Falls that he reached the head of the pass where the track from Portalbion joined the road on which he had traveled southward. He looked down to Castle Drent. In the early evening dusk, the lighted windows showed warmth and shelter. An owl hooted somewhere in the forest, as if welcoming Randolph home. Down in the castle, a gray-bearded figure looked from one of the illuminated windows and saw Randolph as he started down the steep track to the castle gates.

"Well my friend." He addressed a black cat who sat beside him on the wide stone sill of the window. "Here he comes; we had best prepare for his arrival."

Up on the track, Randolph quickened his pace a little. "I'll just sneak in without anybody seeing me," he said to himself. And with that thought and a "fah la la and a hey nonnie no," he strode on, down the hill toward the castle and to the first day of a wizard's lot.

Printed in the United Kingdom by
Lightning Source UK Ltd., Milton Keynes
141484UK00001B/89/P